'Why are you ... the job?'

'Because whatever ... ..., you're as good a doctor as any I ever came across and exactly what I'm needing here,' Dominic answered readily.

'But—but you don't like me!'

'Did I ever say that?'

'No,' Annie had to admit. 'But we never exactly got on, did we?'

Drusilla Douglas qualified as a physiotherapist and worked happily in hospitals both north and south of the border until parental frailty obliged her to quit. When free to resume her career, she soon discovered that she had missed the boat promotion-wise. Having by then begun to dabble in romantic fiction, she worked part-time for a while at both her writing and physio, but these days considers herself more the novelist.

Recent titles by the same author:

CRISIS IN CALLASAY
RIVALS FOR A SURGEON
PARTNERS IN PRIDE
A DOUBLE DOSE
A BORDER PRACTICE

DOCTORS
IN DOUBT

BY
DRUSILLA DOUGLAS

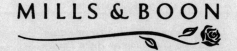

MILLS & BOON

MILLS & BOON, the Rose Device and
LOVE ON CALL are trademarks of the publisher.
Harlequin Mills & Boon Limited,
Eton House, 18-24 Paradise Road, Richmond, Surrey TW9 1SR

© Drusilla Douglas 1996

ISBN 0 263 79603 5

Set in Times 10 on 11 pt. by
Rowland Phototypesetting Limited
Bury St Edmunds, Suffolk

03-9606-44979

Made and printed in Great Britain
Cover illustration by Helen Parsley

CHAPTER ONE

THEY were standing Annie a farewell supper at the bistro opposite the hospital but when the casualty consultant tried to top up her glass again, she covered it with a firm hand and said, 'No, thanks, Jack. It's bad enough to be unemployed without getting nicked for drunk driving as well.'

'I did try, you know,' he told her gently.

'I know that,' Annie responded quickly, 'but they've closed our department in the interests of economy and there's a job going elsewhere for all the medics except me. That'll teach me not to speak my mind to our new masters.'

'You certainly didn't pull your punches, Annie.'

'No, I didn't, did I?' she recalled with a rueful grin. 'And as a result I'm now blacklisted.'

Jack Marshall couldn't deny that so he reminded her instead, 'Glasgow's not the whole world, lass. You'll make out somewhere. Cream always rises to the top.'

'Not these days it doesn't,' she refuted flatly. 'Not unless it licks a lot of boots and bottoms on the way.'

'Thank you,' Jack answered gravely.

Annie elbowed him reprovingly in the ribs. 'Don't give me that—you know fine what I meant. I wish I had one-tenth of your tact,' she added on a sigh.

'You've tact enough for your patients and colleagues,' he said.

'I respect my patients and my colleagues,' Annie returned pointedly.

Jack changed the subject in despair and asked, 'Did

you do anything about that advertisement for an assistant in general practice that I showed you a couple of weeks back?'

'Yes, I applied, but I've not had an answer yet.' Annie didn't add that she'd only posted the letter two days previously—once she'd quite given up hope of getting another hospital job in Glasgow.

Jack tried to hide his dismay with a cheerful, 'Never mind. You're sure to get something soon—a girl with your track record.'

As Annie was thanking him for his faith in her, two waiters were going round switching off lamps and clearing tables. In the face of such broad hints, the hospital party realised that it was time to go.

Outside on the pavement the team crowded round Annie, wishing her luck and telling her how much they were going to miss her. Then they escorted her to her car, calling out more good wishes as she drove away.

Annie's eyes misted over and she dashed away the tears with an angry hand. But for her outspokenness she would have been going with them to the showpiece accident and emergency department at Glasgow's newest hospital instead of applying for jobs in general practice. She'd brought this catastrophe on herself and knowing that was no comfort at all.

She had an attic flat near the university in a graceful Victorian terrace that faced south over wooded parkland. It was her pride and joy but if she couldn't get another job soon she would have to sell it and move away.

Once inside the flat she bent to pick up her letters, sorting through them eagerly. Junk mail and a bill, but nothing about that job. Serves me right for not applying sooner, she acknowledged bitterly, going into the living room and slumping down on the couch. Automatically she reached out and switched on the answering machine to see if there were any messages.

'Dr Duncan?' asked a bright voice. 'This is Laura Carlisle, practice manager at Burnside Health Centre speaking.' Annie sat up straight, her heart thumping. 'Our senior partner, Dr Smith, is familiar with your work and would like to talk to you as soon as possible. Could you possibly call in for a chat this evening any time after six? Thank you.' Click.

It was now nearly midnight and Annie barely had time to tell herself that she'd missed that particular boat for sure when the same voice said,

'Dr Duncan, this is Burnside Health Centre again. As it's now after seven, we're presuming that you were out all day and didn't get our earlier call. Would tomorrow morning at eight be possible? We're very sorry that we cannot give you any longer but it's now nearly a month since the post was first advertised. The other applicants were all interviewed earlier this week and the letters are ready to go out. Thank you.'

Thank *you*, thought Annie, as she phoned the centre and told their answering machine that she'd certainly be there next morning at eight on the dot. Then she sat back to wonder why this Dr Smith was so keen to give her a chance. But no amount of brain-racking brought any likely Smith to mind. Why couldn't he— or she—have had a more unusual name?

Annie got up at six so that she could take her time getting ready. A honey-coloured skirt and jacket and a black, scoop-necked blouse with some discreet touches of emerald were very effective with her thick red hair and tawny, green-flecked eyes. She had never believed that a woman doctor must be dowdy in order to get on. Charm and a smooth tongue would help, though, but she had always scorned such wiles.

And now see where speaking her mind had got her—off the ladder to a promising surgical career and into the dole queue! With this in mind she tried out a few winsome glances in her dressing table mirror, fluttering her long, thick eyelashes for added effect. Then she laughed at herself for looking like a clown. If they liked her the way she was, then great. If not—too bad.

Burnside lay six or seven miles to the south-west of Glasgow. It was one of several satellite towns that had sprung up during the last century in the wake of Glasgow's expanding marine and mercantile prosperity. Once a village, it had developed around the mighty Smith-Jardine marine engineering works.

Annie was near enough now to see that the works had been demolished; redundant, she presumed, like so many others following the decline and death of shipbuilding on the Clyde. In its place stood a few small factory units which couldn't employ more than a quarter of the Smith-Jardine work force.

'So much for progress,' muttered Annie, as she turned off the motorway to look for the health centre. She finally located it on the town's eastern fringe. It was a gleaming new building and surprisingly spacious. Annie's spirits rose as she parked her Metro beside an ageing Granada and bounced eagerly up the steps to the main entrance.

She was admitted by a cheerful little woman in an overall, who asked to see Annie's credentials before leading the way to Dr Smith's consulting room.

'Sorry, Doctor,' she apologised, 'but we need to be awful careful in a place like this with all the drugs and that. Doctor had bars put on all the windows after the break-in,' she ended with obvious approval before tapping on a door and peeping round it. 'See, I've brought ye Dr Duncan, Doctor, dear,' she announced, as though offering her boss the present of a lifetime. Then she stepped back to let Annie in.

A tallish, broad-shouldered man in jeans and a well-worn Fair Isle sweater stood behind the desk. His dark hair was cropped closely, giving him a military look. Piercing dark eyes in a strong, handsome face were wary.

Annie took one look and grabbed at the doorframe for support. 'You!' she breathed in utter disbelief.

Dominic Smith-Jardine folded his arms across his impressive chest, while his expression changed from wary to challenging. 'Didn't you check, then? That's not like you, Annie. So either you've mellowed, or you're desperate.'

Trust him to go straight into the attack. Annie came in and shut the door while searching for words with which to reassert herself. Eventually she came up with, 'I could just as easily ask that of you. The last I heard was that you were heavily into the good life down in London.'

'And I'd heard that you were the apple of Professor Bathgate's eye—as one might expect of so brilliant a student. So why the sudden interest in general practice?'

That was always his way—to ask a question of his own instead of answering yours. So he hadn't changed in that respect, although his clothes and haircut certainly had changed. Well, Annie could ask questions, too. 'Why are you considering me for it?'

'Because whatever else you may be, you're as good a doctor as any I ever came across and exactly what I'm needing here,' he answered readily.

'But—but you don't like me!'

'Did I ever say that?'

'No,' she had to admit. 'But we never exactly got on, did we?'

'Yes, we did. Workwise. At work you could always forget how much you disapproved of me.'

Now it was Annie's turn to ask, 'Did I ever say that?'

'You didn't need to. Only a guy with skin an inch thick could have failed to notice.' He sat down at the desk and waved a hand towards a chair. But Annie stayed on her feet, feeling more in control that way.

Dom shrugged, as if it didn't matter one way or the other to him. 'Let's forget the past and concentrate on the present,' he said. 'For reasons you're not prepared to disclose, you need a job. I need an assistant and I want the best I can get. I've interviewed more than twenty applicants and none of them showed anything like your energy and diagnostic flair.'

It was impossible not to be flattered by that. All the same, Annie felt obliged to point out that it had been four years since they'd worked together. 'I may have changed,' she ended. As you certainly have, she would have liked to add.

'Not in that respect, you haven't,' he returned confidently. 'As soon as your letter landed on my desk yesterday morning I spent half an hour on the phone.'

After which, for all his pretence, he knew exactly the trouble she was in! 'And you *still* think I'm a suitable applicant?' she asked levelly. And is this really Annie Duncan speaking? Sounding so restrained and reasonable. . .?

'Definitely. Just as I knew you would, you've proved yourself splendidly.' He paused. 'Professionally speaking.'

'And personally?' She simply had to ask him that.

A fleeting smile enlivened his face for a second,

softening it and sparking off unwelcome memories. 'By all accounts, you're what you always were,' he answered tantalisingly.

Annie's chin tilted up a fraction as she asked, 'Would you care to expand on that?'

'My sources suggest that you remain passionately eloquent in defence of what you believe to be right.' He glanced at the clock. 'The time is getting on, Annie, and I have a surgery at nine. Are you in or are you not?' Just like that! His eyes held hers in a level hypnotic stare.

She had to sit down then. 'Yes—I'm in,' she heard herself saying with a sigh of resignation. 'So, when do I start?'

'No time like the present,' he told her.

Annie hadn't expected that and she said feebly, 'Well, I don't know. . .'

'The post is vacant and you've finished at the city—' Of course, he would know that '—so what's your problem?'

Annie didn't have one, apart from wondering if she'd been insane to accept. 'I—well, I do live rather a long way off, and—'

'You'll remember that the advertisement stated that this job is initially for a trial period, with the prospect of a partnership if mutually agreeable, so you're not expected to move house immediately if that's what's bothering you.'

It wasn't, but it would do while she got her breath back. 'All the same, the distance could be a problem when I'm on call at night. That's presuming that this practice provides its own twenty-four hour cover.'

Annie watched his lip curl scornfully and remembered the time when he'd railed against practices that didn't.

'I take the view that reasonable folk don't call their doctors out at night unless it's really necessary. Besides, if our patients are seriously ill then, in this practice, we prefer to see them ourselves rather than leave them to the ministrations of some over-tired hospital junior going for an extra buck by doing nocturnal agency work.'

The remembered tirade had been directed at one such junior registrar who had yawned once too often on a ward round.

'My views exactly,' agreed Annie truthfully.

Dom nodded, as though anything else was unthinkable. 'And you needn't worry about accommodation on duty nights. We have a small flat upstairs for that. Apart from convenience, lights on and a presumed presence deters burglars.' Again that rare and attractive smile. 'You'll have noticed that we're not situated at the best end of the town.'

'Hence the barred windows and the hefty fence,' agreed Annie again, smiling back, just as a receptionist looked in to ask if Doctor was ready to start surgery.

Dom said he was and introduced the girl to Annie as 'Carol, our number one receptionist', before asking her to take Dr Duncan along to Laura who had offered to show her round.

The practice manager was as brisk and businesslike in person as she had sounded on the phone. When Annie said that she hoped she wasn't taking up too much time, Laura Carlisle said that she'd rescheduled her morning, knowing how keen Dr Smith was to persuade Dr Duncan to join the practice.

Annie was very impressed by the spaciousness, the equipment and the general air of purpose at the centre, as well as the range of services it offered.

Sensing this, Laura explained proudly, 'None of your

standard layouts for us. Dr Smith designed the place himself. And, now, here's another surprise for you— our own physiotherapy department. No other practice for miles around has one,' she continued, 'but Dr Smith believes that patients get better much more quickly if they are treated immediately instead of having to wait weeks for a hospital appointment.'

'So this is a fund-holding practice then?' Annie asked. Had she been mad to accept a job without even knowing that?

'Oh, yes—and that's another first for Burnside,' Laura confirmed. Clearly, Dom had a loyal supporter in his practice manager. But, then, he never did have trouble eliciting admiration from women. And, to be fair, from his male colleagues as well, remembered Annie, when she was introduced to Craig Patterson, the physiotherapist, who was obviously another fan.

'This will be your room, Dr Duncan,' said Laura, when the tour was complete. 'There are five doctors in all; three partners; a trainee; and, now, yourself— so on-call duty is not too onerous. Did Dr Smith have time to tell you how it works?'

When Annie said no Laura explained about the one duty weekend in five, one other as second-on-call and the weekday evenings in strict rotation.

'At least, that's how it is on paper but they usually juggle about a bit among themselves. Dr Smith doesn't mind as long as there is always adequate cover. He believes in keeping us all happy in our work. But there, I'm forgetting how well you know him already.

'I'm going to leave you now to check your room and if there's anything missing which you think you'll be needing you can tell me later over a coffee. I usually manage a cup about eleven.' And off she went, brisk and efficient to the last.

Annie looked round her consulting room and was delighted with it. It was spacious, well lit, practical and pleasant without being extravagant. And it certainly lacked nothing in the way of equipment. She looked round again, picturing her books in place on the shelf beside the desk, and was startled when the phone rang.

It was Dom. 'Annie? I've got a patient coming in now who I'm sure will interest you. Can you come?'

'Of course,' she answered, with a vivid sense of *déjà vu*. They'd had that exchange so many times during the summer that she had qualified and gone to work as house physician to the dean of medicine. That was a post invariably awarded to the gold medallist of the year and Dom—a past gold medallist himself—was by then the dean's registrar. They had worked together for six months until Annie had to move on to a surgical post, where she discovered her true bent.

Moving on had been a relief. It was impossible not to recognise Dom's brilliance—or to appreciate all she had learned from him. It was also impossible to forget how callously he had treated her particular friend, Lynne, some time before. Lynne had gone completely to pieces after his sudden rejection and had dropped out of medical school. Try as she might, Annie had never been able to trace her.

'You took your time,' said Dom, when Annie eventually knocked on his door.

'I got lost,' she told him evenly, and that was true enough in its way.

He looked at her, his eyes narrowing thoughtfully, sensing the drop in emotional temperature. 'Is there anything wrong?' he asked. 'Anything you dislike about the place?'

His second question was easily answered. 'Absolutely not. I never expected anything so—so comprehensive and up to date.'

'You're still on, then.'

Oh, yes—she was still on. What choice did she have? She couldn't afford to turn down a job because the man offering it had given her one-time best friend a nervous breakdown! 'Yes, I'm still on—thank you, Dr Smith,' she added for the benefit of the small, bright-eyed child who was watching her with such interest.

'She the new'n then, Doctor?' the boy asked curiously.

'Yes, Willie, Dr Duncan is the new'n. I hope you approve,' Dom added gravely.

Willie gave Annie another thorough appraisal before allowing that, in his opinion, she was an improvement on her predecessor. 'So far,' he added cautiously.

'Thank you very much, Willie,' said Annie solemnly. And, then, having been doing some appraising of her own, she asked how long it had been since his accident.

'You telt her, Doctor,' said Willie reproachfully to Dom.

'Not a word,' he returned, much amused. 'All right—be off with you, now. We've kept Mr Patterson waiting quite long enough!'

Was that a rebuke for me? wondered Annie, as Willie asked plaintively, 'Are ye sure I'm fit for the school now, Doctor?'

'For the third time, yes, I am,' smiled Dom. 'But, remember, if there's any trouble with the Clyde Street gang they'll have me on their necks—and fast.'

'Ah reckon they ken that a'ready, Doctor,' returned Willie with relish. 'Be seein' youse then,' he told Annie as he shambled out.

'It's a pity you weren't here in time to see me examine him,' said Dom.

'As I told you, I got lost,' returned Annie, sensing criticism. 'Anyway, I think I've got the picture.'

Dom lounged back in his chair, hands clasped behind his head. 'Have you now?' he returned sceptically.

'The boy has a left-sided hemiparesis, resulting from an injury to his right cerebral hemisphere.'

'That much is fairly obvious,' he considered, unimpressed.

Annie ignored that and went on thoughtfully, 'Those two wee, round depressions are interesting—right temple just above the hairline and the other at the back. He certainly didn't have a fall—or a blow. In fact, if I didn't think it wasn't possible, I'd say he'd been skewered.'

Dom's superior smile faded as he lowered his arms and sat up straight. ' "Skewered",' he repeated. 'That's a very interesting observation.'

'They certainly weren't done surgically and it couldn't have been a bullet,' Annie pursued. 'Yet what else could have passed through like that? I've got to admit I'm stumped.'

Dom smiled briefly. 'No, you're not, Annie, lass— you're spot on as usual. Picture a derelict factory site with boys sneaking in and larking about behind the guard's back. Then one of them picks up something and throws it. . .'

Annie was onto that in a flash. 'Something like a dart. A bolt, perhaps? No, it would have to be something sharp. A metal spike—that's it! And if Willy's skull is abnormally thin, then. . . Is that it, Dom? Is that what happened?'

'Spot on,' he repeated. 'It didn't pass through, of course—not enough velocity for that. The child was rushed to Surgical Neurology in Glasgow with the thing barely protruding at the front.'

'Good grief! And if it had been any longer—or more central then—'

'Curtains,' he finished for her grimly. 'Now you know why we think that he is so special.' He paused. 'And that was a fantastic bit of deduction—even for somebody with your flair. Your new colleagues are going to be very impressed.'

'I hope so,' returned Annie, not sorry to have impressed him so soon. But she was determined not to show pleasure at his praise and merely asked matter-of-factly what he would like her to do next.

He shrugged. 'Anything you like as long as you come to the staff common room at one. Wednesday is our day for a working lunch and general discussion of problems, so it'll be a good opportunity for you to meet those of the team you've not met already.' Before she could comment, he asked, 'How well do you know Burnside?'

'I don't,' she had to admit. 'So I was wondering if—'

But Dom had already decided. 'You'd better come with me now, then. My visits today are fairly well scattered, so if you keep your eyes open, you'll get some idea of the layout.' They stopped at Reception and Dom asked Carol for a street plan as he was about to give Dr Duncan a geography lesson.

Annie followed him quietly out to the car park and couldn't believe her eyes when he unlocked the F-registered Granada she'd noticed earlier. 'What—no shiny sports job?' she asked impulsively, remembering the sort of car he used to drive.

'Use your head, Annie,' he retorted curtly. 'This is an industrial town, not some leafy upmarket Glasgow suburb.'

'I take your point,' she murmured, as she slid into the front passenger seat. And so she did—on a strictly practical level. An expensive car in an area like this would be asking for trouble, as well as being very insensitive. Which thought brought Annie back to her initial amazement. What was Dominic Smith-Jardine doing here at all?

He thrust the street plan into her hands and jabbed it with the car keys. 'There's the Centre and our first patient lives in Archway Street. See if you can find it before we get there.'

This was no time to admit to feeling sick whenever she tried to read in a moving vehicle, so Annie obediently squinted down at the plan. 'First right and then second left,' she was able to say thankfully, quite soon.

'Very good,' said Dom, before spoiling things by telling her that the rest of their destinations would be a lot harder to find.

Annie decided to stay in the car when they got to Archway Street and try committing the plan to memory, but Dom hadn't just brought her along for the ride. 'Come on, then—you'll not want to miss this!'

Mrs Bessie MacMillan lived in the top back flat of a grimy, run-down tenement that overlooked the canal. The walls of the stairway were chipped and stained and the stone steps hadn't seen soap and water for a year or more, but the brass name-plate on Mrs MacMillan's door gleamed brightly in the shaft of sun forcing its way through the dirty skylight. Dom hammered on the door, provoking heavy, uneven footsteps from within.

'I've brought my newest colleague to meet you, Bessie,' he said to the tiny, bird-like woman who opened the door with caution. Her strange footsteps were instantly explained. Bessie had an artificial leg.

She eyed Annie without too much enthusiasm. 'Women doctors and men nusses,' she grumbled. 'I dinnae ken whit the world is comin' to.' She shuffled awkwardly round and led the way to her cluttered but spotless kitchen-cum-living room.

'Bessie is rather old-fashioned,' Dom murmured to Annie with wonderful understatement.

'I haird that,' accused their patient. 'I may be lame and near enough blind, but I'm no dief! Whit are ye wantin' the day?'

'Blood,' said Dom.

'Did I no' give ye some last week?'

'You did—and it told me as plain as plain that you'd not been sticking to your diet or taking your tablets. If you're not a good girl, it'll be the nurse and the needle every day—and you know how you'd hate that. Diagnosis, please!' he fired at Annie.

'Diabetes,' she fired back, earning a look of grudging respect from Bessie.

'Mebbe the two o' youse would like a cuppa tea,' she offered.

Dom thanked her gravely, but said that he'd got a particularly long list of visits today.

'When have ye not?' asked Bessie, baring her arm for the blood-taking. 'He's a good worker—just like his grandad,' she told Annie.

'I didn't know that your grandfather was a doctor,' said Annie, when they were clattering down the murky stairs again.

'He wasn't. He was head of the family business when Bessie started at the works as an office cleaner. She claims he was always first in and last to leave. My father was, too, in his day. Unlike—'

He cut off abruptly and changed the subject. 'And she still does all her own housework and cooking, despite that prosthesis. And I wish she didn't. Her sight is going and I'm terrified that one of these days she'll scald herself—or worse.'

Annie was dying to know what it was that he'd almost said but knew better than to ask outright. 'What's the home help situation in the town?' she substituted.

'Quite good, but Bessie's sent them all packing. She says that they don't go down on their hands or knees, or into the corners.'

'Difficult,' said Annie, hiding a smile.

'As you say, but wait until you've met our next customer before you give Bessie the wooden spoon for cussedness.'

'An even more difficult old lady?'

'No—a fushionless young one.'

They got into the car and, this time, Dom didn't insist on Annie tracing the way on the plan. That was just as well because the route was a complicated roundabout one from the older part of the town to a sprawling run-down housing scheme on the outskirts. He parked between two tower blocks. 'I hope you're in good nick,' he said grimly when he'd pressed for the lift without result and headed for the stairs.

'Poor maintainance?' asked Annie, following.

'Constant vandalism.'

'But why—?'

'Save your breath,' he advised. 'We've a long way to go.'

On the ninth floor, he stopped outside a door which had obviously been kicked in more than once. It was opened by a drab-looking girl who had a pale and fretful infant tucked under one arm. 'Oh, it's you, Doctor. Oh!' she repeated suspiciously, on noticing Annie.

This time, Dom didn't bother with introductions. 'So what's the matter with Tam this time, Tina?' he demanded.

'He's had another of his fits and he fell and hit his head on the cooker, Doctor.'

'Does he never fall against something soft?' asked Dom neutrally.

The girl shot him a look of mingled fright and defiance as she answered, 'He's in here. Sleeping.'

In a gaudy, over-furnished livingroom dominated by a vast television set and video, a boy of three or four lay on the sofa. His face was badly bruised and blood had congealed round a jagged cut on his forehead. The merest glance told Annie that the child was unconscious.

Dom drew in his breath on a hiss as he swooped down to place the child in the recovery position, before ordering an ambulance on his mobile phone. Then he turned to the mother and asked angrily, 'Where's Gary?'

'Out. And Tam fell. I telt ye,' she insisted with more animation than she'd shown yet.

She's got the point of his question all right, realised Annie. 'Is Gary another of your children?' she asked artfully.

The girl sent her a look of pure loathing. 'He's ma boyfriend. Are you from the social?' she demanded suspiciously.

Annie and Dom shared a glance of understanding before he explained that Dr Duncan had joined the practice. Then he turned to the baby which the mother had dumped in an armchair beside two cats. He picked up the child, hefting her in his hands. 'Let me see, Tracy must be ten months old now but she feels no more than five. What are you feeding her on?'

The girl shrugged. 'She's an awful picky eater—and I dinnae get enough from the social to buy the things yon health visitor thinks she should have.'

Dom let his eyes roam round the garish room before they rested finally on the row of bottles and stacks of beer cans on the fancy sideboard.

The girl flushed angrily. 'S'aright for you with yer millions,' she muttered, 'but a body needs somethin'. . .'

'Like a sense of responsibility,' Dom suggested wearily, looking at his watch. 'We can't leave here until the ambulance comes,' he murmured to Annie. 'I'd not put it past her to turn it away.'

'Could I not stay and let you away to your next call?' she offered impulsively.

His face lightened immediately. 'That would be splendid—and you could check the baby over while you're waiting. I'll be in the next block—flat seventy-five. . .' He was already halfway to the door.

'See you there, then,' Annie called after him, relieved. She'd had visions of being stranded indefinitely in this hellhole the minute she'd made her offer.

'I can manage,' the girl said mutinously.

Annie gave her a wide, innocent look. 'My dear, I wouldn't dream of leaving you alone with two sick bairns. Supposing Tam woke up and had another fit? And wee Tracy must be such a worry, too. Tell you what, I'll give her the once-over while we're waiting. . .' So bright, so helpful and so unstoppable.

The baby also showed signs of rough handling so when the ambulance came, Annie sent her to hospital, too. 'Two cases of suspected non-accidental injury,' she told the crew in a low voice.

'You'll be coming too, then,' assumed the leader, smiling at Tina, but she refused. 'Hope he doesn't give her a battering, too,' he said to Annie as they all trooped down the stairs. 'This is not the first time we've been called out for this wee lad.'

Dom let Annie into flat seventy-five with a question on his lips. 'Yes, the baby had also come in for some rough treatment,' she confirmed, 'so I sent her as well. Both with a diagnosis of NAI.'

'Good girl.' Dom was relieved, but also busy now with another problem. His patients here were no more suitably housed than the pathetic girl they had just left.

'The sixties so-called planners have a lot to answer for,' Annie said grimly as they clattered down the stairs. The lifts in this block had also been vandalised.

'I've been pressing for the Browns to be rehoused ever since I took over,' Dom fumed. 'But the answer's always the same. Not enough sheltered housing to go round.'

Having arrived when the consultation was over, Annie only had visual evidence to go on. 'He's obviously a chronic bronchitic and cor pulmonale,' she said confidently, 'but I wasn't sure what to make of his wife. Ankles very swollen and she's rather pale, so—'

'You don't miss a thing, Annie,' he congratulated her. 'Yes, Maisie has left ventricular failure, though it's actually her arthritis that bothers her most.'

'How in the world do they manage?'

'A home help goes in once a week to keep the dust down and a neighbour fetches their groceries.'

'What a life,' sighed Annie sympathetically.

'That depends how you mean that. They're absolutely devoted to one another.'

'How fortunate,' she said.

'And you needn't sound so sceptical,' he reproved

her. 'It still happens. Occasionally.' Dom unlocked the car and they got in.

Annie hadn't been aware of sounding sceptical and she'd have said that if anybody had, it was he. She thought about Dom's wife; so beautiful, rich and fun-loving, and wondered how she liked this new life he'd chosen. Not a lot, if that last remark was anything to go by.

Before she could decide how best to find out, Dom said, 'Now for two suspected cases of flu, a dear old chap with Parkinsonism and a recent stroke victim to complete our morning. I hope you're enjoying the job so far.'

'Is variety not supposed to be the spice of life?' asked Annie as they drove off.

CHAPTER TWO

'Now whom did you not meet this morning?' asked Dom when he and Annie got back to base.

'The other doctors. They were all consulting and, besides, Mrs Carlisle thought you'd prefer to make the introductions yourself.'

'She's got a head on her shoulders, has our Laura,' he confirmed. 'Ten minutes to go,' he added with a glance at his watch, 'so there's just time to fill you in.' He bundled Annie into his consulting room and gave her some quick-fire sketches.

Dr Syme was near to retirement and only worked three-quarter time now. He'd been the Smith-Jardine's family doctor, was one of the old school—caring and wise—and all the patients adored him.

Dr Angus Milne never minded how hard he worked as long as he got his rugby on a Saturday.

Having no family or hobbies, Dr Jane Firth lived only for her work. 'She can be a bit obsessive some-times,' Dom added, 'so you'll be good for her.'

Annie thought that she recognised the type. 'On the other hand, she may resent another woman on the staff,' she warned.

Dom said that, if push came to shove, his money would be on Annie. 'And, lastly, there's Peter Sinclair, our trainee,' he rattled on. 'Peter is all of twenty-five, fresh-faced and eager to save the world. You'll like our Peter.'

'I hope I'll like all of them and that they'll all like me,' Annie returned firmly. 'But, now, if you don't

25

mind I'd like to go and comb my hair before I'm inspected. Baby Tracy just about had it all out by the roots.'

Dom's word pictures of the other doctors had all been spot on and Annie had no difficulty with identification, even before he named names. As well as all the partners, Craig Patterson the physio was there as well as three of the practice nurses and a quiet, competent-looking girl who was introduced as Nan, the health visitor. And of course Laura was there, notebook at the ready.

This proved to be a business meeting rather than a professional one and Annie found it all rather bewildering. Dr Syme noticed this and, afterwards, he attached himself to her before anybody else could.

Annie took a sandwich from the plate he was offering and told him, 'Silly, I guess, but I was expecting a case conference. You know, with everybody describing their trickiest patients and inviting comments.'

'We do confer,' he told her, 'but more informally, and frequently on a one-to-one basis. Dom tells me that you've got your FRCS, so no doubt we'll all be beating a path to your door when wondering whether to refer a patient for a surgical opinion.' He paused before hinting delicately, 'A woman surgeon is still something of a rarity.'

'Prejudice has a lot to do with that,' returned Annie, with feeling.

'And so you gave up the unequal struggle,' he assumed. 'But I mustn't monopolise the new girl. I just wanted to welcome you and hope that you'll be very happy working here.'

So Dom had kept to himself the real reason for her change of direction. Annie just had time to feel grateful to him before Jane Firth beat Craig Patterson for a place at her side. 'Are you interested in women's problems?' she asked in an earnest whisper.

'I'm interested in injury and disease, whatever the sex of the patient,' replied Annie carefully.

Jane pursed her lips before explaining, 'I asked that because I myself have specialised in that area.'

'Then I shall know where to come for advice when up against something I've not met before,' returned Annie, feeling really proud of such tact.

Dom had overheard that and, as Jane moved away, he whispered, 'I forgot to tell you that Jane considers obs and gynae to be her special province, but more of that later. Have a sandwich,' he said aloud.

'Thanks, but I've already had one.'

'So? You're allowed at least two. What did you think of the meeting?'

'It wasn't what I'd expected. All that business about costs—I guess there's much more to general practice than I'd realised.'

'Just like all hospital doctors, I suppose you thought it was nothing but coughs and colds and indigestion—or packing them off to hospital with anything that didn't actually show. Now, there's no need to look so indignant.' Indignant? Annie was seething! 'I felt just the same, Annie, until I learned better. I'll fetch you a coffee. Do you still prefer it black?' He was gone before she could answer.

'I wish I had one half of Dom's energy,' said Craig Patterson from Annie's other side.

She spun round. 'Coming from a physio, that's quite something. Watching you folk at work always makes me feel quite tired.'

'That's certainly the impression we like to give,' he joked. 'Here, have a sandwich.'

Annie took one and said, smiling, 'Everyone keeps

pressing food on me. Do I look so undernourished?'

The look he gave her was very flattering. 'You look absolutely fine to me,' was the verdict. 'In fact, I'd go so far as to say it's a long time since I saw anybody who looked quite so fine.'

Annie preened elaborately. 'You're a smooth talker, Mr Physio,' she purred. 'I can see I'll have to watch myself with you around.'

'Don't bother, Doctor, I'll do that for you,' he was saying when Dom returned with Annie's coffee.

The two men then fell into a highly technical discussion about young Willie. 'That's a very bright lad,' Annie remarked thoughtfully when Craig had been called away to speak to a patient.

'You can say that again,' Dom told her. 'He's got a master's degree in bio-mechanics as well as his physio B.Sc. He's being head-hunted by the college to lecture, so I'm afraid he'll not be with us too much longer.' He fixed her with a bright, probing look. 'What was he saying to you earlier to make you look so pleased with yourself?'

'He was complimenting me on my—er—general appearance.'

'Was he now? I didn't realise he was so impressionable.' The way he said it suggested that, appearance-wise, he himself rated her about three out of ten. Annie knew that, had always known it, and didn't like it any more now than she ever had.

'This coffee is rather bitter,' she said censoriously.

'I think so, too, so I'll have a word with Laura before she lays in any more of it. Now, about this afternoon, Annie. I think I should go a little more deeply into the set-up here—get you properly prepared for the fray.'

'I seem to remember hearing this morning that Wednesday is your half-day.'

'Which is why I've got the time to spare. There are one or two things I must do first, so shall we say my room about three?' And again he was off before Annie could reply. Now there's a technique worth practising, she thought. Apart from anything else, it's a jolly good way of avoiding being contradicted.

'Dr Duncan—' it was Laura Carlisle at her elbow now '—if you've got a minute, this would be a good time to get the paperwork relating to your appointment out of the way.'

'Yes—fine.' Annie followed her to her office. Well, it was fine, was it not? She needed a job and this could be an interesting one. The sticking point was Dom. On the other hand, she wasn't committing herself to more than a six months' trial. Not too long, yet hopefully long enough to negotiate her way back into hospital—in some other city if necessary. As Jack had said, surely with her track record. . .

'Sorry, where do I sign?' she asked when she realised that Laura was holding out her contract.

I've done it now, she realised, as she strolled back to her room to put in the time there until her meeting with Dom at three. And it would be all right. As Dom had said that morning, the two of them always had worked well together. And he'd changed. Quite a lot. Annie wondered why.

Alone and quiet in her room, she let her mind slip back over the years.

How excited she'd been about going to university— the first girl in her family to do so.

'No good comes of educating a girl,' Granny had told Father. Granny had kept house for them all since Mother's death. 'And you'll find it difficult enough helping the three boys through college on a minister's stipend. Besides, I could make good use of her here now I'm getting old.'

But Father had been adamant. Annie was clever and she must have her chance. So Annie had said goodbye to her family and the rambling old manse in the pretty little Clydeside resort where she had grown up, and taken the train to Glasgow.

On her first day at university she'd made friends with Lynne, who had been given the room next to hers in the hostel, and on her second she'd had her first sight of Dom.

As she and Lynne had stood at the gates of the medical school, gazing inwards in excitement and awe, Dom had hooted for them to get out of the way of his wicked-looking sports car with the top down.

'He must be a lecturer,' Lynne had breathed reverently. 'No student could afford a car like that. And did you ever see such a dishy man? I hope he'll be teaching us.'

By supper-time, she'd found out all about him and she'd briefed Annie over spaghetti and chips. 'You *must* have heard of the Smith-Jardines!' she'd exclaimed, when Annie had looked vague.

'They're huge in marine engineering—or used to be. Quite in the millionaire bracket. He's a final-year student; absolutely brilliant and wildly popular and good at everything. And how the blazes am I going to get him to notice me?'

Lynne had soon discovered that Dom was as famous for the number of his girlfriends as he was for his brains, charm and cash, but she had never quite given up hope until Dom had graduated six months later and had passed out of their lives for a few years.

He'd eventually noticed Lynne and Annie for the first time on the wards one day during their second

clinical year. He'd noticed Annie for her brain and
Lynne for the length of her beautiful legs. One date
and Lynne had fallen for him completely; neglecting
work, friends, sleep—everything, just to be with him
or to dream about him when they had to be apart.

Annie had constantly warned her that it wouldn't
last and of course it hadn't. Almost three months to
the day on which he first took her out Dom had
dropped Lynne like a hot potato and, quite soon after,
had married the socially desirable daughter of one of
his father's business associates.

But by then a distraught Lynne had disappeared—
just dropped out of medical school and vanished,
despite all Annie's efforts to find her. She'd had to
comfort herself with the reflection that her friend had
at least been spared all the pain of that fancy cathedral
wedding so soon after being jilted.

Going to work with Dom the following year had
been something of an eye-opener for Annie. Until
then, prejudiced and unforgiving, she had steadfastly
refused to believe that he was really as good at his job
as everybody said. But in that six months he had earned
her deepest respect for his professionalism, although
she continued to disapprove of him as a human being.
And yet here she was, preparing to work with him a
second time

'And I told Lynne *she* was crazy,' she sighed.

'It seems to me that you could do with an accountant
on the staff,' said Annie when Dom had explained all
the paperwork involved in fund-holding. 'It's a wonderful idea in principle because it gives GPs so much more
scope and control, but what happens if they
overspend?'

Dom gave a brief chuckle. 'Trust Annie Duncan to

put her finger on the weak spot,' he said, sounding pleased. 'Fortunately for us, Laura has a very good head for figures and a talent for crisply-worded memos if she thinks any one of us looks like getting carried away.'

'So you're in favour of fund-holding, then?'

'Obviously, or I'd not have applied for it.'

'I didn't know whether it had been instituted by you or your predecessor. And most doctors resent financial restraints on their work,' Annie retorted, giving him two good reasons for her remark—or so she thought.

'Surely, what we all resent is the excessive diversion of limited cash into unnecessarily complicated bureaucracy,' he corrected. 'That's why fund-holding is such a good thing. The doctor holds the purse-strings and only employs enough clerical staff to free him to get on with the job.'

Honesty obliged Annie to admit that he'd put that very well.

'But, then, I always did have a way with words,' he returned, smiling.

'And with people,' she had to add.

'Some people,' Dom retorted pointedly. And Annie got the point.

'I hope we will find we can work together,' she said with a flash of unguarded honesty.

'Of course we will,' he told her confidently. 'We've always agreed on a professional level.'

'Yes—of course,' she agreed quietly. 'And I really should thank you for taking me on.'

Dom fixed her with a searching look. 'But only if you really mean it. I wouldn't want you to endanger your immortal soul.'

'I didn't know you believed in such a thing!' she cried in astonishment.

'That's beside the point. What isn't is that *you* probably do—given your background. And you never did give me the benefit of the doubt on the personal level.'

That was nothing but the truth and, for once, Annie couldn't think of a suitable answer. 'Good heavens! Is that the time?' she cried, jumping to her feet. 'There'll be nothing left of your half-day if you don't leave soon.'

The slow, superior smile which spread over his face told Annie what he thought of that for a cop-out. But all he said was, 'I've pencilled you in for a surgery tomorrow morning. It's an all-appointments affair, so it should be reasonably straightforward. Any objections?'

'Oh, no. Whatever you decide. You're the boss—and a very good organiser, if I remember aright.'

'Thank you,' Dom answered gravely, but there was a hint of mirth in his eyes.

Annie was wondering how to conclude this vaguely uncomfortable interview. 'Is there anything else for today? Because if not. . .' She shut up, afraid that she may have sounded like a clock-watcher.

Naturally Dom couldn't let slip a chance like that. 'I don't think so, so you have my permission to leave as soon as you like,' he returned with barely concealed amusement.

'Thank you,' said Annie, resolving not to lay herself open to any more remarks like that. 'But before I go I'd like to glance over the records of the patients I'll be seeing tomorrow. It's some time since I've treated any but surgical cases and I wouldn't want to be caught out.'

'Now, that is something I really cannot imagine,' he

claimed, 'but I appreciate your forethought. Of course, you'll have noticed that we're computerised.'

'Yes—and in case you were wondering, I'm well used to that.'

'Until tomorrow, then,' he said as Annie left the room.

The clerk on duty was impressed by Annie's request and quickly gave her the patient list she requested. Annie thanked her and returned to her room.

She was halfway through her researches when all hell broke loose somewhere in the building; a confused babble of voices raised in panic, scurrying feet and much banging of doors. Annie rushed out to see what was going on.

The main hall was full of people milling frantically about and it took a minute to decide who was actually hurt and who was trying to help. Other staff were arriving at a run, including Dom. 'Stand still and calm down,' he roared above the noise. Then he pounced on the most serious casualty. 'Peter—Craig—get him to the treatment room. Carol, fetch Dr Duncan—oh, there you are, Annie. That one's all yours. Now, what else have we got here?'

Annie didn't wait to see but followed the trainee and the physio who were half carrying a man who was bleeding copiously from a nasty-looking neck wound. They placed him on the table and cut away his clothing. With nothing now to mop it up, the blood pulsed out like a fountain.

'Craig—prop him up. Peter—a drip. Quickly! And you,' cried Annie to a girl in nurse's uniform, 'get me some instruments, please, while I give him a shot of local.' Having done that, she threw off her jacket and put on a plastic apron. 'We'll soon clear up this mess for you,' she promised the wounded man, while putting on surgical gloves. Then she picked up a probe and some swabs and delicately explored the wound, searching for the severed artery.

She located it after what seemed like hours but could only have been seconds. Not the sub clavian, thank heaven, but bad enough. The poor man must have lost pints. Thankfully, she ligated the damaged vessel and breathed more easily. By then Peter had set up a drip and Annie praised him before asking about blood pressure.

'Eighty over thirty,' said the nurse, which was better than Annie had dared to hope. She worked on, her concentration absolute. Whatever had cut the artery had also partially severed the lateral head of the sterno mastoid muscle. She made a temporary repair and tidied up the wound, having neither the equipment nor the time for a proper job; an ambulance crew was waiting to take the man to hospital.

As she put in a drain and made a temporary closure, Annie was pierced by a shaft of pure envy for the lucky casualty surgeon who'd be tidying up her clumsy emergency job in the calm perfection of the operating theatre.

'That's a really first-class job, Miss Duncan,' breathed young Peter at her elbow.

Annie thanked him for according her surgeon's status but said she was afraid that, actually, it was a bit of a botch-up but at least the bleeding had been stopped.

'Nonsense,' refuted Dom, peering over her shoulder. 'That *is* a first-class job, Annie, lass. I knew I could count on you.'

'You should see me on a good day,' she returned gruffly to hide her pleasure at his praise. His professional approval meant as much to her as ever.

'The paramedics would like a run-down on the patient,' interrupted Craig, so Annie gave them an outline of her first aid before going over to the wash-basin to clean up.

Despite the apron, her clothes were liberally spattered with blood. Over her shoulder she asked Dom, 'Does this sort of thing happen often? Because if so, I'll be putting in for a clothing allowance.'

'Believe it or not, that's the first time we've had such a punch-up practically on our doorstep,' he said reassuringly.

'So that's what it was. What about the other casualties?'

'None as bad as yours. A couple of minor fractures and numerous cuts and bruises.'

'I seem to recall quite a lot of screaming at one point,' said Annie curiously.

'From a fifteen-year-old with a two-inch cut on one cheek which she thinks will put paid to her modelling career.'

'And will it?'

'Lord, I don't know,' said Dom. 'I've never studied that particular subject.' He was looking at Annie's skirt, which was now soaked through after her unsuccessful efforts to sponge off the blood. 'I hope that's not new,' he said.

'Second time on,' she sighed. 'Do you always give the dirtiest jobs to your newest recruit?'

'Problems go to whoever is most competent to deal with them,' Dom corrected firmly. 'And I'm very glad you were here, Annie. That was not a job I'd have cared to tackle—and I doubt that any of the others would have liked it either. Well done! Now come along to the common room. Rumour has it that Laura's made a therapeutic pot of tea.'

The resourceful Laura had also brought along a skirt

of her own which had been destined for the cleaners.
'It's a bit on the short side, Doctor,' she said when
Annie had thanked her and tried it on, 'but it'll save
you from any embarrassment on the way home. You
looked as though you'd just done a murder.'

Angus Milne came in at that point. 'Partying?' he
queried in his breezy way. 'Having seen all that gore
on the waiting-room floor, I expected to find you hard
at work.'

'And so we were a minute ago,' Dom informed him.
'You were lucky to be out visiting.'

'What happened, then?' Angus asked belatedly, but
before anybody could tell him Jane came in, looking
anything but pleased.

'Somebody has made a terrible mess in the treatment
room and I need it for my first patient,' she said
severely. 'Who's responsible?'

'I am,' said Annie, jumping up guiltily.

Dom ordered her to sit down before giving Jane an
account of the dramatic happenings. 'The most seriously injured man had a serious wound at the base of
his neck, which gave Annie the chance to demonstrate
her surgical skills,' he concluded.

'That's all very well,' said Jane, 'but all that mess!'
She looked at Annie. 'Why did you not send them all
straight to hospital? That's what I'd have done.'

'I hope not,' Dom said evenly. 'Annie's patient was
bleeding to death.'

'Then why was he not taken straight to the hospital?'
Jane Firth was clearly one for going by the book.

At any other time Annie would probably have told
her exactly what she thought, but her common sense
was warning her not to start a feud on her first day.

'You may have a point,' she told Jane with tremendous restraint. 'But I just went ahead and did what I

thought was required. I'm straight from an accident
and emergency department, don't forget. No doubt I'll
learn the general practice ropes—given time.'

'Please don't think I was criticising,' said Jane gra-
ciously, now that she'd put the new girl in her place.

'Perish the thought, dear,' murmured Angus Milne,
with a broad wink for Annie.

Then Dom said with quiet authority, 'You weren't
here to assess the situation, Jane, so shall we leave it
at that?'

Nothing could have been more effective. Jane
flushed deeply and agreed. 'As you say. And, now, if
you'll excuse me, I've got a very long list tonight.'

Angus decided that he'd better get started, too, so
Annie and Dom were left alone. 'I'm really sorry about
that,' he said. 'As I told you, Jane is a good doctor
but she doesn't much like the unexpected.' He pulled
a face. 'Also, she was hoping that I'd take on a man
so you're a bit of a disappointment.'

Annie allowed herself a brief smile as she answered,
'I'm not used to sexual discrimination from
another woman.'

Dom raised his eyebrows at such a mild reaction
from one of Annie's fiery disposition. 'When she went
for you like that, I was waiting for you to blow your
top,' he confessed.

'Don't think I didn't feel like it,' she told him fervently, but first day in a new job. . .and all that.'

'You're learning, Annie,' he said, proving beyond
doubt that he knew exactly why she'd been driven to
try general practice.

'Perhaps—but don't push me too far,' she warned,
her tawny eyes glinting dangerously.

Dom merely grinned at her. 'Still the same old
Annie, then, underneath that sophisticated veneer.'

'Folk don't ever change—not really,' she said. 'They just learn to dissemble if they're wise.' She meant him as much as herself.

'I wonder,' he said, half to himself. 'I wonder. . .'

'You do that,' Annie told him briskly. 'I'm off to clean up that treatment room.'

'I'm pretty sure that Rosemary will have done it by now.'

'Who's Rosemary?' Annie asked predictably.

'The nurse who assisted you so ably. She slipped quietly out as soon as Jane mentioned the mess.'

'Then I must find her and thank her before I go home.' She paused briefly. 'What a day this has been— and what a wonderful half-day off you've had!'

'D'you know, I'd quite forgotten I wasn't supposed to be here,' he said.

'You'd better dream up a better excuse than that if you don't want an earful when you get home,' she advised roundly.

'Think so?' he asked, unsmiling.

I've put my foot in it, she realised. 'Well—it seemed a reasonable assumption. After all, somebody is going to wonder where *I've* been all day,' she prevaricated.

'I hadn't heard you were married, Annie,' he said curiously.

'I'm not,' she admitted, breathing more easily now that the awkward moment had passed. All the same, she was glad that Carol came in just then to tell Dom that he was wanted on the phone.

He thanked ber briefly before saying to Annie, 'If I don't see you again before you go, I'd like to tell you how glad I am that you've decided to join the practice.'

'Thanks, Dom—I'm glad, too,' she returned, quite surprised to find that—after all that had happened, past and present—she really meant it.

CHAPTER THREE

'You're a great girl, Doctor,' approved the cleaner, as Annie let herself into the health centre. 'First here— and with the furthest to come.'

'Have I managed to beat Dr Smith to it this morning, Mrs Mac?' asked Annie, feeling pleased.

'Och, no, dear—I wasnae counting him. Times, I think he lives here, the dear man.'

Annie had thought that herself more than once in the past month. She now knew almost all there was to know about her other colleagues, but Dom remained a mystery. The only thing she had discovered was that he lived in a converted barn a mile or two outside the town. And she'd only found that out because one of her patients had mentioned that he was her nearest neighbour.

A discreet question or two would probably have explained things but Annie—never before shy about anything at all—found herself quite unable to reveal her curiosity about Dom.

Word had gone round that the new doctor was very approachable, as well as knowing her stuff, and patients were beginning to ask for Annie when booking in. She would have been pleased if most of them hadn't been on Jane's list.

One such was her first patient that Monday morning. Annie got up and held out her hand. 'Good morning, Mrs Irvine. We've not met before, have we?' When the patient was seated and hopefully at ease, Annie switched on the computer. 'I see that Dr Firth looked

after you when you had that ulcer on your leg. Is she
too busy to see you today?'

Mrs Irvine wriggled uneasily in her chair before saying, 'I've nothing against Dr Firth, Doctor—she made
a real good job of my leg—but I asked for you
specially. Mrs Carlisle says we can see who we like
and the lists are just a formality.'

Oh, dear, here we go again, thought Annie. What
was it that all these women—and they were always
women—had against Jane? Mrs Irvine supplied the
answer when Annie asked what seemed to be the
trouble this time.

After flushing slightly, the patient said, 'Suppose it's
what you'd call women's problems, Doctor. My friend
had the same trouble and Dr Firth asked her all sorts
of rude questions about her—her relations with her
husband. Maggie was that embarrassed, she didn't
know where to look. So she advised me to come to
you. I mean, that's not the sort of thing a respectable
woman wants to talk about, is it?'

Annie said tactfully that it all depended on the con-
text. 'Now, you just tell me what's worrying you and
I promise not to ask any more questions that I
must. OK?'

'Very well, Doctor.' Mrs Irvine glanced first at the
terminal as though she suspected it of eavesdropping.
Then she confided in a piercing whisper, 'It's the—
the *dryness*, Doctor.'

Annie nodded wisely and explained that there was
nothing unusual about that problem when a woman
wasn't just twenty-one any more. 'I'm going to prescribe a cream that I think will be a great help.'

But there was something else that would be even
more helpful if she dared to risk it. 'And if you could
persuade your husband to take his time—court you a

bit first, the way—' The look on Mrs Irvine's face told her that that idea was a non-starter before she said crushingly, 'We never talk about such things.'

Pity, thought Annie, when he's probably one of those who thinks it shouldn't take longer than blowing his nose. She reached for her prescription pad and a pamphlet that would also be helpful if only Mrs Irvine could contrive to bring it to the attention of her disappointing spouse.

'There are other preparations if this one doesn't work for you,' she said, 'and you must promise to let me know how things go. Never endure anything that can be easily remedied.'

Mrs Irvine assured Annie that she would but went out looking only marginally happier than she had when she came in.

As most of Jane's patients who consulted her had gynae-related problems, that suggested a tactful discussion was called for. But how to put things in a way that wouldn't offend Jane? Before Annie had worked that out, her next patient was knocking on the door.

She smiled at the rosy-cheeked old gentleman who came in. 'Hallo, Mr Henderson. How's the pain today?'

'Better, Doctor, thank you, but I'm still hirpling awful bad.'

'I'm afraid you will, my friend. The arthritis in that hip of yours is quite advanced. Have you given any more thought to a hip replacement?'

'I'm no' keen,' he admitted.

A bit of gentle probing on Annie's part brought out the death of a brother on the operating table at the age of nine. She explained carefully that both surgery and anaesthesia had made great strides since those days and eventually won a promise that he would give the operation some serious thought. Then Annie gave him a repeat prescription for Voltarol and buzzed for her third patient.

Everything she'd said to the old man was quite true, but how would she feel if he took her advice and the operation wasn't a success? It had been known. It's easier being a hospital doctor, Annie decided. By the time a patient sees a specialist the wavering time is usually past because the GP has talked him through it.

The door opened and she said, 'Hallo, Mrs Niven. I didn't expect to see you again quite so soon.' Like three days later. . .

'Nor me, Doctor, but who'd have thought the new tablets would drive it into my other shoulder so quickly?'

Not me for a start, thought Annie. Be tactful, now! 'Tell me how the first shoulder is doing,' she suggested.

'It's a bit better,' said the patient, 'but, like I said, the left one's flared up now.'

'Would I be right in thinking that you've been using the left arm more while the right was sore?'

'Fancy you knowing that, Doctor.'

'And then you stepped up your activity when the pain in the right shoulder eased off a bit?'

Mrs Niven replied with a question. 'Have you got a house of your own, Doctor?'

Annie nodded and wondered what that had to do with it.

'Then you'll know how it is. The pelmets were getting awful grubby and as for that ruddy great chandelier we got from his granny's house. . .'

Annie nodded again, her suspicions confirmed. 'I did warn you to go canny,' she reminded her patient. 'You may only have been feeling it in the one shoulder but the trouble is actually coming from your neck. Mr

Patterson is really the one to help you.'

'So you said last time, Doctor, but I'm not that keen on getting my neck wrung.'

'We call it traction, Mrs Niven, and it's no more than a gentle, controlled stretching.'

'All the same, my friend was nearly paralysed when she went to yon man who advertises in the evening paper.'

Everybody in the practice knew about Mrs Niven's friend and her disastrous excursion into the unlicensed fringes of medicine.

'Your friend went to a man who had taken a correspondence course, Mrs Niven, whereas our Mr Patterson has two degrees and is state registered. If he wasn't, we wouldn't have him in the practice.'

And what a pity that would have been, thought Annie on her own account. Craig was making no secret of the fact that he found her attractive.

'*Two* degrees, you say? Well, perhaps, then. . .and if it keeps on travelling about like this. Can I think about it and let ye know?'

'Of course you can, but I'm quite sure that it's physiotherapy you really need—not painkillers to mask the trouble. And let the dust alone for a while, eh? Doctor's orders.'

Mrs Niven said she'd think about that, too, and now would Doctor think she was awful nosy if she asked where she'd got that lovely jacket?

Annie smiled at her and named an exclusive little shop just off Glasgow's Buchanan Street.

'Aye, well, it's got that exclusive look,' nodded Mrs Niven. 'We all get what we pay for.' And off she went, leaving Annie hoping that she knew what was meant by that.

She buzzed for number four and checked the

computer to see what to expect. Good grief! The man had had four abdominal operations in the past three years. No wonder they'd put him on her list.

'Any more bunions and I'm setting up as a chiropodist,' Angus Milne was grumbling when Annie went to the common room for a coffee before starting her visits. 'Fifteen patients this morning and I'm telling you, folks, I never rose higher up the human frame than a varicose ulcer.'

There were appreciative smiles from Annie and the health visitor at such wit, but Jane Firth said pettishly, 'At least you had a good number, Angus. I only got nine this morning.' She was glaring at Annie as she spoke and went on, 'There's a note for *you* on the noticeboard. From the boss. He wants to see you some time today. In his room.'

'What about?' asked Annie as Jane seemed to have all the facts.

'I think I'll leave him to tell you that himself,' said Jane, with an air of smug satisfaction.

'As you please,' said Annie, unfazed, as she poured herself a coffee. 'Is there any more news of the Brightmans, Nan?' she asked, sitting down beside the health visitor. It was Tina Brightman's two children whom Annie had sent to hospital on her very first day.

'They're still in care,' reported Nan, 'and the police have sent a statement to the procurator fiscal. Not that it'll do any good,' she sighed. 'They can't hope to get the case to court unless Tina gives evidence against that dreadful boyfriend—and she'll not do that.'

'Proving cruelty to children is always a problem,' agreed Annie. 'Well, I suppose I'd better go and see if the boss is about.'

'He'll be away on his visits by now,' said Jane

severely, plainly implying that Annie should have gone
without her coffee in order to do the boss's will.

Annie gave her a broad smile in return and said,
'Then I've missed him, have I not?' as she went out.

She met Dom in the doorway of his room. 'Annie,
lass—come away in!' he exclaimed. 'I was just going
to look for you.'

'So I was told. By Jane,' she added, feeling very
sure that this was something to do with her.

'Ah, yes—Jane,' he echoed, closing the door and
leaning against it. 'She's been complaining about you.'

'Because she thinks I'm pinching her patients,'
guessed Annie.

'Something like that,' he agreed.

Annie squared up to him. 'Every time another one
appears in my consulting room I do everything I can,
short of actually refusing to see her.' She paused. 'So
far, they're all women with women's problems that
they are not prepared to discuss at the lengths Jane
considers necessary.'

'I can guess,' said Dom. 'This particular problem
arose before you came to us and in the absence of
another woman doctor on the staff they came either to
Andrew Syme or to me. Hence my decision to appoint
a woman.'

And I'd thought it was down to my skill and not my
gender, thought Annie, absurdly disappointed. And
why hadn't he warned her? She opened her mouth to
ask him that, but he went on, 'I guessed there'd be
defections and I hoped that Jane would either not
notice or else accept the situation. I suppose you think
that was cowardly.'

'That is not for me to say,' returned Annie evenly.
'But Jane feels slighted, so she—'

'Came and complained, obliging me to mention it

to you. Well, I've done that. End of story. Except that I'm really sorry if Jane is giving you a hard time.'

'She's not—not really. And it's only natural that she's peeved at the defection of her patients.' Annie paused to think before proceeding. 'Unfortunately, Jane has no idea how much pre-sixties women are embarrassed by her frank approach.'

'She has now—I told her as much yesterday when she complained.'

'And you don't think I'm at all to blame, then?' She needed to be sure of that.

'No. As I told you, the drift away began before you came. Are you happy here, Annie?' he asked abruptly.

That surprised her. She'd have expected him to ask whether she was settling down all right, rather than whether she was happy. 'The transition has been easier than I expected,' she told him truthfully, 'and I think that's because everybody has been so encouraging and helpful.'

'Except for Jane,' he surmised. 'You don't miss hospital too much, then?'

Oh, but she did. Every moment of every day. . .

'Not as much as I was afraid I would. But then there's such a positive and efficient atmosphere here.'

'You never do things by halves, do you, Annie?' he asked.

'I don't understand.'

'You revelled in your hospital career but now that's in the past you're hell-bent on making a go of this.'

Annie shrugged. 'I never did see much point in half-measures. So I'm either in up to my eyebrows or sitting on the fence.'

Dom burst out laughing. 'If you ever sat on a fence in your life, Annie Duncan, then I never saw you at it.' His smile faded. 'But I can't stand here gossiping.

So many visits. . .' It was almost as though he was reluctant to drop the barriers.

'Me, too,' said Annie. 'All these patients I keep poaching—' But by then she was talking to herself. Dom had grabbed his jacket and disappeared.

As Annie shot by Reception, Carol called out to ask if she could take what sounded like a really urgent call.

'Sure.' Annie went into reverse, took the phone and listened. Carol hadn't been wrong. 'I'll be with you in five minutes,' she said crisply, knowing by then that the patient lived literally just around the corner.

A harrassed husband had the door open before Annie was halfway up the garden path. 'She's awful bad, Doctor, and I'm worried sick. This way. . .'

Annie padded up the stairs behind him, frowning slightly when a voice called out pettishly to know why he hadn't brought her chocolate biscuits with her coffee. The patient was sitting up in bed swathed in a selection of fluffy bedjackets. The bed was littered with magazines and boxes of chocolates and the radio was playing loudly enough to give her a headache, supposing she didn't have one already.

Catching sight of Annie behind her husband, she collapsed limply on the pillows, eyes closed and breathing feebly.

Annie turned off the radio and got out her stethoscope. Then, having listened to the woman's chest, she took her pulse and temperature. 'Is she very ill, Doctor?' asked the poor man anxiously.

'Your wife has a slight cold in the head,' pronounced Annie in a steely voice. 'And it is my opinion that she would be much better up and about.'

'So it's not the flu, then?' he asked doubtfully.

'I can feel it coming on,' warned the patient.

'When—and *if*—it arrives, then call us again,' said Annie firmly. 'But for now, there is absolutely nothing you require from me.'

'I shall report you to Dr Smith,' shrieked the woman. 'I am very ill.'

'We are extremely busy just now and we have no time to waste,' retorted Annie. 'Good morning.'

She found her next patient on the ground floor of the tenement where lived the redoubtable Bessie MacMillan whom Dom had taken her to see on her first day.

'He's awful wheezy, Doctor, and rambling on and off, so I hope I did right not to bring him to the surgery,' apologised his wife as she opened the door to Annie.

Annie didn't like the sound of that. 'You were quite right,' she said, horrified next minute to find an old man with well-advanced febrile pneumonia and a pulse almost too fast to count.

She took out her mobile phone and rang for an ambulance. By rights she should have checked first to see if the hospital could take him but she didn't mean to give them the chance to refuse. There was no way that a case of this severity could be nursed at home, despite his wife's repeated assurance that he wouldn't want to go.

I got it all wrong, worried Annie, as she returned to her car. I should have come here before I went to see that raging hypochondriac. How easy it was, though, to get it wrong when you didn't know the patients. That dear old man's wife had reported 'a wee bit sniffle and some dirty phlegm on his chest,' whereas the tragedy queen's henpecked husband had described somebody close to death. 'And there's two silly heads I'd have liked to bang together,' muttered Annie as she sped off to case number three.

A genuine case of flu this time. 'Bed rest until the fever's away and plenty of fluids,' she advised. 'I'll look in again in a day or two. No—no trouble at all. You were quite right to call me to a woman of your mother's age.'

Now, did she have time to check on that sweet little soul discharged from hospital just three days after a cholescystectomy? It was only just round the corner. But I hope they're not at their lunch. They were, but they didn't mind a bit, and invited Annie to join them. 'You've saved me at least half an hour,' she told them gratefully, before dashing across town to her next three patients. All three lived in a retirement home and all were getting over flu. Annie read the riot act about that. Why had the warden not made sure that all her residents were immunised?

Back in her car, Annie checked her daybook. Two recent stroke cases, a cardiac patient and five more sent home early after surgery to give the GPs more work while helping to massage the hospital's through-put figures. Had the world gone mad?

By the time Annie got back to base, her first patient had arrived for evening surgery. No time for a cuppa, then, though her throat felt like sandpaper. She drank a glass of water in her room and hoped the she wouldn't be called out too often that night.

Laura Carlisle was a motherly soul. When she saw Annie struggling towards the stairs with her overnight bag, her 'rounds' bag and a carrier of provisions, she ran forward to help. But Annie insisted that she could manage. 'Away home with you, Laura—it's good to see you leaving before me for once,' she said. It was getting on for seven.

Laura agreed. 'That's true—my hubby's going to think it's Christmas. Are you sure you've got everything you need, Annie? Milk, bread. . .'

'Quite sure. This is not the first time I've had to stay overnight, remember.'

'I know—and I don't like it. A woman in this great building on her own in a district like this. . .'

'All the others live near enough to wait at home when they're on call. I'm just glad that somebody had the forethought to provide accommodation for one who doesn't.'

'Promise me you'll keep the doors locked,' urged Laura.

'I promise, Nanny,' said Annie with a grin.

The 'on-call suite', as they called it, had been a pleasant surprise. It had a well-furnished and comfortable bedsitter with a pull-down bed, a shower room and a box-sized kitchen. Annie put her prepared meal in the oven and took a shower while it warmed up. She was just about to take it out when the phone rang.

'Awful sorry to bother you, Doctor,' said a worried voice, 'but Jamie's crying with the earache and he's burning up.'

'Name and address?' Annie demanded promptly in case the anxious caller rang off too soon. 'Yes—got that. I'll be about ten minutes. And try not to worry.'

Annie grabbed her bag, thinking how daft it was to say that to a worried mother. How could she help but worry? And please, God, it's not meningitis. Only last week, there'd been two cases reported a mere five miles away.

Shortly afterwards, though, she was able to say reassuringly, 'Yes, he does have an infection in that ear, Mrs MacDougall, but it's definitely not meningitis. I'll leave you a prescription and enough antibiotics to see him through until tomorrow. I don't anticipate any problems but you've only to lift the phone if he doesn't settle.'

Back at the centre, Annie smelled burning as soon as she unlocked the side door which they always used at night. Her supper! She'd forgotten to switch off the stove when that call came in! She raced upstairs, hoping she could save the meal, being extremely hungry by then.

Before she could open the oven, she heard a door being opened and closed quietly downstairs. She froze. Burglars, for sure. It had to be. Keep calm, Annie. They'll be after drugs, so they'll not come up. Phone the police. But even as she dialled with trembling fingers, she heard steps on the stairs.

She looked round frantically for a weapon and seized a heavy saucepan. Then she hid behind the kitchen door, her heart beating wildly as the intruder entered the main room.

'You're back, then,' called Dom.

Annie came out, brandishing her weapon. 'You! What the hell. . .I thought you were a burglar!'

'I guessed that,' he said, eyeing the saucepan.

Annie followed his glance and lowered her arm. 'You're gey lucky you didn't get this between the eyes—creeping about like that.'

'So it seems—and that would have been a poor reward for my thoughtfulness.'

If there was anything thoughtful about his behaviour, Annie hadn't noticed. 'Tell me,' she invited sceptically.

I came back to deal with some paperwork while the place was quiet and as soon as I unlocked the door I smelled burning. When I traced it I realised it was your supper on fire so I went out and got you a replacement. I didn't expect to be assaulted for my trouble. And now we've cleared that up, may I get this onto plates before it gets cold?'

'What is it?' asked Annie, noticing a parcel wrapped in newspaper.

'Haddock and chips—what else? You can't get a boeuf bourguignon carry-out in Burnside.'

'I seem to remember you ticking off a grossly obese patient for eating fish and chips,' said Annie chirpily now that she'd recovered from her fright.

Dom pushed past her into the tiny kitchen, where he unwrapped the parcel. 'You're not obese,' he remarked.

Annie had followed him. 'I soon will be if I eat that lot,' she guessed, gazing at the mound.

'That happens to be two portions,' said Dom. 'One for you and one for me. Would you prefer me to take mine home? Of course, it will be cold by the time I get there but I suppose I could heat it up.'

He sounded so pathetic that Annie had to laugh. 'Oh, Dom, you're such a clown,' she chuckled.

'And you're the hardest, most unfeeling female it's ever been my misfortune to meet,' he accused.

'So what's new?' asked Annie, unaccountably cut to the quick but determined not to let it show. 'I don't have the bottle to shoo you off your own premises, though, so please feel free to eat here.'

'I would hate to inconvenience you.'

'And I'll not let you. If you want to know the truth, I always feel ever so slightly uneasy when I'm alone in the place after dark.' Why had she said that? It wasn't as bad as that.

But it had quite an effect on Dom. 'You do?' he exclaimed. 'Then why on earth didn't you say? I'd have arranged something else for you.'

Like what? she wondered. She didn't see his gorgeous Margot extending a welcome at their place!

He had the food on the plates now and he carried them to the main room. It was very pleasant; close-carpeted in a warm russet shade with matching chintz curtains and numerous lamps shedding a soft, restful light. They ate off the coffee table, sitting side by side on the couch.

Dom seemed in no hurry to go so afterwards Annie made coffee. Then she went to sit in an armchair, feeling safer and more in control there. They had never shared such a cosy, relaxed time before.

After a short silence, Dom said, 'That call you went out for, Annie. Was it necessary?'

She stifled a stab of disappointment at the intrusion of work and thought, how silly. After all, they had nothing else in common. 'Oh, yes,' she said. 'A child of seven with an acute ear infection. One can never be too careful.'

'How long had he had it?'

'It started at school this morning. His teacher sent him home at lunchtime.'

'Then we should have been called sooner.'

'His mother said it didn't become really painful until tea time. And I believed her, Dom. Though I must say if it had been my child, then. . .' With a visible effort she went on brightly, 'Isn't it said that doctors are notoriously neurotic about their own children?'

'But you haven't got any children, Annie.'

'No, I haven't, have I?' she agreed quietly and because that was a secret sorrow and he had probed her sore spot she turned the tables by asking crisply, 'What about you?'

'Hardly,' he said with a bitter, twisted smile.

Heavens, but he was infuriating! What did he mean? Couldn't they have any, didn't they want any, or was Margot pregnant so that 'hardly' meant almost? 'Very illuminating,' she muttered under her breath, looking anywhere but at him.

His eyes were on her, though, and Annie could feel it. When she eventually did look at him, he asked sombrely, 'You didn't know, did you?'

He looked so forlorn, so vulnerable and so utterly unlike himself that Annie said impulsively, 'I'm sorry—really sorry. Your private life is none of my business.' Yet she was bursting with curiosity.

'You thought it was once,' he reminded her with a flash of the old spirit.

'That was different. My closest friend was involved. Now it's—well, it's different.' But she was very glad that he'd reminded her how she'd railed at him for hurting Lynne. For a moment, she'd been ready to pity him.

She sat quietly, waiting for Dom to leave. But when he did get to his feet, it was to go to the kitchen to fetch glasses and a bottle of brandy. 'Want some?' he asked.

'No, thanks. I don't drink spirits—or very much of anything else.'

'I'd forgotten that.' He poured himself a drink and sat down again, his feet well apart and leaning forward with the glass clasped in both hands between his knees. 'Margot and I are divorced,' he said harshly, his eyes riveted on the glass.

'Oh, Lord—I'm so sorry,' she said awkwardly, unprepared for such a revelation.

'Don't be,' he said. 'It was inevitable.'

'I see,' she said, meaning only that she saw why he'd told her not to be sorry. Then she poured more coffee for them both and waited to see if he wanted to say anything else.

'She is incapable of sticking to one man,' he said, after an uncomfortable silence. 'She was always sorry and always going to reform, but she never did. She couldn't. It wasn't in her.'

So the biter was bitten and Lynne had her revenge, however delayed. But somehow that knowledge wasn't as satisfying to Annie as it would once have been. 'Was that why you went south?' she asked gently. 'Did you hope that down there you could start afresh?'

'I didn't want to go—the move was her idea. She has an uncle who's making a packet running a private hospital and she was determined to get me into that. She nagged and nagged until I gave in. She had the quaint idea that in private medicine you can make a fortune without actually doing much work and she couldn't grasp that private patients are ill round the clock, just like all the others.

'She accused me of neglecting her and went out looking for diversion. And, being Margot, she soon found it. It was more of a relief than anything else when she met a South American tycoon who wanted to marry her.'

Annie thought that the expression in his eyes belied his words and she said quietly, 'Now I know why you came home to Scotland.'

'And that was when I got my next shock,' Dom said heavily. 'I thought I only had to ring up the dean to get back on the circuit—but, meanwhile, he'd been training up other whiz kids and had no room for me.' The bitterness in his voice was painful to hear.

'You've got an excellent practice up and running here,' she said gently.

'That was Andrew Syme's idea. He was wanting to

retire and suggested that I take over. Jane wasn't up
to running the show and Angus didn't want the responsibility. Besides, Andrew knew how sorry I was
about the firm collapsing the way it did—so many
thrown out of work. . . ."You can't give them jobs,"
he said, "but you can look after their health and help
them that way."

'It seemed like a good idea at the time. A lifeline,
in fact. For me, anyway.'

'For me, too,' she offered. 'I was feeling pretty
desperate when I switched on my answering machine
that night.'

'And you honestly never suspected?' he asked
quickly, glad to be rid of such painful subjects.

'That you were the mysterious Dr Smith? Not for a
moment. Why did you drop the "Jardine", Dom?'

He gave her a brief, twisted smile and then said, 'It
sounded just right for an up-and-coming consultant,
but a trifle pretentious for an undistinguished GP in a
small industrial town. Especially in a town full of
people with no reason to respect the name.'

'But your family firm gave work to thousands for
generations.' Annie could hardly believe this was really
she comforting Dominic Smith-Jardine, of all people.

'And mass unemployment now. Thanks to my
brother's mismanagement.'

'Surely the recession and changing patterns of indus-
try must have had something to do with it, too.'

'Sure—but Stuart had no head for business. My
father could see trouble coming when shipbuilding
began its disastrous decline, but he was a sick man by
then and Stuart just laughed at his fears. Dad tried to
put together a new management team with plans to
diversify but by then it was too late.' He looked up
suddenly, staring at Annie in amazement. 'God, how

I do blether! But you're such a wonderful listener, Annie, I'd never have guessed. . .'

'I only hope it's helped to talk,' she said simply, although she herself was surprised that he should confide in her—and that she had listened so sympathetically.

'You can't imagine how much,' he said slowly, 'but it's late and you should be getting some sleep while you can. I'll go now.'

'There's no need! I mean—I never sleep properly when I'm on call, so. . .'

That was quite true, but Annie was aware how much she wanted to prolong this new accord between them.

But Dom was already on his feet. 'You're very kind, Annie, but it's way past midnight.' When she followed him to the door he said, 'I'm so sorry I startled you earlier. I should have thought.'

She was disappointed. 'Oh, that, I'd quite forgotten. It was—nice to have company. . .'

A slight spasm distorted his features for a second. 'Yes. . .' He bent forward and, for a crazy moment, Annie thought that he was going to kiss her. But he only raised his hand and gently stroked her cheek. Then, with a muttered goodnight, he turned away, leaving Annie standing there in a welter of mixed emotions.

CHAPTER FOUR

'Busy night, Doctor?' asked Carol next morning.

'Only two calls,' Annie told her. 'And both of them are patients of Dr Milne's. Is he in yet?'

'He whizzed by about five minutes ago.' Carol wrinkled her nose. 'There's another one of Dr Firth's asking for you. . .'

'Is my morning list full?' Annie asked hopefully.

'To bursting.'

'Then be a dear and divert her, would you? I've also got a lot of visits to make—and this is supposed to be my half-day.'

'OK, I'll do my best,' promised Carol with a saucy wink.

She knows there's a problem, Annie realised, but it would be tactless for either of us to spell it out.

Having given Angus Milne the run-down on his two patients she'd seen last night, Annie went to her own room the long way round in order to pass Dom's door. She wanted to see how he would react after last night's leap forward in their relationship, but his door was shut and he was obviously on the phone.

While she was waiting for her first patient, Annie went through her in-tray but her mind kept wandering to the previous evening. Dom's confidences had been surprising and rather touching. Had he just needed to talk, or had he wanted to unburden himself to her personally? There was quite a difference and Annie was impatient to find out which it was.

She was considering the chances of synchronising

59

their coffee breaks when her first patient came in, putting a stop to such meanderings.

Mrs Govan was a real professional at the health game and Annie's heart sank as she forced a bright smile and asked, 'So, how are we today, then, Mrs Govan?'

'I can see you're just fine, Doctor. Me, now, I'm that ill I should really be in my bed.'

That'll teach me to hide behind stock phrases, Annie told herself, as she asked what the matter was.

'It's ma stomach, Doctor. It's all over the place.'

'In what way, Mrs Govan? Pain, wind, sickness. . .?'

'Aye, all o' that—and the flatulence and regurgitation.' She kept a copy of *Home Doctor* on her bedside table.

'But the tests were all negative, so I'm afraid you're one of those unfortunate souls who need to be extra-careful with their diet. No hot, spicy foods and only a little fat. Are you following the diet plan I gave you?'

'The family'll no' stand for it and I haven't the time to cook something separate for myself. Surely there's a pill for a case like mine?'

'You've already tried most of them, Mrs Govan— and in any case, prevention is always better than cure. You really must study your—your delicate constitution and stick to a diet that'll not upset it.'

Mentioning a delicate constitution had been a big mistake. Mrs Govan discoursed at length on her diverse sufferings over the years. Backache, headaches, palpitations, dizzy spells and an ingrowing toenail. When she could get a word in, Annie reassured and advised her. Taken all together—except for that toenail—the problem could easily be psychosomatic; masking perhaps a family problem or money worries.

'Is everything all right at home?' Annie probed delicately. 'Because sometimes—'

Mrs Govan shut her up with a full-scale glare. 'You and that Dr Firth,' she snapped. 'I don't know who's the worst! I'll be asking for one o' the men next time.' She flounced out, obliging Annie to run after her with her prescription.

At least I got the worst one over first this morning, Annie reflected some two and a half hours later after a succession of genuine, no-nonsense consultations. And now she could go looking for Dom. He wasn't in the common room, though, and she only had time for a five-minute break before she started her rounds.

There were three new cases of flu today and all in different parts of the town. If she added on calls to the most serious cases she'd seen the day before there was no way Annie could finish by lunchtime. She decided not to bother with a meal and just press on. She felt sure that her patients would understand if she called in the middle of their meal.

The patients did understand but not the boss, as it turned out. Annie met him as she was coming out of one of the tower blocks and he was going in. 'Is this not supposed to be your half-day?' he demanded brusquely, without a greeting.

He'd sounded almost angry and Annie was hurt. 'I'm only making priority visits—as instructed.'

'It's getting on for three.'

'Is it really? Well, no matter—that was my last case.'

'It's no accident that half-days follow nights on call whenever possible, Annie.'

'I know that—and I think it's a *wonderful* idea!' Mild words, but delivered very crisply because, by then, Annie was angry too.

'I could have done that last visit for you,' he said reprovingly.

'And I'd have appreciated that, but how was I to know you also had a patient here?'

He acknowledged the truth of that. 'All right, but get home now and get some rest in what's left of the day,' he advised, shouldering his way into the building.

Annie frowned after him. She'd been wondering all morning how he would react next time they met. Well, she knew now—and if there was one thing certain in this world, it was that Dom Smith-Jardine regretted his late-night confidences. No burgeoning friendship then. But did he have to be so spiky? All she'd done the night before was listen—and he'd praised her for that!

'Busy night, Doctor?' Carol was asking Dom as Annie arrived next morning.

'Not a single call,' he told her. 'First time ever but not the last, I hope.' He turned, having heard Annie come in, gave her a brief 'Good morning' and hurried on.

'Two early calls came in for you, Dr Duncan,' Carol told her.

Annie swallowed her disappointment at Dom's snub. 'Will they keep until after surgery?' she asked practically. Carol said she guessed so as they both thought they'd come down with flu.

Annie said, 'Good,' but then, mindful of yesterday's mix-up, she checked the previous medical history of both callers before buzzing for her first patient.

Among the usual collection of aches and pains and coughs and sneezes was a man with a recent back injury who was a clear case for Craig's attention. Annie sent the patient along to Physio with a note. As she was tidying her room after her last case, Craig came to see her—ostensibly to talk about the new patient. Annie hid a smile. He was finding it more and more necessary to discuss their mutual patients at length and she wondered how much longer it would be before he asked her out.

Having told her that he'd had the man X-rayed and found him to be a prime case for manipulation, he then mentioned with studied carelessness that he'd overheard her telling Laura that she'd missed out on *Four Weddings and a Funeral*.

'Yes—and I'm mad about that. Now I suppose I'll just have to wait for it to come out on video.'

'That could be ages—and it's showing at the Carlton in the high street this week.'

'Really? Then I hope I can fit it in.'

'I'm thinking of going tonight, so why not come with me?'

'That's a good idea but what time does it start?' she asked. 'I've got an evening surgery.'

'That's all right—the film is only being shown once nightly, at eight. There might even be time for a quick chow mein at the Golden Orient first.'

'What could be nicer?' asked Annie.

And she enjoyed her evening very much. Craig was charming and amusing—and very good for her ego, unlike some she could name!

So when he asked her to have dinner with him on Saturday, she accepted. That was fun too. So was ice-skating the Wednesday after that. All the same, Annie meant to keep these outings from the rest of the staff as long as she could.

Unfortunately, Craig was not so reticent and by the following Friday everybody knew that Annie and Craig were keeping company—as Mrs Mac the cleaner put it. As Annie was thinking of going for coffee that morning, Dom rang and asked her to go and see him.

'Come in and shut the door,' he said crisply. And when she'd done so, he added, 'I've been hearing things.'

Annie knew exactly what he meant but she told him not to worry as tinnitus was easily treated these days.

'Oh, very funny,' he growled. 'But if you need it spelled out—and I'm quite sure you do not—I was referring to you and Craig.'

'So what about me and Craig?'

'He's very impressionable,' said Dom.

Annie stiffened. 'Well, he must be, mustn't he?' she asked tightly. 'Otherwise he'd not have taken a fancy to me!'

'Don't be silly—that's not what I meant, and you know it.'

'I'm not sure that I do,' she returned haughtily.

'Well, do you know that he's rather younger than you—and still with some growing up to do?'

'My brother is a lot younger than his wife—and he thinks she's a cross between Cleopatra and Helen of Troy!'

'*You're* looking ahead!' he exclaimed, looking rattled.

'No, I am not. I was merely pointing out that a three-year age difference is not necessarily a bar to friendship. If it were, there'd be far more lonely people around than there are already.'

'Granted, but are we merely talking friend-ship here?'

'*I* am,' she retorted, 'but I can't be held responsible for what's going on in your head—or Craig's.'

'But you admit to knowing that he finds you attractive?'

'Of course I know! Look here, what *is* this? And

why do you think you have the right to interfere?'

'I have a responsibility to keep staff relationships harmonious,' he returned pompously.

Dom *pompous*? Annie would never have believed that possible. 'And that gives you the right to interfere in my private life, does it?' she asked grimly.

'I happen to think it's a good idea to avoid emotional involvement with one's colleagues.'

Annie had the feeling that he wasn't just warning her to lay off Craig. 'Oh, really—since when?' she asked dangerously. 'I can think of quite half a dozen of your fellow workers whom *you've* left languishing along the way! Including my friend, Lynne.'

Dom seemed to swell with rage. 'One of these days, I'll tell you the truth about your friend Lynne!' he threatened.

'No time like the present. I'm listening!'

'Good! Because we hadn't finished our discussion when you trotted out that red herring.'

'Red herring be damned! You said—'

'I know what I said—and it's because of one or two unfortunate personal experiences that I came to the conclusion I did about emotional involvement with colleagues.'

Oh, very neat! 'And because *you* can't handle such a situation, you think that gives you the right to veto them for your underlings!'

'Don't be absurd!'

'I'm being no more absurd than you are!'

'And please don't shout! There's no need for the entire staff to know that we can't hold a simple discussion without arguing!'

'And we never will if you require me to accept your ruling on every aspect of my life—personal as well as professional.'

'You're shouting again,' Dom sneered with an irritating superiority which had Annie longing to smack his smug face.

'You'd make a saint shout!' she hissed. 'And if I'd remembered how infuriating you can be, I'd never have taken your stupid job!'

'And if I'd realised that you'd overreact so hysterically every time I had to ask for your co-operation, I'd never have offered it!'

They glared at one another, both equally furious now. 'Right, that's it, then!' snarled Annie. 'My resignation will be on your desk first thing tomorrow morning.'

'There's no need for quite such haste,' he said loftily. 'I'm going away for the weekend and I'll not be back until Tuesday.'

'Then you'd better have it before you go,' she retorted. 'You'll enjoy your weekend so much better then!'

That was a pretty good exit line, Annie decided, as she marched back to her room to get herself together. But what wouldn't she have given to recall it! She needed this job desperately, yet she'd put it on the line. And for what? Craig wasn't all that important to her.

It wasn't just him, though. There was a principle at stake, too. Dom couldn't be allowed to get away with laying down such draconian rules. And certainly not in such a high-handed manner.

So, instead of going for coffee, Annie got out all the *BMJ*s in her room and pored over the 'Appointments Vacant' columns. One for a locum surgeon in Mauritius caught her eye. Re-advertisement, it said, so they might be desperate enough to employ even her! Moreover, Mauritius had the merit of being a long, long way from Burnside and Dominic Smith-Jardine!

*   *   *

Fewer home visits than usual that day meant that Annie would have time for tea before evening surgery. First, though, she must write out her resignation. That didn't take long.

Dear Dr Smith,
   Our irreconcilable differences have made my position in this practice untenable. Therefore I offer my resignation, to take effect at the end of next month.
   Yours sincerely,
   Anne C. Duncan MB FRCS

Annie slid the single folded sheet into an envelope, addressed it to Dom and placed it in the exact centre of the blotter on his desk before going to the common room.

Only Andrew Syme was there. 'Ah, Annie, lass,' he said, getting up courteously and smiling as she entered. 'I've been meaning to ask you for weeks. How are you settling down?'

That was ironic to say the least in view of what had happened that day. Annie replied blandly that everybody had been very kind and helpful, making the transition from hospital to general practice less traumatic than she'd anticipated.

'Yes, you've adapted wonderfully well,' the old man congratulated her. 'But then Dom assured us you would when Jane expressed doubts about your change of direction.' He poured tea for them both and chose adjoining chairs.

'I've seldom seen Dom so pleased about anything as he was the day your application landed on his desk,' he continued. 'He'd already made a choice from the other applicants but he told Laura to hold everything until he'd seen you.'

Annie knew that already, but that Dom should have been so pleased was hard to believe. Especially now. 'Would you not all have welcomed the chance to look me over first?' she asked, remembering her own surprise at the speed of her appointment.

'We trusted Dom's judgement,' Andrew Syme answered simply.

'I was very surprised to discover that Burnside's Dr Smith was the Dominic Smith-Jardine I'd worked with in Glasgow,' said Annie, more to keep the conversation going than anything else.

It proved a fruitful remark: 'No more surprised than I was when he turned up in my surgery that January day last year and announced his intention of returning to Scotland and going into general practice.'

'You already knew one another,' she recalled.

'I've known and liked Dom all his life,' Andrew said warmly. 'Never dreaming what was in his mind, I told him about a friend of mine who was looking for a partner for his practice in Bearsden but only Burnside would do for Dom.

'The family firm went to pigs and whistles after his brother took over. Stuart had absolutely no head for business and the firm went into liquidation. Dom wanted to do something—however indirectly—for the people whom he felt had been let down.'

It was impossible not to notice that Andrew Syme's version of the move was a lot more flattering than Dom's own modest one.

'He built this place with money left to him by his grandfather, and it took every last penny he had. He's a born administrator and it's my belief that if Dom and not Stuart had gone into the business then Smith Jardine's could have survived. But that's another story and you must be sick of an old man's senile ramblings, Annie.'

Annie protested at the very idea and sent his opinion of her soaring by praising an article that he'd written for the *BMJ*. Then she said that if she didn't soon get started on her evening surgery she'd be getting the sack, nearly choking on the last words as she realised the poignancy of what she was saying.

Surgery that evening was an undemanding succession of follow-up visits and repeat prescriptions and it wasn't until the door closed behind her last patient that Annie realised what a strain the day had been. Now, though, she had only to negotiate the mid-evening traffic to Glasgow and she would have the whole weekend in which to reflect on the disastrous quarrel with Dom and its even more disastrous consequences.

She was supposed to be spending most of the time with Craig but decided to phone and cancel. She'd need all her time for job-prospecting. Would she seem too eager—or desperate—if she was to send a fax directly to Mauritius? More than likely. . .

She rang Craig as soon as she got home but got no answer. After a scrappy supper and a leisurely bath she tried again, letting his phone ring for ages before remembering that he'd mentioned an evening out with the boys. So she'd have to catch him in the morning. I'd have remembered every damn thing he'd said to me if I was really interested, she told herself shrewdly.

She picked up a book and curled up with it on the sofa, but her thoughts persisted in returning to her quarrel with Dom. He had no right to veto her friendship with Craig—if that's what he was actually doing. Or had he merely been advising her to be discreet?

No matter! Whichever it was, he had behaved with quite unnecessary high-handedness so it was no wonder that she'd lost her temper and reacted so violently.

But Annie was thinking more clearly now and could see that her anger was less about Dom's objection than his reason for it. He'd claimed that her relationship with Craig could jeopardise harmonious staff relationships, but the woman in Annie had wanted him to be jealous! That was why she'd overreacted so spectacularly and pushed things to the point of no return. . .

Annie was trying to read herself to sleep hours later when she heard the entryphone. Some drunken prankster, she assumed, and ignored it. But when it rang again and went on ringing, she wondered if somebody in the Terrace was ill; all the neighbours knew that she was a doctor. So she scrambled hurriedly out of bed and went to answer it.

It was Dom. 'Annie, I know it's late, but I have to talk to you before I go away.'

Annie didn't know whether to laugh or cry. Had he come to thank her for resigning—or to talk her out of it? 'Will it not keep—whatever it is?' she asked uneasily.

'No,' he said tersely.

Annie pressed the release button and went to fetch her dressing gown. She had the flat door standing open by the time he reached her landing. One quick look at his face told her that his thoughts were as grim as his voice had sounded on the intercom.

'Can I get you something?' she offered in an effort to postpone the crunch. 'Tea, coffee—a drink. . .' Her voice tailed off in the face of his frown. 'The living room is this way,' she muttered.

Dom followed her and planted himself in the middle

of the hearthrug, fixing her with a steady, solemn stare as though trying to read her thoughts. At last he said heavily, 'We have to clear the air.'

Annie thought they'd done that this morning, but if he didn't. . . A tiny flicker of hope sprang to life to be extinguished by his next words.

'You simply must realise that this constant wrangling makes things impossible, Annie,' he said intently.

She started and turned to face him, her remarkable tawny eyes huge pools of doubt. For almost the first time in her life, Annie had absolutely no idea what to say.

'I—I don't mind admitting it would have been a help—career-wise—if I could have completed the six-month trial period,' she got out at last. 'But in the circumstances—'

To her horror, she could feel tears pricking her eyelids. She, tough Annie Duncan, who hardly ever cried—and certainly not over a *man*!—was about to go to pieces. With a supreme effort she stumbled on. 'I'm grateful for the chance you gave me and I'm sorry it didn't work out. But, then, given how very different we are. . .'

Now she really had to stop. She turned away, fighting back her tears.

'So you really are determined to go, then,' Dom said heavily. 'Well, perhaps, after all, that's best.'

How like a man to get his own way and then dodge any blame by making out that the decision was all yours! In a flash Annie's mood switched from resignation to rage.

'Yes—I'm leaving,' she said in a much stronger voice, 'but let's be quite clear why. You've shown me more than once that you regretted taking me on, although this morning was the first time you actually

said so. So I'm leaving,' she repeated, 'mainly because
that's what you want.'

She rushed out of the room, shouting over her shoulder, 'What *you* want. So don't pretend otherwise.
That's dishonest!'

She had the flat door wide open by then but Dom
hadn't followed her. After an uneasy wait of a minute
or two, Annie shut the door and crept back reluctantly
to the living room. She should have guessed that he
wouldn't allow her the last word, but how much more
of this could she take?

He was still standing in the middle of the hearthrug.
'You came to clear the air,' she said through stiff lips.
'Well, we've cleared it. So why don't you leave?'

'But we haven't,' he said. 'Not altogether.'

'Surely you didn't think I'd let you get away with
pretending that this was solely my decision?' she challenged.

He waved that aside. 'I lost my temper this morning,'
he said, 'but then so did you—and very dramatically.'

'You provoked me!'

'Perhaps I did,' he allowed, to her astonishment.
'But I didn't know then what I know now.'

'I—don't understand,' she temporised, hoping that
she'd not given herself away completely.

'You don't really want to leave the practice, do you,
Annie?' he asked in a much gentler tone.

If she'd given herself away as much as that, how
much more had he guessed? She must be very, very
careful now. 'Well, no,' she began with pretended
reluctance. 'I'm enjoying the work a lot more than I
thought I would. But that's not the real issue, is it?'

'Then what is?'

'I get on your nerves—and that weighs a lot more
with you than having me on the team.' As soon as

she'd said that, she felt herself yearning foolishly for him to deny it. 'Well, come on—that is the problem, is it not?' she demanded impatiently when he didn't answer.

'There are times when I could cheerfully strangle you,' he said slowly. 'And others when I'd be— appalled if you walked away. Now, tell me what you make of that.'

Annie knew exactly what she'd like that to mean but that was about as likely as going on a package holiday to Mars. She also knew that whether or not she could stay depended on finding the right answer now.

'You seem to be saying that my usefulness and my— my irritation quotient are more evenly balanced than I'd thought. If so, does that mean that you'd quite like me to stay in the job?'

'You got the question right at least,' he said after a pause. 'So, what's it to be, then?'

'I think—yes, I really think that we should give it another go,' said Annie, hoping she looked as detached as she'd managed to sound.

Dom had relaxed visibly, but his response was guarded and low-key. 'I don't mind admitting that's quite a weight off my mind.'

Was it, now? Yet, only a second before, he'd claimed to be appalled at the thought of losing her! 'Because it would have been such a nuisance having to replace me so soon?' she asked, hoping to be contradicted.

'A nuisance? Yes. Apart from anything else, applicants would be bound to wonder what was wrong with a practice that couldn't keep its assistants.'

Having won his point, he now retreated out of reach. But then, hadn't that always been his way with women? To flatter and cajole until he got what he wanted from

them? Be fair, though, she told herself. This is what
you want, too. Except that it wasn't all she wanted. . .
Annie reined in her wayward thoughts. Dom couldn't
have made it plainer that this was a professional
relationship and would never be anything else.

'Have you far to go?' she enquired briskly. He
looked blank. 'Tonight. You were on your way
somewhere.'

'Yes. To Skye. For my mother's seventieth birthday
lunch tomorrow. She moved there to be near my
married sister after things fell apart down here.'

'And you're going tonight? That will take hours.'

'I know but I like night driving,' he said. 'The roads
are so much quieter. Besides, I couldn't go any
earlier—I had a meeting.'

So he wasn't late calling because he'd been trying
to find the courage—she was just one more business
headache. Annie, what a complete and utter fool you
are! she said to herself. 'Then I must apologise for
having delayed you still more,' she said stiffly.

'It was worth it to get things sorted out,' he
answered. 'Still, I'd better be off. Sorry I got you up,'
he apologised belatedly.

'It doesn't matter—I was still awake. Have a good
weekend. . .' But all the time she was thinking, we
could be the merest strangers. Is this how it will always
be from now on?

Annie was only just back in bed when her
entryphone buzzed again. Now what? she wondered
crossly.

'Sorry, but it's me again,' Dom announced. 'Would
you believe my car won't start? And I've lent my car
phone to Angus for the weekend. May I come up again
to ring the AA?'

'Yes.' Annie pressed the release button. 'Has your

car been giving trouble recently?' she asked when he appeared on the stairs.

'No—and it's only just been serviced. I can't understand it.'

'Very annoying for you. Well, you'll find my phone in the living room beside the sofa.' Annie left him to it and went to make coffee.

He joined her in the kitchen shortly thereafter. 'They think it'll be at least an hour before they can get here,' he said, frowning gloomily. Then he spotted the cafetière. 'You shouldn't have bothered. I would have waited in the car.'

'Whatever you prefer,' said Annie, 'but I wasn't planning to throw you out, although I am going back to bed.' She put coffee, milk, a mug and some biscuits on a tray and handed it to him, telling him to make himself at home. 'And in case the coffee isn't enough to keep you awake, you can put on the telly,' she told him. 'The soundproofing in these old houses is first-rate so you'll not disturb anybody.'

'I'm not sleepy,' he said, looking anywhere but at Annie in her clinging silk nightie. She'd forgotten her dressing gown this time. And then he added, 'You're being very good about this. . .'

'I'm not always bitchy. My friends say I'm a sweetie. But now I'm going back to bed.' Against all the odds Annie actually dozed off, to wake with a start when she heard her entryphone for the third time that night.

Dom was very apologetic when she came out of her room, yawning and rubbing her eyes. 'That was the AA arriving. I knew I should have waited in the car,' he said. 'I was actually looking out at first, but then I must have dozed off. . .'

'Don't be daft—there's a heavy frost tonight and you'd have got frozen. What will you do if your car can't be fixed?' she was minded to ask.

'Hire a Rolls,' he said. 'But don't worry, Annie. I'll
not be bothering you any more tonight. And thanks
again.' He bounded down the stairs.

Of course, being Annie, she couldn't leave it there.
She dressed quickly and followed him down in time to
hear the mechanic telling him how sorry he was but
that this was definitely a workshop job. Dom's reply
was predictably colourful, but he stopped swearing
when he saw Annie. 'Guess what?' he sighed, as the
AA man drove off.

'No need—I heard. And I must be psychic. Look.'
She held out her car keys.

'No!' he said violently.

'Why not? I'm off this weekend, so I'll not be needing my car. And you'll never arrive in time for that
lunch if you hang about in Glasgow until some car-hire
firm opens for business.'

He was tempted. 'That's true, but how will you get
to work on Monday?'

'I shall take a taxi and charge it to the practice.'

'I really can't let you do this, Annie.'

She pretended to misunderstand. 'Then I'll just have
to get a bus.'

Wonder of wonders, that provoked him to a little
grin. 'You know I meant that I can't take your car.'

'What's your alternative?' she asked pragmatically.

When Dom admitted that he didn't really have one
she dropped the keys in his pocket, saying they'd both
freeze if they stood there any longer.

'You can be so generous,' he said then.

'And also very irritating, it seems, but then who's
perfect? Now for heaven's sake be off with you before
my friendly neighbourhood cop comes by and thinks
I'm being mugged.'

Annie hadn't been joking about freezing; her face was smarting with the cold. But she stayed there until he'd driven away. By lending him her car, she'd put him in her debt. And she meant to do her damnedest to see that it stayed that way!

CHAPTER FIVE

WHEN Annie told Dom that she'd not be needing her car that weekend, she'd quite forgotten the small matter of her weekly visit to the supermarket. She solved the problem by walking into town and stocking up in a side street of smart but expensive little specialist shops. She was just coming out of the delicatessen when somebody yelled her name. Annie spun round to see a girl who had been in the hostel with her and Lynne in student days.

'That looks like a decent little café across the road,' said Claudia, when they'd finished exclaiming at the coincidence. 'What do you say to some catching up over a coffee?'

Claudia had read modern languages, graduated with distinction, and promptly landed a wonderful job with an international conglomerate based in Geneva. As a result, she had a very exciting lifestyle to describe and Annie was very envious. 'So why on earth did you come back to Glasgow?' she asked after the recital.

'But I haven't, silly! I'm only visiting for my sister's wedding. And now it's your turn to tell,' she commanded.

Annie made the best she could of her earnest preparation for a surgical career and her present sidestep into general practice.

Claudia nodded sympathetically. 'Poor old Annie— what a shame! But, then, surgery was always regarded as a male preserve, so what else did you expect? And medicine must have played havoc with your social life.

Lynne had the right idea—getting out when she did. Did you know she's just opened her ninth shop? In the middle of Rome—lucky thing!'

Annie said that she hadn't heard a word from Lynne since the day she dropped out of medical school.

Claudia screeched her disbelief. 'I don't believe it— you were always such chums, even though you were so different from each other.'

Annie defended Lynne from old habit. 'I know, but she was totally shattered when Dom Smith-Jardine dropped out of her life.'

'I remember—but then what else had she expected?'

'Because he was such a flirt—'

'I meant the baby! That was no way to try and catch a fly guy like Dom. He wanted her to have an abortion, you know, but she wouldn't. And he's such a gorgeous child, as blond as a Viking and with eyes as blue as periwinkles. Her husband's very complacent about him—'

Claudia dropped her voice to a piercing whisper. 'Quite middle-aged, my dear. Bald and stout—and very grateful to get such a lovely young wife, one supposes. Even though he wasn't first past the post by a long chalk. What ever is the matter, Annie? You've gone quite green. Damned if I haven't shocked you!'

She giggled delightedly. 'Still Puritan Annie, then, as the boys on the top landing used to call you. Or didn't you know?'

But Annie had hardly heard that. She was still trying to take in the fact that Lynne and Dom had had a child. No wonder Lynne had been in such a terrible state when he dumped her. 'I wish she'd told me,' she said. 'I would have helped her.'

'Darling, you were the last one she'd have gone to!

A scene and a sermon were the last things she was
needing just then.'

Annie ignored that slur on her charity and asked,
'So what happened then? I mean, where did she go?
I know she didn't go home.'

'To an elderly relative in deepest Cumbria—very
Victorian! Then, soon after the birth, she left the boy
with a foster-mother and went off to Paris to learn the
rag trade. When she was earning enough, she got wee
Dominic out of pawn. Then, a couple of years ago,
she married and now they're all three living happily
in Italy. Apparently.'

It had given Annie a nasty jolt to learn that Lynne
had named her son after his father although, knowing
how she'd adored Dom, it was only to be expected.
She pulled herself together and smiled at Claudia. 'This
has been wonderful,' she claimed, 'but I really do have
to go now. I've got somebody coming to lunch.'

She managed to get a taxi straight away but, in the
dense Saturday traffic, it took some time to get home,
which gave Annie time to come to terms with what
she'd heard.

That was just as well because when she got to Park
Terrace Craig was already on her doorstep. 'Are you
always this extravagant, Annie?' he asked, having read
the prestigious names on the carrier bags he'd just
toted up the stairs for her. 'I'm too poor to shop anywhere but Tesco's.'

'I only break out like this now and again,' she said
reassuringly. She saw no point in telling him why she
hadn't got her car. 'It adds spice to my otherwise dull
and exemplary existence.'

'I'd rather hoped that I was doing that,' he said.

Annie would rather have been told that nothing
remotely connected with her could possibly be dull but

she was discovering that Craig was rather self-centred. Not that he's any different from most other men in that respect, she hastened to tell herself.

He asked her what they were having for lunch and she delved into her carriers. 'How about carrot and coriander soup, followed by prawn Marie Rose baguettes, followed by mangoes?'

'Heavens above! I was expecting a tin of Heinz tomato soup and a cheese sandwich!' he exclaimed.

'I told you—I'm having one of my exotic phases. Now, if you really want to go trailing all the way out to Kilmarnock for a football match you'll pass me that saucepan, or we'll be late.'

Annie was not a keen football fan and had only agreed to go with Craig this afternoon in exchange for his company at a somewhat avant-garde concert the following evening. For the most part their leisure interests were entirely different and sooner or later, she supposed, they would grow tired of such compromises.

As things turned out, it was sooner.

'Call that music?' scoffed Craig as he parked as near to Annie's home as he could get the following evening. 'I've heard better tunes played on a pub piano!'

'People said things like that about Beethoven—and look how he's lasted.'

'So have the Rolling Stones.'

'You're a philistine!'

'And you're a flippin' blue-stocking. Am I coming in for a coffee?'

'I think I might manage that,' agreed Annie in a tone that should have told him that that was all he was getting.

But she soon discovered that it would have been better to spell it out. Craig pounced before the coffee was even ready for pouring. 'That wasn't very subtle,' she remarked, when she'd managed to free herself from his first clumsy embrace.

'You weren't exactly co-operating,' he complained.

'I wasn't trying to. I'm just not in the mood.' That was kinder than telling him point-blank that he didn't attract her.

'When are you ever? Look here, Annie, I've been very patient. Do you not think it's time you stopped playing hard to get?'

'For heaven's sake! You sound like somebody in a soap opera,' she told him irritably. 'I've told you more than once that I only see you as a friend—nothing more. Why can you not accept that?'

'Because I fancy you rotten—that's why! What's the matter with you? I thought that women doctors were liberated.'

'Liberated, yes. Promiscuous—not in my case. Now, will you please just—Craig!' she yelled, but he was a lot stronger and fitter than she and he soon had her pinned down on the couch.

Then the doorbell rang, distracting him just enough for Annie to give him the full force of her flexed knee just where it would hurt most. While he was coping with that, the doorbell rang again. Annie wriggled free and went to answer it, buttoning up her blouse as she went.

Naturally, she expected to see one of her neighbours on the landing but it was Dom who was leaning nonchalantly against the bannister rail. 'You!' she breathed. 'A day too soon. . .and how the blazes did you get in?'

'The outer door wasn't properly latched—you should get it seen to. And it looks as though I'd better apologise for coming back too soon.' He didn't need to say more. His expression was enough as he took in her dishevelled appearance. And it was a safe bet that he'd seen Craig's car in the road.

Despite knowing now the full horror of his treatment of Lynne, Annie was actually pleased to see him—in the circumstances. 'I've just made some coffee,' she explained with forced brightness. 'Would you like some?'

'I wouldn't want to intrude,' he said pointedly, while strolling past her into the flat.

She collected another cup and saucer on the way and followed him to the living room. She found Craig standing awkwardly behind the sofa, while Dom lounged with studied ease in her best armchair. He was dangling her car keys ostentatiously from one finger, then he dropped them onto the coffee table where they landed with quite a clatter.

Just in case Craig still hadn't got the message, Dom said, 'I was very careful with your car, Annie. And of course I've filled the tank.' Then he looked at Craig and said silkily, 'Annie's so generous. It's not everyone who'd lend out their car when your own refused to start at three in the morning, is it?'

Craig could only manage a confused shake of the head in reply.

Dom was noting Craig's awkward posture with a knowing grin. 'You seem to be in some discomfort, old chap,' he remarked sympathetically. 'Is there anything I can do for you—professionally?'

Craig looked quite appalled at the idea. 'Er, thanks, but I really must be going,' he muttered. 'An early start tomorrow. . .

Annie would never have believed that he could be so awkward and ill at ease.

When she came back from seeing him out, Dom had

poured the coffee. 'But then he's still very young,' he murmured, as though he'd read her thoughts.

'We'd been to a concert,' she found herself explaining, against her will.

'Really? Now if you'd said a wrestling match. . .' Again that cool appraisal of her untidy appearance. He's got himself on a tight rein but he's really nettled, she realised. And by what right?

'Do you monitor the private lives of all the staff as carefully as you seem to be monitoring mine?' she asked tightly.

His eyes flashed fire. 'Don't provoke me again, Annie!'

'Why not? You're definitely provoking me!'

'You know how I disapprove of messy intrigues between colleages,' he hissed.

Annie clenched her fists. 'You sanctimonious bastard!' she exploded. 'How dare you call a harmless friendship a messy intrigue! All right, so he did make a pass at me tonight,' she conceded, on noting the contemptuous curling of his lip. 'But I dealt with it and it wouldn't have happened again. He's not a monster. Anyway, who are you to sit in judgement—the way *you* go on?'

'And what way is that?' he demanded dangerously.

'Littering the world with unwanted children— that's how!'

To her utter bewilderment, he actually burst out laughing. How could he be so unfeeling? And to think how near she'd come to believing in him until yesterday. . . 'Don't you dare to pretend you didn't know Lynne had a child!' she ordered cuttingly.

He sobered right down at that. 'So we're back to that, are we?' he sighed. 'That girl has a lot to answer for.'

'You can bluster as much as you like, but I know very well that you knew!'

'That Lynne had a baby? Oh, yes—I knew that. She told me herself—couldn't wait to, in fact.'

'Yet you tossed her aside like—like an old shoe!'

'Good Lord, Annie, where do you get such expressions from? I did not toss her aside. I was very sympathetic—at first. I even gave her the money for a private abortion.'

'How could you be so cold and unfeeling? She adored you!' She frowned. 'And what do you mean by "at first"? That's a very peculiar attitude to take.'

'Not when you know the facts,' he refuted. 'I stopped being sympathetic when I realised that she meant to pretend it was mine.'

'You'll be telling me next that you never slept with her,' sneered Annie.

'No, I will not—because I did. She was a very attractive girl and quite desperate to hop into my bed. And I'm as normal as the next man.'

'Huh!' snorted Annie, a world of derision in her voice.

Dom pushed her down in a chair and loomed over her. 'I know it'll break your heart to find out I'm not as black as you'd like to think, but you're going to listen! You owe me that.

'By the time we started dating Lynne was already pregnant and when she told me the news impossibly soon, I knew that the baby couldn't be mine and I just thought she wanted help. So I arranged for her to see a gynaecologist who was a friend of mine.

'Knowing I'd been seeing her, he jumped to the wrong conclusion—just like you—and gave me all the details. Dates and so on. After that, for all her insistence, she couldn't go on pretending it was mine. She begged and pleaded and I did everything I could to help, but there was no way I was going to be trapped into an unwanted marriage.'

'It's a good story,' said Annie, who by then had got back both her breath and her nerve. 'But if it's true, why did she call the baby after you?'

'How do you know that?' he asked sharply.

'Because yesterday I bumped into a girl who used to be in our hostel. She sees a lot of Lynne—abroad. She's also met the boy. She says he's gorgeous; "as blond as a Viking and with eyes like periwinkles"—' She stopped abruptly at the look of triumph spreading over his face.

'Blue eyes,' he said scornfully. 'Not very likely, is it?'

Not unheard-of but, as he said, unlikely when both he and Lynne had brown eyes. Suddenly Annie remembered the Swedish exchange student Lynne had been seeing before dropping him for Dom. Add that to the gynaecologist's report and. . . Annie collapsed like a pricked balloon.

'What—no smart comeback?' Dom asked smugly after a minute. 'Now, there's a first.'

Annie stared past him, biting her lip. 'If you must know, I'm feeling rather a fool,' she muttered.

Dom stopped looming and dropped down on the arm of the couch. 'Another first,' he murmured.

She shot him a suspicious glance. 'And if you crow, then I'll—I'll—'

'I have to admit that I'm tempted to—now that I've got you on the ropes.'

If he believed that, then she'd better sharpen up. 'There's nothing like a good fright for making someone see the light,' she pronounced, sounding more like herself. 'It will be the—the unfortunate brush with

Lynne that decided you never again to get involved with a colleague?'

'Yes,' he agreed grimly, after a noticeable pause.

But he doesn't sound too happy about it, Annie decided. I'd not be at all surprised if he hasn't been tempted.

As if he could read her thoughts, he said, 'Don't forget I was married for most of the time since.'

Yes. Married to a woman who wasn't too particular whose bed she slept in. Life hadn't been all that rosy for Dom Smith-Jardine, despite Annie's long-held belief. Much more of this sort of thinking and she'd start feeling sorry for him again! 'Somehow, I got the impression that you were also taking Monday off,' she said, to change the subject.

'I may still do that. I only came back today so as not to inconvenience you too much.'

'But I told you—'

'I know. And I appreciated it.' He got to his feet. 'I think I should be going now.'

'How will you get home?'

'I've a friend living quite near here who owes me a favour.'

Male or female? was her instant reaction. 'What would we do without our friends?' she asked satirically.

'Especially when they lend us their cars. I hope I thanked you properly.'

'Oh, yes—more than adequately,' she returned pointedly, as his thanks had been as much for Craig's benefit as hers. . .

A smile flickered over Dom's face—to be gone in an instant.

'I'm so glad I can sometimes get it right,' he said. 'No, don't get up. I'll see myself out. And thanks again. That was a great kindness on your part.'

After he had gone, Annie remained curled up in her chair for some time. She'd known Dom—on and off—for ten years. Or had she?

First as a shining, popular figure at university to be admired and talked about. Then his brief affair with Lynne. How she had envied Lynne! Why not admit it? But that had soon been forgotten in wholehearted sympathy for her friend and utter disgust for Dom when Lynne had been rejected and had run away. How far she'd been from realising that both sympathy and disgust were so misplaced.

Two years had passed. She'd qualified and found herself working closely with Dom in her first job. Six long, busy and demanding months in which to learn the other side of him, the serious side he kept for his work. A time that had left her grateful for his help and encouragement and for his respect and admiration for her own skill. She'd been piqued, though—piqued by his continued inability to see her as a woman.

Annie was being very honest with herself now, but would it do her any good? They'd done nothing but fight ever since she joined the practice. His decision to keep her on could be due as much to reluctance to admit that he'd been wrong to appoint her as to his avowed appreciation of her work.

Annie wished that she'd had more experience of men than the odd flirtation and one half-hearted affair. But, unfortunately, the rigorous pursuit of her life's ambition had left her too little time for in-depth researches of the romantic kind.

Annie hardly recognised her car the next morning; it was so bright and sparkling clean, inside and out. As well as filling the petrol tank, Dom must have treated it to the most expensive programme at the car wash round the corner. And on the driver's seat was a large box of Belgian chocolates. She looked forward to thanking him when he returned to work tomorrow.

Annie's first patient that Monday morning was old Mr Henderson. He was hirpling worse than ever today but before she could raise the question of a hip replacement again, he said, 'I've decided, Doctor. I'm going to have it done.'

'I'm so glad!' enthused Annie, much relieved. 'It'll make a tremendous difference to your quality of life and as we're a fund-holding practice we should be able to get it done for you quite soon.'

'Save the money for some other puir soul,' he advised. 'Ma son's won quite a bit on the lottery and he's making me his first priority. Mind you, that stuck-up wife of his would rather he bought something flashy like a Jag, but he says a nice Volvo will do them just fine. So I'm to get ma new hip with the balance. Is that not grand?'

'It certainly is, Mr Henderson. There are several surgeons in Glasgow who specialise in hips so I'll find out which one can see you soonest.'

'Aye, m'lass, the sooner the better. The Smith-Jardine Pensioners' Club's away to Spain in July and I'd like fine to be going with them.'

What a change of heart! The last time they'd talked he'd been very reluctant to have the operation. Now he couldn't have it soon enough.

By half past ten, a series of follow-up visits and repeat prescriptions had Annie longing for a patient she could really get her teeth into—medically speaking. Her prayers were answered when her next patient walked in.

Annie looked up, her welcoming smile becoming fixed as her suspicions were aroused by the unusual pigmentation of Mrs Leckie's skin. When she went on to describe her continual tiredness, weight loss and recent 'tummy upsets' Annie was almost sure.

When she commented on her patient's unusual skin tone, Mrs Leckie blamed it on a new face cream. Never alarm the patient unnecessarily, Dom had told her on her first day as a doctor. 'How long have you been using it?' she asked mildly.

'About six weeks.'

'And your skin was all right before that?'

'I wouldn't say that, Doctor, but it certainly wasn't this bad.'

Annie asked her to undress and found, as expected, similar changes in skin colour in other areas subjected either to light or to pressure from clothing. Her doubts resolved, Annie explained gently that some of the glands were not working quite as well as they ought but that a course of steroids would soon sort that.

Mrs Leckie looked puzzled. 'But that's what my mother gets for her arthritis, and nobody's said anything about her glands.'

As briefly as possible Annie explained the different uses of cortico-steroids, reserving till last the news that it was the patient's own cortisone-producing glands that were under pressure. 'Did you understand what I was saying?' she asked hopefully.

Mrs Leckie shook her head. 'But I'm hoping that you do, Doctor.' She coloured at her own lack of tact. 'I didn't mean to be rude but I'd feel happier if I could have a word with Dr Syme. He's been my doctor sonce I was a bairn but they told me at the desk that he's only seeing a few patients now.'

The new-girl syndrome in operation, supposed Annie. 'I'll see that you get an early appointment with him—and, yes, I quite understand. I'd feel the same

myself in your place,' she added, sending Mrs Leckie
away happy.

What Annie did mind was the way that one lost sight
of the most interesting patients in general practice,
whereas in hospital you could follow up people like Mrs
Leckie right down the line. Stop it, she told herself. Be
grateful that you've got a job at all.

Mrs Irvine was next and Annie was surprised to see
her back so soon. While she was divesting herself of
numerous bags and parcels, Annie very nearly asked
her, 'Any joy?' Am I mad? she wondered, remembering why Mrs Irvine had come to see her in the first
place and the unpromising details gleaned of that poor
lady's intimate life. 'Did you find the cream effective?'
she asked instead.

Mrs Irvine blushed and looked down at the floor.
'He says it's giving him a rash,' she volunteered at last.

Annie didn't like the sound of that. 'But is it effective
from your point of view?' she asked delicately.

Mrs Irvine blushed some more and said it might have
been, had she been allowed to keep on with it.

'Never mind,' soothed Annie, 'I'll prescribe something else when I've taken a look at you.'

Mrs Irvine stiffened and said that she'd rather not
put Doctor to the trouble if it was all the same to her.

Annie sighed at the disappearance of her chance to
find out if Mr Irvine had passed on his mysterious rash
to his wife. 'This rash of your husband's,' she said.
'You haven't got it too, have you?'

Mrs Irvine said that she definitely had not and as
she obviously hadn't got the point of her question
Annie didn't press the point. She just gave her a prescription and urged her to come back if the problem
continued. Then Annie sat back in her chair and wondered how on earth Mrs Irvine managed to be so

innocent and modest in the face of all the explicit material coming daily over the airwaves in the name of entertainment.

She must have what doctors called the ostrich complex. Unless, of course, she didn't have a television set. Annie vowed to ask her next time. And ten to one she'd ask if Annie thought TV was responsible for her problem!

Craig was in the common room when Annie went for her coffee after surgery. So were Laura and Angus so she just gave Craig a quick smile in passing and went to talk to the others.

She told them about Mr Henderson's stroke of good fortune, thanks to his son. This prompted Angus to launch into a diatribe about the ironies of a system that kept pensioners hanging on in pain while teenagers who claimed to be psychologically traumatised by the tattoos they no longer wanted were able to get plastic surgery at the drop of a hat.

Annie blinked at such vehemence. 'Phew!' she said when Angus had gone. 'I wonder what on earth brought that on?'

'A lad with "Darlene" tattooed all over his chest and who has now fallen violently in love with a church elder's daughter called Agnes,' explained Laura, who always knew everything.

Annie burst into laughter. 'I can see his problem,' she agreed. 'But Angus is quite right. It's a funny old world, right enough.'

'And remember that neither joint replacements nor such sophisticated plastic surgery had been thought of when the NHS was set up,' observed Laura shrewdly. 'Is it any wonder that the poor old dinosaur is constantly strapped for cash?'

'But we're better off than any other practice around

here—thanks to Dom,' Annie reminded her, getting a vicious look from Craig as he left the room. Fortunately Laura didn't notice.

I must straighten out that boy when I've got a minute, resolved Annie, as she set out on her rounds. She forgot all about him, though, when she saw her first patient. He was a boy of about eleven and he lay breathless on the hall floor, wheezing violently. Annie flew to put him into a sitting position while asking urgently, 'Where's his inhaler?'

'He hasn't got one,' said his mother, as though it was no more important than a packet of crisps.

Annie propped the boy against the wall and, opening her bag, took out some ephedrine which she gave him by mouth. Then she watched and waited anxiously for it to take effect.

'So it's not just his temper, then?' queried his mother, who was now sitting on the stairs nursing a large ginger tom.

'"Temper"?' echoed Annie. 'Good God, no! Your son is having an asthmatic attack—which is quite likely due to that chap you're making such a fuss of.' I shouldn't have said that, she told herself. But honestly! Some mothers just didn't deserve their children.

'He's looking better,' said the mother. 'There! I told you there wasn't much wrong with you, didn't I?' she shouted at the child. 'Little devil'll do anything to get off school. That's why I asked for a call. The doctor will soon stop this malingering, I told him.'

'Your son is seriously ill,' Annie told her, the woman having shown herself quite equal to the shock. 'And I'm sending him to hospital for treatment and allergy tests.' She glared at the cat which might or might not have been responsible, but who certainly ranked higher in his mistress's esteem than her poor little son.

'Hospital? Well, there's a turn-up for the book,' returned the mother as Annie dialled for an ambulance. 'I suppose I'd better pack him a bag, then. This would damn well happen on washing day! I don't think he's got any clean pyjamas. . .' she went grumbling up the stairs, still clutching her pet.

In view of his mother's lack of concern, Annie felt that she must stay with the child until the ambulance came. She put in the time writing an explanatory note for the hospital.

'I don't know what his dad will say about this,' sighed the mother, as she watched her son being taken away.

'As the child is going to hospital and is not in disgrace, I hope his father will be suitably worried,' was Annie's parting shot.

By then it was lunchtime and, realising that she'd have difficulty making all her calls before evening surgery, Annie bought some fruit and ate it as she drove. As always when she got behindhand, things went from bad to worse. For instance, a call on one patient involved a call on the man next door, too.

'Ach, I jest telt him not to bother the surgery when you were coming to me anyway,' explained Annie's own patient when Annie had confirmed that she was definitely over her post-flu bronchitis and could start getting out and about again.

'So has he also got the flu?' asked Annie, thinking it likely.

'No! The ole fool was digging in his garden and cut off a bit of his foot with yon steel spade he's so proud of,' was the horrifying explanation.

Annie flew round the corner with her heart in her mouth. 'No real damage done—not even one little bone broken,' she was able to report three minutes later. 'That good stout boot took most of the damage.'

The boot was cut through to the lining, though. 'Thank goodness you weren't digging in rubber boots as so many gardeners do.'

Tidying up the damage took time, though, and Annie positively fled back to her car and away to her next case with a screeching of tyres.

'Dr Smith's picked a good one there,' remarked one neighbour to the other as they watched her go.

And then who'd have thought that popping into the baker's for a loaf would bring such grim consequences?

'Just groaned and dropped down at my feet, Doctor,' said the shocked assistant, pointing down at the unconscious man behind the counter. 'He'd just finished fixing the bread slicer—and thank heaven he had or the boss would've gone spare. . .'

By then Annie had stopped listening and was on her knees beside the man. A CVA, of course—and a bad one by the look of things. 'He's had a stroke,' she rapped out. 'Now, where's your phone?

'No, I don't know his name. He's a workman on a job. No, I don't know if he's registered with us.' What kind of idiot was this on the other end of the line? 'Just tell the controller that Dr Duncan wants an ambulance immediately to MacNab's the baker's in the high street for a patient with a major CVA—or else Dr Smith will be wanting somebody's head on a plate!'

Annie had been in Burnside long enough now to know that the mere mention of Dom's name had near magical powers.

As with the asthmatic child that morning, Annie was desperate to leave but she couldn't leave until she'd seen this man safely away to hospital. She still had four more patients to see and not one whom she'd feel happy about leaving until tomorrow.

'I'm so sorry,' she panted, when she finally arrived

back at base a good half-hour late.

'Don't apologise to me—save it for your first patient,' advised Carol's new assistant, who all the doctors had decided was a touch too cheeky. 'The poor man is absolutely furious at being kept waiting.'

'Is he now? Well, I'm fairly furious myself, so that makes two of us!' Annie retorted grimly as she pelted on down the corridor.

CHAPTER SIX

'GOOD morning, Annie. There's a record number of new patients coming your way these days,' said Carol brightly on Monday morning, two weeks later. 'Word's going round that you're gey clever.'

'That's nice,' returned Annie. 'I could do with a pick-me-up.' As soon as she'd said it, she knew it was a mistake. She and Craig were so scrupulously polite to one another these days that all the staff had guessed that there had been a falling out. Now, of course, Carol would be laying on the comfort.

'Poor Annie,' she soothed, right on cue. 'You need an interest. Have you thought of joining something?'

Annie said that was a good idea but she was a bit long in the tooth for the Guides and as she sang like a corncrake in pain no church choir would touch her.

Carol's appreciative hoot of laughter followed her down the corridor to her room. She hung up the jacket Mrs Niven had admired so much and picked up her mail but her mind wasn't on her letters; it was on the boss, where it was showing a deplorable tendency to linger these days.

Last Tuesday week, she'd made a particular point of thanking Dom really prettily for returning her car in such sparkling condition. 'It hasn't looked so good since the day I bought it,' she had said, before going right over the top and telling him that she'd be happy to lend it to him again at any time.

'You're very kind, but that'll not be necessary. I'm taking delivery of a new one in a day or two,' he had

answered gravely. 'And as for getting yours cleaned—
that was the least I could do. Skye and back is a gey
long way and some would say I should have paid you
the going rate of hire.'

That was when Annie's hopes of a better relationship
began to wither. 'I'm very glad you didn't,' she said
quietly. 'That would have been an insult in the face
of—of a well-intentioned gesture.' Then she walked
out quickly before he thought of something else
unkind to say.

And it had been the same every time their paths
had crossed since, which hadn't been all that often.
Annie found that so irritating that she actually considered reviving her friendship with Craig. If nothing
else, it might prod Dom out of his indifference. But
after his double humiliation, first from Annie and then
from Dom, Craig would have none of it. And who
could blame him?

So Annie knew now where she stood with Dom,
which was precisely where she'd always been; a valued
colleague and nothing more. He knew exactly how to
butter her up to keep her sweet and also how to keep
her in line if she looked like overstepping the mark.

In the face of that knowledge, only a fool would go
on hoping for anything more. And, whatever I am, I
am not a fool, Annie told herself firmly, as her first
patient of the day tapped on her door.

In walked a girl of fourteen, both new to the practice
and new to Annie. She was followed by her mother,
who began explaining and apologising even before
she'd shut the door.

'. . .So in the end, I said to him, "Doctor," I said,
"My daughter's not just another neurotic teenager trying to get out of gym and if you'll not take her seriously
then I'll find a doctor who will!" So here we are.'

Annie had already noticed the girl's swollen and mauve-tinted eyelids. That, together with a stiff and awkward gait more reminiscent of a pensioner than a teenager, had sparked off suspicions. Now she invited mother and daughter to sit down and chatted generally to put them at ease before asking Leanne Burns how long she'd been feeling poorly.

It was difficult to take a history with the anxious and voluble mother chipping in all the time but eventually Annie established a history, going back several months, of proximal muscle weakness and tenderness, bouts of low grade fever and occasional shortness of breath. 'Have you ever had any kind of rash?' asked Annie, to complete the picture.

'Now and again she has,' Mrs Burns chimed in. '*He* said it was an allergy and told me to dab it with calamine lotion.'

'And I expect that was very soothing,' Annie replied, determined not to let any breath of criticism of another doctor escape her.

Then, as clearly and reassuringly as possible, she explained the significance of all Leanne's symptoms. 'So I'm going to arrange for her to be seen by a rheumatologist as soon as possible,' she wound up. 'We'll soon have you feeling more like yourself, dear,' she told the girl, getting a grateful smile for answer.

When they had gone Annie wrote a note to Dom, briefly outlining Leanne's symptoms and asking if he would like to see her. As she put it in her 'Out' tray, Mrs Niven came in.

'You were long enough with yon lassie, Doctor,' she said curiously.

'Not everybody is as good as you at describing their symptoms,' Annie answered, quick as a flash.

Mrs Niven was delighted and promptly launched into

a highly charged account of her present state. 'So you
see, it's on the march again, Doctor. Knees, feet,
hands—the lot. Are you still quite sure it's not the
new pills?'

'If it is, then that's a first,' said Annie. 'But I did
warn you that this is a generalised condition, did I
not? And it takes longer than we've given them for
the pills to make a difference. Now then—let's have
a look at you.'

Mrs Niven was visibly embarrassed. 'You examined
me last time, Doctor—and I'm not wearing ma
good slip.'

Annie promised not to notice, gave her the once-
over and repeated that, given time, the new pills would
soon bring all her wayward joints under control.

'Right, then—thank you, Doctor.' Her eyes strayed
enviously to Annie's jacket, hanging on the back of the
door. 'I see you're wearing your lovely jacket again,
Doctor. I reckon you could go anywhere in that. But,
then, I've always said you've got to go to the little
shops if you want something really stylish. Well, I
mustn't hold you up, must I?' And off she went after
a final longing glance at the jacket.

Annie was still smiling about that when her second
new patient appeared; a sulky-looking schoolboy with
what his mother called a dodgy knee. Annie soon had
him out of his jeans and trainers and up on the couch.
She examined the knee in question and then palpated
the insertion of the big quadriceps muscle group on
the tubercle of the tibia. As she expected, he let out
a sharp yelp. 'Are you keen on cycling or climbing?'
Annie asked acutely.

'Both, the little terror,' said his mother. Did
all Burnside mothers always answer for their
offspring? 'And I've told him and told him he'd stand

a much better chance of getting a job when he leaves school, if he'd just stay in and do his homework properly.'

'Well, Sean,' said Annie firmly, 'I'm afraid you'll be doing just that for the next wee while. This knee is not going to settle down if you don't rest it. All that exercise makes the muscles on the front of your thigh pull extra hard on this tiny little bit of bone—and that's why it's so sore to the touch.'

She frowned ferociously at him, raising a wintry smile. 'And if you don't do as I say, m'lad, it's a heavy plaster stookie and a visit to the bone specialist for you. D'you hear?'

Then she reassured his mother by telling her that he would grow out of it as his bones matured—as long as he did what he was told now.

'Hear that?' asked the mother, before telling her son that if he didn't do as the doctor said she'd tan the living daylights out of him, big as he was.

On their way out, they passed Peter Sinclair coming in to ask Annie's advice about a patient with a suspected gastric ulcer. Explaining the latest thinking on helicobacter pylori and the efficacy of amoxycillin took up precious time in an already crowded morning. As now seemed par for the course, Annie was late starting her rounds.

Her first call was to the hypochondriac with the henpecked husband to whom she'd read the riot act some weeks before for calling her out to a head cold. This time she'd fallen and hit her head on the kitchen table and Annie was very surprised to hear that the woman had asked especially for Dr Duncan.

She opened the door herself and she looked dreadful. The right side of her face was grossly swollen and discoloured. If a table did that then I'm no doctor,

thought Annie. Following the patient to the living
room, Annie she noticed that she was limping badly
and guarding her left side.

'I'll just draw the curtains and examine you here,
as it'll be rather painful for you climbing the stairs,'
said Annie.

'Oh, but it's only my face, Doctor,' she protested.
The change from tyrant to mouse was astounding.

Having satisfied herself that the damage to the face,
though spectacular, was superficial, Annie set herself
to probe further.

Then it all came out. Having tried her husband's
patience once too often, he had turned on her and
delivered a chastisement that had taken her completely
by surprise. While feeling a sneaking sympathy for
the long-suffering little man, Annie couldn't overlook
three fractured ribs and some nasty bruising over the
spleen. 'I understand that you don't want this to go
any further, my dear,' she said firmly over more pro-
tests, 'but you've simply got to go to hospital for
X-rays.'

Annie had already decided that it would be quicker
to drive the patient there herself rather than call an
ambulance. Besides, left alone, the woman would
probably have turned it away.

'A domestic disagreement,' Annie whispered to the
casualty officer, 'though I doubt there'll be any charges
brought.'

That was an assault waiting to happen, decided
Annie, as she drove to her next case; a woman with
a deep venous thrombosis in the left calf.

She found her patient up and about. 'You did say
just to rest until the leg got soft and went away,' she
paraphrased when Annie queried her mobility.

'Did I really say that?' asked Annie, hiding a smile.

'All the same, I'd like to see for myself that it's really gone.'

'Yes, that's fine, Mrs McCabe,' she confirmed, after careful inspection and palpation. 'But you must finish your course of tablets and then report back to me at the surgery. That wasn't the first DVT you've had. Clot,' she translated, at which Mrs McCabe looked indignant. 'Clot in your leg,' Annie amended hastily. Oh, the pitfalls of the English language. . .

All the other doctors were there before her when Annie went to the common room for tea before evening surgery. Andrew was holding forth with Peter hanging on his every word, while Jane and Dom were in the middle of an animated conversation which was making them both laugh a lot.

He doesn't mind letting his hair down with *her* then, thought Annie indignantly, as she crossed the room to talk to Angus, who was sitting by himself in a corner and staring gloomily up at the ceiling. 'Could you do with some company?' she asked.

He came out of his dream and smiled at her. 'If it's yours—then, any time,' he declared.

Annie told him about her *faux pas* with Mrs McCabe, provoking a guffaw which had all heads turning their way. 'My God, Annie, you're a tonic and no mistake!' puffed Angus. 'Promise you'll never leave us.'

'I make no promises I may be forced to break,' she replied, after meeting Dom's disapproving eye. Was he now squaring up to reprove her for having designs on Angus? Talk about a dog in the manger. . .

'I'd like a word with you before surgery, Annie, if you can spare the time,' said Dom, appearing to confirm her suspicion.

'I'll make time, Doctor,' she responded courteously. Extreme courtesy epitomised her present attitude to him. She had an inkling that he found it as irritating as she found it difficult to keep up.

Her opening remark was on the tip of her tongue as she knocked on his door soon afterwards and spilled out as she entered. 'I know that Angus is married; I've met his wife; we got on like a house on fire and I've offered to babysit!' And now tell me *that* will jeopardise harmonious staff relations!

If he had been ready to deliver a rocket, his surprise was very well done. 'That was kind,' he returned mildly, 'and surely much appreciated. Actually, I wanted to congratulate you on diagnosing that child with dermato-myocitis.'

Annie contained her annoyance at being wrong-footed yet again. 'You've seen her already, then,' she surmised.

'Good Lord, no! She's your patient and I have complete faith in your diagnosis. I gave Dave Carswell a ring. Remember him? He's making quite a name for himself in rheumatology at Glasgow General. He's agreed to see her early next week. That was what you wanted of me, wasn't it?'

'Yes—thank you. . .' She hesitated, before telling him, 'I saw another interesting child this morning—a boy of twelve with Osgood-Schlatter's disease.'

'I'm glad that you're getting some interesting cases. I was afraid you were finding general practice rather dull after all the drama of hospital life.'

Heavens! Was he boiling up to edge her out again? 'And two on the one day,' he went on. 'You're lucky. I've had nothing but coughs, colds and compensation cases today. Well, thanks for coming,' he added, after an awkward pause which he seemed unable or unwilling to fill.

'No problem,' said Annie, turning to go. And if that's all he had to say to me he could have said it in the common room, she thought as she went. Now they'd all be thinking I was getting a row. Annie almost wished she had been. Anything was better than this polite non-conversation which was all that passed between them these days. At least when they were quarrelling, she had his undivided attention!

Evening surgery was shorter than usual and, being on call that night, Annie looked forward to a lull with her feet up before the rush—if there was one. But having gone upstairs to the flat, Annie barely had time to unpack her overnight bag before the phone rang. 'Oh, Dr Duncan, I'm so glad it's you.' Annie recognised the voice of the warden of the sheltered housing complex on the other side of the town. 'One of our ladies has had a nasty fall and can't get up.'

'Ten minutes,' returned Annie, hoping that the situation wasn't as bad as it sounded as she grabbed her bag and dashed off.

The warden was hopping anxiously about on the doorstep when Annie arrived. 'This way, Doctor. What a thing! And we're always so careful.'

But not quite careful enough, thought Annie, as she dropped to her knees beside the casualty. After the briefest of examinations Annie phoned for an ambulance. Then she fetched a pillow and the duvet from the bedroom to warm the old lady up. 'Yes, the neck of the femur is definitely fractured,' she said, in answer to a frantic question, 'but she's also very cold. How long has she been lying here?'

'Not long,' said the warden.

'Since lunch, I shouldn't wonder,' chipped in the

next-door neighbour. 'She didn't come in to me for
her cup o' tea as usual at three.'

'You should have told me!' cried the warden.

'I tried, but you were away to the hairdresser's. And
then I dozed off and didn't come to till I heard the
shouting.'

'I thought they all had personal alarms to wear in
case they fell and couldn't reach the cord,' said Annie
to the warden.

'That's right, but Mrs Hunter wouldn't wear hers.
She said it got in the way of her knitting.'

Another instance of human nature thwarting good
intentions, thought Annie, storing up this example for
the next staff meeting.

Just as she was leaving, she got another call; a suspected heart attack this time—and only three streets
away. The patient had sustained a major coronary
infarct so, with every second counting, it was providential that Annie was nearby. A shot of streptokinase
and he was stabilised by the time the ambulance
arrived. 'My word, you're keeping us busy tonight,
Doctor,' said one crew member as he shut the doors
of his vehicle.

'That's because I didn't want you sitting about getting bored,' she quipped as she unlocked her car.

Annie was surprised to see Dom's car still in its
allotted place by the main entrance when she returned
to the centre. She was even more surprised to find him
in the tiny upstairs kitchen taking a pre-packed meal
out of the oven. But she just said a casual 'Hello,'
from the doorway and left him to it.

'That was a long call,' he threw over his shoulder.

'Two, actually—and both needing hospital admis-
sion.' She told him briefly about the heart case who
was one of his patients.

'That's his third,' he said sombrely. 'It was very lucky you were on the spot.'

When he came into the main room carrying the food on a tray, Annie slipped into the kitchen to make some coffee to go with her own supper. After a minute he called out, 'What are you doing? Your supper is getting cold.'

'My. . .? But I thought you were heating that up for yourself.'

'I had mine some time ago.' He was halfway through the door by then.

'How kind of you. But you didn't need to—'

'One good turn deserves another,' he said gruffly. 'Hope you have a quiet night.' Then he shut the door and went downstairs before Annie could come up with a suitable reply.

She ate the food and it was absolutely delicious. She wondered where he had got it and was debating whether to make coffee now or later when the phone rang.

'We need a doctor. Bad,' said the voice on the other end of the line. A girl's voice, strangely muffled.

'Name and address, please,' said Annie instinctively.

'The thing is—we're not on your list, Doctor.'

'Do you mean that you're just visiting Burnside?'

'Yeah—I guess. It's an emergency,' she added, with more emphasis.

'Then why not go to Casualty at the hospital?' Annie suggested. 'That's definitely your best bet.'

There was some whispering at the other end before the girl said, 'No transport.'

Then an agonised wail in the background had Annie saying urgently, 'All right. Just give me your address.'

Another pause and more whispering before the girl

said, 'We're at the cottage by the old waterworks. Know it?'

'Yes, but—'

'See you, then. And hurry!' The girl rang off before Annie could say she'd thought that cottage was derelict.

Annie slipped on her jacket, grabbed her bag and hurtled down the stairs; but once in the car she felt vaguely uneasy. There had been something just not quite right about that call. Something she couldn't put her finger on.

She felt more uneasy still when she reached the cottage, which looked even more dilapidated than she'd remembered. But the caller had mentioned an emergency, so she grabbed her bag and sped up the overgrown path. As she reached out to knock the door swung open, a hand shot out and she was pulled inside. She was thrust roughly against a wall and steel glinted close to her face. 'Do as you're told and you'll not get hurt,' said the man who was threatening her with a knife.

Annie was terrified but also furiously angry. 'Do you need a doctor or not?' she demanded bravely.

'We need what you've got in that bag,' said another male voice from the shadows.

My God, they're druggies, Annie realised, too late. 'I don't carry much medication,' she said.

'Your prescription pad will do nicely, dear,' said the girl who had made the call.

'I don't carry one at night,' Annie lied bravely. 'Here, look for yourself.' She held out her bag, praying that they wouldn't make her turn out her pockets. That was a vain hope. They bundled her into an inner room where she was roughly stripped to her bra and pants.

'Here, these'll keep you warm, Jude,' said one of

the men, tossing Annie's skirt and sweater to the girl. 'And what's this?' He pulled Annie's car keys and prescription pad from her jacket pocket before giving the jacket away as well. 'Bloody little liar,' he said without heat. 'You can't trust nobody these days. Come on then, you lot.'

'Where to?' one of them asked.

'Who cares? We got wheels now.'

'Are you just going to leave her?' asked the girl.

'She'll cause a riot, walking back to town like that,' sniggered the man who had brandished the knife.

'Tie her up, then,' said the leader. 'That'll give us time to get clear.'

'What with?' asked the girl.

'Anything. There's a pile of stuff in the next room. But make it good.' He'd been rummaging in Annie's bag all the time they were talking. 'Hey, look! There's enough stuff here to give Sharon her fix.'

'What—now?'

'Nah! She can wait till we get clear.'

The same wail that Annie had heard over the phone came now from somewhere behind the man. He swung round and hit the girl Sharon across the mouth. 'Shut up! We've gone to a lot of trouble to get you this.'

By then, the girl called Jude had fetched some strips of coarse plastic binding from the other room. Realising that it was now or never, Annie tried to make a dash for it but somebody stuck out a foot and brought her down with a crash that shook the rotten floor. She banged her head in falling and saw stars.

Annie came to with a blinding headache. She was also shivering with cold. They had made a good job of binding her up and she lay on her side, trussed like a chicken. They hadn't bothered to gag her so she shouted as loudly as she could, but there was no answer. Then she tried to wriggle free, but she had been expertly bound. Besides, the floor was rotten, she was half-naked and every movement that she made on the splintered wood was agony. She wondered how long she'd lain there but her hands were tied behind her back and, in any case, they had stolen her watch along with everything else.

A soft rustling nearby made Annie think of mice. Or worse—rats! She had a horror of rats and she screamed at full power. The rustling stopped but her headache had trebled in intensity. She also felt sick and dizzy. I mustn't faint—I mustn't! But I'm cold. . . so cold. . .

Annie came to again with a violent shudder. All around were sirens, blazing lights and scurrying feet. 'In here,' shouted a voice and next minute a burly policeman was down on his knees beside her, untying her hands. 'It's all right, Doctor, ye're all right now, lassie,' he said soothingly. 'Is there a blanket in the car, Dougie? They've pinched her clothes, the bastards!'

'And my bag—and car,' sobbed Annie, half laughing and half crying in her relief.

'There, there,' said her rescuer. 'We've got the lot and the buggers should be in the cells by now. That's a good lad, Dougie. Now help me get her up. The poor wee soul's that cold and stiff she cannae move.'

The big one called Dougie scooped Annie up in his arms and carried her out to the police car. 'Straight to the hospital, you reckon?' he asked his partner.

'No, the sergeant said we were to take her to the health centre,' replied the man who had found her.

In the warmth of the car, Annie relaxed onto the back seat and sighed with relief. She'd have hated to go to hospital with all the publicity and fuss that would have caused. And Dom would have been even more furious than he was going to be anyway. 'What time is it?' she asked anxiously.

'Half past one, Doctor.'

'Thank you. . .' So she'd been in that hell-hole less than four hours. Dom would have gone home long since and with luck there wouldn't have been any more calls. Things could be a lot worse. Unless—! 'You don't suppose this will get into the papers, do you?' she pleaded.

'Aye—I reckon, and you'll come out like a heroine,' said Dougie, having quite the opposite effect from what he'd intended.

First, virtual dismissal from hospital and now this! How could her career survive? Annie was overtaken by a violent, nervous shivering.

When they got to the centre, it seemed to Annie's anxious eyes that every light in the place was blazing. And Dom's car was still there. Would she have been better to go to the hospital after all? By now she could see clearly just how foolish she'd been not to tell anybody where she was going when she got that strange call.

Dom was waiting on the doorstep. He looked very angry. 'Take her upstairs to the rest room,' he said in answer to Dougie's question. 'My God, what have they done to her?' he breathed when he saw Annie wrapped in the blanket and supported like a rag doll between the two police officers. Her hands and face were streaked with grime and her hair was a wild tangle.

'Frightened the life out of the poor lass, I shouldn't wonder,' said Dougie, having swept her up in his arms again before Dom had recovered from shock. 'But they didn't beat her up, or anything. At least. . .' He looked down on Annie anxiously.

'No, they just robbed me—and tied me up,' she said, striving to keep her voice steady and not succeeding.

'That's right—on the sofa,' ordered Dom when they were all upstairs. 'And you can put that away,' he added when Dougie's partner took out his notebook. 'No questions until she's recovered.'

'I think I'd rather get it over, please,' faltered Annie. Anything would be better than being left alone with Dom in his present angry mood.

So, while Dom fumed in the background, Annie tried to tell her story but reliving the experience so soon was too traumatic and Dom soon put a stop to it, promising that they could talk to her again next day after she'd had a good sleep.

'You're very cross,' sighed Annie when she and Dom were left alone.

'Of course I'm cross! What else would you expect? Here—take this!'

'What is it?'

'Mogadon. You must get some sleep.'

'I couldn't—not like this. I feel so soiled. . .' As she spoke, the blanket slipped from her shoulders.

Dom gazed in horror at her slender body, so scantily clad. She was badly scratched and bruised, as well as filthy, after her frantic struggles to free herself on that dreadful floor.

Annie also looked in horror at herself then back at him, pleading, 'Please—I must get clean. Please!'

He realised that her desperate need for cleansing was largely psychological. 'But could you cope with a shower?' he asked. 'If only I'd had the sense to put in a bath. . .' He looked stricken.

'But you couldn't have thought of anything like this.' Annie struggled to her feet, swaying. Dom caught her and she clung to him for support. He half carried her to the shower, dragging a chair after them.

'No, not in the water—it'll ruin it,' she fretted when she realised what he intended.

'It doesn't matter.' He put the chair in the shower compartment, sat Annie down on it and helped her out of bra and pants. Then he handed her a sponge and turned on the water.

'Please don't drown, little one,' he said unsteadily.

He waited outside and Annie could hear him padding up and down. 'You're taking a long time,' he said at last. 'Are you all right?'

'Just coming.' But Annie couldn't dry herself. Her hands and wrists were too sore and all her muscles felt like jelly. She staggered out of the shower with the bath towel draped uselessly over one shoulder, obviously still very wet. When she reached for her dressing gown, Dom said, 'No, not yet. . .'

He dried her so carefully as she stood there with eyes half-closed, passively accepting his ministrations. At first. Then, despite her recent ordeal and inevitable nervous fatigue, Annie was conscious of a growing excitement. The feel of Dom's hands, gently but firmly caressing her body through the soft towel, was more erotic than anything she had ever known. Her eyes roamed over him hungrily, searching for signs that he too was aroused.

Then suddenly he threw aside the towel and bundled her into her dressing gown. 'Into bed with you, now,' he said with a forced, awkward brightness. 'I'm going to fetch something for those abrasions.'

Annie did as she was told. She lay there obediently, her whole body aglow and tingling from his touch. Her eyes fastened on the door, awaiting his return.

He was away some time and when he returned he was completely switched off; entirely the doctor deal-

ing with a patient. He dressed her chafed limbs with
scrupulous care before dosing her with Mogadon,
washed down with brandy.

'We tell patients not to take alcohol with drugs,' she
breathed, in a pitiful attempt to be her usual self.

He put the glass to her lips again. 'I know what I'm
doing,' he returned evenly. 'I want you to sleep. And
soundly.'

'And then I'll not be any more trouble.'

'True—but that's not quite what I meant. You've
had a dreadful experience and now you need to rest.'

'Do I?' Her body was still aroused, but less so now
in the face of his detachment.

'Of course you do! Where's your professionalism?'
he asked.

'I seem to have mislaid it. Sorry. I should have managed better. No wonder you're so cross with me.'

'How can you say that?' he asked roughly. 'I'm not
cross *with* you—but *for* you. Now go to sleep—and
don't be afraid. I'll be downstairs.'

How had he meant that? Don't be afraid because
you'll not be alone—or don't be afraid because I'll
be keeping my distance? 'Please stay with me,' she
whispered, but not loud enough for him to hear.

'Hungry?' asked Dom, coming quietly into the room
next morning and seeing that Annie was awake.

She'd been awake for several minutes and was feeling humiliated beyond measure by her memories of
the night before. Now she was desperate to regain
some dignity.

'I was very foolish last evening,' she began. 'I felt
there was something wrong about that call and I should
have left word where I was going. I've caused a lot of
trouble for a lot of people and I'm very ashamed.

Naturally, I shall leave this practice immediately.'

Dom crossed the room and stared down at her. Hunched up as she was with the covers pulled up round her, she looked small and childlike and very vulnerable. 'Immediately?' he asked gently. 'That *would* add spice to the tale. For one thing, you don't have anything to wear. Or had you forgotten?'

'When I said "immediately", I meant today. Quietly. By the side door with as little fuss as possible. And, of course, dressed.'

'Have you finished?' he asked in the same gentle voice.

'Finished what?' asked Annie, mystified. She thought her spur-of-the-moment apology had been splendid from one so recently traumatised. And she'd even spared him the embarrassment of sacking her.

'You forgot "in disguise and after dark",' he said softly.

Annie eyed him covertly, trying to decide if he was serious or not.

Dom sat down beside her on the bed. 'You'd only just woken up when I came in,' he guessed. 'Otherwise you'd have been thinking more clearly. To imagine that being attacked in the course of duty is grounds for dismissal is just plain daft.'

Annie gazed at him, torn between hope and doubt. 'Are you sure? People are so funny,' she said at last. 'If an ordinary woman got ambushed and beaten up, then the public would be up in arms and yelling for blood. But doctors are supposed to be superhuman— infallible. Especially if they're female. They'll think that I've been stupid and inefficient and— What are you doing?' she asked when he took her head in his hands.

'Looking for signs of injury,' he said. 'Only a severe

dunt on the head could account for such drivel as you're pouring out this morning.' Then he took her by the shoulders, rocking her gently as though she were a bewildered child. 'Now, listen to me, Annie. You were right about one thing. If you were doubtful about the validity of that call, it would have been better to call at the police station and ask for an escort. But that's all. You're a damn good doctor and an asset to this practice. So let's have no more nonsense about resigning.

'And now we've cleared that up, you're going to have some breakfast, after which I'm sending you home in a taxi.' He got up then and went into the kitchen.

Annie liked the sound of that, but felt obliged to point out that the police wanted to talk to her.

'Then they can talk to you at home,' he decreed.

Annie settled back on the pillows. In the ordinary way she resented being ordered about, having complete confidence in her ability to run her own life.

Or, rather, that had been the case until recently. She'd been too outspoken in her last job and had paid the ultimate penalty. For the same reason, she'd almost lost this one as well. Then last night she'd been attacked and that had shown her how vulnerable just being a woman could make her—something she'd never quite believed before.

So all in all it was very restful, not to say wonderful, to be having her decisions made for her. Especially by Dominic Smith-Jardine.

CHAPTER SEVEN

ANNIE edged up to her living room window and stood on tiptoe to peer over the parapet and down into the tree-lined street. The view was restricted. Newshounds could still be lurking down there and out of sight from attic level.

At midday they'd overwhelmed the postman and swarmed up the stairs to hammer on her door and call through the letterbox.

'Come on, Doctor—tell us your story.'

'What's the matter, Annie—got something to hide?'

'The gutter Press is aptly named!' she'd bawled back, forgetting the advice of her new policeman friends to keep quiet and pretend that there was nobody at home.

She'd come home dressed in a pair of over-tight jeans, which she'd intended to pass on to any patient down on her luck, and an old shirt of Dom's which hung off her shoulders and reached her knees. 'You look like a student,' he'd said as he put her in a taxi.

She'd been barely five minutes in the flat when Dougie and Sam arrived. They had listened and nodded and made notes as Annie recounted the events of the previous night. 'What I don't understand,' she'd continued,' is how you found me so soon.'

'Now, there we had a bit of luck,' Sam had explained. 'It seems they stopped for fish suppers at the chippie in the high street and your patient, Mrs—' he'd stopped to consult his notebook '—Mrs Niven, was queueing behind them. She noticed that one of the girls was wearing the identical jacket you'd been

117

wearing that day. She thought that was a bit of a
coincidence so she struck up a conversation so as to
ask her where she'd got it.

'When the girl said "Down the market" and her
boyfriend told her to shut up and mind her own business, Mrs Niven was suspicious and looked out to see
which way they went. When she saw them getting into
your car, she came straight round to the station.
We put out a call and they were stopped by a traffic
patrol car a couple of hours later on the East Kilbride
road.'

'Bless her!' Annie had exclaimed. 'I've a good mind
to give her that jacket—she's earned it.'

'They're not professional criminals,' Dougie had
chimed in. 'Just a pack of youngsters gone wrong
through drugs and that. They were glad enough to tell
us everything when they were brought in.'

You should know, Annie had thought, but I was in
no position to appreciate the finer shades of criminal
behaviour. Aloud, she'd thanked them again for finding her so quickly and had repeated her hope that the
papers wouldn't get hold of the story.

That was when they'd advised her to stay quiet and
send out for anything she needed—just until the excitement had died down.

Annie peeped out of the window again and saw three
men who were reporters obviously conferring earnestly
on the opposite side of the road. She was still under
siege, then.

She rang the health centre for the fourth time and
asked to speak to Dom, but he was still unavailable.
Then she had to listen to Carol's highly charged
account of police comings and goings and visits from
the Press. She seemed to think that it was all great
fun. 'You're famous,' she said enviously, to which

Annie replied that that sort of fame was something she could do without.

After some muffled whispering, Jane came on the line. 'Poor, dear Annie,' she cooed. 'You must be feeling awful about the trouble and publicity. Would you like me to come and cheer you up after evening surgery?'

The last thing Annie wanted was a dose of Jane's spurious sympathy, so she invented an old friend who'd already offered.

When the phone rang almost immediately after she'd put it down she snatched it up eagerly, sure that it was Dom. 'We know you're there, Annie,' said the same detestable voice she'd heard through the letterbox. 'Just tell us your story and we'll go away.'

Annie gave him the only Polish phrase she knew— a query about a remedy for piles if she remembered aright—then banged down the phone. With luck, that wretched man would think he'd misdialled. Then she switched on the answering machine, discovered that it was on the blink again, swore and yanked the phone out of its socket. She'd ensured relief from nuisance calls but she'd also cut herself off from her friends.

She was debating her chances of escape after dark when the paper boy pushed a note through her door, along with the *Evening News*. Her name was written in large letters on the envelope in Dom's strong, clear hand.

'Have sent the Press on a wild goose chase,' ran the note. 'Pack a bag as fast as you can and come out before they realise. I'll be waiting at the kerb. Dom.'

Three minutes later Annie was hurtling down the stairs. Not a reporter was in sight and Dom was there in his car as promised, with the engine running and the passenger door open. Annie leapt in with a fervent 'Thank you!' and they were away.

'The least I could do,' he said. 'If I'd had the sense I was born with, I'd have anticipated all this hullabaloo and sent you to a secret hideaway until it was all yesterday's news.'

'You can't blame yourself—I never dreamed of this either. But how on earth did you get rid of them?' she asked eagerly.

'With lies and bribes—how else? A call to Central Cabs, ordering a taxi to the service lane behind Park Terrace to pick up a Dr Duncan, and then a tenner to your paper boy to tell the vultures about the taxi waiting for you at the back entrance. By the time they find out it's all a con, we'll be well away.'

'Brilliant!' breathed Annie. 'I'd never have thought of anything like that.'

'I know,' Dom said. 'That puritanical streak that makes you keep on resigning would never have allowed it.'

Annie didn't feel like debating his reading of her character right now. 'Brilliant,' she repeated. 'I just hope they don't take it out on the cabbie—or the boy.'

'Why should they? The cabbie was sent by his firm and the paper boy is in the clear if he sticks with what I told him to say.'

'Which was?'

'There's a taxi in the back lane, waiting for Dr Duncan. And so there is.'

'What a clever, devious devil you are, Dom Smith!'

'Was that a compliment?' he enquired.

'Of course it was! I was going mad cooped up in there and it's wonderful to be free. Where are you taking me?' she thought to ask as they streaked across the Kingston bridge.

After a minute he said carefully, 'It seems to me

that the last place they'll think of looking for you is my country hideaway.'

Annie was ashamed of the surge of excitement she felt then. 'Brilliant,' she managed for the third time. 'I don't know how to thank you.'

'You'll be required to work your passage,' warned Dom, provoking another deplorable surge of excitement.

'I'm told I make a mean omelette,' she offered experimentally.

'I don't like omelettes,' he said. 'Now shut up, there's a good girl, while I pick a way through this lot.'

The traffic was certainly heavy and fast-moving enough to need all his concentration, which left Annie free to get his surprising rescue in perspective. As senior partner, and for the good name of the practice, he would naturally want all the fuss to die down as soon as possible, she reasoned. That alone was sufficient cause for his gesture. Wasn't it?

When Annie was told that Dom lived in a barn, she'd never dreamed of anything so picturesque. When she admired it he shrugged and said that it wasn't finished yet; for instance, he'd not yet fixed up the spare room, but not to worry. She could have his room and he would sleep on the sofa.

A small square hall gave onto a large, raftered sitting room with roughcast walls, an open fireplace and a south-facing picture window that framed a splendid rural scene of fields, woodland and distant moors. Through an open door, she glimpsed a dream kitchen.

Dom tossed her bag onto a sumptuous sofa, which could have held four sumo wrestlers in comfort, and pointed out the phone. 'There must be somebody you'd like to know your whereabouts,' he said. 'And I'll not be listening.' He went into the kitchen and closed the door.

Annie rang a neighbour to explain about the old friend who was putting her up until interest in her abduction had faded. 'Quite near the health centre,' she said in answer to the obvious question, 'but if anybody asks, would you mind saying Helensburgh or Stirling or somewhere else on the north side?'

The neighbour thought that was a good plan so, having covered her tracks, Annie strolled over and tapped on the kitchen door. 'You did say I had to work my passage,' she called out.

She was promptly invited in to set the table. This room was L-shaped with the larger side half screened off as a dining room. It also looked out to the south but, as it was now getting dark, Annie switched on some lights.

'Draw the curtains,' Dom told her.

'In case the neighbours see me and wonder?'

'In case those rogue reporters are brighter than I gave them credit for,' he corrected.

'Sorry—I never thought of that. Bringing me here could add another dimension to the story.'

'If they tracked you down, that would certainly make a nonsense of it,' he corrected again. 'I hope you like chicken in a wine and tarragon sauce,' he said, taking plates from the microwave.

'Sounds wonderful. Did you make it yourself?'

'You're joking! It's the work of the nice wee widow who does for me and keeps the freezer well stocked. This just happened to be at the front.'

Now Annie knew where he'd got the super meal he'd given her the night before. 'Why is it that only a man can find the perfect domestic treasure?' she wondered, as they sat down at the table.

'Because women find it easier to work for a man,' he returned provocatively.

'Surely that depends on the man,' retorted Annie.

'This could become personal,' he murmured thoughtfully.

'And you wouldn't want that. . .'

'Not unless the verdict went in my favour.'

'I will say this,' allowed Annie. 'No boss, male or female, could have been more helpful and understanding than you've been this past twenty-four hours.' She hadn't dared to be more personal for fear of risking their new understanding. Why couldn't I have fixed on a more likely man than you to light my fire? she wondered, not for the first time. Yet here we are, about to pass a second night under the same roof. . .

'You're thinking serious thoughts, Annie,' said Dom, watching her intently across the table.

'I was just—just wondering what the other doctors made of last night's adventure,' she invented. 'After all, they've had to cover for me ever since.'

'Not quite. Today was your half-day, remember. The fact is, they're all very indignant on your behalf. Peter stepped in most willingly overnight and we all took a share of your morning surgery patients and calls. As for Jane, we had the greatest difficulty persuading her not to write a fiery letter to the *Herald* about the appalling risks faced by women GPs when making night calls.'

'That would have played right into the hands of the die-hards who still insist that medicine is no job for a woman,' Annie surmised shrewdly.

'There are no flies on you, my girl,' he approved with a chuckle. 'Come on—let's leave this lot and have our coffee in the other room.'

'To continue the theme,' said Dom from a chair by

the fire while Annie settled down on the enormous
sofa, 'do you think that prejudice played a part in your
unfortunate exit from the hospital scene?'

Annie sighed. 'No—it was my own big mouth that
brought that about. Although. . .' Should she tell him
or would he think she was only trying to gain his
sympathy? 'Sex did have a small part to play,' she
murmured, half to herself.

'It helps to talk,' he prompted softly. 'I got the gist
of it from Jack Marshall, but—' He left it there, waiting
to see if she was ready to tell him.

Annie had always known that Dom was curious and
there'd probably never be a better time than this to
tell the story.

'The straw that broke the camel's back was a
Mercedes 300,' she began surprisingly. 'We'd had the
sort of night in A and E which makes "Casualty" seem
like a peep into the first-aid tent at the Highland
games. Three stabbings, a motorway pile-up, a couple
of dog bites, domestic punch-ups—and a cardiac arrest
for good measure. Then at about four am an infant of
eighteen months was brought in with horrific non-
accidental injuries.'

Annie bit her lip hard, remembering the scene. 'I'd
not have believed that a baby could sustain such injuries and live. Anyway, I worked on the wee mite for
over an hour, only to be told that the paediatric ICU
was full. Apparently two cots had been axed the week
before in the interests of economy—or rationalisation,
as they like to call it.

'While we were phoning desperately around the city
to find a unit that could take her, the wee mite died—
there on a table in the so-called recovery room.'

Her voice caught on a sob. 'I went off duty at nine
and the first thing I saw was our new overlord getting

out of his new Mercedes. That was bad enough but
the bastard had to show off, calling out for me to come
and admire it—and assuming that now he'd got it I'd
not be able to resist his invitations.'

Annie could hardly continue, remembering how
she'd felt then. 'I saw red. Literally,' she said in a
choked voice.

'I ran up to him and I beat him with my fists, shriek-
ing that babies were dying to pay for his wretched toy.
I went on and on, pouring out all the disgust I felt for
a system that puts cars and expense accounts and plush
new offices and bloated salaries before the welfare
of the people it was set up to care for. And all this
when the day staff were coming in and dawdling to
enjoy the spectacle.

'Well, of course, after such a performance as that
his pride demanded that I should be punished—especially as everybody knew he'd been chasing after me
from the day he arrived.

'He persuaded the board that I should be sent for
psychiatric assessment, no matter what Jack and all
the department had to say about it. But the professor
of psychiatry assessed me himself and reported that if
all his patients were half as sane as I was then he
would be redundant. So they couldn't discharge me for
insanity—but they could refuse to renew my contract.'

Annie gazed at Dom, her expressive eyes full of
sorrow. 'I'm a good surgeon, Dom, but skill is no
longer the main requirement for the job. I'd given a
jumped-up little squirt, who wouldn't know a patient
if he fell over one, a well-deserved set-down. Worse—
I'd rejected his sexual advances. Therefore, I had to
be taught a lesson. And now you know exactly what
sort of assistant you've taken on.'

'There's only one thing wrong with that scenario,

Annie,' said Dom, crossing over and dropping down beside her on the sofa. 'You didn't torch that bloody car!'

During that painful recital, Annie had been strung up to near-breaking point. Now, with his remarkable reaction, all the tension drained out of her on a wonderful upsurge of laughter. She laughed until she cried, then mopped her eyes and clapped a hand over her aching diaphragm.

'Splendid. Priceless,' she gasped as soon as she could. 'Oh, Dom—thank you! Thanks a million times over.' She sagged against him, still shaking. 'You understand. You really truly understand. I never dreamed. . .'

He put an arm around her and hugged her affectionately. 'I don't know anybody else who'd have gone so bravely into battle without any thought of self. You're a one-off, Annie, girl, you're unique!'

'Thank you, thank you,' she said again. 'I'm very flattered, but Jack Marshall thinks I must have a death wish.'

'But not me, Annie—not me,' he denied firmly.

Annie could hardly believe it. 'You don't think I'd have been wiser to say all that in private—or not at all?'

'Wiser? Definitely. But I admire the way you struck out.'

'Because you'd have done the same?'

'Because their loss was my gain.'

He meant that and she knew that he did. 'My lifeline,' she murmured. 'What would I do without you?'

'Sink,' he suggested, laughing down at her. Then he ruffled her hair playfully and kissed the mess he had made of it.

'Brute,' charged Annie, not meaning it in the least. She was quite intoxicated with the result of her confession. 'If you're going to treat me like this, I'll start wondering again if I was wise to come and work for you.'

He looked at her again—really looked—and was transfixed by the change from sensible, no-nonsense career woman to playful tigress. Her abundant auburn hair framed a face of startling vitality in which her amazing tawny eyes were alight with mischief.

'My god, Annie,' he said hoarsely. 'Why did I never realise what a fascinating little witch you are?'

'Because I was—kind of right under your nose,' she suggested breathlessly. Her heart was hammering wildly as his arms went round her, pulling her close.

No matter that they'd never kissed before; to Annie, it was like a homecoming after a long and lonely absence. Her fervent, ready response fanned the flame leaping in him. They kissed and kissed until they had to stop for breath. 'You're amazing—wonderful,' he murmured. 'Who'd have thought it?'

Annie liked the ardour, but could have done without the astonishment. 'Not me, anyway,' she claimed defensively. 'There were times when you hated me.'

'I wonder,' he returned slowly, holding her face between his hands while his eyes drank in all this sudden and unexpected beauty.

That was better. It might after all be possible that he was feeling all the love and wonder that she was. 'What do you wonder? All that fighting. . .'

'We don't bother to fight with people we're indifferent to,' he said in the same bemused way. 'It was there all the time, Annie—it must have been. Only buried so deep that we didn't know.'

'Know what, Dom, darling?' she crooned, so sure now of what was coming.

'The sexual attraction. I fancy you, lovely, wonderful

Annie Duncan—and you fancy me. So don't deny it.'

He couldn't have hurt her more if he'd struck her.
Fool that she was, she'd been expecting a declaration
of love. But as it had all her life, her ready tongue came
to her rescue now. 'Denial would be a bit pointless, I
guess, when I've not been exactly discouraging.'

She leaned back and assessed him as coolly as she
could manage. 'Yes, you're definitely an attractive
devil, Dom Smith—as if you didn't know! No—don't
you be getting carried away,' she said when he looked
like starting again. 'This could complicate things. And
you're on call, too—or had you forgotten?'

'Yes, I had,' he groaned. 'You could make a man
forget his own name—you fascinating minx.' He
rubbed his cheek against hers and teased her earlobe
with his lips until she thought she'd scream with frustration. 'But I'll be off tomorrow night,' he murmured.

'But will my bruises be better? I'm still aching all
over from my dreadful experience.' If only she didn't
need to keep him at arm's length like this, but Annie
had never been one of your modern women who could
separate sex and love like a man apparently could.
And she needed time to see whether she could manage
it for him. . .

'Blast!' growled Dom when the phone put an end
to his urgings and her confused thoughts.

'All in the day's work,' she said with amazing non-
chalance.

'I wish I could take this in my stride as easily as you
can,' he sighed, releasing her unwillingly to pick up
the phone.

Annie was both sad and resentful at being so mis-
understood when she'd thought for one brief and
wonderful moment that all the years of division and
duelling were at an end. How stupid could she be?

'With luck, I'll not be too long, sweetheart,' Dom said, kissing her swiftly before going.

'Famous last words,' she responded brightly, keeping up the act to the last.

She listened to him driving away and then went to feed the dishwasher and tidy the kitchen. Then she returned to the living room and made up the fire. She'd no sooner switched on the television than the phone rang. She turned down the sound and slithered along the sofa, prepared to answer a professional call.

'Are you feeling as lonely as I am tonight, lover?' asked a husky female voice before Annie could say anything.

'That depends,' she heard herself replying, provoking an audible gasp and the slamming down of the receiver.

Misdialled, poor soul, and now feeling ridiculous, Annie thought, as she turned up the television volume again.

Seconds later, the phone rang again. This time, Annie forestalled the caller with a prompt hello. Again, the caller hung up.

Annie sat back, frowning thoughtfully. The woman had called again, solely to make sure she'd dialled correctly the first time. That was the only explanation. She had a rival, then. Given Dom's potent charm and attraction for women, it would have been surprising if she hadn't. Well, forewarned was forearmed—or so it was said. Thank God she hadn't disclosed her true feelings to him earlier. At least the playing field was still level!

Annie took care to be in bed with the light out when Dom returned. When she heard the slight click as he opened the bedroom door, she simulated the slow, soft breathing of sleep. He came across to the bed and bent over her. 'Annie,' he whispered. 'Annie, darling—are you asleep?'

It took all her resolve to maintain the pretence, but she did it. After a silent second or two he bent down, kissed her very gently on the cheek and crept away.

'And where d'you think you're going?' Dom demanded next morning when he came into the bedroom with a breakfast tray to find that Annie was up and dressed.

'To work, of course,' she returned perkily. 'Is that for me? Oh, Dom—how sweet!'

'Nothing is too much trouble for you, my favourite witch. And you can forget work—you need at least one more day off.' He set down the tray and would have taken her in his arms but she dodged away after planting a quick kiss on his cheek. Having woken very early, Annie had done some constructive thinking and decided there was nothing to be lost by keeping this situation light until he showed his hand.

She picked up the tray and carried it to the kitchen, where they continued to wrangle light-heartedly all through breakfast about whether or not Annie should go to work.

Annie won. 'And you'd better drop me off before we get there, my hero,' she decided. 'If we're seen arriving together then tongues will wag.'

'Why? They'll know you can't have walked from Glasgow.'

'If anybody asks, I came by bus. OK?'

'Lord, but you're bossy,' he sighed. 'I'm not sure I can cope with being ordered about like this.'

'Time will tell,' she said. 'But we'll not be rushing our fences meanwhile—huh?'

'You're having second thoughts,' he challenged, looking nettled.

'Call it natural caution,' she retorted. 'We were both fairly—euphoric last night.'

'Surely you don't want to go back to the bad old days?'

'Heaven forbid! I just want us to be sensible, that's all. Last night was all a bit—sudden.'

A huge, impish grin broke over his face. 'I get it—you want me to court you,' he decided.

To her horror, Annie felt herself blushing. 'Don't be daft!' she growled. 'It's just that if we get this wrong, I really will have to leave. Had you thought of that?'

'No. Because discovering the cause of our eternal wrangling will make things easier, not worse, you goose!'

Goose, indeed. And last night he'd called her a witch and a minx. Was that how men usually addressed the loves of their lives? How Annie wished that she'd devoted less time to surgery and more to personal relationships. 'I thought you respected my intellect,' she said frostily.

'So I do—most of the time. But you're talking an awful lot of waffle this morning. Finished breakfast? Good. We'd better be leaving. If we're caught arriving late as well as together tongues really will wag.'

'And you wouldn't want that,' Annie said provokingly.

'What I want seems to be neither here nor there,' he retorted. '*You're* the one who's laying down the ground rules!'

Shifting the initiative like that left Annie exactly where she'd been before. Completely in the dark.

CHAPTER EIGHT

'JUST look who's here!' cried Carol excitedly when Annie arrived well after Dom, having nagged him into setting her down a couple of streets away. 'We were just dividing out your morning patients. Oh, heavens!' she exclaimed, on noticing Annie's injuries.

Andrew Syme was concerned, too, but very relieved that she wasn't more seriously hurt. Angus said that he'd back Annie against your average mugger but four would have been a handful, even for her.

It was Jane who asked Annie if she hadn't been just the least bit suspicious. 'I mean—such a dreadful old cottage, dear. . .' She left a charge of folly hanging in the air.

But hers was the only qualified greeting. Peter admired Annie for her dedication in turning up for work so soon, while Laura said that she'd expected nothing else.

'Thank you for not having me down as an absolute twit,' said Annie, hoping that the patients would be as understanding.

She had her usual bright greeting ready for the first one, but Mrs Soutar said, 'Never mind me, Doctor. How's yourself?' Then she reversed roles by coming round the desk to inspect Annie's battle-scars more closely. 'This is what comes of banning the tawse in schools,' she decided. 'What are ye putting on yon? My granny used to swear by arnica, though I've not tried it myself. Now then—'

Annie broke in to thank her for her advice and slide in some of her own. 'Are you still taking the painkillers regularly, Mrs Soutar? You were hirpling quite badly when you came in.'

Mrs Soutar looked guilty. 'The fact is, I've been sharing 'em with the auld yin—his back's been awful bad—and we ran out at the weekend, only I couldn't manage to get in before today. Do you think you should be working, Doctor? They're saying you were knocked out and left for dead.'

'Not at all! You know what the newspapers are for hyping everything up. Anyway, after a lazy day off, I've almost forgotten all about it. But that's by the way. I'm very cross with you. The ketoprofen was prescribed especially for you and if your husband—'

'Ma faither, Doctor.'

'Your father, then. If he's in trouble, he should consult us. What suits you may be contra-indicated—I mean, quite unsuitable—for him. Is he housebound?'

'Naw! He gets the length of the pub, no bother.'

'Well, then, I think you should make an appointment for him on your way out.' Annie had been writing busily while she spoke, and passed over a new prescription. 'You'll see that I'm only giving you a week's supply this time so you'll not be tempted to share them again. They're not sweeties, you know.'

While agreeing in principle, Mrs Soutar added that she wouldn't mind betting that Annie would have done the same if she'd been putting up with the old man and his complaining.

A new patient next; a smartly dressed, plumpish matron from the best end of the town. 'What seems to be the trouble?' asked Annie when the patient had finished apologising for coming.

'Heart failure,' replied Mrs Adam confidently.

Annie said she'd need to reserve judgement until after an examination.

'Yes, I'm afraid you will have to get undressed, Mrs Adam. Just pop behind that curtain and give me a shout when you're ready.'

'So, what makes you think you've got heart failure?' she asked about twelve minutes later.

'Why, ma ankles, Doctor. See how swollen they are already? By evening they'll be out like balloons.'

'That is certainly one symptom but, in the absence of any others, I think this is the most likely culprit.' Annie picked up her patient's strongly elasticated pantie girdle, which was at least three sizes too small.

'It's obviously restricting the return blood flow and causing a backlog in the peripheral blood and lymph vessels—that is, the ones in your feet and lower legs. Come over to the mirror and look at these red marks. See? It's as though you'd been tightly bandaged at the top of your thighs.'

Mrs Adam needed some persuading before she agreed not to wear her girdle for a few days and test out Annie's theory. 'But how am I to keep my stomach flat without it?' she worried. So Annie gave her a note for Craig, explaining that he would teach her some useful exercises.

Then she buzzed for the next patient. Oh, help! Another one of Jane's. . .

'And where do you think you're going?' asked Dom, coming into Annie's room after surgery to find her putting on her jacket.

'Visiting, of course!' she returned crisply—and that was his fault as he was standing much too close and she could feel his breath on her neck; so very unsettling for a girl who was trying to be sensible. She reminded herself that he didn't know she knew about his other girlfriend.

'If you're going visiting, you'll need your bag,' he advised.

'Of course—and the nurses are making up a temporary one for me, so—' Annie had just remembered that she was also without her car. 'Blast!' she muttered. 'Jane's quite right. I am an idiot.'

'When did she say that?' Dom asked sharply.

'She didn't—just sort of implied it. And it's true, if I can forget things like having no car.'

'I don't agree. You're putting on a great show, but you're probably still slightly shocked. That's why I didn't want you to work today.'

'But I'm managing fine—honestly. And if Laura can't lend me her car then I'll hire one.'

'You are now going to put your feet up on the couch and I'll send somebody along with a coffee,' he decided, looking his most implacable.

Annie liked his concern, but felt obliged to protest a bit. 'You're very kind, but—'

Dom put a stop to that most effectively by kissing her firmly on the mouth, leaving her all weak and woozy. Then he scooped her up in his arms and put her on the couch. 'Stay there until I tell you to move,' he ordered. When she simply gazed at him wordlessly, he went out looking like a cat that had got at the cream.

The promised coffee having been delivered and drunk, Annie got up to phone the police station to ask how long it would be before she got her stolen property back.

By good luck it was Dougie who answered, although he couldn't answer her query and advised her to hire a car. 'Your insurance will pay,' he said.

Annie hoped that he was right. She'd battle that out

later. First she consulted the Yellow Pages for a car-hire company and ordered delivery of a suitable vehicle forthwith.

And that was how she happened to be out on a visit when Dom returned from his morning calls. The usual Wednesday working lunch was already under way when she got back. She could tell that he was angry with her, but trying hard not to show it. He waited to explode until he'd followed her back to her room after the meeting. 'Damnit, Annie, where did you go? We'd already divided out your visits between us!'

'So I discovered, but when this call came in from one of my patients naturally I went. He'd fallen down-stairs and I'm pretty sure there are no bones broken but, with his history, I sent him to hospital for X-rays—just in case. You know Donald Muir, so you must see I was right. . .'

He was looking anything but approving. 'How?' he barked.

'What do you mean—"how"?' she retorted.

'He lives on the other side of town—and you've no car.'

'I've hired one.'

'Already? How very efficient!' he said sarcastically.

'I *am* very efficient. That's why you hired me.' But she was taking risks, going on like this. Supposing he asked her if she thought it was efficient to answer dubious calls without leaving word where she was going? He didn't.

After glaring at her in angry frustration for some seconds, he said grimly, 'I'm only thinking of you, Annie. If you were a patient, I'd have put you off work for a week after an experience like that!'

'Then why when you fall off a horse do they tell you the best thing is to get straight back on?' Oh, why am I provoking him like this? But, in her heart, she knew why. Her natural independence apart, she couldn't forget those mysterious phone calls the night before. They were staying with her like an aching tooth.

'You just can't bear to be wrong, can you?' Dom asked heavily. 'OK, then—go and volunteer for every emergency call that comes in this afternoon! And tell Andrew there's no need for him to take your evening surgery—even though he insisted. Then tell Jane you'll take her night duty, why don't you? I'm going home!'

The weary disgust in his voice wasn't just hurtful, it was terrifying. She'd decided to keep things light for a while but this wasn't light—it was open warfare and if she went on like this she'd lose him altogether; handing him over to the other woman on a plate.

She got to the door before him, barring his exit. 'Dom—please listen! I know I'm being pigheaded and—and aggravating, but I'm only trying to show that I can cope. It's my way of keeping my end up. Can't you see?' she pleaded, clutching at his lapels with her bruised fists.

'What I can't see—after last night—is why you still think you've got to keep it up with me,' he answered in hurt perplexity.

But she couldn't tell him that, could she? This was definitely not the time. 'I guess I need time to adjust,' she said inadequately.

'That's more or less what you said at breakfast,' he reminded her. 'You've had a whole morning and half the afternoon. How long do you think you'll need? We've already wasted almost ten years—and we're not getting any younger!'

Encouraged by his weary but bantering tone, she allowed, 'You could be right—about my being in shock. So could you manage to humour me—just for a little while?'

He covered her hands with his own and it hurt, but what did that matter when his eyes were overflowing with warmth? 'I'm sorry if you think I'm pushing you too hard, sweet girl. Just tell me what you want and I'll do my best to see you get it.'

'Just—just don't rush me,' she begged, shy of telling him that she wanted his love in case she frightened him off.

'Into bed, you mean,' he said bluntly. 'Or would you also rule out a cosy candle-lit dinner?'

'Oh, no—I'd really love that. . .'

'I was right, was I not, when I said you wanted me to court you?' he asked mischievously. 'No, don't answer that if it embarrasses you.' He held her closer and gazed searchingly into her eyes. 'Oh, Annie—why can't you be as glad and happy as I am at this amazing thing that's happening to us?' Then he kissed her before she could answer and his kiss was even more wonderful than the promise in his eyes.

So it was a great shame that they started wrangling again almost at once.

Annie said that she simply must go back to Glasgow and fetch something smarter than the workaday clothes she'd got with her.

Dom said that was rubbish—she looked just fine to him in that nice blouse and skirt.

But Annie insisted so Dom said that he'd drive her up to town and she could pack a nice big suitcase.

Annie asked why she would need a large one and he said that he thought she should stay with him for at least a week to save herself the fatigue of travelling.

Annie replied that cutting out the travelling was a good idea but why did she not stay in the on-call flat as nobody else needed it because they all lived so near?

To her surprise he agreed to that, but the next minute she was wishing she'd never suggested it. Too late, she had realised that staying with him would have made it easier to suss out her rival's position.

'And I must admit that, for once, compromise makes sense, dear heart,' he went on. 'Some of our older patients would be rather shocked to hear that we'd shacked up together.'

'Not only the patients,' she returned thoughtfully.

'You mean the partners, I suppose.'

She didn't, she meant Sultry Telephone Voice, but she said, 'I'm pretty sure that Jane woundn't approve and possibly Andrew might raise an eyebrow.'

'So this way we get the best of both worlds; only two or three miles apart and no eyebrows in danger of dislocation,' he said, making her wonder if that wasn't really what he'd intended all along.

At that moment, Annie's phone rang. She answered it, listened for a minute, then told him, 'There's a man from the home and health department waiting for you in your room.'

'Damn,' he said. 'I'd completely forgotten asking him to come on my half-day so as not to waste good patient time. You'd better forget about that suitcase, darling.'

'Get to your meeting and don't worry about me,' she advised. 'I'll see you later—Prince Charming.'

The journey up to town in her hired car went smoothly, though Annie stayed longer at home than she'd intended. Having a bath, making phone calls, visiting the neighbours who were keeping an eye on her flat and then remembering at the last minute to empty the fridge all took longer than she'd envisaged. Then a lorry shedding its load on the motorway more than doubled the usual time for the return trip.

Dom was waiting for her in the on-call flat when she arrived back and was none too pleased, judging by his expression. 'Where the hell have you been?' he demanded. 'It's way after six.'

'And it's nice to see you too,' she returned satirically.

'Oh, very funny! I was worried,' he said, instantly defusing the situation. 'Didn't you realise I would be?'

'I'm sorry I spoke like that,' she said quickly. 'There was an accident on the M8, which slowed things up. I can be ready in ten minutes.'

'No rush but, having calculated that you'd be back at least an hour ago, I got myself in a bit of a state—that's all.'

'Oh, Dom. . .' Annie ran forward, put her arms round him and kissed him spontaneously for the first time.

He wasn't slow to respond and if Carol hadn't buzzed to say that the car alarm driving them all mad down there was on that wee Vauxhall Annie had hired and would she please come down and stop it, then they would probably not have got out to dinner at all!

Dom had booked a table at a fairly new restaurant in a pretty little village to the south of Burnside.

'I wouldn't mind living here if I could afford it,' said Annie, admiring all the delightful houses in their well-kept gardens.

'Margot's parents live here,' said Dom.

For one mad moment Annie wondered if it had been his former wife on the phone last night. 'Do you ever hear from her, Dom?' she asked offhandedly.

'Of course not! Besides, she's on the other side of the world—as I told you.'

'Sorry—I just wondered. . .'

'Well, you can just stop wondering. That part of my life is over.' He snatched a quick sidelong glance at her. 'It occurs to me that we've got a lot of catching up to do, my Annie.'

'Have we?' she asked wondering what else he'd got to tell her.

'Of course we have.' He slowed the car and turned off the road to park by the restaurant—a long, low building tacked onto an old watermill. 'Surely you realise how curious I am about what you've been up to all these years? There must have been men. . .'

Naturally he was curious, But why did he want to know now? Was it just a diversion to get away from discussing his ex-wife?

'Annie?' he prompted gently.

'One or two. Well, just the one, really—on and off. He was a teacher and in spite of all the fuss they make about all the marking and preparation, he had much more free time than I—especially when I was working for my fellowship. He never understood that and in the end he got fed up and married a history teacher with a guitar and buck teeth.'

Dom broke into laughter and Annie shot him a wounded look. 'I was fairly upset at the time,' she reproved him.

He slid an arm round her shoulders. 'Never mind— you'd soon have realised that a man with such poor taste was all wrong for you.'

A bit ambiguous, that, but on balance Annie decided that it was really a compliment. 'To be truthful, I wasn't all that attached to him,' she admitted, 'but it was useful to have somebody to go about with. I'd probably have looked for a replacement sooner if I'd had the time.'

Dom pulled a comical face. 'You sound as though

the man in your life is no more important than the car or the vacuum cleaner. Do you always sit and wait for them to drop down from the trees, rather than take positive steps to annex one you really like the look of?'

'I suppose I do,' she agreed, while knowing exactly why. The one she'd always most fancied had never looked her way until now.

He kissed her; a long kiss which she returned with interest because he'd caught her in the middle of a sentimental thought.

'Three cheers for guitar-playing, dentally challenged history teachers,' he said, laughing softly. 'But for one such, I'd have had to fight that stupid man for you. Do you have any more confessions to make, my dear little witch?'

'None worth the time it'd take to tell,' she said, but before she could ask whether he had any he had kissed her again, said to hell with the past and now they were getting on with the present.

Annie had never been one for drinking; largely because even very little alcohol made her all giggly and reckless and she preferred to keep her wits about her. But Dom had arranged for a bottle of nicely chilled vintage champagne to be waiting for them and it slipped down so beguilingly that she forgot to keep track of her consumption. So, what with that and Dom at his wittiest and most charming, Annie was soon away on a cloud.

Dom was enchanted by this second appearance of Annie at her most relaxed and defenceless and did all he could to encourage her with more wine, and soft compliments that got more and more extravagant as the evening wore on.

Annie hardly noticed what she was eating—or that the waiter had just removed the second empty champagne bottle. She planted her elbows on the table—with great difficulty because she seemed to be floating inches off the ground. Then she supported her chin in her hands, sent Dom a dreamy look and asked, 'What is the male equi—equi. . .opposite of a witch, please?'

Dom did a double-take before telling her, 'It's a warlock, darling, but why on earth do you want to know that just now?'

'Because I think that's what you are. I'm just completely—be-warlocked!' Annie smiled and chuckled and twinkled at him. Then she noticed her empty glass. 'Unless I'm drunk—oh, Dom! Tell me I'm not drunk!'

'You're not drunk,' he said. 'Relaxed, happy, uninhibited, perhaps, but not drunk.'

'If you say so. I trust you, you know,' she confided.

'And about time, too, my treasure. Have you enjoyed your evening?'

'The best of my entire life,' Annie declared dreamily.

'Then this is the right moment to go home,' he murmured.

He himself had drunk little, so the drive home was quite uneventful.

Annie was still too transported to notice that they had stopped outside Dom's house and not the centre. 'Thank you for the most lovely, lovely time,' she said, winding her arms round his neck as he guided her erratic steps towards the bedroom.

He kissed her fondly. 'My pleasure, sweetheart.'

'Mine, too. . . Oh, Dom—I think I love you!'

'And about time, too, my treasure. . .' And, then, because she seemed inclined to loll there all night in his arms, he undressed her gently and laid her tenderly under the duvet.

But by the time he'd undressed and would have got

in beside her Annie had passed out, wearing nothing
but a blissful smile.

Annie was awakened by the crowing of a cock. She
knew she was dreaming because nobody kept chickens
in the middle of Glasgow. She opened her eyes. She
wasn't dreaming and she wasn't in Glasgow. Memories
of the night before filtered back. She turned her head
with a mixture of eagerness and doubt but she was
alone in the big bed and the pillow next to hers was
plump and undented.

She lay and thought for a while because that wasn't
what she'd expected. She thought some more, getting
as far as the moment when they had stood beside the
bed in one another's arms. . . Then, nothing. So she'd
drunk too much and passed out, yet surprisingly she
could feel no trace of a hangover. Dom must have put
her to bed and left her. Was that because he loved
her or because he was disgusted that she couldn't
hold her liquor?

There were other questions. How would it look when
she turned up for work in her slinky evening dress?
Most of the staff would cope with the sight but darling
Mrs Mac, the cleaner—who was constantly holding
her up as an example to all womankind—would be
terribly upset. Worse—Mrs Mac was a champion
gossip.

Suddenly Annie saw the way to spare everybody's
feelings. By the time she had dressed it was still barely
six o'clock. She tore a page off the phone pad on the
bedside table and wrote quickly, 'Call me a puritan if
you like, but to avoid any dislocated eyebrows I'm
walking into Burnside. Last night was wonderful.
You're a terrible man, but I think I love you. Annie.'

Then she tidied the bed and placed her note in the

middle of the duvet. She couldn't resist taking a peep at Dom before she left. He lay sprawled on his back on the opened-out sofa, most of the covers having slipped off onto the floor. She watched the rise and fall of his magnificent chest in the slow, even breathing of sleep and was tempted to fling caution to the winds and throw herself on top of him. But only for a second. She was sober this morning—and their moment must surely come soon.

Annie saw nobody she knew on that walk into town, which was just as well. She looked a strange sight in her high-heeled sandals and an old plastic mac several sizes too big, which she'd taken from Dom's cloakroom to hide her skimpy dress. Her feet were excruciatingly painful and she kicked the sandals off the minute she'd let herself into the centre by the side door, which she re-locked. Then she limped upstairs to the sanctuary of the on-call suite.

Half an hour later, after muesli and a shower, she was ready to call to the cleaner from the top of the stairs, 'Just didn't want you to get a shock, Mrs Mac, but I'm staying here for a few days to save myself the travelling.'

'That's a good idea, dear,' Mrs Mac called back. 'And now I know what that strange car's doing outside.' She never missed a thing.

'I hired it,' explained Annie. 'Just until I get my own back. Would you like a cup of tea before you start? I've just made some.'

But Mrs Mac tut-tutted at the very idea. 'I'd rather have everything nice for them coming in, if it's all the same to you, dear.'

By the time she heard Dom's car screech to a halt in its usual place under her window, Annie was seeing her first patient of the day. He'd slept in, then; something she'd never known him do before. She wondered what he'd thought of her dawn flight. Was he amused, impressed or annoyed?

'So what is it then, Doctor?' asked the bright little woman Annie had just examined.

She pulled herself together. 'It's what we call a sebaceous cyst, Mrs Armstrong. They're quite common and completely harmless. Usually we leave them alone but yours is right under the fastening of your bra so I'm going to remove it as soon as surgery's over. Or would you rather come back some other morning this week after eleven?'

Mrs Armstrong decided the sooner the better. 'So I'll just pop along to Tesco's and come back later.'

Annie warned the duty nurse that she'd be doing a minor op later, then waited a few minutes before buzzing for her next patient in case Dom couldn't wait to see her.

Apparently, he could wait. The next tap on the door heralded Annie's second patient. She recognised the quiet man who kept the open-all-hours corner shop that supplied their Wednesday sandwiches. 'Why, hello, Mr Khan. We don't often see you this side of the counter. What seems to be the trouble?'

He was embarrassed. 'Perhaps I will be coming back another time, Doctor. See Dr Smith or Dr Milne. . .'

Annie guessed his problem and how to deal with it. 'Oh, come now, Mr Khan. I'm a doctor—just like your pretty daughter. What do you think Nahreen would say if I were to tell her you didn't trust me because I'm a woman?'

'You know Nahreen?' he asked, surprised.

'Sure. We were on the same team at Glasgow

General for a while. She's a very good doctor—and she thinks I'm a good doctor, too.'

He wrestled a while longer with his cultural attitudes before saying, 'It's my back, Doctor.' Annie had already guessed that from his awkward posture. 'I was lifting a big crate. . .'

It was quite a common story and it didn't take long for Annie to pinpoint the spot and decide that this was a case for Craig. She wrote a referral note and gave it to the shopkeeper. 'And don't worry, Mr Khan,' she said when she'd explained what was wrong. 'Our physiotherapist is a man.'

He smiled at her and said, 'You are very quick-witted, Doctor—just like my daughter. It is not easy for a man like me to accept this. My wife gets impatient with me. It was she who insisted that Nahreen should go to university.'

'And now you're very proud of her,' Annie guessed shrewdly.

'Yes—and, as I said, you are very quick, Doctor. And I thank you for your skill and patience.'

As he left, Annie picked up the phone to tell Craig that she was sending him another patient. It wasn't strictly necessary but he'd been avoiding her so carefully that she'd decided it was time to stop that. When she'd said her piece, he said, 'That should be all right. And if it's as you say, then I should be able to put him right before I leave.'

'You're leaving?' Dom would be very sorry about that.

'Yes. I've accepted a teaching post.'

'And will you like that?'

'It will be preferable to my present post,' he returned pointedly.

So he was still smarting and there was nothing Annie

could do about that. 'I'm sure you know I wish you well,' she offered.

'I didn't, but if you say so I'll try to believe it. Was there anything else?'

'No—not just now. . .'

'Then I'll say goodbye,' said Craig, and rang off.

Annie didn't begrudge him the last word. Besides, she had something much more pressing on her mind. But when she went to the common room for coffee Dom wasn't there, and she missed him at lunchtime, too. It was unsettling, but surely she would see him before evening surgery?

He finished before she did that night and, glancing out of the window at the sound of a car engine, she saw him driving away. By then, Annie was really upset and could hardly concentrate on Mr Kerr's long-winded account of his quarrels with his mother-in-law, which he blamed for his heart condition.

She roused herself to disagree. 'Family stress of that sort can be an aggravating factor but it's not the cause, Mr Kerr. The blood supply to your heart is not as good as it should be but a simple operation can put that right, so I'm referring you to a cardiac surgeon who is an old colleague of mine.'

And heaven forgive me for calling any operation simple—as a surgeon, I should know better—but why burden him with technical details?

'Did you catch what I said, Mr Kerr?'

'Aye, I'm hearing you, lass. Anything you say. You're the doctor.'

When he had gone, Annie's thoughts homed in on her own heart condition. Why had Dom dashed off like that without a word to her? And why had he been avoiding her all day? She knew definitely now that that was what he'd been doing. And it didn't make sense when the night before they'd been so happy.

Automatically she tidied her room as she did at the end of every day and forced herself to dictate a few necessary letters. Then she decided that she would go home and be miserable in comfort. What was the point of staying here now?

She had found her case and had pulled down the bed to make a surface to pack on when she heard the side door open and shut, followed by the sound of somebody running upstairs. Seconds later, the door burst open and Dom was filling the doorway.

'Why should I let you get away with it?' he shouted. 'You're damn well going to explain—and, by heaven, you'd better make it good!'

'Explain what?' asked Annie in genuine bewilderment. 'What am I supposed to have done *now*?'

'You know damn well what you've done! Are you trying to drive me mad?'

Annie's own ready temper was on the rise now. 'I could ask *you* that,' she spat. 'You're mad about something—that's clear. But instead of saying why, you sulk all day—then crash about and shout! Not everybody's gone home yet and I'll bet they're really enjoying this.'

'It's women like you who drive men to murder!' roared Dom, heedless of her warning. 'I've every right to be angry—sneaking off like that without a word! Carol thought I was mad when I rang her first thing to ask if you were here. After telling everybody yesterday that you'd be living in for a bit!'

'You didn't go into the bedroom,' said Annie, thinking she had found the reason for his anger.

'Don't be silly—I looked everywhere!'

'But you didn't see my note?'

'There wasn't any note.'

Annie understood now. 'Oh, Dom—how could you think I'd be so unkind? I left a note for you on the bed. Telling you that I was walking to work early. To get changed. I mean, how would it have looked— coming to work in that dress?'

Her disjointed explanation had calmed him down a bit. 'You had only to wake me and I'd have driven you in. Walking all that way—and in such silly shoes. . .'

'I can see now it would have been better if I had but it's only two miles and it was such a lovely morning. Oh, Dom! Why do we always get so steamed up with each other?'

'Do you really not know why?' he asked unsteadily, reaching out for her.

She went into his arms and he held her tightly, frantically—like a man who had been drowning and had suddenly found a lifebelt. Then he began to kiss her— her face, her eyes, her neck, her shoulders, and each touch of his mouth evoked a shiver of delight. Annie had never felt such desire; it was as though she'd only been half-alive until now.

'You're sure?' he was asking feverishly. 'There'll be no going back this time. . .'

'Yes, yes,' she breathed, moving against his eager body. Something she'd never done before; something she hadn't known she knew how to do.

Skilfully he undressed her, every brush of his hand adding fuel to the flame of her desire. Then he laid her on the bed, drinking in every line of her while he undressed himself. Annie pulled him down to her eagerly. This was their moment; the moment she'd been waiting for all her adult life.

She awakened alone. Dom had gone. Even when she remembered that tonight he was to address a meeting of other fund-holding principals, she still felt deserted. Reading the tender little note he had left for her helped. It would have helped more, though, if he'd mentioned that he loved her. . .

CHAPTER NINE

'Now for the last item on the agenda,' said Dom. 'The request from the west end practice, asking us to team up with them to provide night and weekend cover. Andrew?'

Andrew Syme was against the idea, seeing more advantages for the other practice than for theirs.

Angus voted next, saying that his wife was in favour of anything that would give him more time off. So he voted for. So did Jane. She believed that the women registered with the other practice would welcome the chance to consult a woman.

Dom didn't point out that that could only happen if they managed to be ill out of normal surgery hours. 'So we're evenly split then,' he said, revealing his personal dislike of the scheme. 'And with Peter just visiting pro tem the casting vote is yours, Annie.'

'I'm against the idea,' she revealed. 'I prefer that our patients always be seen by one of us. Continuity of care is so much easier when there is easy access to records—not to mention personal discussion. Besides, we run an unofficial second-on-call scheme here and I doubt they'd want to join in that when it's clear they want to cut down. They must be very busy in a two-man practice but by all accounts they've got very full lists so the remedy is obvious. Take a cut in income and employ another doctor—if they don't want to use an agency for night cover.'

'That's it then,' said Dom with obvious satisfaction.

'So one of your nice tactful letters then, please, Laura.
And that's it for today, folks.'

He kept Annie back with a hand on her arm as the
others left.

'Thanks for agreeing with me,' he said. 'That doesn't
happen too often these days.'

Annie ignored the allusion to their continuing differences. 'No problem,' she returned. 'In a nutshell, I
just don't fancy either of those two monkeying about
with any of my patients.'

'And also "in a nutshell", neither do I,' he agreed.
'What time do you think you'll manage to finish today?'

Annie shrugged. 'Half past six—seven, perhaps—
provided my evening surgery list hasn't grown since
last I looked at it.'

'Life was simpler before you insisted on moving back
to your own place,' he grumbled. Annie had moved
home about a week after the attack on her.

'Perhaps you should get yourself a mistress a bit
nearer home,' she countered.

Dom contrived to look both scandalised and hurt.
'You can be very coarse when you put your mind to
it,' he told her angrily.

'Only because I was brought up to call a spade a
spade, m'lad. So will I see you tonight or not?'

'You'll see me.' His voice was strained. 'You know
damn well that I can't keep away from you.'

'Flatterer,' responded Annie, sounding a lot calmer
than she felt. 'And now I must get on. I'm not the
lucky one with the half-day.'

But she didn't immediately start again on her visits.
Things were quieter since the end of the flu epidemic
and she only had four calls scheduled for that
afternoon.

Back in her room, Annie put her feet up on the

desk and thought. That wonderful night, now almost
two weeks ago, that they'd first made love had seemed
to her then the pinnacle of all her hopes and dreams.
But it hadn't taken long for her to realise that going
to bed together hadn't really solved anything, for her.
She was certain that Dom would be perfectly content
if she could only plunge into this affair with his frank
enjoyment and lack of commitment. Annie couldn't
do that. She was in love; painfully and quite hopelessly.

First, there was the business of the visit home. They
were both off the weekend after the attack on her
and its momentous results, and Dom had planned a
romantic weekend at a fabulous hotel.

'But I can't, my treasure,' Annie had wailed. 'I
simply must go home. It'll be Dad's thirtieth anniver-
sary in the parish and the congregation are giving him
a celebratory dinner. But for that I'd not be off, anyway—I changed with Angus especially for it. Why
don't you come with me?' she had then asked eagerly.
'It'd be a splendid chance for you to meet my family.'

His look of embarrassment had been more revealing
than his bland reply. 'I don't think so, dear—some
other time perhaps. When your father doesn't have
anything official on. . .'

'All right, but what will you do here—all by
yourself?'

'I'll survive,' he said. 'After all, I had to before you
came into my life.' With the help of the Other Woman?

On the following Sunday Annie escaped early from
her family, pleading pressure of work, and hurried to
Dom's house only to discover that he was out. When
she told him next morning he merely said casually, 'I
went away too, after all.' Annie was too proud to ask
where, torturing herself instead with thoughts of that
wretched woman.

She'd chosen her moment with care to broach the matter of those phone calls. But either she'd been too subtle and Dom hadn't got the point or else he'd got the point all right—and skilfully pretended that he hadn't.

They had their next more serious disagreement when Annie told Dom that she was moving back to her own flat. 'We agreed I should stay at the flat only until I was over the shock. Well, I'm over it—and this is too cramped for a prolonged stay,' she'd pointed out reasonably.

'Doesn't our life together mean anything to you?' Dom had asked plaintively.

'We don't have a life together,' Annie had returned, with a painful little stab of regret. 'We just work together—and sleep together. Glasgow is not at the end of the world and I'd like to think I'm worth a bit of inconvenience. But if not. . .'

'Tell me what you want of me, Annie,' he'd demanded then.

'Right now, nothing but a bit of peace!' she'd snapped back, hurt.

The weekend after that Annie had been on duty, with Dom technically second-on-call. He'd persuaded her to stay at the barn and to let him share the work. That way there had been time for leisurely meals, short rambles on the nearby moors within range of their communications system—and, of course, lovemaking in the huge bed. There were never any doubts or differences in bed.

But Annie's doubts had resurfaced when he'd said, 'This is how it would always be if you were nearer.'

'How could I stay on indefinitely in the on-call suite?' she had asked.

'You couldn't—I know that. But if you're still so

set on having your own place, there's usually something suitable for sale in the villages round about. I know how much you love your flat, but you knew you'd have to sell it eventually if you stayed on in the practice.'

'That's true,' she'd admitted, without committing herself. He hadn't suggested Burnside itself as a suitable place to live, and Annie had thought she'd known why. In Burnside it would be too easy for partners and patients to suss out what was going on!

'I've been thinking,' she'd said, but by then Dom had got tired of talking and had stopped her mouth with a kiss.

The sound of bells ringing and scurrying feet roused Annie from her unhappy thoughts and took her right back to the drama of her first day here. She ran out into the corridor, almost colliding with Carol. 'It's Willie,' she sobbed. 'The boy who got the spike through his head. He's h-having a fit—in my office.'

Annie took off, with Carol on her heels. Willie was lying on his back with his knees drawn up—about the worst possible position. The fit had subsided, but he was ominously grey in colour. Annie rolled him over and thumped him hard on the back, producing a stream of vomit, after which his colour and respiration improved dramatically. Thank heaven! He'd been choking but now there'd be no need to aspirate his lungs. Then she cleaned him up and when he was sufficiently recovered she questioned him about any previous attacks.

'Not had none—ever, Doctor.' Willie was adamant about that. 'I didna feel well, so I came lookin' for Dr Smith. Tha's all I remember.'

But that had been a fairly spectacular episode for a first. Having dosed him with Epanutin, Annie phoned

Surgical Neurology and asked for his next follow-up appointment to be brought forward as a matter of urgency.

'So it was serious, then,' concluded Carol, calmer now that the emergency was over. 'And am I glad I spotted your car! I thought you were all out.'

'Epilepsy is a frequent complication of serious head injury,' Annie explained. 'I guess it's lucky this has not happened before.' She turned her attention to Willie again. 'And now, young man, you and I are going to the chemist's to get you some pills. Then it's home to your mammy with strict instructions for a careful watch on you.'

'Will I be better to stay off the school now, Doctor?' he asked hopefully.

Annie smothered a smile. 'Until the end of the week, anyway. After that, it'll be up to Dr Smith.'

'That's smashin', Doctor,' said Willie, beaming right across his cheeky face.

Annie wished that she could agree with him but only time would tell whether his epilepsy was temporary or with him for life.

Coping with Willie, as well as her remaining visits, meant that Annie was late starting evening surgery.

Arriving home eventually, she was surprised to see Dom's car already parked outside. Has my little bid for independence shaken him, then? she wondered, as she got out and went to meet him.

He kissed her, regardless of the twitching curtains in the nearest house. 'And if you'd only given me keys, as I asked, I could have had the dinner ready by now,' he said.

'I told you—I'd have to get more cut. Anyway, I don't have a key to your house.'

'You shall have one tomorrow,' he promised. 'Now, what's for supper?'

'Nothing—I've not had time to shop. Unless you'll settle for an omelette. . .' Which she knew he wouldn't.

Dom pulled the expected face of disgust. 'Let's go to that nice Chinese place in Byres Road,' he suggested. 'The walk will do us good.'

'Suits me,' said Annie, perking up at the thought of not having to cook. 'Only I must pop in first and leave my bag.' No doctor would dream of leaving a bag unattended in a car, even in a respectable district like this.

When they were seated and waiting to be served, Dom said, 'You were much later than I expected, my witch, and I was getting worried, with the motorway so busy tonight. That's another reason why I wish you'd move.'

Annie ignored the last bit. 'Yes, the traffic was heavier than usual. There's a match re-play at Greenock tonight—I expect that's why.'

He returned to his last point. 'If you were nearer, you'd not have to cope with so much traffic every day.'

'Ah!' said Annie, and then sought to divert him by telling him all about Willie's fit.

It worked. 'It's a damn good thing you were there,' he said when she'd finished.

'Yes, wasn't it? Another minute and I'd have been away, though. What worried me was Carol's reaction. She was terrified and had no idea what to do. Do you not think a bit of in-service training in the basics is indicated for the non-professional staff?'

He looked rather offended. 'We do run a course— about every three months. Carol must have forgotten in the heat of the moment what she'd learned.'

'That's not so surprising when these things happen so rarely. All the same—'

'I'll see to it,' he said with finality. 'And now for something completely different.'

'But we always have the sweet and sour,' said Annie, picking up her chopsticks. Eating Chinese-style was one of the few things she did better than Dom.

'I meant the conversation—not the food,' he corrected, refusing to compete and asking for knife and fork. 'Have you heard of Seacliffe Castle?'

'No—is it a stately home?'

'Not any more. Now it's a stately hotel in deepest Galloway. It's been creaming off all the awards. You know the sort of place—log fires, oriental rugs, regulation ghost and every bed a four-poster. Do you fancy having me in a four-poster?' he asked whimsically.

Annie fancied having him anywhere—and that was her main trouble. 'Only if the ghost doesn't fancy you, too,' she returned lightly.

He laughed, startling the other diners. 'What an unearthly thought—especially as it's supposed to be male! But, seriously, would you really like to go there this coming weekend?'

'Yes, *please*,' said Annie, determined that somehow there should be time for some serious talking amid all the teasing and lovemaking. If I don't soon find out where I stand I think I'll go mad, she thought.

It was very pleasant walking back to her flat through the lush rolling parkland around the university. Everywhere leaves were bursting out of their buds and birds sang frenetically. 'Why go away at all with country like this in the middle of Glasgow?'

'But no four-posters, my little witch,' teased Dom.

'And no ghosts either—as far as I know,' she returned, laughing.

Back at the flat they went straight to bed and, as always, Annie's doubts dissolved. Dom was a considerate lover—always as aware of her needs as of his own. I should be grateful, thought Annie, staring into the darkness after he had gone. There must be thousands of lonely women out there who'd give ten years of life for what I've got. Then she turned on her side and quietly cried herself to sleep.

Fridays were second only to Mondays for their workload. Carol said that patients liked to come on Fridays in case something went wrong over the weekend and then on Mondays because it had.

'You're quite the little philosopher,' Annie had told her when she heard that theory, but today looked like bearing it out. 'I'll be lucky if I so much as get to the loo before nightfall,' she muttered when she'd looked over her lists.

'It's your own fault—you shouldn't be so nice to them and then you'd not be so popular,' Carol was saying, as Jane came through the swing doors with Dom just behind.

Jane took her lists without a word to Carol but a full-scale glare for Annie as she swept on.

Dom was too busy staring at Annie's severe black suit to take in the atmosphere. 'You look more like an advocate than a GP who's got the weekend off,' he considered. 'What's the idea?'

'My assailants are to appear in the sheriff court on Monday and I'm trying out a suitably sober outfit—in case I don't manage to get back to Glasgow before then,' she ended on a whisper as Angus rushed by with a couple of hearty greetings.

'What time?' Dom asked keenly.

'Ten o'clock, I'm afraid, so I'll have to give morning

surgery a miss. And I'd asked particularly for eleven-thirty at the earliest, but was told they couldn't upset their schedule to take account of my work.'

'Damn!'

'Yes, I know it's very inconvenient but I can't help it—'

'Of course you can't—I know that! And it's damnable because I'll not be able to come with you as I'd intended. Will you be all right, little Annie?' he asked with sudden tenderness, and Annie was touched.

'Yes, I'll be fine,' she answered gently. 'I'm used to court appearances after all those spells on Casualty.'

'But not as the victim. Defence counsel could give you a hard time.'

'Just let him try!' she snarled, looking fierce.

Dom gave her an admiring smile. 'Yes, you'll be all right if you take that line. All the same, I really wanted to be there for you. . .'

He can be so sweet and understanding, she thought, as she prepared for surgery. Maybe things *will* work out in the end. Perhaps—after this weekend away. . .

'Oh, good morning, Mrs Irvine. And how are you today?'

'Fine, thank you, Doctor. He's left to go to a job down south.'

What did she mean—her husband had left? While Annie was trying to decide whether she was supposed to sympathise with or congratulate her, Mrs Irvine said, 'It's ma knee, Doctor. I think I must have hurt it at the bingo.'

'Really?' That was almost as difficult to comment on. 'I'd better take a look at it, then. Yes—both legs out of your tights, please. I'll need to compare them.'

The problem knee was very swollen, as well as shiny and warm to the touch. Annie didn't like the look of it at all, nor the other one either, though Mrs Irvine insisted that it was pain-free.

'You're going to an awful lot of trouble, Doctor,' she said when Annie had also examined her feet, ankles, hands and arm joints. 'Ouch!' she exclaimed as Annie tentatively elevated the right shoulder joint. 'That one's been giving me twinges when I lift it, so I stopped. I mean there's no sense, is there? What are you going to do now?' she asked fearfully when Annie went to the trolley for some sample bottles and syringes.

'I'd like to send some of your blood away for testing—just to make sure there's no underlying cause for these twinges you're getting. You're at what we women call our awkward age, when our joints do sometimes protest a bit—along with other things. It's all the hormonal changes, you see. . .'

Soothing words, while she hoped against hope that she was wrong, but Annie was very much afraid that Mrs Irvine was experiencing the first symptoms of rheumatoid arthritis.

'Yes, I do get tired easily these days,' she admitted, in answer to further questioning. 'But I was putting that down to my age, too. Who'd be a woman, eh?'

'Good question,' agreed Annie. 'The thing is, what are we going to do for you? Something soothing for the pain, of course, and a diet sheet—to make sure you're getting all the right minerals and vitamins. And that's about it until we get the results of the tests. Make an appointment to see me again next Thursday. I should have them by then.'

'Thanks, Doctor. You're awful thorough—I'll say that for you. Thursday, you said?' And off she went, leaving Annie smiling wryly at the backhanded compliment.

'Well, and if it isn't young Sean back again,' she said when the boy with Osgood-Schlatter's disease in his right knee came in, propelled by his mother. 'I've brought him in to get that plaster stookie on it, Doctor. Twice I've caught him sneaking off on his bike. Twice! So it's the only way, I reckon. Short of chaining him up!'

'Let's see if he's done any damage first,' suggested Annie, while thinking that the stiff, tight jeans he was wearing must run plaster of Paris a pretty close second.

'No stookie necessary,' she decided, to the mother's disgust. 'That is definitely a last resort because the muscles get so lazy when a limb is in plaster.'

'But you said for him to rest his muscles, Doctor.'

'Not rest completely, Mrs Christie—just cut out all that strenuous exercise he'd been doing. There's a big difference between moderate walking, say, and putting him in plaster and inhibiting any muscle action.'

'Did you hear what the doctor said?' she yelled at her son. 'You've got away with it this time, you wee terror, but that's not to say you always will!'

'No long cycle rides and no rough walking,' Annie added. 'It's important that you stick to the rules. That knee's got to last you a long, long time.'

'I'll try—honest, Doctor. But it's awful hard when you see yer mates going off somewhere. . .'

'That's life, I'm afraid,' said Annie. 'There's a down side to everything in this life.' And she wasn't just thinking of Sean as she said that.

The morning streaked by with the usual selection of aches and pains and dizzy spells; none of which turned out to be as potentially serious as Mrs Irvine's arthritis.

'When I went to the other practice about ma ears,

they set the nurse on me,' claimed Annie's last patient
of the morning.

'What for?' she wondered, dazed.

'To syringe ma ears.'

'This is probably just another build-up of wax, then,'
said Annie, reaching for her auriscope. 'Yes, there's
quite a lot—' She syringed his ears and looked again.
The right tympanic membrane was very inflamed and,
without any history of recent infection to explain that,
Annie told him that she'd like him to see a specialist
in Glasgow.

He was delighted. 'That's the ticket—I could just
be doing with a nice day oot.'

'Then I hope you enjoy it,' said Annie as he solemnly
shook her hand. Just as I hope to enjoy my weekend
when it comes. . .

Because Jane followed her out of the gate that evening,
Annie took the Glasgow road. So did Jane. Damn!
Now what to do? In the next urban sprawl she came
to, Annie stopped by a row of shops and waited for
Jane to pass. Then, in case Jane was using her rear-
view mirror, Annie got out and went into a shop where
she bought some toffees she'd never eat in case they
pulled her fillings out.

She looked up and down the street to make sure
that the coast was clear before turning west and south
and finally got on the road to Dom's village.

Not surprisingly, he'd got there before her and he
came out of the house as she drove into the garage.
He had already changed into casual clothes for the
journey. 'What kept you?' he asked, opening the boot
of her car to transfer her luggage to his own.

Annie got out and kissed him lightly before saying,
'Not that bag yet, hon—I need to change. Unless you

want the folk at Seacliffe Castle to think we're having a business meeting.'

'In a four-poster? Anyway, what kept you?' he asked again.

'Jane. She followed me out of town so I thought it best to pretend I was heading for home. But I shook her off by stopping at a wee shop. She's suspicious, Dom.'

'Good. It might stop her inviting me to her place for dinner every other blasted week! I'm running out of excuses,' he called after Annie as she dashed into the house.

Dom had no pity and no sympathy for the unwanted attention. That's the difference between men and women, thought Annie, as she exchanged the black suit for trousers and a chunky sweater. We deflect unwanted attentions, too, but at least we feel sorry. She dragged a brush through her hair and re-did her lipstick before repacking her bag and dashing outside again.

'We're going to be late for dinner,' said Dom as they set off.

'Then we'd better stop somewhere on the way,' suggested Annie.

'I'd rather not,' he said.

'Why?'

'You'll see,' was all he'd tell her.

'Put your foot down, then—there's hardly any traffic just now.'

'And land up in court? No, thanks. One court case in the practice is enough for one month.'

Annie was hurt and didn't try to hide the fact. 'You've changed your tune!' She protested heatedly. 'You were all sympathy when I was mugged. Now you seem to be suggesting I was somehow to blame!'

'Nonsense! But if I got nicked for speeding it would certainly be my fault. *That*'s what I meant.'

'I see.'

'When you say "I see" in that particular tone, I always know that you don't. Good God, Annie— what's the matter with you? I thought that once we'd gone to bed together everything would be all right between us, but we seem to be going from bad to worse. Just say if you want to end it!'

The mere thought of that was enough to freeze her blood. She'd been wondering if she could settle for sex without love and commitment. Now she realised that half a loaf would always be better than no bread— with Dom.

'Not before I've seen Seacliffe Castle—and had you and that ghost in a threesome in a four-poster, you great big, gorgeous brute you,' she managed with frenzied brightness.

Dom dissolved into laughter and pulled over on to the hard shoulder to recover. 'You can always get round me,' he confessed, chuckling. 'You really are a witch and I'm completely in your power.'

If that was really true then things were definitely looking up. Annie hugged him thankfully and kissed him over and over.

'That's a nice little wood over there,' he suggested, when he'd returned her affection with enthusiasm.

'Down, Rover!' she ordered. 'You want to get there by dinner-time and I'm not settling for anything less than a four-poster tonight!'

The weekend was perfect—to begin with. Dom had ordered a champagne supper to be served in their room, which was so huge that the four-poster looked no bigger than a single bed. And they could have held a dance in their bathroom it was so big. The bath being to scale, they bathed together and that was so exhilarating that they could hardly wait to get dry before falling into bed.

The next morning was just as carefree; sleeping late, having breakfast in their room and then going for a long walk along the shore in blazing sunshine.

It was when they went back to the castle for lunch that things changed.

Annie and Dom had almost finished their meal when somewhere behind them she heard a woman say to her companion, 'Now, was that not quite delicious, Hughie?' It was a voice that Annie had known all her life. The speaker and Hughie lived next door to her father's manse and Annie went rigid with shock.

'What's wrong, darling?' asked Dom at the sight of her shrinking visibly in her chair.

She gasped, waggled her eyebrows and jerked her head backwards over her shoulder.

He grinned at her and asked her where the pain was and she muttered through clenched teeth, 'I know the couple behind us. No—don't look!'

But of course he did and said, 'They look perfectly respectable to me. What's the problem?'

'*That*, you fool! He's an elder in our church,' she mouthed. 'Oh, what am I going to do?'

Dom took another look. 'Too late—you've been spotted, but leave this to me,' he returned confidently, just before Mr and Mrs Hughie Tennant ranged themselves either side of Annie like arresting constables.

'I just *knew* it was your back view, Annie, dear. Didn't I say so as soon as I stood up? That lovely bright hair of yours—so distinctive.' She was addressing Annie but her eyes, alight with interest, were on Dom.

'My p-partner, Dr Smith,' quavered Annie. 'We work together,' she added hastily, after realising how ambiguous that word had become. 'Dom, Mr and Mrs Tennant from my home town.'

Dom was already on his feet, charming them. 'Are you on holiday?' he asked, smiling blandly. 'What glorious weather you're having. Annie and I? Oh, just a fleeting visit—for a wedding.'

'A wedding,' cooed Mrs Tennant. 'How romantic. It's so lovely that some young people still believe in marriage, isn't it, Hughie? Well, we mustn't keep you when you're not even dressed yet.'

Was that meant ironically? agonised Annie. 'Are you staying here?' she asked anxiously.

'Oh, goodness me, no, dear—we can't afford these prices. We just had lunch for a wee treat on our way home from our usual guesthouse in Newton Stewart. So nice to meet you, Doctor. Is Annie settling nicely into general practice, then? And we all thought she'd end up a top surgeon. How things do turn out. . . Now, you mustn't keep us any longer—such a long drive ahead. . .'

We've got away with it, Annie was thinking, when the waiter who brought their coffee asked Dom if he wanted a bill or would he charge it to their room number?

Mrs Tennant didn't hear that, but Hughie did. 'I'll tell your father we've seen you,' he promised Annie, meaningfully.

'Yes—please do,' she murmured faintly.

'There, now—that wasn't too bad, was it?' asked Dom as the dining room door swung to behind the Tennants.

'Not so *bad*? When the waiter asked for our room number—*and you told him*?'

'Sorry—I guess I'm not much of a deceiver after all,' he said, in a tone that suggested he deserved a pat on the back.

'And you told me to leave it to you,' she groaned, ignoring the interruption. 'I knew I should have dealt with them myself.'

'That would have been something to see—you'd almost lost the power of speech!'

'My father will be shattered.'

'Oh, come—and besides, they'll probably spare him the sordid details.'

'Some hope! Hugh Tennant is the most dedicated muckraker I've ever met.'

'And I thought he looked a harmless little man.'

'Huh! Anyway, it's not him I'm worried about— it's my father. He's a good man—almost innocent. Old-fashioned by your standards, of course, but a good man. I wouldn't hurt him for the world. Oh, how I wish we'd never come here!'

'You're a hypocrite, Annie,' he said quietly. 'You don't actually mind being here with me—you just hate being found out!'

'Yes, you're right—I am a hypocrite,' she echoed with such an anguished look that she stifled his anger.

'Come on, darling, dry your eyes,' he said gently. 'Perhaps they believed my tale about the wedding. I know! You must say we just took a room to get changed in, if that helps.' But she went on sniffling, so he said, 'Look, if you're really so upset we'll go home now—this afternoon.'

'What good would that do?' she asked. 'The damage is done. And I'm all right in myself. It's my father I'm so upset for. He thinks I'm perfect, you see.'

'That must have made life very difficult for you. Even though you are, nearly. Some of the time.

Except, of course, for that blistering tongue of yours. . .'

He was rewarded with the beginnings of a smile and continued to coax and flatter her until she recovered. She was quieter than usual, though and when he reached out for her in bed that night she took a while to respond. But she gave in at last. I'm so weak where he's concerned, she realised sadly.

'I'll be in as soon as I can manage it,' said Annie for quite the sixth time as she waved Dom away to work on Monday morning.

'I know you will, my angel,' Dom said. 'If there's one thing I'm sure of it's that work will always come first with you. After me, of course?' he added on a questioning note.

'Don't fish,' she commanded. 'And now be off with you or you'll be late.'

'You're a hard woman, Annie Duncan,' he called out as he drove away.

Annie went back into Dom's house to shower and dress. She put on the black suit she'd brought especially for the court hearing and had picked up her luggage when she heard the sound of a key in the back door. Walking into the kitchen, she found herself face to face with one of the neatest, most gorgeous blondes she had ever seen. A blonde, moreover, who had just let herself into Dom's house with her own key!

Annie stared at her, bemused, as the woman exclaimed with apparent astonishment, 'Good heavens! Dom never told me we'd got a visitor. You must be Clare.'

'Clare?' Annie echoed faintly.

'His sister. Not Clare, then. Inter-est-ing. . .' she drawled.

Bitch! thought Annie, as that feistiness Dom admired in her came to her rescue. 'I'm Dr Duncan— a colleague of Dom's. And you are. . .?' But Annie had already guessed. She'd heard that voice before.

'I'm Dom's—housekeeper, for want of a better word. Sylvia Ross. . .' She was enjoying the effect that had had on Annie.

Annie was shaken. The sultry woman caller and Dom's housekeeper were one and the same! So much for the stout motherly widow of imagination!

'Now I seem to remember hearing you were coming,' the woman was saying. 'Otherwise, we might have gone away again this weekend.' Dear God! Had he taken *her* that other weekend, then? 'I've kept on my house in the village for the time being. It's such a small place and you know how people talk. And of course the divorce was an additional reason for caution. We couldn't afford to give any ammunition to that awful wife of his. But now that's all behind us. . .'

'We'—'us'—'caution'. . . With so much unsought information showered on her, Annie was left in no doubt about the relationship between Dom and his housekeeper. 'Quite!' she managed. 'Well, as I told you, Mrs Ross, I am a colleague of Dom's. And I'll not be getting in your way because I'm just leaving.'

That provoked a peal of silvery laughter. 'Goodness me! Surely you don't think I *clean*? No, no—I just keep the freezer stocked—and so on. . .'

The woman was a past mistress at innuendo. 'I've got the picture,' promised Annie grimly.

At that, the set smile on Sylvia Ross's beautifully made-up face relaxed a bit. 'Good,' she said. 'It's so embarrassing if one has to spell it all out, don't you think? Yet one is entitled to defend one's corner. . .'

'Quite,' repeated Annie. She was getting over the

shock now. After all, the woman had only confirmed
her suspicions. 'Though I do wonder how sure you are
of yours, if you feel the need to defend it against every
house guest Dom happens to have!'

That's given the bitch something to think about,
decided Annie, as she went out to the garage. Not
that that was much comfort. Annie had only been
speaking the truth when she said she'd got the picture.
She had—every damned last square inch of it. No
wonder Dom had so skilfully avoided discussing those
mysterious phone calls!

Of all the deceitful, double-dealing, dyed-in-the-
wool, devious devils—but why was she so surprised?
And what price these famous brains of hers if she could
be so easily bamboozled, despite what she knew of his
past? You'll pay for this, Dom Smith-Jardine, vowed
Annie. Oh, yes—you'll pay.

But first I've got to go to court and listen to some
smart defence lawyer trying to make out that getting
tied up and robbed was somehow all my own fault.

CHAPTER TEN

ANNIE came out of the courthouse and paused on the steps for a few deep breaths. The hearing had been an ordeal, even for one of her fibre. The defence lawyer had been just as hard on her as Dom had feared but she felt that she'd stood up to him well.

Not as well as Mrs Niven, though; she'd been brilliant. What was it she'd said to him? 'No, young man, I am not mistaken. There's nothing wrong with my eyes and I know what I saw. I'm not needing fancy great glasses like *some* folk who cannae see the wood for the trees!'

The fact that she was allowed to run on like that without being warned should have told Annie what the sheriff thought of the case but she was still too shaken by her own encounter with the fierce, bespectacled young man to be that rational.

'You were great, Doctor,' said Dougie, coming up behind Annie to pat her on the back. 'You fair took the wind out o' yon laddie's sails. You were great,' he repeated.

'Not as great as Mrs Niven. She was your star witness.'

'Aye. A few more with her courage and we'd win more cases,' said Sam. 'But honest folk are mostly so astonished at being heckled in the witness box that they go to pieces. Well, thanks again, Doctor. I hope we meet again some time.'

Annie said she hoped so, too, but in happier circumstances. 'I couldn't have wished for kinder rescuers than you two,' she added warmly. Then, after more compliments all round, they parted to get on with their respective jobs.

Annie's main concern was to put off a meeting with Dom for as long as possible so she got straight on with her visits when she got back to Burnside. A call to Carol would ascertain whether any more calls had come in for her that day. There was a sticky moment when her mobile phone buzzed as she was waiting at traffic lights. It was Dom, very relieved at having got hold of her at last.

A monumental screeching of brakes from a juggernaut drawing up beside her caused Annie to jump so violently that she accidentally pressed the cut-off button. Providential, she thought, not being nearly ready yet to deal with him as coolly and crushingly as he deserved. When the phone bleeped again, she ignored it.

Her eventual return to base was timed perfectly. Almost all the staff were having a pre-surgery cup of tea in the common room, making it easy for Annie to avoid Dom's eye and plunge into animated conversation with the people nearest the door.

Of course, they all wanted to know how things had gone in court and she made much of Mrs Niven's spirited and unshakable performance.

'But that man would have been less aggressive with you—the victim,' assumed Carol.

'Don't you believe it! Having failed to prove that I was nearly as blind as he'd tried to make out Mrs Niven was, he made out such a good case for provocation on my part that I couldn't decide how best to deal with it. "Do you not feel that you were at least partly to blame for this alleged attack?" was one question.'

There were exclamations of outrage and horror from

all sides. 'I hope you put him firmly in his place,' said Laura.

'I don't know about that, though I did give him a sob story about being conditioned both by training and upbringing to help the sick and needy whenever and however I could, without stopping to think of the consequences. "So if that's what you mean by provocation, then I suppose I am partly to blame," I said. The public gallery loved it, even if I had made myself out to be too good to be true.'

Annie had told her story lightly and amusingly, deliberately suppressing the hurt and indignation she'd felt at such an outrageous reading of the situation.

'I hope they didn't get off?' exclaimed Angus.

'Oh, no—there was too much evidence against them when they were arrested in my car, with their fingerprints all over it and my bag and the cottage—not to mention the small matter of the girls wearing my clothes.'

'And now they're safely locked up?' he asked.

'No, bound over for social and psychiatric reports. Apparently they've never been in trouble before.'

'I knew I should have been there,' said Dom heatedly, having managed to escape from Jane. 'I could have told them how shocked and battered you were.'

'Dougie and Sam did that,' Annie answered. 'And you wouldn't have been allowed to say anything as you weren't a witness.'

There was an edge to her tone which had him staring at her and frowning. But he didn't comment—not with all the others there.

He's saving it up, she realised, and she still wasn't feeling strong enough for the showdown. 'Well, I must be off,' she said with false heartiness. 'I'm seeing two of my most pressing cases from this morning before surgery proper. Thanks for the tea and all the sympathy.'

She had taken Dom by surprise and got safely clear. He followed her to her room, though, pausing frustrated in the doorway when he realised that she already had a patient waiting. 'I'd like a word after surgery, please, Dr Duncan,' he said with commendable restraint.

Annie agreed in the same restrained way and Dom eyed her in sombre silence for some seconds before shutting the door.

As always, Annie shelved her personal problems when confronted with a professional one.

'You say that stomach trouble is in your family, Mr Guthrie, but that doesn't make it any less bothersome for you. I want you to go to hospital for some tests we don't have the equipment for here. Just a matter of popping a thin tube down your throat with a wee light on the end so that the surgeon can take a good look at your stomach lining. You'll be nicely sedated and hardly know anything about it.

'I do feel it's very important to make quite sure what it is we're dealing with,' she added persuasively when he looked like refusing.

'Indigestion,' returned Mr Guthrie doggedly.

'Yes, I know, but indigestion is a symptom not the actual problem. Probably all that's needed is to cut out some particular food or foods that don't agree with you but let's be sure, shall we?'

Annie eventually persuaded him, just as she usually did manage to persuade her patients but when he'd gone she wondered anew at the diversity of the human race. So often, the patient who worried most about himself turned out to have the least cause. She hoped the reverse wouldn't turn out to be true of the stoical

Mr Guthrie. He was such a nice man with a lovely family who'd be devastated if their dad was seriously ill. So unfair. But since when was life fair?

Annie put the Guthries out of her mind so as to give all her attention to her next patient.

Dom was still consulting when Annie finished her surgery. She was stealing herself for the big showdown when an urgent call came in. 'Thirty-two Winton Terrace—a wee boy's been badly scalded,' relayed Carol.

'On my way,' responded Annie, unable to squash a stab of relief that the stormy meeting with Dom must be delayed. Patients came first.

The door was opened by a girl who looked ill enough to be a patient herself. 'In the back kitchen, Doctor,' she said needlessly—the child's screams were pointer enough. 'I know I shouldn't have left him, but Mother was calling for the toilet and doesn't like to be kept waiting. . .I'm a rotten mother,' she ended. She seemed to be reciting a lesson well taught.

Next minute a banging and shouting came from upstairs that had the girl scurrying off. 'Excuse me— she's wanting to go back to her room.'

The child was lying in a big pool of water beside the enormous pan he'd pulled over himself. Annie turned on the cold tap to fill the sink and whipped off his clothes. Then she sat him in the icy water, splashing it all over his arms and back. It was crude but effective first aid. His cries had died away by the time his mother returned. She was relieved but said worriedly, 'I should have thought of that. . .' and ended in a fit of weak but bubbly coughing.

The one I'm really worried about is you, Annie was thinking as she said soothingly, 'You mustn't blame yourself. Hardly anybody knows that cold water is the best thing for superficial scalds and burns—it dulls the sensory nerve endings. There are only one or two places where the skin is actually broken so I'll dress the worst bits then we'll dry him off with a soft towel. If you keep him in loose clothing and put him to sleep on his tummy for a night or two, he'll soon be fine.'

The boy began to cry again when Annie dressed his most painful spots but a lollipop produced miraculously from her bag worked wonders.

'Oh, dear—Mother doesn't let him have sweets because of his teeth,' whispered the harassed girl.

She's a nervous wreck as well as very sick, Annie realised grimly. 'Is he your child?' she asked.

'Yes,' answered the girl, looking puzzled.

'Then why does your mother make all the decisions? Are you afraid of her?' Annie asked bluntly, that often being the best way to get at the truth.

It worked. In no time at all she had the whole story. A gentle, compliant daughter of a domineering mother who drove away first her own husband and then her daughter's. Never feeling well or getting anything right, too little time for her child and her mother so heavy and helpless. . . They were all Jane's patients, though, so there was little Annie could do now that she'd dealt with the emergency. But the girl must have medical attention—and very soon.

'That's a very nasty cough, my dear,' she began. 'Have you seen Dr Firth about it?'

'Oh, no. Mother says it's just my nerves. I've always had nervous trouble. . .'

I'll bet—and no wonder, thought Annie. 'Well I'm absolutely sure your nerves have got nothing whatever to do with that cough,' she said firmly, 'and you must make an appointment as a matter of urgency.'

'You're very kind,' said the girl, 'but I can't. I can never leave mother—she gets so upset—and so we have everything sent.'

'What's the matter with her?'

'Arthritis—she can hardly move some days and she's that heavy; but I mustn't grumble.'

'Why not?' asked Annie. 'You've got plenty to grumble about, it seems to me. I'll have a talk with Dr Firth and I'm sure she'll be able to sort you all out once she's aware of the problem. And if there's anything else we can do for you meanwhile, don't hesitate to call.'

'Goodbye, then, doctor—and thanks ever so much. All right, I'm coming, mother. . .' The old lady was banging for attention again.

'I'll see myself out,' said Annie, longing to go upstairs and sort out the matriarch but that was Jane's job.

God, what a can of worms I've opened there, she thought as she returned to the centre. An arthritic old lady too infirm to be looked after by a sick daughter half her size—a daughter with severe pulmonary TB, if Annie was any judge. It would be a miracle if the child hadn't contracted it, too—he was small and pale enough. But how was she going to put all this to Jane?

'Oh!' she exclaimed on opening the door of the on-call suite to see Dom there, waiting for her. 'I wasn't expecting to see you—'

'I can see that. But why not?'

'I've just been out on an emergency call to a patient of Jane's. An intolerable situation and I think you should—'

'Later!' he rapped out, silencing her. 'First I need to know why you've been behaving so strangely all day.'

Annie gazed at him, quelled as only he could quell

her. 'The court appearance wasn't exactly a—a picnic,' she muttered.

'Is that a fact? I could have sworn you enjoyed it—hearing the wonderful story you made of it for the staff.'

'Yes—well—' Annie sought another excuse. She'd thought that it would be so simple to tell him about Sylvia's appearance and all that she'd learned from her but she was still trying to come to terms with the appalling fact that they had been sharing him. Desperately she clutched another excuse out of the air.

'Meeting the Tennants upset me more than I'd realised. My year didn't christen me Puritan Annie without reason, it seems. I'm just not cut out for the kind of relationship we've been having!' What's the matter with me? Taking the blame like this. I meant to give him such a drubbing. . .

'I think I always knew it couldn't last,' Dom said heavily, in a tone of despair. 'I must have been mad to think it was mutual. I see now—I caught you at a bad moment. Your defences were right down after being attacked. All you needed was a shoulder to cry on—any shoulder. And mine just happened to be there. If I hadn't been so besotted I'd have realised that from the way you started back-pedalling almost straight away.

'Damn you, Annie—I wish you'd never come back into my life!' He pushed past her roughly and stumbled out of the room.

Annie was too astonished to move. He'd sounded so sincere that she almost had to believe him. But when she eventually stirred enough to run after him, her mobile phone rang. Then she heard his car start and, running to the window, she saw him drive away.

*   *   *

Next day Annie set off for home soon after three, more thankful than she'd ever been for the half-day that followed a night on call. It had been a relatively quiet night but she was deathly tired all the same.

After Dom's dramatic outburst she'd felt very remorseful. Because of her indecision, her lack of trust—everything. But by morning everything looked very different. Today she could see that he might just as easily have been cleverly shifting the blame onto her. A carefully disguised parting of his own choosing, in fact. Because there was no getting round his steadfast and clever refusal to tell her about Sylvia, despite all the chances she'd created.

Arriving home, she automatically switched on her repaired answering machine, paying scant attention to a message from a neighbour about a stray cat. But then she heard Jack Marshall, her old chief, telling her that he had to see her as soon as possible.

She phoned him immediately, getting him just as he was leaving the hospital. They arranged to meet for a drink that evening and, in her present gloomy state of mind, Annie was expecting some unpleasant sequel to her brush with that poisonous administrator.

In her anxiety to know what other dreadful thing Fate had up its sleeve for her, she arrived early at the rendezvous. 'So what's up now?' she asked Jack when he eventually arrived.

He kissed her and gave her a hug. 'You'll never guess,' he said, 'so I'll tell you straight out. He's going, love. The bastard's got the push.'

She stared at him in hope and doubt. 'You can't mean—you do!' She relaxed against his solid, tweedy warmth and began to laugh. 'He's upset somebody more important than me—is that what you're telling me? Oh, bliss!'

'That's putting it mildly. He's been given the sack! His new assistant has uncovered a string of blunders as long as the West Highland Way! You'll like him, Annie. He's already taken over and we soon discovered he believes that the hands-on staff actually know more about patient care than he does!'

'He sounds like a dream come true,' agreed Annie, 'and I'm very happy for you all. But I don't see how this affects me.'

'My present senior registrar is off to try his luck in South Africa. So the job is yours, Annie—if you want it.'

If she wanted it! 'Oh, Jack! But there'll be dozens after it.'

'Naturally—but I'll bet my pension that there'll not be another to touch you for skill and flair.'

That gave her a painful stab to the heart, being so close to Dom's tribute when explaining why he wanted her in the practice. She forced herself to point out, 'That man did a pretty thorough job of discrediting me, Jack.'

'And now he's completely discredited himself. I can tell you, Annie—unofficially, mind—that the board is falling over itself to make amends.'

'They are? How wonderful! I can't tell you what a relief. . .' She was practically crying by then.

'Knowing you, you'll have done your damnedest to adapt but you're hating general practice, aren't you?' he asked.

'It's been—a very useful experience,' she returned cautiously, 'but surgery will always be my first love.' Professionally speaking.

'That's settled, then,' he said. 'And all before we've even ordered. What are you drinking, Annie girl?'

*   *   *

Annie decided that she must do the thing properly so she asked Laura to arrange a meeting for her with Dom. Laura was clearly surprised but she agreed and when Annie got back from her morning visits she found a note on her desk, suggesting a time that afternoon immediately after the weekly working lunch.

Today there seemed to be more to discuss than usual at the meeting and, while Dom appeared to be completely calm, Annie could feel herself getting more and more strung up. And she was furious with Jane, who was querying every point and delaying the scene to come.

But at last it was over and with a grave, steady look that gave nothing away Dom told Annie he'd see her in his room in five minutes.

'There!' breathed Jane triumphantly. 'Now you'll see where your spiteful tale-carrying has got you!'

'I don't know what you mean,' said Annie firmly.

'Don't pretend you never told him about seeing the Winton Terrace family because I know you did. He spoke to me about them this morning. He was very concerned—he doesn't like tale-bearers.'

'I merely mentioned in passing that I'd seen them,' she said. 'But when I looked for you this morning to tell you what I'd found, I was told you hadn't come in yet.'

'What's wrong with them now?' asked Jane, who was clearly spoiling for a fight.

'Aren't you forgetting that I'm about to be carpeted by the boss?' asked Annie. She didn't doubt the imminence of a showdown, though it wouldn't be along the lines Jane hoped. Still, her problem family would do for openers, after which she would tell Dom that she was leaving before he could demand her resignation.

'About those patients of Jane's whom you saw last night,' he said, seizing the initiative before Annie could even shut the door. 'I spoke to her this morning and now I'd like to hear what you found.'

Annie's chin jutted out. 'I was called out to the boy who had sustained mild but extensive scalding which I treated. However, I was much more concerned about his mother who—from observation only—seems to be suffering from fairly advanced pulmonary TB. She is also exhausted from caring for an elderly, severely arthritic mother who dominates her completely.'

'You seem to have found out more in one visit than Jane has in several. She was prepared to accept the old lady's version of events. Just as well—Jane has asked for them to be put on your list.'

'She *has*?' Annie was astonished. 'But—why?'

'Reading between the lines, I think she's terrified of the old lady.'

'I see. Well, in the normal way I'd be glad to take them over, but—'

'Exactly. You'll not be here much longer. But thank you for bringing them to my notice. Urgent action is needed—and I've already seen them.'

'Who told you I was leaving?' she demanded.

'I can hardly believe you wish to stay here now, so—'

'I'm going back to the hospital,' she cut in quickly, determined not to be dismissed. 'Jack Marshall is arranging it.'

Dom looked grim. 'That didn't take long,' he said. 'But it's probably better for us both if—'

'I can see it will be much more convenient for you if I back out without a fuss,' Annie returned scornfully.

'"Convenient"?' he echoed. 'How the devil can it be convenient?'

'Because juggling two women at once must have been a strain—even for you!' Oh, I didn't mean to do it this way! Now he'll think I'm jealous—and I am!

'I'll admit to being disappointed that you and Jane don't seem able to hit it off, but—'

'I'm not talking about Jane!' Annie spat out.

'You're not? Then I don't know what in blazes you *are* talking about!'

'If I say the word "housekeeper", will that help at all?' asked Annie sarcastically.

'No,' he said, but it seemed to her that there was a flicker of uncertainty in the syllable.

'Your housekeeper, as she calls herself, arrived just as I was leaving for the court on Monday and we had a very—enlightening talk. I gather that her duties are more than usually comprehensive.'

'Ah!' said Dom. 'I suppose that means she told you that we slept together.'

'Which was, of course, a wicked lie,' sneered Annie.

'Not exactly because, technically speaking, we did— once. She was being more than usually sympathetic and I was feeling particularly depressed. I had also drunk more than enough to impair my powers. So nothing happened. I made it very clear that there would never be a second time and she said she quite understood. Otherwise I'd never have kept her on.'

'All the comforts of home—and from such a beautiful source. I can't think how you found such self-control!'

He was very angry, but managed to curb his rage. For now. 'I might not have—but for one thing.'

'She snores,' jeered Annie. 'Did she snore when you took her away for that weekend—instead of me?'

'Now what are you going on about, you madwoman?' he demanded furiously, giving up the struggle to remain calm.

'As if you didn't know! That weekend when I had

to go home, you took her instead of me. Don't deny it—she told me!'

'And you'd rather believe her than me. Thank you very much for your trust!'

'She's more convincing than you!' shrieked Annie, running out of his room and taking refuge in her own.

He came after her, taking up the quarrel where she'd abandoned it. 'You've had enough of me and you want out so you're looking for an excuse. If you'll not believe me—and that wouldn't suit you—maybe you'll believe Andrew. Ask him where I was the weekend you went home. Go on—ask him!'

'You've obviously primed him to give you an alibi so what's the point?'

All the fire went out of him then. He slumped, beaten, against the wall, his eyes dark pools of despair. 'If you'd rather question the integrity of a man like Andrew Syme than believe me then there's no hope,' he said. 'I've been living in a fool's paradise.'

Annie wouldn't—daren't!—be taken in by that. 'You had your chance,' she told him starkly.

'I know—and I blew it.' A spasm of pain distorted his face for a second. 'Put it down to inexperience. I'd never had to work so hard at charming a woman before.'

'I meant you had your chance to explain—about that woman. I told you about those mysterious calls and when you shrugged them off I naturally thought there was more to them than you were willing to admit.'

'But there wasn't so it seemed less upsetting all round just to play it down. I was afraid of losing you!' He laughed harshly, without mirth. 'Funny how I can say it now that I have. But I *was* afraid of losing you and I really didn't know what to do for the best. I thought, like a fool, that if I just went on trying to please you, trying to make you happy, then you'd come to love me as much as I loved you.

'I'd had one miserable marriage; it couldn't all have been Margot's fault. And I was determined to get it right with you—so much more dear to me. . . But you always seemed to be holding back—even when we were closest!'

He turned to go, then stopped and took a packet from his pocket which he dropped on the desk before going out and shutting the door with a dreadful finality.

It was some time before Annie steeled herself to look at what he'd thrown down. It was a packet of snapshots. She picked it up, thinking vaguely that it must have some professional significance.

The first print she looked at was of Andrew's wife Mary and Dom, frowning into the sun in front of a small cottage.

Next, Dom and Andrew pushing out a boat. Then Andrew and Mary sheltering under a golf umbrella. All three of them having supper, Andrew and Dom in shorts, chasing sheep out of a garden. . . What did it all mean?

There was one sure way to find out, provided Andrew hadn't gone home yet. He was in his room, dictating letters. He looked up and smiled when he saw who had looked in. 'I found this in the common room,' Annie improvised. 'I had to look inside to see whose it was and I decided it must be yours.'

Andrew took it, recognising the folder. 'Ah, yes— the record of our recent weekend at the cottage. Mary never goes anywhere without her camera and I was supposed to give this to Dom.' He looked worried. 'I must have forgotten—yet I was so sure. . . Never grow old, dear Annie,' he sighed. 'The third age is very much overrated. Is there anything wrong? You look so tired. . .'

'No, there's nothing wrong,' she denied. 'Nothing. And perhaps it was Dom who dropped them. I'll give them to him. . .' She hurried to Dom's room, praying that he'd be there.

He was standing by the window, hands in his pockets, staring moodily out. He swung round as she opened the door. Annie opened her mouth to speak but it was too dry so she just laid the packet of snapshots on his desk. 'I'm sorry,' she managed to whisper.

'So am I,' he said bleakly. 'That was a cheap piece of theatre on my part and I wish I hadn't done it. They're not dated, so what do they prove?'

'Andrew said—he said they were taken on their most recent weekend at the cottage.'

'Just as I told him to, of course. Good old Andrew!' The bitterness in his voice cut her to the heart.

'Dom—don't,' she pleaded. 'Andrew would never lie—I know that.'

'Since when?'

'Since—always, really. I was angry. And hurt. . .I didn't know what I was saying.' Oh, God—this was so difficult and so very important. 'I was scared, too,' she admitted. 'Terrified, in fact. Don't you see? I so wanted it to be all real and true. I wanted it so much. Yet I didn't dare believe. . .'

They stared at one another, hope dawning in their eyes, yet afraid even now to be sure.

'How could we get it so terribly wrong?' he asked at last.

'Easily—being us. We got off to the worst possible start. Not now—years ago—and we were too proud to admit it. That's really been the whole trouble, you know. The way I see it. . .' Annie was getting into her stride now but Dom marched over and stopped her in mid-flow with a long and thrilling kiss. 'What was that for?' she asked.

'Just showing you how I mean to shut you up in future when you talk too much.'

Annie was bubbling over with happiness. 'So now I know what to do when I want to be kissed,' she said, determined—as ever—to have the last word.

And he let her. Just for now. . .

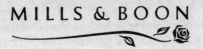

MILLS & BOON

MEDICAL ROMANCE

The books for enjoyment this month are:

A PRIVATE AFFAIR	Sheila Danton
DOCTORS IN DOUBT	Drusilla Douglas
FALSE PRETENCES	Laura MacDonald
LOUD AND CLEAR	Josie Metcalfe

Treats in store!

Watch next month for the following absorbing stories:

ONE STEP AT A TIME	Caroline Anderson
VET WITH A SECRET	Mary Bowring
DEMI'S DIAGNOSIS	Lilian Darcy
A TIME TO CHANGE	Maggie Kingsley

Delicious Dishes

Would you like to win a year's supply of simply irresistible romances? Well, you can and they're FREE! Simply match the dish to its country of origin and send your answers to us by 31st December 1996. The first 5 correct entries picked after the closing date will win a year's supply of Temptation novels (four books every month—worth over £100). What could be easier?

A	LASAGNE			GERMANY
B	KORMA			GREECE
C	SUSHI			FRANCE
D	BACLAVA			ENGLAND
E	PAELLA			MEXICO
F	HAGGIS			INDIA
G	SHEPHERD'S PIE			SPAIN
H	COQ AU VIN			SCOTLAND
I	SAUERKRAUT			JAPAN
J	TACOS			ITALY

Please turn over for details of how to enter

How to enter

Listed in the left hand column overleaf are the names of ten delicious dishes and in the right hand column the country of origin of each dish. All you have to do is match each dish to the correct country and place the corresponding letter in the box provided.

When you have matched all the dishes to the countries, don't forget to fill in your name and address in the space provided and pop this page into an envelope (you don't need a stamp) and post it today! Hurry—competition ends 31st December 1996.

Mills & Boon Delicious Dishes
FREEPOST
Croydon
Surrey
CR9 3WZ

Are you a Reader Service Subscriber? Yes ❏   No ❏

Ms/Mrs/Miss/Mr _____

Address _____

_____

_____ Postcode _____

One application per household.

You may be mailed with other offers from other reputable companies as a result of this application. If you would prefer not to receive such offers, please tick box.   ❏

C396
F

Byke
Heartbreak for Donna

BYKER GROVE

HEARTBREAK FOR DONNA

BBC BOOKS

Byker Grove is a Zenith North Production

Published by BBC Books,
a division of BBC Enterprises Limited,
Woodlands, 80 Wood Lane, London W12 0TT

First published 1990
© Carrie Rose 1990
ISBN 0 563 36066 6

Set in 10/12 Baskerville by
Goodfellow & Egan Ltd., Cambridge
Printed and bound in England by
Clays Ltd, St Ives Plc
Cover printed by Clays Ltd, St Ives Plc

CONTENTS

CHAPTER ONE

Donna Bell wished she hadn't chosen the same table in The Copper Kettle that she'd sat at six months ago. Her mum hadn't shown up then either. She flipped through the pages of her magazine, attempting to look relaxed and casual while she felt her stomach churning.

'Donna, lovie, I'd spot that hair a mile off.'

Putting down the magazine, Donna sat for a moment feigning coolness as her mother wove her way eagerly through the tables. Donna was still angry with her for being so late. Polly, looking not much older than her sophisticated daughter, chattered nervously. 'Sorry I'm late, only I got this great big ladder in me tights and I had to buy a new pair and dive into the ladies to change them. I didn't want you seeing me for the first time in ages thinking your old mum's turned into a right slut. Let's have a look at you.'

Donna hesitated, then leapt up and ran over to her mum.

'Oh Donna lovie.'

'Oh Mum.'

They fell into each other's arms. Donna had waited a long time for this.

Trying not to look too pleased, she sat down and ordered a meringue from the waitress. Polly had a little struggle with herself, then said she'd just have a lemon tea.

When the meringue arrived, Donna noticed Polly eyeing the fresh cream that oozed out of it so temptingly.

'Go on, have one. You know you will.' Donna knew her mother too well.

'I really mustn't,' Polly protested. 'I've put on pounds since the accident.'

Donna said she hadn't and bet that she could still borrow her mum's clothes. Polly smiled, remembering how things used to be when they had lived together as a family. 'You used to be a little devil for that in the old days.'

'Before you ran out on us, you mean?' came the cutting reply.

'I wish you wouldn't say that, lovie.'

'Well it's true.' Donna bit her lip but she couldn't help it. She loved her mum but she was still angry with Polly for leaving her and her dad and, if she was honest, hurt too. For once, Polly couldn't think of anything to say. She changed the subject, trying to lighten the atmosphere.

'Used to be our favourite place this, didn't it pet?'

'I know. It was where we were supposed to meet that day. I waited hours.' She wasn't going to let her mother off the hook that easily.

But Polly felt Donna was being a bit unfair. 'What could I have done, lovie, lying in that hospital? After all, I had just been knocked down.'

'By a BMW,' Donna couldn't help commenting. 'Trust you, Mum. Anyone else would have been knocked down by a scruffbag in a tatty old van.'

Polly smiled as she felt her daughter warm towards her. She'd often felt guilty about leaving her, especially when Donna wouldn't answer her letters or speak to her on the phone. Now Polly wanted the two of them to be close again. She reached over with her teaspoon and swiped the end off Donna's meringue.

Outside Byker Grove, Spuggie stood, watering can in hand, surveying her kingdom. It wasn't so much a kingdom, more a scrubby little patch of ground, but to her it seemed like a kingdom. And she was growing sunflowers in it. Alison, one of the Byker Grove helpers, wandered past on her way to the office.

'They'll not grow if you keep looking at them every five minutes, Spuggie.'

Spuggie, who spent her life hearing people tell her what she couldn't do, replied with conviction. 'Yes, they will. They have already.'

'Wouldn't you prefer something smaller than sunflowers? Then you can put them in a vase,' Alison asked.

'No.' Spuggie told Alison that anybody could grow titchy little pansies and stuff. Hers were going to be something amazing.

Alison smiled to herself. That Spuggie was one determined kid. Nobody could dissuade her once she put her mind to something. 'Good for you Spuggie,' she told her. 'I like your style.'

When she'd finished her watering, Spuggie went inside. As she walked into the club room a helium character balloon with grinning face and legs bounced its way towards her. She stood for a moment surveying the bustle, her face screwed up in disgust. 'Huh,' she sniffed.

As was often the case with Spuggie, no one took any notice. They were all too busy preparing for Donna Bell's party that evening. The room was already partly decorated with pink, purple and orange streamers and balloons. A red-faced Speedy was blowing up more balloons, while Ian hung them on the wall in brightly coloured bunches. Cas, balanced precariously on a ladder, was about to hang up a banner.

'Where shall I put this?'

'What does it say?' Spuggie demanded. Cas held out the banner which read 'Happy Birthday Donna' in large purple letters.

'Huh,' was Spuggie's response.

9

'Belt up, Spug,' said Cas amiably. 'You sound like a flippin' Indian squaw. Heap Big Spuggie Running Water.' The others laughed but Spuggie was not amused. She wanted to know why Donna always had such a fuss made of her. Speedy replied reasonably that it *was* her birthday.

'So why are you lot doing all the work then? Why isn't she here?'

The decorating team looked at one another and shrugged. It was a good question.

Each colourful shopfront was more enticing than the one before. Julie Warner never got tired of the Metro Centre – it was huge and full of plants and flowers and great things to buy. She remembered for a moment the first time she'd come here with her dad, all those months ago. She'd been dying to explore the shops, but determined that she wasn't going to give her dad the satisfaction. She'd hated Newcastle, longed to be back in Wimbledon. Now she loved the place, especially the Metro Centre.

She and Nicola Dobson were shopping for a birthday present for Donna. It wasn't easy. Nicola pointed to a particularly flimsy, frilly pair of knickers in the window of a trendy lingerie shop. 'D'you think she'd like them?'

Julie grinned, 'Knowing Donna, she'd love them.'

Nicola peered at the price tag. They were fifteen pounds – far too much.

'Would you wear something like that?' she asked Julie.

'Not for anyone to see,' Julie replied.

Nicola looked amused. 'Isn't that meant to be the whole point?' she asked.

They gave up on the idea of sexy underwear and trooped into Boots instead. At the jewellery counter,

10

Nicola picked up a large, garish bangle, wondering aloud whether it was Donna's taste.

'It's very Donna,' Julie laughed. 'Bright and flashy.' She and Donna had never exactly been the best of friends and there were times when Julie couldn't resist having a go at her. 'Anyway, I've got to go now,' she said, looking at her watch. 'Hope you'll find something. See you tonight.'

'OK, see ya,' Nicola replied.

She turned back to the jewellery counter as Julie walked away. 'What the heck d'you get for a girl who's got everything?' Nicola muttered to herself. She was rapidly getting fed up with present buying.

A little later Nicola was in a newsagent's looking at magazines. She hadn't noticed the tall blond boy with film star looks who was watching her thoughtfully from behind a postcard rack.

Jan had spotted Nicola across the magazines, thought she was pretty and, equally important, alone. He'd never have had the courage to chat a girl up it she was with a friend. Girls always giggled in pairs even if they fancied you. He picked up a postcard, took a deep breath, and marched over to Nicola.

'Please can you tell me where is this?' He held the postcard out for Nicola to inspect.

'It's Bamburgh Castle,' Nicola replied, trying to stay cool. He was quite a dish.

'It is far from here?' Jan asked.

'Not very. You should go, its got a fantastic beach.' Nicola thought how sexy his accent was. 'Where are you from?'

Jan explained that he was from Copenhagen and over here on an exchange visit. He told her that he hadn't been in Newcastle for very long, so he didn't know many people. Nicola couldn't believe her luck, a gorgeous blond hunk who was *unattached*. Then she realised she didn't even know his name. 'I'm Nicola by the way, Nicola Dobson.'

'And my name's Jan Petersen. I am glad I have met you, Nicola.' They looked at each other for a moment, neither of them wanting to go, but stuck for something to say.

'Look,' Nicola blurted out finally, 'my friend's having a party tonight. Why don't you come along? It'll be a good way to meet people.'

'But I don't know her.' Jan protested.

Nicola grinned 'That's all right, you know me. It'll be OK, honest.'

Jan still felt like he'd be gatecrashing but on the other hand Nicola *was* very pretty and the first possibility of a date since he'd been over here. Also, he was on holiday and what's a holiday without a bit of romance? 'Why not?' he said. 'Tell me where to meet you.' He fished in his jacket pocket for a scrap of paper and a biro and gave it to Nicola. Finding nowhere to sit down and write, Jan presented her with his back to rest the paper on while she scribbled down the details.

'Suddenly I'm looking forward to this party a whole lot more,' Nicola thought happily. 'What the heck am I going to wear?'

Back at The Copper Kettle, Donna was scraping the last morsels of meringue off her plate. 'I'd best get back if I'm to make meself gorgeous for tonight.'

Polly took a gulp of tea and wished her daughter a wonderful time at her party.

'Dad wanted me to have it at home but there's more room at the Grove. Besides I didn't want *her* hanging around,' Donna explained.

12

'What's she like? Is she pretty?' Polly asked, trying to sound casual but dying to know.

Donna hesitated, then decided to tell a bit of a white lie. Well, a blimmin' big one actually. Much as she disliked Lisa, she had to admit she was very attractive. 'Nah. Dead naff,' she replied, suddenly feeling embarrassed and hoping fervently that Lisa and her mum never bumped into one another. 'Thanks for tea, Mum. And me pressie.'

Polly reached across the table and impetuously grabbed hold of her daughter's hand. 'Meet me here tomorrow. We'll have another of them cream cakes.'

Donna was surprised and pleased. She'd assumed this was a flying visit, just long enough for her mother to make it up with her and then get straight back to *that* bloke. She honestly didn't know who she hated more, Lisa or Him. 'You're staying over then?'

'For a few days.' Polly waited to see her daughter's reaction. She was obviously glad but then a certain look came over her face. Polly remembered that look, it meant trouble.

'Is *he* with you?' Donna asked sulkily.

'No, he's not.' She hesitated, then, 'You never would say his name, would you? One of these days when you're older, maybe you'll understand.' Polly wished they could change the subject. On top of the guilt she still felt for leaving her daughter, she couldn't really explain herself why she'd done it. Why on earth had she left a man who provided her with all the little luxuries she enjoyed so much, who probably still loved her too, for a hopeless romantic with hardly two pennies to rub together?

'Try me now,' Donna suddenly said, in a different tone.

Polly drained her tea cup. 'Your dad was taking me for granted, there was no excitement in my life any more. Then Ken came along and suddenly I felt young again.'

All the hurt and anger Donna had felt when her mother first left came flooding back. She lashed out at Polly, 'Yeah, I suppose it must have been dead boring having a thirteen-year-old daughter to look after.'

'I never stopped loving you, Donna hinny. I wanted to take you with me but your dad wouldn't let me.'

'I wouldn't have come anyway. I never want to meet him, so don't ask me to.' Donna wasn't one to mince her words.

A shadow crossed her mother's face. Donna would almost have said she looked embarrassed but it took a heck of a lot to embarrass Polly Bell.

'I won't,' was all that Polly would say, before briskly changing the subject. 'Now promise me you'll have an absolutely smashing time tonight.'

Donna said of course she would, she was the star of the show, and hugged her mother goodbye. But she couldn't help feeling, as she left the café, that there was something Polly wasn't telling her.

In the grounds outside the Grove, the lads were having a brill time practising for their upcoming football match against Denton Burn. Brad, their coach, wasn't feeling quite so optimistic. He could see that the boys had a long way to go before they were anything like decent. Still, what they lacked in skill, they made up for in enthusiasm. If only that could win you football matches. He decided it was time for a break. Nothing to do with the boys, he'd just seen Alison, the love of his life, wandering out of the office.

Spuggie stood on the sidelines feeling miserable. She wished they'd let her play football. She'd often asked if she could kick a ball around with the lads but they

14

always laughed at her and called her names. She bet she could play better than some of them – if only they'd let her. And Duncan McDonald, the closest thing she had to a boyfriend, and that wasn't very close, had disappeared yet again. 'You're always mizzling off lately,' she'd told him earlier. 'Have you got a girlfriend?'

'Don't be daft,' he'd replied dismissively.

But Spuggie wasn't giving up that easily. If it's not a girlfriend then what is it?'

'No law says I have to tell you everything,' Duncan finally retorted before sneaking off to his secret destination. And then there was Brad and Alison. Spuggie idolised them both but, as she watched them chat together, she felt a sudden pang of jealousy. It wouldn't be long before they were going out together, just like all the other couples. It wasn't fair. Spuggie wanted a boyfriend too. And not like the boyfriends Donna and the girls at the Grove had. She wanted a proper sweep-you-off-your-feet romance, like in the old films they showed on telly.

If Spuggie had only known, the path of true love wasn't running as smoothly as she thought. Brad was struggling against a strong desire to reach out and touch Alison as he talked to her. He wanted to stroke her cheek, her hair, anything to break down the barrier that she always seemed to place between them.

'It'll be a needle match, this one. There's no love lost between Denton Burn and our lot,' he dimly heard her say.

Without thinking, Brad replied, 'Speaking of which – have we fallen out?'

Alison looked distinctly uncomfortable. 'Don't be silly,' was all she'd say.

But Brad wasn't letting her get away with it that easily. 'You've been avoiding me lately,' he told her bluntly.

15

'I haven't. I've seen you here nearly every day.' Alison's response was a mixture of indignation and evasion – and Brad knew it. He'd set off along the road and he wasn't going to stop now.

'I'm not talking about here. When are you coming out with me again, Ali?' This time there was no reply. Alison went very quiet and for a few seconds Brad thought he'd got through to her. But no such luck.

'You know I can't,' she said finally, 'Mike . . .'

Brad had had enough. He wanted to be with Alison badly but he had his pride and he wasn't going to beg. 'One of these days you're going to have to make your mind up between us, sweetheart.' He walked off back to the football practice but his words had hit home. Alison stood alone, tears in her eyes. Brad was right, she couldn't bear this much longer.

Julie was loaded down with parcels, rolled-up posters and a large pot plant as she approached the big, dilapidated old house with a mixture of fear and excitement. What would her mother say if she knew her boyfriend lived in such a grotty place? 'She'd go up the wall,' Julie thought with certainty. Good job she was hundreds of miles away in London. Her dad, on the other hand, hardly uttered a word of protest these days.

Poor Dad. Julie felt sorry for him. Even at fifteen she knew she could out-argue him. And she could see now why her mum had left him. He was a kind man but there was also something weak about him.

Not like Gill. He was a different kettle of fish, tough and determined. Perhaps that's why she'd fallen for him in the first place. And yet, when she thought about it, Gill was also an old softie at heart. She hoped he'd like the things she'd bought for his new home – well, it was just a room really.

Julie rang the bell but there was no answer. Then she saw that the door was already ajar. She pushed it open and walked up to Gill's room. What a tip. Overflowing cardboard boxes, a battered holdall and several dirty coffee mugs lay amid clothes strewn on the floor and across the bed. The wallpaper was peeling at the corners and a couple of patches of damp were spreading across the revolting flowery pattern. Julie dumped her packages on the bed and got to work.

When Gill walked in an hour later the place was hardly recognisable. Julie had tidied up the clothes, stacked the cardboard boxes neatly in one corner, washed the coffee mugs, hung posters on the walls to cover the damp spots and even found a place for the pot plant. Gill was gobsmacked.

'What?' was all he could say, as he stood in the doorway staring at the transformation.

'Surprised?' asked Julie, suddenly worried that he might be angry with her for meddling with his things.

'I am,' Gill replied. Then he smiled, 'Come here.'

'What for?' Julie asked suspiciously.

'So I can thank you properly for all this.' Julie moved closer and Gill put his arms round her neck and kissed her. She loved the way he kissed her, it felt so strong and passionate. Not that she had that much to compare it to, she'd hardly been allowed out with boys in Wimbledon. She felt herself drifting away, wanting the kiss to go on forever, but then she became aware that Gill was edging them towards the bed. He sat them both down on it without breaking the embrace. Suddenly Julie felt nervous and she pulled away. 'I must get back.'

Gill masked his disappointment by teasing her, 'Still worried about what Daddy will say?'

This really irritated her but she was determined not to rise to Gill's bait. Instead she said coolly, 'I've got to get ready for the party. I'll meet you at the Grove around six.'

Gill watched her walk out of the room. He knew by now not to push Julie too far, otherwise she'd fly off like some scared little bird. She'd changed a lot since she'd been in Newcastle but not *that* much. And the last thing he wanted to do was lose her. He cared about her a lot. Gill grinned at himself for being so soppy. What would his mate Winston say?

Make-up was scattered across Donna's dressing table as she sat in her shortie bathrobe with a face pack on and bendy curlers in her hair, dolling herself up for the party. There was a knock at the door. 'Who is it?' Donna asked impatiently, nearly smudging the nail she was painting. She didn't want to be interrupted, especially if it was Her.

'It's me, Lisa. Can I come in?' Donna would have loved to simply say 'No' but she didn't want to get on the wrong side of her dad so she grudgingly agreed. Lisa came in carrying a beautifully wrapped parcel with a silk rosette.

'Blimey,' she laughed when she saw the state of Donna.

'You doll yourself up too!' was Donna's indignant response.

'I know, but don't tell your dad. We girls have got to have some secrets from the fellas. Right?' Donna hated it when Lisa tried to be matey with her. It got right up her nose and it wasn't going to work. She wanted her mum back with her dad and Lisa out of their lives for good. She wished the girl would just get the message and go.

'What do you want?' Donna asked rudely. Lisa handed her the package and wished her happy birthday. Donna just managed a quick 'Ta', then went back to

18

painting her nails. As she was obviously no longer welcome, Lisa started to leave the room.

Then, on impulse, she turned back. 'Donna. Why can't we be friends?'

What a question! thought Donna. Doesn't the silly cow know the answer to that one? She bit her lip and said aloud, 'Because I don't want to, all right?' Then she turned and appeared to study her face with extraordinary concentration in the dressing table mirror. She smiled to herself at the hurt look on Lisa's face as she left the bedroom. Perhaps she was getting the message after all.

The girls' loo at Byker Grove was quiet for a change. The only person there was Spuggie, attempting to put on some make-up for the party later. She smudged her lipstick, muttered to herself, then scrubbed it off with loo paper and started again, wondering why she even bothered. Then, looking at herself one more time and hating what she saw, Spuggie ran out of the loo and bumped straight into Alison.

'You look nice, Spuggie.' Somehow Spuggie didn't quite believe her. 'Can I make a suggestion?' Here it came, she knew it. 'Perhaps a touch less lipstick?' She was secretly relieved as she wiped the gooey pink stuff off her lips with the back of her hand.

A few minutes later she was in the club room and Winston was trying to flog her a Byker Grove rosette for the match against Denton Burn. That was typical Winston, he never missed a chance to make some cash. No way was she going to buy one of his tatty bits of paper, even if she had any money, which she didn't – as usual. She'd just told Winston politely to 'get lost' when she spotted Nicola coming into the room with a tall, very good-looking blond boy. She went over immediately.

19

'Who are you?' she asked. Spuggie was never one for beating about the bush.

Nicola smiled at the boy. 'This is Spuggie, Jan. I should have warned you about her.'

'What do you mean, warned him about me?' Spuggie asked indignantly. Having found out where Jan was from and what he was doing in Newcastle, Spuggie's curiosity was satisfied and she wandered off to find other amusements.

The Grove was starting to fill up with people coming for the party. The club room was looking great by now – everyone had done a really good job of putting up streamers and balloons and banners. Julie and Gill walked in. Gill had made a special effort to spruce himself up and Julie was looking exceptionally pretty. Nicola introduced them to Jan who was rapidly becoming the star attraction.

'Where are all the other lads?' Gill wondered. Alison, who was passing by with a tray full of sandwiches, solved the mystery.

'In the gents poncing themselves up,' she grinned. 'I walked past and nearly got gassed from all the after-shave and deodorant wafting through the door.'

Over in the boys' loo, the air was heavy with talk as well as deodorant. The forthcoming match against Denton Burn was the cause of the excitement. Though the more honest amongst them admitted that Denton Burn were an ace team, the Byker Grovers' morale was high and they were still convinced that they would beat their rivals.

'Ah, we'll smash 'em to bits, no danger,' Ian declared, sounding far more confident than he felt. 'Right Cas? Cas?' But Cas wasn't listening, he was peering anxiously at his hair in the mirror.

'It's definitely falling out,' he said in a worried tone, as he parted it different ways looking for bald spots.

'What is?' asked Speedy, never very quick on the uptake.

'Me hair.' Cas showed everyone his comb with at least four hairs in it. 'Look.'

The others laughed, telling Cas that everyone gets hair on their comb. He wasn't getting much sympathy. 'I bet I'll be bald by the time I'm twenty,' he fretted.

'Will you, heck.' Ian dismissed this thought scornfully. But Speedy had other ideas.

'He might. Some people do. Look at Mr T.' This was greeted with hoots of derision from the others.

'He shaves his, you prat,' said Ian.

Finally, the lads were reasonably satisfied with their appearance and began to troop out into the Grove general room. Only Cas and Speedy were left, Cas still examining his hair in the mirror.

'And there's Duncan Goodhew,' Speedy tried to reassure him. 'And Kojak. There's loads. And you could always wear a hat like Elton John.'

Cas threw Speedy a withering glance. 'Just belt up, eh?' was his final comment, before he too decided to join the gang. He left Speedy wondering what the heck he'd said that was so wrong. He was only trying to help.

In the club room the pile of presents lay unopened on the table. The sandwiches were still under snapwrap. 'Where is she?' Cas asked Nicola. Nicola grinned, telling Cas he ought to know Donna better than that by now. She was the star of the show tonight and Nicola knew she would be the last to arrive, making a grand entrance in some amazing new get-up that she'd have 'forgotten' to tell Nicola about.

It was mostly the girls who were dancing – as usual. Brad was doing a great job of being DJ but even he couldn't get the boys bopping.

'Right, now, everyone on the dance floor. We're going to really swing to Lisa Stansfield.'

'He'll be lucky,' Nicola said. 'They'll just stand against the wall posing.'

'Trying to look macho,' agreed Julie.

Jan tried to defend his sex. 'I think perhaps you are being unfair. Boys are more self-conscious than girls. They don't like to look stupid.' But his reasoning wasn't going to wash, even with Nicola.

'Girls don't like to look stupid either,' she told Jan bluntly. Then she took his hand and led him over to where everyone else was dancing. 'Can you dance?' she asked.

'Not so well,' Jan grinned. So Nicola showed him how it was done, giving it all she'd got. After a minute or two Jan began to follow her lead and soon the two of them were bopping together like they'd been doing it forever. Then Jan leaned over to Nicola and shouted above the noise of the disco music that this was a very strange party. Puzzled, Nicola asked him why.

'Because the girl who is having the party is not here.' Nicola laughed at that and explained to Jan that Donna always had to make an entrance, that she had to be the star of the show. But he wasn't listening, he was looking over at the far corner of the room. Nicola turned to see what he was staring at. 'I think the star of the show has arrived, no?'

The bendy curlers and face pack had certainly paid off, Donna looked knockout. She was wearing a figure-hugging, off-the-shoulder red dress, her wild hair was set off with a scarf tied in a big bow on top of her head, and her make-up was expertly applied – tips she'd picked up from Lisa although she'd never let on. She stood posing in the doorway, holding the package Lisa had given her and waiting until all eyes were upon her.

Nicola sighed as she saw the look on Jan's face. 'Yep. That's her.'

Donna had caught sight of Jan at about the same time too and was now making a beeline for him and Nicola.

'Who's this?' The question was addressed to Nicola but Donna didn't once take her eyes off Jan.

'He's called Jan, he's from Copenhagen. Jan, this is Donna.' Jan was obviously delighted to meet her. Nicola told the story of how she'd met him in the Metro Centre that afternoon, and Donna was clearly impressed by her friend's boy-pulling powers but even more impressed by Jan himself. An awkward threesome soon began to develop.

'Right guys and gals, I hope you're hot to trot with the latest chart entry from New Kids on the Block.' Brad was enjoying his new role as Byker Grove's DJ. Alison watched him lining up the next record and then went over, Coke can in hand.

'Here,' she said, handing over the Coke. 'Talking that much has to be thirsty work.'

'I'm a multi-talented man. I can dance too,' Brad replied with a wink. 'Care to take a turn around the floor?' He bowed low before her – Alison laughed but refused the offer.

Donna, standing nearby, wasn't going to let that pass. 'Go on Alison, have a dance with him. You've got to, it's my birthday.'

Sometimes Alison wished the little madam would mind her own business. Life was complicated enough as it was. But at the same time she had to admit that she did want a dance with Brad. 'Just one, then,' she finally conceded. Before she knew it, Brad had changed the fast dance record for a slow smoochy number and had taken her in his arms. Trapped!

Meanwhile Donna also seized the opportunity. She

moved seductively over to where Nicola and Jan were dancing together.

'Excuse me.' Donna stood in between them, and made it clear that she wanted Jan to partner her for the next dance.

An irritated Nicola asked her, 'Who says so?'

'I do,' Donna replied. 'It's my birthday.'

There was no arguing with that. And besides, Nicola noticed that Jan wasn't exactly unwilling to go with Donna. Sometimes my best friend can be such a cow, she thought angrily.

The party was in full swing by now. Everyone, with the exception of Nicola, was having a great time, dancing, chatting, eating and drinking. Brad and Alison were dancing cheek to cheek. He had let go of Alison only to change the record each time but she wasn't protesting any more. This was the third slow record and she was secretly wishing it would go on for ever. Suddenly she pulled away, with a look of shock.

'Hi, Mike. What are you doing here?' she said rather too brightly. Brad was also thrown for a moment. Mike stood in the doorway of the crowded room but the only people he saw were Alison – and Brad.

'I thought you might want a lift home,' he replied lamely. 'It's raining heavily.' It was an excuse, and they both knew it. How long has he been there watching Brad and me dancing? Alison thought with horror. She took a deep breath and tried to sound casual. 'Mike, this is Brad.' She had to introduce them, there was nothing else for it. They said hello to each other in polite, strained tones. Meanwhile Donna, unable to resist this kind of intrigue, had temporarily deserted Jan to gossip with Nicola.

'Think they're going to fight over her?' Donna couldn't help sounding excited at the thought.

'I hope not,' Nicola said, meaning it. 'Mike's nice.' She wasn't into high drama like Donna. But Donna persisted, declaring 'Brad's sexier though.' There was a pause while Donna enjoyed a little fantasy about having two men fighting over *her*. She couldn't think of anything that would please her more. 'Men *do* fight over women. I think it's exciting,' she declared, with conviction.

But Donna wasn't about to get her wish this time. Mike was far too mild-mannered and sensible for a brawl. Instead he settled for standing with his arm round Alison as everyone watched Donna opening her presents. Alison was irritated by this. She knew it was Mike's way of saying 'She's mine so lay off,' which should have made her proud – but didn't.

Donna was in her element, the centre of attention, as everyone waited eagerly to see what was inside each package. She loved Ian's gift which was a framed photo of herself taken at camp the previous summer. 'That's her favourite view of all time,' Gill commented with a grin. Everyone laughed but Donna could forgive them today. Besides – they were right. She showed the photo to Jan, flirting outrageously as she asked him how she looked in it. 'Very pretty,' Jan replied, with feeling.

Nicola, wanting to break up the cosy twosome, handed Donna another package. 'Here, what's this one? You came in with it.' Donna seemed strangely unwilling to open it but eventually tore the paper off. Inside was a video cassette called 'Your Guide to Health and Beauty'. The girls were impressed, the boys less so.

'What did your dad get you?' Spuggie asked Donna. 'A video recorder,' Donna told her, so she could watch stuff in her room without her dad and Lisa gobbin' on. 'But you need a telly for that,' Ian pointed out. 'She's got one,' Nicola told him. Spuggie was gobsmacked, she couldn't believe how lucky some people were. Her own telly? And her own video recorder? Blimmin' heck!

People like Donna Bell seemed to have all the fun. It wasn't fair. Why couldn't something go right for Spuggie for a change? Look at this party, for instance. Here she was, on her own feeling miserable, as per usual. Duncan had promised he'd be there but Geoff had seen him sneaking off ages ago. And I bet I know where he's blimmin' gone, Spuggie thought crossly.

Half an hour later Alison stood in the hallway with Mike. She couldn't bear being around him *and* Brad any longer and was trying to persuade him to leave. But Mike was being quietly subborn and insisted on waiting until Alson had finished for the evening. He told her he'd wait in the office with Geoff and have a cup of tea with him. The sounds of 'Happy Birthday' drifted along the corridor from the club room.

'You'd better go back inside,' he told her.

'You don't mind?' Alison asked, wondering what she'd do if he said he did.

'Course not. You're just doing your job,' Mike replied. Alison wasn't sure how to take this so she said nothing and headed back into the club room.

Everyone was gathered round the table with the birthday cake on it. The candles had been lit and Donna was enjoying every second of the noisy rendition of 'Happy Birthday'. Cas had his arm around her waist but she constantly glanced over to where Jan was standing with Nicola. Julie and Gill were apart from the gang, with their arms round one another. Ian too was holding hands with a partner he had found that evening.

Alison walked back into the room and her eyes met Brad's, yet another romance noted by lonely eagle-eyed Spuggie. Donna blew out the candles on her cake. 'Make a wish Donna!' Spuggie shouted. Donna screwed up her eyes hard and clenched both fists. Wishing for your parents to get back together again took every ounce of energy you had. 'What did you wish for?' Spuggie asked. Donna silenced her with a look. No one was going to find out about *that* wish.

The next day Spuggie was coming out of the Grove, watering can in hand to water her seedlings, when Duncan reappeared. Coming straight to the point she asked him crossly where he'd mizzled off to the night before. He was strangely evasive, simply telling her that he didn't like parties. But Spuggie wasn't giving up that easily. 'Did you go to see a girl?' Duncan denied this indignantly. 'So where *did* you go?'

'Mind your own business,' he retorted.

Spuggie retaliated with the only weapon she had. 'Well, don't think I'm your friend then, 'cos I'm not.'

Suddenly she spied Popeye, Cas's dog, happily digging up her seedlings. Horrified, she yelled 'Popeye, *scoot*!' That did the trick but now she had to replant her seedlings.

'Don't just stand there like a lemon, give me a hand,' she demanded of Duncan. Indignant, Duncan began to point out that he was no longer Spuggie's friend, she'd just given him the push. But Spuggie simply fixed him with a beady glare. It was more than a boy could stand. 'OK, OK, piggin' females,' he muttered as he knelt down and began to help her repair the damage.

Later that day a very energetic football practice was underway outside the Grove. Brad still had a lot of work to do if his team were to have any chance of beating Denton Burn. Winston, in the meantime, was conducting a chanting session with some of the younger kids on the sidelines.

'Who's going to win?'

27

'The Grove.'

'Who's rubbish?'

'Denton Burn.'

'Who's the best?'

'Byker Byker Byker *Grooooove*!'

Alison wandered nervously over to Brad. They hadn't spoken since Mike's arrival the previous evening.

'That should put the fear of God into them,' she joked, trying to lighten the atmosphere.

Brad cut through her small talk. 'Funny, Mike turning up like that.' He paused for a moment, looking Alison straight in the eye. She didn't know what to say. 'Seems like a nice guy,' he added. 'Trouble is, I'm a nice guy too. Right?' Alison gave him a helpless look as he walked away. Brad was right. What a position for a girl to be in, two great men both wanting to be with her. It was one of those situations that sounded wonderful as long as you weren't the ones involved.

Brad's coaching was beginning to pay off – the boys were performing some excellent passes. Cas came pelting along towards the ball and gave it an almighty kick towards the goal. It sped through the air but he'd misjudged the direction by about ten yards. The ball was heading at speed towards the seedling patch. Ian made a heroic leap to head the ball and save the little plants but unfortunately slipped and crashed to the ground – right in the middle of Spuggie's garden.

There was a silence and then the sound of a stifled giggle, rapidly followed by more laughter. Spuggie was furious. 'You're horrible. I hate you all!' Brad tried to reassure her that it was an accident but the continuing laughter did nothing to back him up. 'I'm going and I'm never coming back,' she shouted angrily.

Winston told everyone she was bluffing because she didn't have anywhere else to go, which made Spuggie even more furious. 'That's what you think Winston Cleverbonce! I have got somewhere else to go. I'm going to Denton Burn.' Genuinely shocked, Speedy declared, 'You can't go there! They're the blimmin' enemy!' But Spuggie's mind was made up and what's more, her pride was at stake. She marched off, her head held high. She had to go to Denton Burn now.

Outside the Byker Arms, Donna's dad's pub, a taxi screeched to a halt and Polly Bell stuck her head out of the window. 'Donna! Donna!' she yelled. A surprised Donna came running out, still in her school uniform. She wasn't expecting to see her mum until later at the café but then Polly had always been nothing if not unpredictable. 'What the heck are you doing here?' she asked, baffled.

'Change of plan,' Polly replied mysteriously. 'Get in. I'll tell you about it on the way.' It turned out that they were heading for the station. It also turned out that Polly had been doing some 'serious thinking'. Donna giggled at that. 'You?!' she asked. Polly ignored her daughter's cheek, she was used to it, and went on to explain, 'Thing is, Kenneth's all dazzle and promises. And at my age a girl can't live on promises.' Donna had a feeling that life was bout to do a rapid U-turn. Birthday wishes worked pretty fast, she thought happily.

Half an hour later Donna came running back into the pub to find her dad and Lisa sorting glasses behind the bar. Lisa was the last person she wanted to see just then. She tried to sneak up the stairs without being seen but Lisa looked up with a smile. 'Hiya. Listen, I'm going shopping for a new frock on Saturday. D'you fancy coming with?'

Do me a favour, Donna thought. You're the last person on earth I'd want to go shopping with.

Her dad was holding out a ten-pound note, 'You'll

enjoy that, pet. Get yourself something as well.' No way was he going to bribe her to like Lisa.

Donna decided that now was the perfect time to deliver her bombshell. 'If I want to go shopping I'll go with me mum when she comes back to live.' She paused for effect, waiting for what she'd just said to sink in. 'She's leaving that bloke and she's coming back to Newcastle. She'll probably get a flat round here, seeing this is where she knows everyone.' Delighted by the look of horror on Lisa's face, Donna headed for her bedroom. Her parting shot came from halfway up the stairs. She turned round and aimed her words directly at Lisa. 'Won't that be nice?'

CHAPTER TWO

The pile of furniture by the roadside was growing by the minute. A rather scrawny-looking young man delved into the back of his removal van and brought out a pink frilly-skirted dressing table. 'Right lady. That's the lot.'

Polly surveyed her worldly belongings parked awkwardly on the pavement as proudly as if they were valuable antiques. She picked up another carton to take inside as Donna came running up. 'Mam! What have you fetched all this lot for? It's a furnished flat.'

Polly smiled and winked at Colin, the removal man. It was easy to see where Donna got her flirtatiousness from. 'I couldn't do me face at the ugly thing they've shoved in there.' She turned mischievously to Colin. 'A girl's boudoir ought to be a place of beauty. Don't you think so, pet?' The poor man swallowed nervously and hurried inside with the dressing table while Polly and Donna stood on the pavement giggling at each other.

Inside the flat, Polly's possessions were strewn all over the place. It wasn't very large or very modern but it was obviously going to be *very* Polly, once her furniture and numerous bits and pieces were in place. Donna said she thought it was smashing. Colin was out of earshot, struggling to get the rather large dressing table through her bedroom door, and Polly turned to her daughter, looking as though she was about to tell her a huge secret. 'Don't laugh, pet, but I'm scared.'

Donna was amazed. 'What of?' she asked, genuinely baffled.

'I've never lived on me own before,' Polly replied. 'I was with me mam and dad till I got married. Then ever since I've been with Ken.' Donna stopped to think about that, it hadn't occurred to her before. She knew one thing though, she was going to have a place of her own before *she* got tied down. And she told her mum that too.

For once Polly looked serious. 'You're stronger than me, lovie. Me, I need a man to lean on.' She paused, then tentatively asked, 'Do you think your dad ever misses me?'

Donna felt awkward. She *hoped* he did, of course. But she had to admit that she wasn't so certain since that cow Lisa had appeared on the scene. Of course that wasn't what she told her mum. 'Course he does,' she said just a bit too brightly, then asked Polly if she still cared about her dad.

Polly sighed. 'What's the point? I doubt if he could ever forgive me for what I did.'

In her eagerness to see her parents together again, Donna was prepared to overlook all the evidence. 'I bet he would. I'm sure he still loves you, Mum.' Was she telling the truth or was it just wishful thinking? Donna really didn't know. But one thing was for sure – Polly wanted to believe it.

A little later Polly's flat was beginning to take shape. Most of the pieces of furniture had now found a home but there were still several cardboard boxes overflowing with possessions which needed to be unpacked. Polly was not a woman who lived simply.

'Mind if I go now?' Donna had been helping her mum for an hour or so and was starting to get bored with playing house. 'Only I promised to meet my mates at the Grove.'

Polly said of course she didn't and asked her to come round the next morning so they could go shopping together like the old days. Feeling apologetic, Donna explained that she couldn't because of the Byker Grove v. Denton Burn football match. 'And,' she added with a touch of embarrassment, 'there's this lad I hope'll be there.'

Her mother laughed and said she might have known. 'What's he like?'

Donna's eyes lit up. 'Really fantastic,' she replied with enthusiasm. Polly wondered what had happened to Cas. She knew he'd been flavour of the month not so long ago. Donna explained. 'Cas is OK, but he's a bit boring. He's not dead exciting like Jan.' Polly nodded but said nothing. Wanting excitement was something she identified with – to her cost.

'Who do we hate?'
'Byker Grove.'
'Who's going to win?'
'Denton Burn.'
'Who's rubbish?'
'Byker Grove.'
'Who's the best?'
'Denton Burn Y.C. Yeaaaaah!'

A small crowd of Denton Burners stood on the street corner taunting Ian, Speedy, Nicola and Winston who were on their way to the Grove. The Grovers immediately retaliated by setting up their own chant. The chanting grew louder and louder, neither side was going to be outdone. This was going to be some football match!

Finally the Denton Burners walked up the pathway to their club, watched by a small red-haired girl. Hanging back at a safe distance, Spuggie heard them chatting and laughing together. She felt very alone and scared but she was *determined* to do it. She screwed up her courage, took a deep breath, and followed the crowd into Denton Burn club.

*   *   *

Geoff felt like he needed at least two extra pairs of hands. He was manning the snack bar, which seemed to mean pouring drinks, serving crisps, making tea and taking money all at once. Alison came rushing into the general room looking puffed out. She apologised for being late, explaining that she'd borrowed Mike's bike and it had a puncture. Mary O'Malley, Nicola's gran and the Grove's volunteer all-round helper, came in carrying a broom. She'd been ill for a while and this was her first day back.

'Nice to see you, Mary. Place wasn't the same without you.'

Mary of the eagle eyes had already noticed that Spuggie wasn't around. 'She's usually the first one here. *She's* not poorly too, is she?'

Speedy piped up scornfully, 'Only turned traitor, hasn't she?' When Alison explained about the unfortunate episode with the seedlings and Spuggie's subsequent departure to Denton Burn, Mary replied that she wasn't surprised. 'Poor little mite,' she said with feeling. 'How would *you* like it if everyone was forever teasing *you*?' That made everyone go quiet for a few moments. Mary had a way of putting things that really hit home. Finally Geoff broke the silence. 'If I know our Spuggie, she'll come back in her own good time.' He hoped he was right.

Over in the boys' loo a few minutes later, Cas was worriedly examining his hair again. A female voice from outside shouted, 'I'm coming in.' It was Mary the demon cleaner, mop and bucket in hand. Cas muttered to himself, hesitated in the doorway, then headed for Geoff's office. Seeing Geoff sitting at his desk he went in and closed the door behind him. Geoff looked up in surprise, the kids usually waltzed in and out without ever thinking of closing the door behind them. This must be serious.

34

'Can I ask you something?' Cas looked sheepish.

Geoff told him to 'Fire away.'

Cas stared at Geoff for a moment, feeling unsure and embarrassed, then blurted out, 'How does my hair look to you?'

When Geoff had recovered from the shock of the question – he was expecting a terrible confession at the very least – he replied that it could do with a trim. He didn't know what else to say as he hadn't a clue what Cas was getting at but it was obviously important to him whatever it was. Now he'd started on the subject, Cas couldn't back out. So he confided to Geoff that he thought his hair was getting thin. In fact, worse that that, he thought it was falling out all the time and he'd soon be bald. 'When I wash it there's always some down the plughole,' he informed Geoff.

Geoff knew better than to treat this lightly. To Cas it was deadly serious. 'I bet you're worried about spots as well,' was all he said.

Cas was surprised. He *was* worried about the number of zits that kept on popping up all over his face. But he thought he'd keep that quiet and deal with the most pressing problem first. Now he was certain that they must show up really badly.

Once he saw the look on Cas's face at the mention of spots, Geoff knew what he was dealing with. 'When I was your age, you know what?' Cas shook his head. Geoff continued, 'I worried I was fat. I worried I was clumsy. I worried I had dandruff. I worried I had pimples. I worried I had sweaty feet. I worried when girls wouldn't talk to me. I worried when they *did*.' He paused, Cas was beginning to get the message. 'You name it, I worried. And shall I tell you something, Cas, there isn't a lad who doesn't.'

There was a knock at the door and Ian stuck his head

round looking exasperated. 'You coming to this footie practice, or what?'

Cas replied that Ian didn't have to do his nut and he was coming in a minute. Turning to Geoff, he grinned, 'You're wiser than you look, you. Thanks, mate.' Then he scooted before Geoff could cuff him one.

The gleaming red Ferrari looked distinctly out of place on the walls of Gill's dingy bedroom. Gill was positioning the poster so that it had pride of place amongst the others. Standing back to look at it for a moment, he felt both envy and admiration. That was one beaut of a car.

He switched on the kettle, then picked up some pieces of wood he was carving into pigeons for Julie. It had long been a hobby of his and it pleased him to be making something for his girlfriend. As he carved, Gill began to fantasize about picking Julie up from school in the red Ferrari. He could see all her gobsmacked schoolmates and Julie's look of pride as she stepped into the car. In the distance her snotty mother was staring in disbelief as they drove off like a flash of lightning, Gill, his bird and his amazing mean machine.

Winston walked through the half-open door and the phantom red Ferrari instantly disappeared. Irritated, Gill tried to hid his pigeon woodcarvings.

'Don't you ever knock, man?'

'Why, what you doing?' Winston immediately suspected something. He caught sight of the pigeons. 'What're they?' Gill tried to pass it off as nothing much. However, seeing his embarrassment, Winston put two and two together and realised he was carving the pigeons for Julie. 'Could flog them down the Sunday market,' he told Gill, with his usual eye for a fast buck. But Gill dismissed them as 'rubbish' and suggested that they go out for some grub as he was starving. Winston was delighted. 'Just the two of us? No Jooooolie?'

'No Julie,' Gill replied.

'Fell out with her?' Winston asked hopefully. But that was expecting too much. Gill explained that she had loads of homework and then shoved the pigeons under the bed. 'What you doing that for?' Winston wanted to know but he was only told to keep his gob shut. So he was right, they were for Jooooolie. He wished she'd disappear down a big hole forever and him and Gill could be back the way they were.

A tension-filled game of Monopoly was underway in the Grove general room. However the tension wasn't coming from the game but from the players, Nicola, Donna and Jan.

Donna was being her usual flirtatious self and Nicola was heartily sick of it. Jan had landed on Covent Garden and was telling the girls about Stroget which he thought was the same sort of place only in his country. Donna sat listening all wide-eyed as though Jan was telling her something amazing. Then when he'd finished describing Stroget, she turned to him. 'I'd love to go to Copenhagen one day. Would you show us round?' She was being so obvious that Nicola wanted to be sick.

'Stop nattering and get on with the flippin' game, will you?' she said crossly.

Cas came over fresh from football practice to check on the game's progress. 'Who's winning?' he asked.

'She is,' Donna pointed at Nicola. It was Donna's turn next. When she landed on Community Chest she decided she'd had enough for one day and they should all go to Frank's fish and chip shop. Nicola wasn't keen as she'd already had an enormous tea at home and Cas said he was off home soon. Donna teased him, 'Ah, got to be a good lickle boy and go to beddybyes, has he?'

Nicola sprang to his defence. 'That's not fair Donna. Brad wants them all fighting fit for the match tomorrow.' But Donna felt like teasing Cas and wouldn't let up. She started teasing him about his hair and even easy-going Cas got angry. Donna's response was to link arms with Jan. 'Right, come on Jan, if these two wet wellies won't. I'll show you where they make the best chips in Newcastle.'

Nicola couldn't hide her indignation. 'Hang on, Jan's with me.' Donna craftily pointed out that no one was stopping Nicola from coming and besides, she said, giving Jan a particularly flirtatious look, 'He's a free agent, aren't you Jan?'

There was a long moment as both girls waited for Jan to make his decision. Finally he stood up, a little shamefaced, and turned to Nicola. 'I'll see you tomorrow, Nicola.'

'Don't piggin' bother!' she replied, close to tears as a triumphant Donna walked out arm in arm with Jan.

Donna was still high from her triumph when they walked into Frank's place. It hadn't occurred to her to waste time worrying about how Nicola might be feeling, *she* was on top of the world. Her spirits were only slightly dampened when she caught sight of Gill and Winston eating at a table in the corner.

'Oh heck, not them two.' She pulled a face at Jan who wondered what was so wrong with them. Donna explained that they were both apes. They didn't have any style, not that many lads round Newcastle did. When Jan told her he wasn't sure what she meant by this 'style', Donna turned to him with her most seductive smile. 'I mean like you, Jan. You're not a silly kid like them. You know how to go on.'

Jan thought about this and then decided this was because he was older and had lived in several different places. Donna, in return, confided that *she* was more mature than most of the girls she hung around with, adding slyly, 'I mean Nicola's very nice but she's not exactly *sophisticated*, is she?'

Satisfied that she'd planted and watered the seed of dissatisfaction in Jan's mind, she turned her attention to the menu chalked on the board behind the counter.

Back at the Grove, the football practice had finished and Brad and the rest of the boys trailed across the room to get some cold drinks. They were immediately chased out again by an irate Mary who'd just cleaned the floor. Standing in the doorway, Brad took off his boots and walked over to Alison. 'Coming to support us tomorrow?'

'Of course,' Alison told him.

Then, with a touch of mischief, Brad added, 'Nice to know you'll be there, cheering me on.' When Alison corrected him, saying she was coming to cheer the *team* on, he grinned. 'Naturally.' Then, 'When are you going to stop fighting it, Bright Eyes?' he asked. Alison told Brad she didn't know what he meant and walked away. She knew exactly what he meant but she didn't know what on earth to do about it.

Wise old Mary O'Malley had been listening to all this. 'Don't push her, pet. It's the worst thing you can do,' she advised.

Uncharacteristically dropping his guard for a moment, Brad told her, 'I know. But I love the girl, Mary. And she loves Mike, or thinks she does. Right little mess all round, isn't it?' With a sad smile he went out to join the boys.

* * *

'Thank heaven it isn't pouring buckets,' Brad thought as he peered through the bedroom curtains the following morning. He had enough to worry about without a muddy, rainy football pitch to contend with. And the morning stayed warm and bright as kick-off time drew near.

The Byker Grove team were in fighting spirit and had convinced themselves that they were going to win. Winston, always ready to make a few extra quid, wanted to take bets until Ian pointed out scornfully, 'Us lot are hardly going to bet on Denton Burn winning, are we, you wally?'

The Byker Grove supporters had turned out in force to cheer their team on. Everyone from Mary O'Malley to little Debbie Dobson, Nicola's sister, was there sporting the crêpe paper rosettes Winston had been busily flogging.

Debbie stood by her big sister scanning the crowd. 'So where's this amazing new lad then Nic?' For the millionth time Nicola wished she'd kept her mouth shut at home. Whenever she mentioned anything in front of her kid sisters she always regretted it.

'I never said he was amazing. And don't call me Nic,' she snapped. Suddenly Debbie caught sight of Donna who had arrived with her arm firmly wrapped around Jan's waist. 'Who's that yummy boy she's with?' Debbie wanted to know. A feeble 'Just somebody' was all Nicola could manage in reply. Debbie, used to the traumas of her sister's relationship with Donna, was quick to catch on. 'You two haven't fallen out again?' Nicola had had enough by this time, told Debbie it was none of her business, and wandered off, desperate to escape her busybody kid sister's questions.

Meanwhile Donna had spotted her dad in the crowd and was dying to introduce this handsome hunk to him.

And she had to admit she wanted to show him off to Lisa too. She guided him over to where they were standing chatting in the crowd. 'Dad, this is Jan, Jan, this is me dad.'

They exchanged hello's, then Jan stook looking awkwardly at Lisa, waiting to be introduced to her too. Finally Mr Bell asked, 'Aren't you going to introduce Lisa?'

'Oh yeah, I forgot,' Donna replied, lying. 'Lisa,' she muttered and immediately drifted off into the crowd again with Jan. Lisa sighed and told Jim that it was no use, she had tried but Donna was worse than ever. Jim could only reply that she should take no notice, his daughter would come round eventually. He wished he could sound more convincing, even Lisa hadn't seen Donna at her *most* stubborn.

'Rosettes, get your colours here, support your team . . .' Winston was still doing a roaring trade with his rosettes, flogging them to loyal Grove supporters. Suddenly he spotted Spuggie who had her back to him. 'Spuggie,' he called out, surprised at how pleased he was to see her. As she turned round to find out who was shouting her name, his mouth fell open in shock. Spuggie was wearing a huge Denton Burn rosette.

'What's that you've got on? Looks like a blimmin' cabbage! Winston couldn't believe that she'd really turned traitor.

'I'm doing what you said, Winston. I'm supporting my team,' Spuggie told him sweetly.

'Piggin' traitor,' Winston muttered before he sped off to spread the news to the rest of the Grove gang. Spuggie stood for a moment looking uncertain and more than a little upset. Then she turned her back on the disappearing Winston and marched away to her new friends.

41

Kick-off time was approaching. The two teams trooped onto the pitch, each with cheers and shouts of encouragement from their supporters. A coin was tossed and the match began. So did the chanting.

'Who do we hate?'

'Denton Burn.'

'Who's going to win?'

'The Grove.'

'Who's rubbish?'

'The Denton Burners.'

'Who's the best?'

'Byker Byker Byker Groooooove!'

As the match got underway, Debbie Dobson turned to Spuggie who was standing next to her. 'I thought you went to the Grove?' she said eyeing Spuggie's rosette with a puzzled look.

'I used to,' was the abrupt reply. Further interrogation was getting Debbie nowhere when a couple of the Denton Burn gang walked past. 'Hiya Kirstie,' one of them greeted Spuggie. Winston, who was hanging around nearby, burst out laughing. '*Kirstie*?' he repeated incredulously.

Spuggie turned to him with as much haughtiness as she could muster, 'What's so hilarious? It's my name.'

'Nobody flippin' calls you Kirstie.' Winston was still laughing.

'They do now.' Spuggie replied firmly. 'Not that it's anything to do with you.'

Elsewhere in the crowd, Donna was watching Jan who kept on glancing over to where Nicola was standing. She told him he needn't feel bad, it wasn't as though they'd been going out together. But Jan hadn't forgotten how kind Nicola had been when he didn't know anybody.

Wondering how to shake him out of feeling guilty, Donna suddenly saw her mother arrive on the scene.

Any problems with Jan immediately disappeared in the light of this one – Polly, Jim *and* Lisa together in the same place. Flippin' heck. She whispered to Jan that she had to go somewhere but she'd be back in a couple of minutes and then shot off to talk to her mother.

'Mum, what're you doing here?' she asked nervously. Polly said she'd come to cheer Donna's mates on. 'I used to get on very well with your gang in the old days,' she reminded her daughter. Then she asked whether the tall, blond handsome lad was Donna's new man. When Donna said he was, she laughed. 'You've certainly inherited your mum's good taste.'

Donna wasn't overly concerned about Jan at that moment. 'Only me dad's here,' she told her mum awkwardly. Polly scanned the crowd. It didn't take her long to pick out Jim standing next to Lisa. She narrowed her eyes. 'Who's the blonde next to him? She can't be his girlfriend surely, she's much too young?'

Donna swallowed hard and decided to lie. 'Oh her, she's Brad's girlfriend. He helps out at the Grove and he coached the team.' She pointed him out to her mother, hoping she'd successfully changed the subject but Polly was determined. 'Your dad's bit of stuff not come along, then?' Donna assured her that she wasn't at the match, while wondering what on earth she'd say when her mum found out. She decided she'd deal with that one when it happened. But worse was yet to come, now Polly wanted to go over and say hello to Jim. What the heck could she tell her? She fished around for something brilliant to say. In the end the best she could do was to tell her mum it would be great if she and Jim got together for a natter but not in public, with everyone watching.

She held her breath while her mother thought about it, then almost sighed with relief when Polly finally agreed with her. 'Perhaps you're right.' Then she added

43

dreamily, 'A quiet drink somewhere on our own would be nice.'

'Goooooool!' The Denton Burn crowd whooped and shouted. Their team had scored a goal in the first five minutes. Spuggie, standing with the rest of the Denton Burn gang, deliberately cheered loudest of all. The Byker Grovers turned to look at her with disgust but she glared back at them defiantly.

'Shut it Spuggie!' Winston shouted across at her.

'What's his problem?' One of the Denton Burners asked. Spuggie explained that they didn't like her being with them because she'd been to the Grove 'once or twice'. The Denton Burn gang were taken aback to hear this. You simply didn't do that. You went to one or the other club but never *both*. 'What's it like?' they asked curiously.

'Rubbish,' Spuggie replied without conviction. 'Denton Burn's much better.' Spuggie was lying, she missed the Grove a lot but no way was she going to let on to *them*.

Alison wasn't overly surprised to see Mike wander up, obviously looking for her. He'd started to ask a lot more questions about the Grove and he'd turned up at least twice since Donna's party to pick her up. It was beginning to get on her nerves. She felt as though she was being spied on.

'Hi, how're we doing?' Mike asked.

'Down one nil,' Alison replied, without much warmth. She knew she was being unfair. Mike was perfectly entitled to come along and support the kids if he wanted to. But that wasn't why he was there.

'You're keen on him, aren't you?' Mike's question came like a bolt of lightning out of the blue. Then she realised that she'd even been watching Brad whilst Mike had been standing next to her.

44

'Of course not,' she said, flustered. 'We work together, that's all.' But Mike wasn't going to be fobbed off that easily. He reminded Alison that one thing they'd never done was lie to one another. Alison felt trapped. She didn't want to lie to Mike but she wasn't ready to say anything yet until she'd sorted out her feelings. Stalling for time, she said, 'If there was anything wrong I'd tell you.' Mike still wasn't convinced but he knew he couldn't push it any further – for now.

Ten minutes into the second half there was another roar from the Denton Burn supporters as their team scored another goal. The Byker Grove gang let out an equally loud groan. Two goals down. The Byker team needed to get their act together – and fast.

'What was your mam doing here?' Jim Bell was standing with his daughter as Lisa chatted to Jan. Donna told him that Polly was just passing, then added that she didn't think he'd want her to stop, not with Lisa there. Her dad didn't see the problem – after all he and her mother *were* divorced. Deciding that now was as good a time as any, Donna told her dad that Polly wanted to go out for a drink with him. But he didn't think that was a good idea at all.

'Why not?' Donna demanded to know. 'I s'pose cos *she'd* throw a wobbler. Just because she's all jealous and possessive doesn't mean you can't be friends with me mam.'

Jim remained calm but firm. 'Lisa isn't jealous. Or possessive.' That did it as far as Donna was concerned. She couldn't bear to hear her dad defending Lisa.

'She thinks she owns you,' Donna burst out. 'I heard her talking to her pals about you that night at the fashion show.' Jim was about to lose his temper with his daughter, something he rarely did. He told Donna that he wouldn't have her talking about Lisa that way. 'She's a lovely girl and she's very fond of you.'

'Well I'm not very fond of her! She's only after you because she thinks you've got money,' were Donna's final words before she dragged Jan away from Lisa, then stumped off angrily. She hated being on the wrong side of her dad especially where *she* was concerned. Donna needed to win Jim over to her way of thinking if he and her mum were ever to get back together again.

The game ended without another goal being scored either by Denton Burn or Byker Grove. The jubilant Denton Burners did everything they could to rub in their two nil victory. The Byker Grove gang did their best to ignore it but it wasn't easy. Their team joined them and people began drifting off home for lunch.

Spuggie stood alone, watching wistfully as the Byker Grove group headed off towards the Grove. Alison and Mike were about to leave too when Alison spotted Spuggie. Telling Mike she'd catch up with him in a minute, she wandered over.

'All by yourself, Spuggie?' she asked gently. Spuggie replied that Duncan was meant to come but he hadn't turned up.

'Come back with us then,' Alison suggested in a deliberately casual manner. Spuggie was clearly tempted and was on the verge of saying she would when Winston and Speedy wandered by.

'Traitor! Blackleg! Fink!' Winston shouted at her as he walked past. Alison told him to shut up but it was too late, the damage was done.

'No chance,' she told Alison with a determined stare. Alison knew Spuggie well enough to realise that there was no changing her mind there and then. She said goodbye and left Spuggie, the last lonely little figure on the pitch.

*　　*　　*

The respectable middle-class Volvo looked distinctly out of place in this run down street full of dilapidated houses. Mr Warner, Julie's father, read the house numbers as he drove slowly along the road. Finally he found number 35, the one he'd been looking for. He stopped the car, switched off the engine and looked out at the grotty, crumbling facade of the house where Gill lived. Shaking his head, he got out of the car. How could his daughter be mixing with someone who lived in a place like this?

Julie spotted him walking down the path as she and Gill were coming along the road from the football match. She ran up to him. 'Dad! What are you doing here?' Her father said simply, 'Can we go inside?' Julie looked at Gill who shrugged, and led the way to his room.

As they walked along the hallway, Gill hoped that at least he'd left it in a reasonable state. He knew Julie's dad thought he was a bit of a yob, he didn't want him thinking he was a slob as well. Thankfully he *had* made a reasonably good job of tidying up before he'd left for the football match. He smiled, he also had Julie to thank. She was forever tidying up.

Julie repeated her question. 'Dad, what *are* you doing here?'

'I wanted a word with . . .' Mr Warner couldn't quite bring himself to say Gill's name.

'Gill?' Julie enquired, making her father suffer. She wanted to know what about but Gill interrupted, 'I think I can guess.' Mr Warner then launched into the speech he'd been preparing ever since he'd decided to come and find Julie and tackle Gill head on. He told Gill that someday he might have kids of his own, daughters perhaps.

'And I'll want blokes to treat 'em with respect, right?'

Gill could see where Julie's father was heading before he'd got there. He turned to Mr Warner, 'I daresay this'll be a surprise to you, coming from a yob like me. But I *do* respect Julie.' Julie backed him up immediately, telling her father in no uncertain terms that *he* was the one who didn't respect her, spying on her the way he had.

Mr Warner could see all his well-rehearsed arguments falling to pieces as his daughter defended this young lout. Feeling horribly inadequate to deal with the situation, he played his final card, 'Apart from anything else, what do you think your mother would say if she saw you in a place like this?'

Julie replied coolly, 'She'd probably have a fit.' Mr Warner looked at this headstrong young woman who used to be his shy little daughter. He was completely at a loss.

The pond was always a good place to come if you wanted to be on your own. Spuggie loved watching the ducks weave their way through the tall reeds. 'Come to think of it,' Spuggie realised, 'I've been on me own a lot these last few weeks.' She'd been to Denton Burn a few times. They were all right but they weren't like the Grove lot. Even if they did tease her, she felt at home there where she knew everyone. Spuggie didn't know what to do, she wasn't going to go back to Denton Burn and she *couldn't* go back to the Grove.

Some kids sped past on roller skates, Debbie Dobson amongst them. Seeing Spuggie she called out 'Hiya' and skated over to her. 'I thought you were going back with the Denton Burn lot,' she said as she wheeled round on her skates.

'Well I didn't,' Spuggie replied glumly. Debbie, who always knew everything, knew that the Denton Burners were having a party to celebrate their two nil victory! and she asked why Spuggie hadn't gone. Spuggie wasn't in the mood for the younger girl's questions and simply said that she couldn't be blowed. Realising that she wasn't going to get rid of Debbie in a hurry, Spuggie sat down by the water's edge. Debbie sat next to her. They sat looking out over the water for a moment before Debbie's next question popped up. 'What's it like there anyway?'

'Really good,' Spuggie said very quickly but not very convincingly. Then, tired of pretending, she admitted, 'No it's not, it's horrible.' Understandably, Debbie wondered why she bothered going then. And, if she hated it so much, why didn't she go back to the Grove?

'I can't,' Spuggie told her wretchedly. 'They'll only say "I told you so" about Denton Burn.' Debbie didn't see that that was a problem at all.

'Big deal,' she said. 'If *I* wanted to go somewhere there's nobody'd stop me.' Spuggie looked over at the determined little girl. Maybe she had a point?

The atmosphere at the Grove was, for once, pretty glum. Nobody was really in the mood to sit around chatting, especially Nicola, who was deliberately keeping her distance from Donna and Jan. Winston was the only one with anything to smile about as he sat at a table counting the profits from the sale of his rosettes and putting the coins in a large brown envelope. Ian, Speedy, Cas and several other lads were sitting round holding a post mortem when Brad walked in.

'If Cas had been half awake he'd never have let Wilson past him for that first goal.' Ian glared at Cas accusingly.

Cas wasn't having any of that. 'You're joking, I didn't stand a chance. We should never have given their winger so much space down the left.'

49

Brad came over to them, having overheard the last two jibes. 'It's not down to any one player,' he told them. 'It's a team failure.' This piece of information did little to lighten their spirits but it did at least stop them from bickering amongst themselves for a few minutes. Brad went to get a cup of tea and Winston wandered up.

'Should have got me dad's mate to give you a few tips.' The others groaned. The last thing they wanted to hear about was one of Winston's dad's shady mates. Only Speedy was curious enough to ask, 'Who's that then?'

When Winston replied, 'Gazza Gascoigne', the famous ex-Newcastle United player, the boys nearly fell off their chairs laughing. Winston kept his dignity and simply repeated that his dad was a personal friend of the football hero and why shouldn't he be? Gazza was entitled to have friends, he wasn't a flippin' alien from outer space. But the others weren't having any of it. They'd needed a good laugh after the disastrous match and now they were having one. Winston walked away trying to look as though he wasn't bothered.

Outside the Grove, Spuggie walked up to the gateway and stood hesitantly looking down the drive. Mary O'Malley came up behind her, she'd brought some of her home-baked cakes for the kids. They didn't ever get eaten – they were as heavy as lead – but the kids never let on.

'Hello pet, enjoy the game did you?' Mary asked Spuggie casually as though she'd never been away from the Grove.

Spuggie shrugged and looked uncertain, 'It was all right.' Mary stayed and chatted a couple of minutes longer. She asked how her brother Fraser was and whether she was having a good time. Spuggie's response of 'Yeah, fantastic,' was obviously untrue but Mary didn't push her. 'That's the ticket,' she told Spuggie as she headed up the path to the Grove to deposit her goodies. Spuggie stayed rooted uncertainly to the spot.

Over in a corner of the general room, Gill and Brad were having a chat together. Gill admired Brad, he was cool and had style like his own older brother, the Man. He had secretly hero-worshipped the Man whilst they'd lived at home together. Then he'd gone off to London, got himself a great job, a posh pad, an ace car, and no doubt dozens of birds. Yeah, Brad definitely reminded him of the Man, bet he had lots of women too.

'How's the YTS thing going?' Brad was asking.

'Horrible,' Gill answered truthfully. Brad said surely it couldn't be *that* bad but Gill made it plain that it was. He explained that he didn't mind the hard graft 'But a blimmin' robot could do what I do.' Sympathetically, Brad asked Gill what he'd really *like* to do. That wasn't something he'd considered recently. It all seemed to be about what was available and who would have him. But he didn't have to think long, there had always been one thing he'd loved working with.

'Cars,' he told Brad without hesitation.

'Driving them?' Brad asked. Gill agreed that that was part of it. But what he really wanted to do was work on classy cars. 'Stuff that purrs along at a ton and you think you're moving at fifty.' Brad suggested that Gill tried to get on a training scheme but he'd already done that. 'No chance.'

Alison walked into the room and Brad stood up. But before he went over to her, he gave Gill one last piece of advice, 'Don't give up so easily. If it's worth doing, it's worth making some effort for.' He left the younger lad deep in thought.

'Mike's around a lot lately.' Brad tried to make it

sound like a casual statement but they both knew what he meant. Alison came up with some lame reason but Brad wasn't buying it.

'Is it because he's keeping an eye on me?' he suggested. Alison told Brad he was being ridiculous but he persisted. He wanted to know what Mike had been saying and wouldn't give up.

Finally, after much pestering, Alison confessed, 'He thinks I'm keen on you.'

'And are you?' Brad asked bluntly. Alison had had enough. Mike was constantly questioning her at home these days and now Brad wouldn't let up. Between the two of them they were driving her crazy.

Brad stuck to his guns. 'It's a simple question,' he told her. Alison was beginning to look quite panic-stricken.

'I can't answer it. Don't make me. I don't *know*,' she virtually shouted as she hurried out of the room.

Donna was standing alone, looking thoughtful. She wasn't going to give Jan up but she hated falling out with Nicola who was, after all, her best mate. And she had enough sense to know that Nicola wasn't going to be the one to make up. She crossed over to the corner of the room where Nicola was sitting with some other girls.

'What's up with you?' Donna asked. As if she didn't know. But she had to start somewhere. Nicola ignored her. Donna repeated her question. Still no reply. This was too much for Donna. 'What did I do that's so terrible?' she blurted out. 'He wasn't your blimmin' boyfriend.'

Jan, who'd been getting a Coke, hurried over when he realised the argument was over him. 'Nicola, Donna . . .' He looked upset. 'I don't mean to cause trouble.' Nicola told him not to worry, he hadn't done anything, it was *her* who did nothing but. Donna wasn't taking that lying down and was about to defend herself when Nicola jumped in.

'She's just like her mum,' Nicola told Jan with unusual bitterness. 'Has to have every feller she sees.' Donna stood looking at her, for once gobsmacked.

Then, after a moment, she got over the shock. 'You leave my mam out of it!' she shouted at Nicola.

'Why should I?' Nicola replied, 'She's a blimmin' flirt and everyone knows it. They all used to talk about her . . .' That was more than Donna could stand. She slapped Nicola across the face, hard. And, half-frightened by what she'd just done, she left the room determined that no one would see how upset she was.

As Donna swept down the hallway she barely noticed Spuggie, standing even more uncertainly than she had at the bottom of the path. Spuggie watched Donna disappear, squared her shoulders, stuck her head in the air and marched inside.

The stunned silence which followed Donna's dramatic exit was eventually broken by the sound of Spuggie coughing loudly. She couldn't bear to have actually walked into the room without anyone noticing she was there.

Winston was the first to comment. 'Well, well. Look what the wind's blown in.'

When she felt that most eyes were upon her, Spuggie announced, 'As it happens, I've got some very important news.' Seeing that no one was about to take her seriously, she continued hurriedly, all in one breath, 'They're growing prize leeks and they're going to enter them for the Garden Festival and they're going to win a hundred pounds.'

The others finally extracted from the excited Spuggie that she was talking about Denton Burn. She delivered her final call to battle. 'And they said it's no use the

Grove doing it because they couldn't grow mould on a piece of cheese.' That was enough. All previous fights were temporarily forgotten as Nicola turned to the others with a glint in her eye.

'Are we going to let the Denton Burn wallies get away with that?'

She was met with a loud chorus of, 'No we're blimmin' not!'

The bell rang and rang. Donna tried knocking on the door, then ringing once again but there was no reply. She was in tears as she hammered furiously on her mother's front door. 'Mam! It's me, Mam! I need to see you . . . Mam?' Finally it dawned on her that Polly wasn't there. Somehow her mother was always missing when she needed her most. A very dejected Donna turned away and walked slowly down the street.

CHAPTER THREE

Donna was going to miss the Metro if she didn't hurry. Rushing along the platform in front of her, she saw Julie and her friend Hayley Oduru. They were also running to catch the train. 'Hiya!' she shouted out, as she caught up with them. She'd never liked Julie but, things being the way they were, she couldn't afford to be too choosy about her friends. 'Where're you going?' she asked.

'Shopping,' came the rather abrupt reply from Hayley. She'd never had much time for Donna either. Donna said she was going shopping as well and wondered if they were looking for anything special. Julie told her they were just mooching.

'I'll mooch with you,' Donna told them decisively. She always found a way of getting what she wanted.

Inside the Metro Centre, the three of them paused to stare at a weird and wonderful window display outside a boutique. Hayley grabbed hold of Julie's hand. 'Come on,' she urged. Julie wasn't sure but then Hayley reminded her of their real reason for coming shopping – to change Julie's image. Donna's sarcastic snigger was all Julie needed to propel her towards the clothes rails.

She'd soon chosen several items and disappeared to try them on. A few minutes later the cubicle curtain parted slowly near the top and Julie's worried-looking face appeared. 'I can't come out,' she told the other two girls.

'Why? Got your zip stuck?' Donna asked. Julie said no, she just looked too ridiculous, but eventually they coaxed her out.

Hayley's first comment was 'Wow'. Julie stood in front of her in black leather mini skirt laced up the sides and black leather biker jacket with fishnet tights and black ankle boots.

Donna was less enthusiastic. 'I think she looks a right tater.' Secretly she thought Julie looked great too but she wasn't going to give her the satisfaction. Hayley tried to persuade Julie to buy the gear but she laughed, said she wasn't convinced, and went back into the cubicle to peel it all off again.

The boys were kicking a football around when Mr Dobson, Nicola's dad, arrived. Nobody had been in the mood to practise seriously since the disastrous match but it hadn't put them off footie altogether. 'Hey up, Mr Leek himself,' Cas commented with a smirk as they carried on dribbling the ball. Nicola's dad soon came over and rounded them up to go and have a look at the proposed leek patch. Being a champion leek grower himself, what he saw didn't impress him. 'This land's not been dug over since Adam was a lad.'

Winston didn't see that as a problem. 'All it needs is a bit of muscle power. I can organise that.' The other boys groaned. They knew Winston too well. That meant him doing the bossing around and *them* doing the dirty work.

Alan Dobson explained to the growing crowd that their competitors had an advantage over them because they'd started preparing their trenches months ago. However everyone was still determined to have a go. Then Mr Dobson suddenly spotted another patch a short distance away and went over to examine the soil. 'Now this is more like it. Soil's in good condition, been looked after this has.' Duncan tried to interrupt but everyone was getting carried away with Mr Dobson's enthusiasm.

'Right then lads, X marks the spot.' Cas was all set to go and find a spade when Winston suddenly remembered, 'Isn't that Spuggie's patch?'

Duncan breathlessly confirmed what he'd been trying to tell them all earlier. 'Yep. She's going to kill us.'

Nevertheless, preparation for the leeks was soon in full swing. Alan Dobson was supervising with his self-nominated assistant Winston. Ian, Speedy and Cas were digging the leek trenches, while Nicola and the Grove's new assistant, Gwen, heaved sacks of manure and fertiliser out of Mr Dobson's van. Nicola muttered something about lugging heavy sacks around being man's work, only to hear Ian mutter about equality between men and women. If she *really* wanted to do some heavy duty work, he said, why didn't she try digging?

Nicola was wondering if it was all worth it anyhow. 'We don't really stand a chance. There's people been growing leeks round here for years.' Gwen, who seemed pretty square and serious, said that in her opinion beating a rival wasn't the point. Winston couldn't understand this at all. Weren't they only doing it to show Denton Burn a thing or two? And of course for the hundred quid.

Never too far away from the action, Spuggie walked up the Grove path with her new friend, fourteen-year-old Kelly, who had recently moved into town. Kelly's dad had worked on a farm but he'd been made redundant. He'd come to the city to find work which Kelly was delighted about – she was bored stiff out in the country. But her parents weren't so chuffed, especially her dad. He hated living in town. She and Winston had met on the Byker Grove camping trip last spring.

Winston saw them both coming, waved at Kelly and whistled to Spuggie, 'Here, Spug.'

'I'm not a blimmin' dog,' she yelled back. 'What do you want?'

For once Winston came running over to *her*, dragging Speedy along with him. 'Got a job for you,' he told Spuggie. She eyed him suspiciously. Winston's 'jobs' tended to turn into disasters and usually paid next to nothing.

'How much?' Spuggie got straight to the point. Winston explained that it wasn't *that* kind of job. 'We want you to go back to Denton Burn,' he said.

Spuggie's response was short and sharp. 'Not blimmin' likely.' At this point Speedy, who'd been brought along to back Winston up, joined in the persuading. 'We need you to act as a spy,' he explained. 'Like in war films,' he added as if she didn't know what a spy was. Spuggie was slightly more intrigued now they put it like that. Being a spy had an edge of excitement and adventure to it. Realising they were making progress, Winston and Speedy told her they needed her to find out what Denton Burn were doing with their leeks, what fertiliser they were using and that sort of thing.

'They think you're still one of them,' Winston said.

'Please Spuggie, you're the only one who can do it?' Speedy pleaded.

The thought of being the heroine of Byker Grove was rapidly becoming very appealing.

Kelly suddenly looked over to where the rest of the gang were busy digging in the distance. She turned to Spuggie, sounding confused. 'I thought that was your patch?' 'Where?' Spuggie asked and looked over to where Kelly was pointing. Saying nothing, she marched over and found Duncan busy shovelling soil with the others. He stopped dead in his tracks, a look of fear on his face. 'I did try to stop 'em Spuggie. Honest,' he muttered feebly in his defence. In reply Spuggie thumped him across the chest and silently walked off towards the Grove.

A few minutes later Nicola came in to get a cup of tea for her dad. 'Thirsty work is leek work,' he always told Nicola, which usually meant that he wanted her to make him some tea. She went over to her gran, Mary, and ordered one.

'That man's obsessed with his leeks,' Mary grumbled. 'I don't know how your mam puts up with it.'

'She'd sooner he spent his time with a leek than another woman,' Nicola grinned cheekily, knowing she was shocking her gran. Then she left for the leek patch, cup of tea in hand.

On her way out she was surprised to see Polly. 'Nicola, pet, remember me?' she asked. Of course she did. Who could ever forget Polly Bell once they'd met her? Nicola told Polly that Donna wasn't there but it seemed she already knew that. She didn't want to see her daughter, it was Nicola she'd come to see. 'Can I have a word, pet? In private, like.' Nicola nodded, handed her dad's cup of tea to Kelly to take to him, and left the Grove with Polly.

It was a glorious sunny day outside but Nicola wasn't enjoying it one bit. She felt embarrassed being with Polly after everything she'd said about her. Nicola was sure that Donna hadn't told her mum but even so, she'd still been rude about her. And, if the truth were known, she liked Polly. You couldn't help liking Polly. She was silly and scatty and a flirt it was true, not the way Nicola wanted *her* mum to be at all. But she was also good-hearted, as she was proving now.

'I don't want to see you falling out,' she told Nicola. 'Not over a lad you'll have forgotten in a couple of months.' Nicola pointed out that Donna had started it, to which Polly replied, 'Well, maybe you're the one that can finish it.' Then she let Nicola into her little secret – a party she was organising for Donna at her flat that night.

'She only had one last week!' Nicola exclaimed. But Polly explained that that was her dad's treat, she wanted to do one of her own. She'd asked all Donna's friends to come, 'Most of all, pet, I want you to be there. Please say you will?'

Flippin' heck, thought Nicola. What's a girl to do?

Meanwhile Duncan was recovering from his ordeal by standing at the snack bar counter stuffing crisps into his mouth as fast as he could. He saw Spuggie coming over and wondered if there was anywhere he could hide but it was too late.

'Tried to stop 'em? You were blimmin' helping 'em,' she accused him indignantly.

Duncan tried to defend himself once again. 'Spuggie, I did try to . . .' But Spuggie didn't want to hear.

'I'm not speaking to you,' she told Duncan and was about to walk off still in a huff when Mary, who'd overheard the conversation, came to their side of the counter. Gently she told Spuggie that it wasn't Duncan's fault. Then she delivered her winning stroke.

'Just think, when they win the prize it'll all be down to you. They said they'd not stand a chance if it wasn't for Spuggie's patch.' Spuggie had to admit that she liked the sound of that but she wasn't about to let go of her grumpy mood that quickly.

'Who said?' she asked suspiciously.

'Everybody,' Mary replied and then went about her washing-up, leaving Spuggie to decide whether she was still angry or whether she'd prefer to be the Byker Grove heroine after all.

Later that day the gang still hadn't given up on Spuggie being their spy. Duncan was having a go at her now.

'So are you going to be the spy?' he asked. It occurred to Spuggie that this meant a lot to the gang. She suddenly realised she was in a position of power and she was enjoying it. 'Might,' she replied. But Duncan immediately put the dampers on any thrill she might have felt at taking on the assignment. 'If you get caught they'll torture you. That's what they do with spies,' he said ghoulishly. Spuggie looked at him. She wasn't sure whether he was being serious or not.

They walked over to the leek patch where trenches had now been dug but nothing had yet been planted. Hayley joined them. 'Is that it?' she asked disappointed. Cas was indignant. 'What d'you mean, is that it?' He told her they'd been breaking their backs for an hour to get the trenches looking the way they did. Hayley still wasn't impressed. 'Not much to see, is there?'

Meanwhile Ian's little brother Sammy was scrabbling around in the dirt, as usual. Ian was often lumbered with taking Sammy and Sally, his sister who was even younger, to the Grove. Coming from a one-parent family with his mum working full time there was often no one except Ian to look after the little ones. He'd grown used to his role as full-time unpaid babysitter and mostly accepted it without much moaning. But there were times when he got totally fed up with the kids. Like now. They'd been playing in the leek trench all afternoon and he knew his mum would go potty when he took them home filthy.

Sammy had found something in the soil. He picked it up and handed it to his big brother who he adored. Ian told him to put it down and to stop getting so mucky but Cas saw what he was holding and took it from him.

'Blimmin' heck,' he said. Julie peered over to see what he was so excited about.

'It's a bit of Roman pottery,' she told everyone. She'd just done the Roman Empire in history and had seen lots of photographs of similar pieces of pottery. Winston's eyes lit up. 'Is it worth anything?' he asked hopefully. Everyone groaned. If Winston found a whole dinosaur skeleton in his back garden his first question would be how much money he could get for it. Julie dashed his hopes by telling him that there was Roman pottery buried all round the area, this was nothing special. Winston was still caught up in fantasies of buried treasure though and suggested that there might be more stuff around, perhaps even something that was dead valuable.

Speedy picked up something else he'd just seen lying on top of the soil. Beady-eyed Winston asked him what he'd found.

'Nothing,' Speedy answered, about to throw it away. 'Just an old bottle top.' But Winston was too quick and wrestled the object out of his hands. He scraped the dirt off it and shouted excitedly, 'Blimmin' heck, ain't no bottle top, man. That's a gold coin!'

Ian told him he was bonkers but Winston insisted he was right. Spuggie was dying to have a look. She tried to grab the coin from Winston but he pushed her out of the way.

Speedy, who'd been looking thoughtful for the last couple of minutes, suddenly interrupted. 'The Professor'd know if it was gold.' Everyone turned to look at him. Who on earth was he talking about? Speedy told them about a boy who'd come to live at his foster home who was 'dead clever, he knows all about that Roman stuff, and everything.' Cas was all for giving the coin to Speedy for this lad to check out but Winston wasn't having that.

'No he's blimmin' not. It might be worth a fortune that. Tell him to come down here.' Everyone agreed.

In the meantime Hayley thought it would be a good idea to remove the coin from Winston's hot little hand and give it to Geoff to lock up in the office. Reluctantly, Winston had to agree.

*　　*　　*

Donna surveyed her reflection in the mirror. Not bad at all, though she said so herself. She'd had her hair cut in a new style and she thought it was a definite improvement. Lisa was calling her from downstairs.

'Donna! Your boyfriend's here!'

She took one last look in the mirror, then raced down the stairs, eager to get Jan's verdict on her hair and ignoring Lisa as she stood posing for him.

'Well? What do you think?' she asked. Jan didn't know what to say. 'What about?' he said finally. Impatiently Donna pointed out her newly coiffed hair, hoping that Jan would then heap the compliments on her. But no. 'It's very nice,' was all he would say.

'I'd have settled for amazing, knockout, sensational,' she replied as she pulled Jan through the bar past Lisa and her dad, 'but very nice will do.' Donna said goodbye to her father as they headed for the front door, once again completely ignoring Lisa.

Jim Bell followed them to the doorway to ask Donna whether they were off down the Grove. She was pleased to be able to tell him that they were going to her mum's for tea. 'It'll be better than that horrible muck Lisa makes,' she added spitefully. Mr Bell told his daughter off sharply. Lisa often went out of her way to cook meals that Donna liked and she knew it.

'Well she needn't bother,' was Donna's parting shot as she left the Byker Arms.

Her dad stood watching her and her latest flame walk off down the road and felt completely at a loss. He loved his daughter to pieces, was proud of her independent spirit and her strength of mind. But she was driving him potty over Lisa. When would she accept that this woman was a part of his life, someone he cared a lot about? He sadly suspected that she never would.

Jan was quiet for the first few minutes of the journey.

He seemed to be deep in thought. Finally he turned hesitantly to Donna. 'I think perhaps you are a little unkind to Lisa,' he said. Donna was shocked. Firstly she no longer noticed how nasty she was being to her dad's bit of stuff and secondly she was shocked to hear Jan criticise her. She started to worry. Did that mean that he didn't like her any more because of the way she talked to Lisa? If that cow had lost her a boyfriend as well as everything else . . .

Donna leapt to her own defence. 'She's a dumb blonde, wraps all you men round her little finger.' Jan wasn't convinced, he told her that he thought Lisa wanted to be her friend. But she remained as stubborn as ever – there was no way she was *ever* going to be Lisa's friend. Forget it.

They arrived at Polly's flat and Donna was slightly surprised to see how dressed up her mum was. She'd put on a rather sexy low-cut cocktail type dress together with high-heeled shoes and she was wearing one of her more outrageous pairs of earrings. But Donna was used to her mother's quirkiness by now so she thought little of it. She kissed her mum 'hello' and Polly told her to go on into the living room.

As she and Jan entered the darkened room, Polly switched on the lights to reveal a room full of Donna's mates, piles of sandwiches, crisps and bottles of cold drinks and booze together with a jug of punch.

'Surprise, surprise!' they all yelled. For once Donna was lost for words. She stood there open-mouthed and finally managed to ask, 'Mam! What's all this?' Polly told her it was to celebrate the two of them being friends again and gave her a big hug. Donna was overwhelmed, especially when she saw how many of her pals had turned up. She looked around the room quickly – except for one. Nicola Dobson wasn't going to spoil this party for her, no way. She'd still have a brill time even if her ex-best friend wasn't there.

Polly asked for some help with pouring the drinks and it was then that Gill spied the bottles of vodka, gin, rum and whisky. 'She ain't kidding when she says drinks,' he muttered to Cas. 'Have you clocked that lot?' Overhearing this, Polly said that she didn't mind the older lads having a sip or two of something stronger but there were also soft drinks in cans. The boys couldn't believe their luck.

Back at the Grove, the new helper, Gwen, stared glumly into her tea. Mary came in, fastening up her coat ready to leave. She looked over at Gwen knowingly and then wandered over to her. 'I shan't be sorry to get to me bed tonight,' she said to break the ice. Gwen smiled and said she'd heard that Mary had been ill and wondered if she should have come back to work so soon. Mary explained that she'd been feeling sorry for Geoff, what with Alison being on holiday.

'*You're* not finding it too easy, are you?' she said. Gwen looked up, surprised that anyone should have noticed, particularly Mary who always seemed to be chatting or gossiping.

'I don't know. I'm not very good at getting through to them,' Gwen admitted ruefully. Taking a moment to sit down, as she was still feeling tired from her illness, Mary explained that the kids didn't want a teacher, 'They get enough of that at school. Be more of an older sister,' she suggested. The advice was spot on, and Gwen knew it. Funny how the most unlikely people could often turn out to be the wisest. She'd dismissed Mary O'Malley as a nosy old woman up till now.

'Give it a chance, pet, you've barely been here a week,' Mary said as she got up to go but Gwen was deep in thought, mulling over what she'd just been told. She smiled absently at the older woman.

'And pet?' Gwen looked up this time. 'Cheer up, eh?'

Donna's party was going a bomb. Some of the kids were snogging in corners, others were dancing with one another, and a crowd of them were gathered round the buffet table munching what was left of the sandwiches and crisps. Donna looked over at Cas and suddenly felt something unusual for her – guilt. Deciding that now was as good a time as any to try and patch things up, she walked over to where he was sitting.

'Didn't think you'd come,' she told him honestly. Cas grinned and said he never missed a good bash especially one where there was so much booze around.

It was now or never. 'Sorry if I was a bit rotten to you.' This was the closest Donna would ever come to a full-blown apology.

'A bit rotten? You blimmin' dumped me!' Cas teased her good-naturedly. Feeling embarrassed at having this pointed out so blatantly, all Donna could do was apologise again.

But it turned out that Cas didn't really mind anyway. After all 'It's not cool to get tied down at our age,' he told Donna who felt relieved that at least *one* friendship seemed to be on the mend. She took his hand and led him to the least crowded space in the room.

'C'mon,' she smiled. 'Let's dance.'

Over in a corner, Spuggie and Kelly were confiding in each other that they didn't like parties much. They were both feeling left out because they had no one to snog with. Spuggie plucked up the courage to ask Kelly if she'd ever been kissed by a boy. With typical honesty Kelly replied that she had 'sort of' but she didn't like it much. And she told the boy as much. Spuggie was open-mouthed that she would do such a thing. Then Kelly asked her the same question. Looking unusually embarrassed, Spuggie also muttered 'sort of'. But she was a terrible liar and immediately confessed, 'No, not really.'

'I'd worry I wouldn't know where to put me nose,' she added. And in a final attack of honesty she told Kelly, 'Anyway, nobody's tried.'

In the kitchen Gill was helping Polly to mix a drink, and apparently being chatted up by her at the same time. This didn't go unnoticed by Hayley who was sitting with Julie. 'Do you mind her flirting with Gill?' she asked curiously.

'Why should I?' Julie replied, 'He'd never fancy a common thing like her.' Hayley looked at Julie and couldn't decide whether she was being bitchy or simply honest. Either way, Hayley noted, Polly might be common but she certainly had something, 'You can see where Donna gets it from.'

An hour later Kelly had decided that she ought to go home. When Winston offered to walk her back, Spuggie immediately piped up that she'd come too. Winston, feeling a bit merry, had remembered that he quite fancied Kelly. He was hoping for a quick snog on the way back so Spuggie's presence was less than welcome. And he told her so.

'I won't be a goosegob,' Spuggie protested. 'It's not like you'll be doing any snogging, is it?' Winston looked crushed and asked Spuggie how the heck she knew that.

'Kelly told me,' she said bluntly.

Helping herself to another cocktail, Donna looked on as Jan chatted to Julie. Ian came over and shyly asked her if she wanted to dance. She was about to turn him down when she saw Jan doing the same thing with Julie. Giving Ian a flirtatious smile she said, 'I'd love to Ian.'

While they were dancing he said he thought it was a cracking party and that her mum was amazing, always smiling and that. Donna was in the middle of telling him, 'That's us Bell girls, always the life and soul of . . .' when the door opened and Nicola stood there in the doorway. There was a long silence as the two of them looked at one another. Finally Donna shouted over, 'Well, don't just stand there, Dobson's kid, get one of these down you!' She grabbed a cocktail, plonked two straws in and handed the glass to Nicola.

A shaft of sunlight filtered through the curtains the next morning. Donna turned away from it, groaning softly. Her father was shouting from downstairs, but all she could do was lie in bed clutching her head.

'Donna! Eight o'clock and you're still not up!' She heard her dad's footsteps coming up the stairs and closed her eyes once more.

He came into the room, telling her again that she was going to be late for school, then opened the curtains. Donna let out a yell as the room filled with the glare of sunlight. She wanted to crawl back under the sheets and hide.

Jim Bell was concerned. 'What is it, pet? Are you not well?' he asked as he pulled the covers back and peered at Donna's face.

'I think I'm going to be sick,' came the response. One look at his daughter's pale complexion and bloodshot eyes and Jim put two and two together.

'What you've got is a king-sized hangover.' Donna immediately denied that it was anything of the sort. 'I didn't have that much to drink . . .' she protested. But Jim knew a hangover when he saw one and this was *some* hangover. He was furious with Polly. 'That woman is totally irresponsible,' he fumed. Again Donna was on the defensive. The last thing she wanted was for Polly to be in her dad's bad books. She tried to tell him that it wasn't her mum's fault but Jim wouldn't listen. 'No? Then whose fault is it? Mine? Lisa's?' he demanded as he stormed off angrily.

Donna groaned loudly and pulled the sheets back over her head. She thought she was going to die – at the very least.

The round discs of Alka Seltzer went plop then fizzzzz in the two glasses of water. Gwen watched them dissolve into a white froth and then carried them through to the Grove general room where the casualties were waiting. Ian and Cas had both had a lousy day. Neither of them had ever known a headache like it and Ian had been sick twice. Now they were sitting quietly, still hungover and feeling very delicate. They reached out for the glasses Gwen offered them and thanked her.

'It's stupid to abuse your body like that,' Gwen began. Both boys groaned, not for the first time that day. 'Alcohol is a poison. Alcohol, nicotine, caffeine, drugs, they're all poisons.' Ian and Cas looked at one another, the last thing they wanted right now was a flippin' lecture. All they were concerned about was whether they'd ever feel like normal human beings again.

Nicola came in with the news that her dad was outside and needed some help with the leek beds. Cas and Ian groaned even louder.

The next stage in the leek-growing process was well underway. Small leek plants had now been placed at regular intervals in the trenches and several of the kids were starting to build a windbreak with wire netting and sheets of polythene. Wooden stakes were being driven into the ground as Spuggie arrived, looking full of self-importance. She'd finally agreed to go spying at

Denton Burn and had come back with her precious information. But when she delivered her first nugget, that Denton Burn were growing two kinds of leeks, pot ones and blanche ones, she was greeted with scorn by Winston, 'So are we, you pillock. Them's the club rules.'

Undeterred by this minor setback, she imparted her second piece of information, 'And they're feeding 'em with . . .' She consulted a piece of paper on which she'd written the details. 'Fish blood and bonemeal,' she said triumphantly. Winston was scornful once again. 'They're having you on!'

But Alan Dobson put him straight on that, telling him that Spuggie had got it right and that *was* what the leek plants were fed on. Winston still wasn't impressed, 'Not much of a spy that only finds out stuff we already know.'

'So you blimmin' do it then if you can do it better!' Spuggie replied huffily.

Winston was about to answer her back when he saw Speedy coming up the path, pushing a boy of about fifteen along in a wheelchair. None of the gang had ever seen him before.

'Have you found any more coins buried?' Speedy wanted to know. His question met with various responses. Cas thought the one they'd found was just a fluke and there was no way they'd find any more. Winston though, ever optimistic about making his fortune, decided that there were 'probably hundreds of 'em down there. Doubloons, pieces of eight . . .' 'Them's not flippin' Roman,' Ian laughed but Winston pointed out that they'd still be worth something. What he really wanted to know though was where this Professor was.

'Oh you mean Robert,' Speedy said. 'This is him.' The others stared at the boy in the wheelchair. 'Him?' they asked in chorus. 'Hi,' said Robert cheerfully.

*   *   *

70

Jim Bell had been furious with Polly all day. Lisa had tried to calm him down, telling him that she was sure Donna wouldn't do the same thing again in a hurry. But Jim said that wasn't the point and Donna wasn't at fault, her irresponsible mother was. Finally, when his daughter came home from school still looking decidedly green, he told her to get in the car. They were going to her mother's. Lisa watched the car disappear and sighed. Why couldn't she have had a nice simple relationship without an ex-wife and difficult daughter to contend with?

Polly wasn't feeling so hot herself when the doorbell rang. She hadn't done her face and knew she looked a mess, so she was less than delighted to find her ex-husband on the doorstep. However, not wanting to seem inhospitable while there might be a chance of them patching things up, she invited Jim and Donna inside.

No sooner had Polly closed the living room door behind her than Jim launched into her. 'What the heck do you think you were playing at, Polly?' Donna tried to defend her mother but Jim wasn't having any of it.

'It was a party,' Polly said weakly. She claimed that she hadn't put alcohol in any of their drinks. It had simply been there on the sideboard and she wasn't going to lock it away. 'They're not babies,' she told him.

Donna interrupted to tell her dad that she was fine now, but her father was determined to make his point. 'What kind of mother encourages her teenage daughter to get paralytic?' he asked angrily.

Polly had had enough. She felt like a stupid child and she couldn't bear Jim speaking to her like this. 'Stop yelling, Jim. Is it any wonder I left you?' she told him.

This was all too much for Donna, whose hopes of seeing her parents back together again were rapidly disappearing. She exploded, 'I've had enough of both of you! You go on about the way us kids carry on, but you want to listen to you two!

Not wanting them to see just how upset she was, Donna ran out of the flat in tears. This wasn't what she'd planned at all. She felt like it was all her fault that her mum and dad were now shouting and yelling at one another instead of having that cosy drink in the country pub that had once been their special place.

Back at the Grove, the kids had all squeezed themselves into Geoff's office. Geoff handed Robert the coin and everyone gathered round as he examined it. After a thorough inspection, turning the coin over several times, Robert finally made his pronouncement. 'Yes,' he said with conviction.

Winston, standing impatiently next to him, couldn't bear the suspense. 'Yes *what* man? Is it gold?'

'No,' came the response and there was a groan of disappointment. But then Robert went on to tell them that the coin was Roman, 'a bronze sestertius' he said. He knew that because it had Hadrian's profile on it.

Not wanting to give up completely, Winston asked hopefully, 'Must still be worth a bomb then?' The reply came back, 'About two pounds.' Winston couldn't believe it, he *knew* that anything antique was worth pots of dosh. But Robert patiently explained that was only if they were in mint condition or a gold coin like an 'aureus'.

By this time Ian was getting bored with the whole discussion. As far as he was concerned the coin they'd thought would make their fortunes worked out at about 20p each. 'But we haven't found an aureus, we've found a sisterwhatsit,' he said impatiently.

'Well, they *have* been found together,' Robert replied thoughtfully. That was more than enough to set

Winston off again. He was all for getting the spades and making a start straight away. Until, that was, Nicola realised just *where* he would be hunting for the coins.

'Hey, you're not digging up our leeks!' she shouted, chasing after him as he ran to get a spade.

This was war. The two camps stood on either side of the leek trench. One side: Winston, Ian, Speedy and Robert, had spades in their hands. The other: Nicola, Kelly, Spuggie, Cas and Duncan, looked ready to do battle without spades.

Winston was trying to appeal to their sense of history and to their greed. 'You can't put a few manky veggies before a priceless treasure trove!' He appealed to the rest of the gang to see reason. But The Other Side weren't having it.

Nicola was as determined as ever that the leeks should stay put until the competition. She was backed up by Cas who'd felt humiliated enough when Denton Burn beat them at football. No way were they going to win the leek competition too.

By this time Winston's head was swimming with thoughts of Serious Money – 'Thousands, millions!' – and nothing was going to deter him. He began to dig but he hadn't reckoned on the wrath of a woman scorned.

Grabbing a spade off Speedy, Nicola brandished it menacingly at Winston. It was a pretty terrifying sight, scary enough to make him put down his spade for a minute.

At this point, thinking no one was watching, Duncan decided to sneak off. After he'd been gone a minute or two, eagle-eyed Spuggie, who didn't miss a trick where Duncan was concerned, quietly followed him.

Nicola made the position crystal clear to Winston. 'My dad put them leeks in,' she told him, 'And nobody's digging 'em up.' Then in case Winston wasn't getting the message clearly enough, she added, 'Not even if the blimmin' Crown Jewels are buried underneath!' Just one glance at the threatening look on her face was enough for Winston to know that Nicola meant business. He put his spade down and accepted defeat – for now . . .

Meanwhile Spuggie was doing a good job of following Duncan. He was pretty easy to trail – he never looked behind him like they did in the films. She was beginning to quite enjoy her private detective role when Duncan suddenly disappeared. Flippin' heck, she thought crossly, I haven't trailed him all this way to lose him now. As there were only three or four buildings he could have gone into, she began peering inside each of them.

In the third one, which was an amusement arcade, she found Duncan playing on an electronic game. She watched for a minute or two, waiting to see if he was joined by anybody. But when no one arrived, she went over to him.

Duncan was not overly delighted to see her. 'What the heck are you doing here?' he asked. Not the least bit phased by Duncan's obvious irritation, Spuggie asked him the same question. 'Nothing,' he answered abruptly. This certainly wasn't going to satisfy Miss Private Detective who pointed out to Duncan that he'd been mizzling off for weeks.

Finally, seeing that he wasn't going to let on, Spuggie said triumphantly, 'You're waiting for a girlfriend, right?' but Duncan flatly denied it. Spuggie, who'd been convinced that this was why he kept on creeping off, wouldn't believe him. 'If I had a boyfriend I'd tell you,' she pleaded.

Duncan was getting very fed up by this time, 'I've not *got* a flippin' girlfriend,' he said in exasperation. How much longer would she stay there nagging him?

Realising that she was getting nowhere fast, Spuggie decided to cut her losses and get back to the Grove. She flounced off in a huff, telling Duncan, 'All right, keep your blimmin' secrets. See if I care.' He watched her go, secretly wishing he *did* have a girlfriend but delighted that Spuggie hadn't guessed the real reason for his regular disappearances.

When Spuggie got back to the Grove the great leek debate was getting even more heated. More kids than ever were standing round the leek patch as word got out about the conflict. Julie was sensibly arguing that if the coins had been there since Roman times they were certainly still going to be there after the leek competition. Gwen decided that the only democratic way to handle the situation was to take a vote on it which the others reluctantly agreed to. Raised hands were counted and the 'leek digger uppers' had the largest number of votes – by one vote. Delighted, Winston, Speedy and Ian went to grab their spades. But then Gwen spotted Donna walking up the path. In the interests of fair play, she told them all, Donna had to vote too. The boys pulled faces but put down their spades for a minute.

'Donna,' Gwen yelled to the figure approaching them, 'We've got a leek stalemate. Can we have your vote?' No one was prepared for the answer which came back, least of all Gwen.

'Stuff the leeks, you stupid woman,' Donna told her. 'There's more important things to worry about than blimmin' leeks.' Gwen stood there open-mouthed and very hurt, as Donna disappeared into the Grove. There had been no need for that outburst, she'd only asked the girl for a vote.

Then Geoff walked up with Nicola, much to Gwen's relief, and she explained the situation to him. There was no debate as far as Geoff was concerned. Nicola's dad had spent time and money helping them grow prize leeks. He'd also asked them all if they were serious and they had said they were. So *he* was going to decide democratically what they should do with the leek trenches. 'We'll leave them be, that's what we'll do!' he told the assembled crowd, to general moans from the boys.

Everyone began heading back to the Grove. Everyone except Winston who was holding a strange object wrapped in sacking. Well used to the boy's antics by now, Geoff spotted him lurking behind. 'Winston!' he shouted and Winston reluctantly walked away slowly.

Once he was sure that everyone was back inside the Grove, Geoff included, Winston crept out again and pulled the sacking off his metal detector. He began scanning the leek trench with great excitement, when suddenly a voice came out of nowhere. 'Winston, you've been told!' He'd been so engrossed in what he was doing that Geoff had managed to creep up right behind him without him noticing.

'Yeah, yeah, all right,' Winston finally gave up, packed his metal detector away and skulked off. Watching him go, Geoff had to grin. You had to hand it to the lad, he never gave up trying. He was the type that would either end up a millionaire or in big trouble.

The incident with Duncan had upset Spuggie. She'd hoped to get to the bottom of his disappearance but instead she felt shut out – once again. Feeling left out wasn't a new experience for her but she'd hoped it might be different with Duncan.

Gwen had noticed her looking miserable. 'What's the matter, Spuggie?' she asked. Spuggie tried to pretend that it was nothing but she was a hopeless liar. In the end she told Gwen simply, 'Friends, who'd have 'em?'

Not knowing quite what to say next, Gwen said she was going to Bamburgh at the weekend, and would Spuggie like to come too? Spuggie wasn't very keen at first, even when Gwen added that they could go to Farne Island and see the puffins. But Kelly, who'd just joined them, said enthusiastically, 'I've been there, there's seals and millions of birds. It's fantastic.'

Seeing her friend's reaction, Spuggie decided it might just be worth a try and Kelly said she'd like to come too. Feeling quite excited now, Spuggie said she had to go home to tell Fraser about her trip. Speedy and Robert were leaving too so they decided to walk back together.

On the way home Spuggie, being Spuggie, asked Robert how long he'd been in his wheelchair and what was wrong with him. Robert wasn't at all phased by her directness and explained, 'It's called partial dislocation of the neck. I call it a blimmin' nuisance.' He told her he'd done it in a football accident and Speedy added that he'd been a brilliant player. But he was determined that he was going to recover completely – *and* play football again.

The boys had come to their road. They said their goodbyes to Spuggie and headed back.

Spuggie was ambling along, thinking about the trip to Bamburgh, when a shadowy figure wearing a hooded anorak suddenly leapt out of some bushes by the road-side. Before she had time to react he grabbed hold of her from behind. Putting his hand over her mouth, he rifled through her jacket pockets until he found her purse. Spuggie somehow managed to sink her teeth into the hand clamped over her mouth. Then she screamed.

CHAPTER FOUR

'I've got news for you, Dobson. You snore,' Donna giggled. Nicola had been staying the night, now that they were friends again. But she was indignant at this accusation and immediately denied it, telling Donna that *she* talked in her sleep.

Want to know what you said?' Nicola asked mischievously. Donna said she didn't, then changed her mind.

'Ooh, Jan, kiss me Jan, I love you Jan . . .' Nicola mimicked Donna, clasping her hands to her heart and fluttering her eyelashes. Donna in turn, grabbed the nearest pillow and whopped Nicola over the head with it. They both fell onto the bed laughing.

'S'pose we'd best get dressed,' Nicola said. 'Knowing her she'll be dead on time.'

Gwen had invited Nicola and Donna to join Spuggie and Kelly on the trip to Bamburgh. Somehow she'd caught them with little else to do and they'd looked at one another and said 'yes'. Now Donna was regretting it, wondering why she'd ever said she'd go with 'Miss Piggy'. 'She's like something out of the ark,' she sneered. Nicola tried to convince her that it would be a laugh and that they didn't have to stick with Gwen.

It *would* be a laugh, Donna knew that. Things were always a laugh when she was with Nicola. With unaccustomed sincerity she turned to her friend. 'Hey, Nic. I'm glad we're mates again.'

Nicola grinned before replying, 'Maybe I'm just waiting me chance to push you off the boat on the way to the island.' That did it. This time the pillow fight was a full-scale one.

By half-past eight the pillows were more or less back on the beds and Donna and Nicola were almost ready for their day trip. Donna, however, was having great difficulty deciding which of her many jackets to take. When Nicola sensibly suggested taking the warmest one, Donna complained that it was 'well knackered'.

'Blimmin' heck, girl, it's not a fashion parade! It'll be freezing on that sea.' Nicola laughed at her friend's never-ending concern with her appearance. She was already the trendiest by far in their crowd and Nicola wondered why she sometimes had to go to such great lengths to stay that way. Nicola liked clothes too but she wasn't obsessed by them the way Donna was. 'And besides,' she thought with only a trace of envy, '*I* don't have the money to buy the stuff even if I wanted it.'

There was a knock at the door and Donna grudgingly allowed Lisa in to tell her that her mother was on the phone. She hurried downstairs to find out what Polly wanted.

Lisa sat on the bed as Nicola brushed her hair. She hesitated, then turned to the younger girl. 'She can't stand me, can she?' It was more of a statement than a question. Donna had made it perfectly clear for a long time that she didn't want anything to do with Lisa.

Blimmin' heck, thought Nicola, how do I answer this one? She felt that she had to be loyal to her friend but at the same time she was sorry for Lisa. Donna did treat her lousily, it was true. And she didn't deserve it. In fact Nicola quite liked her – not that she'd *ever* let on to Donna.

'I don't know,' she answered evasively. But Lisa wasn't fooled for a minute. The two girls were best friends and she knew that Donna would have made her opinion of Lisa crystal clear to Nicola.

In an unguarded moment, Lisa told her, 'She's no time for me at all. It makes things very awkward. I've tried, I really have.' Lisa hadn't meant to say so much but it had been getting increasingly difficult to handle and she felt it was unfair to talk to Jim about it. She knew he cared about her a lot but he was also a doting father and she didn't want him to feel torn in two.

For the first time Nicola saw how hard it was for Lisa. She wanted to say something to help her, but what?

'I think it's just that . . .' she began. She didn't know how to carry on but Lisa was impatient to know. Eventually Nicola confided that Donna felt she was trying to take her mum's place. When pushed a little further, she also admitted that Donna wanted to see her parents back together again. Lisa was shocked to hear this. As Jim and Polly were already divorced, she'd never imagined that Donna might still dream of their remarrying.

Suddenly the door flew open and Donna burst in looking very worried.

'Nic, me mam's in some kind of bother,' she told her friend in a fluster. 'I've got to go round there.'

They agreed that Nicola would meet Gwen as arranged and ask her to hold on for Donna for a while. Meanwhile Donna would call as soon as she knew what was happening. She rushed out of the bedroom a minute later, leaving Lisa and Nicola looking at one another not knowing what to say. The moment of shared confidences had been shattered.

Spuggie stood outside the Grove fidgeting impatiently with her knapsack. The mugging was already more or less forgotten. Her attacker hadn't managed to get her purse after all. She'd given him a good hard kick and he'd gone hobbling off down the road with an agonised yelp, leaving Spuggie a little shaken but flushed with victory.

She still didn't know who he was but at the moment she didn't much care. The main thing on her mind was getting to the castle and seeing all the amazing birds Gwen had told them about. They'd been hanging around the Grove waiting for Donna for at least half an hour. Then Gwen appeared telling them they really should leave soon if they were to have a full day. But Nicola was reluctant to leave without her, especially as she didn't know what kind of trouble Donna's mum was in. She asked if they could stay for just a few more minutes.

This didn't go down too well with Spuggie, who was fed up that Donna and Nicola were going with them at all. She was even more irritated that they were 'stood here like pimples waiting for *her*.' People were always doing things for Donna Bell. Spuggie bet that if it was her, nobody would have waited. They'd have gone without her. 'Trust Donna Bell to knacker it for us,' she grumbled.

Now Geoff shouted to Nicola that Donna was on the phone for her. After a minute or two Nicola came out of Geoff's office with the news that Donna couldn't come. 'Good', said Spuggie, not bothering to hide her feelings. Nicola told her she was being rotten but Spuggie didn't see it that way.

'She always gets everything she wants. Won't hurt her to miss out for once,' she told the others as they piled into Gwen's car.

Polly's eye was bruised and swollen. She examined it in the mirror fretfully. 'I can't put any make-up on, I'll look a fright.'

Donna wasn't taking any notice, she was too angry with Ken, her mum's ex-boyfriend. He'd come round early that morning to try and patch things up but Polly had insisted their relationship was over for good. Ken wouldn't take no for an answer and Polly had finally told him a few home truths. Her ex-husband was twice the man he'd ever be, she said, at which he promptly hit her – in the face.

'Why on earth did you leave me dad for *him*?' Donna wondered. Polly said she wished she knew. At the time, going off with Ken had seemed like a new and exciting start to her life. But it certainly hadn't ended up that way.

Donna's next question was the one she *really* wanted the answer to. 'Do you still love me dad?' she asked. But Polly wasn't going to lay her heart on the line that easily, she wanted to know more first.

'Remember you said you thought he still loved me?' she reminded Donna anxiously. Donna certainly did. She remembered at the time crossing her fingers and wishing it were true. Her mother asked her if she'd really meant it. 'Course,' Donna replied, trying to sound convincing. Then when Polly went on to ask about Lisa, Donna dismissed her as 'nothing'.

Suddenly feeling more hopeful, Polly turned to her daughter and confessed the dream she'd secretly been cherishing for a long time now. 'Just imagine me moving out of this grotty dump back into the Byker Arms, the three of us a family again.'

Donna didn't reply. She was too busy imagining the scene too. It was something she wanted every bit as badly as her mother.

The first glimpse of Bamburgh Castle had left even Spuggie dumbstruck. Now she, Gwen, Nicola and Kelly were standing admiring the majestic castle which still stood proudly on top of a high crag, its huge silhouette dominating the skyline. Gwen reached for the guide book she'd brought with her and began reading some of the castle's history out loud to the girls.

But that wasn't what Spuggie was interested in. 'We don't need a blimmin' history lesson, Gwen,' she told her. 'Let's go and explore.' And she ran off towards the castle, calling to Kelly to come and race her to the entrance. Gwen smiled at the enthusiastic pair and buried her head once again in the guide book. Only Nicola remained staring at the castle, still captivated by its ancient magnificence.

They finally caught up with one another on the castle's terraces and wandered round exploring. Making another attempt to educate her team, Gwen began reading from the guide book again. But this time, when Spuggie attempted to shut her up, she was overruled by Nicola who couldn't wait to hear more. The castle had really caught her imagination.

'Think of all them battles . . . the Romans, the Scots, the Vikings.' Nicola closed her eyes tight and began to see the battles taking place in her mind's eye. 'It's as if you're part of a huge jigsaw puzzle in time . . .' She opened her eyes quickly and laughed at herself, wondering what Donna would have said if she could have heard her.

The next minute, rounding one of the battlements, she suddenly saw the words 'Kevin and Danny were here' being sprayed onto the castle walls by a denim-jacketed lad of about seventeen. He and his pal laughed together as he sprayed the letters with a large can of red aerosol. Nicola was furious and didn't stop to think before she shouted. 'Here! What d'you think you're doing?'

Both lads laughed at her and told her to mind her own business but she was determined not to walk off and leave them to their mindless vandalism. 'You've no right to damage this place,' she told them angrily. The boys sneeringly asked if the castle was hers. When she had no answer to that, they told her to 'naff off' and returned to their paint spraying.

This time it was Gwen who stepped in. She marched over to the lads and snatched the spray can off the one called Kevin. Not stopping there, she told them crossly that the castle belonged to everybody. 'It's been here for centuries,' she said. 'And yobs like you aren't going to wreck it.'

Taken aback for a moment, Kevin then recovered and asked menacingly who was going to stop them. Nicola was beginning to get quite scared by now. After all, they were big lads and neither she nor Gwen were a physical match for them. She looked around. Apart from Spuggie and Kelly running round in the distance, there was nobody in sight.

But Gwen didn't seem daunted. She stood her ground with the boys and told them that if they didn't clear off she'd call the police. At this point Kevin threatened to 'thump the pair of you.' Even then, when Nicola would have liked to run off, Gwen refused to budge.

'Try it. Want to land up in court?' was her response. Seeing that threats of brute force weren't getting him anywhere, Kevin made a last ditch attempt to stare Gwen out. But by now it was pretty clear who was winning the battle of wills. Finally he skulked off with his mate, muttering something about it being a lousy dump anyway.

Nicola looked over at Gwen who had gone to lean against the wall. Suddenly she didn't look quite so strong or brave.

'You were fantastic, Gwen,' Nicola told her with feeling.

Gwen managed a weak smile as she confessed that she'd been scared silly. 'But,' she said, 'what else could I do?' As they walked off to catch up with Spuggie and

Kelly, Nicola was starting to rethink her impression of the Grove's newest helper. Gwen wasn't such a wet sponge after all.

Round at Julie's house, she and Hayley were about to go off shopping for the day. Mr Warner was trying, as he often did, to have a friendly conversation with Julie. But these days she only ever answered him in monosyllables, giving him the essential information and no more. Today, Hayley had already told him that they were going shopping but when he asked what for, his daughter was as evasive as ever. He did the only other thing he could think of, pulled out his wallet and counted out some cash for Julie. Unfortunately this had completely the wrong effect.

'Dad, you give me enough money . . .' Julie felt guilty about taking the notes. She knew her father did it because *he* felt guilty but sadly it only left her despising him. On the rare occasions when he chose to disagree with her about anything, Julie would usually win the argument. She had little time or patience for her father these days. Shrugging, she took the money and left with Hayley.

Today however, she felt particularly guilty about the reason for her shopping trip. When she told Hayley this she was accused of 'bottling out' before she'd even done anything. That was enough. She wasn't going to be accused of being a coward. Taking her friend by the arm, Julie marched into the Metro Centre.

They stood facing each other outside The First Snip, a unisex hairdresser's. Julie looked uncertain.

'Oh, I don't know, Hayl. Perhaps I'll just settle for a trim?' she suggested unconvincingly. But Hayley wasn't letting her off the hook that easily.

'Who wanted a new image? Who said she felt a prat in

her little Fair Isle jumper?' Julie could see that Hayley was enjoying this bossy role and she told her so. Hayley laughed and said Julie was right, she hadn't had so much fun in years. Then she prodded her friend gently but firmly in the direction of the entrance.

An hour later, as they left the hairdresser's, Julie couldn't resist glancing at her reflection once again in one of the mirrors. She'd had several inches chopped off her hair and it was now fashioned in one of the trendiest styles Hayley had seen in ages. A far cry from her 'sweet' bob with a fringe. Julie was none too sure about her new look yet. 'I look a complete wally,' she told Hayley, and meant it. Right now she'd have been quite happy to have her Fair Isle sweaters back.

But her friend replied that she looked brilliant. 'Honestly, I wouldn't say it if I didn't mean it,' she added, with conviction.

Apart from worrying that she looked stupid, there *was* one other thing bothering Julie. She knew her dad would go bonkers. 'Well, if he's going to go bonkers anyway,' Hayley said, laughing, 'we might as well give him something he can *really* go bonkers about.' And she pulled Julie over to the shop they'd been in with Donna, the one with all the black leather gear in it.

When they got back, Mr Warner was finishing a conversation with Julie's mum. Julie gestured to Hayley to keep quiet as they eavesdropped from the hall.

'She's fine,' he told his wife. And then went on to tell her, almost apologetically, that their daughter was still seeing Gill. 'But I think we have to let that run its course,' he added, hoping to appease his wife. It obviously didn't work because Julie then heard her father saying, 'I *have* tried, Clare, of course I have.'

When would they stop trying to split her and Gill up? Julie wondered. Although her father no longer put up much resistance to her plans, she was fed up with being disapproved of by both her parents. She wished they'd stop meddling with her life and get on with sorting out their own.

Mr Warner put the phone down and stared in disbelief at his daughter. The pretty young lady had disappeared. In her place stood a girl dressed from head to foot in black leather. Black leather biker's jacket, black leather mini skirt with thongs up the sides. Julie was even wearing short black leather lace-up boots and fishnet tights. Her hair was stiff with gel and she'd gone to town on her make-up too. It was far more daring than she'd ever worn before – red lips, black eyeliner and lashings of mascara.

'It's the new me. Don't you like it?' Julie asked, sounding far more confident than she felt. She wasn't at all sure about this new look that Hayley had persuaded her to try out. The last thing she needed was her father's disapproval.

The look on his face said it all before he even opened his mouth. But in case Julie hadn't got the message, he replied, 'No, I do not. Go upstairs and wash that stuff out of your hair and put some decent clothes on.'

There was a silence which, to Hayley, seemed to go on for an eternity. She was feeling extremely uncomfortable as it was, particularly as she had definitely had a large part in creating the new-look Julie.

Julie was thinking hard herself. In the old days she'd have gone and done what she was told, even though she might have sulked a bit. But the old days were gone. Nothing was the way it used to be – including her. And it was about time her dad recognised that. Finally Julie told her dad, 'I'm sorry but no, I won't. I don't see why I should have to look the way you want me to.' She was amazed at herself. At one time she'd *never* have spoken to her father like that.

Mr Warner was struggling to deal with the situation. It was especially at times like this that he wished his wife were still around. He tried to sound strict but he sensed that he'd already lost the battle. Julie would just ignore him. 'I'm not staying here to be treated like a silly kid,' she said as she left the house with Hayley. Mr Warner sighed. If only he knew how to treat his increasingly rebellious daughter these days.

The trip to Farne Island by boat was windy and choppy but Nicola, Kelly and Spuggie were too fascinated by the wildlife to mind. Once on the island they wandered along the beach to get a better view of the puffins, oystercatchers and other seabirds that played along the water's edge.

Spuggie and Kelly liked the strange and wonderful puffins which reminded Spuggie of huge parrots. But Nicola was the one who was really fascinated, and then horrified, when Gwen told them that human beings were killing off these beautiful birds, amongst many others.

'We're slowly wrecking this planet of ours. And wild creatures are amongst the victims,' she continued. No one teased her this time. They all sensed she was right.

Nicola wanted to know how exactly we were killing off the seabirds and Gwen explained about birds' wings getting clogged up with oil which meant that they couldn't fly and then they drowned. She gave other examples too, like birds getting poisoned or seals not being able to breed properly because of the oil spillages, nuclear waste and pesticides polluting the sea.

Standing by the water's edge with the wind blowing in her hair, Nicola realised, not for the first time that day, that she was glad Donna wasn't there. She knew her friend wouldn't take all this seriously, she'd find some way to laugh about it. Or more likely she simply wouldn't want to listen and would be off hunting for boys instead.

'How can we help them?' she asked Gwen, who told her that cleaning up the worst areas of coastline and making sure the pollution problem didn't spread would be a good start. Nicola realised something else – she was really beginning to respect Gwen's opinion.

'You know so much about all this,' Nicola said. It was a statement rather than a question and intended to be a compliment as well. Gwen smiled and said that her brother, who was a vet, was also very concerned about the environment. She paused before asking Nicola, 'The kids think I'm boring don't they? Boring and square?'

The younger girl's heart went out to her and she suddenly felt very guilty about all the times she'd laughed at Gwen behind her back. Feeling even more guilty for lying, she denied what Gwen had just said. 'No, they don't,' she answered. Then she hesitated and decided to stick a little closer to the truth. 'Well, it's only 'cos they don't really know you.'

Gwen knew a white lie when she heard one, though she appreciated Nicola trying to save her feelings. She turned to her and grinned. 'Well, I *am* boring and square!'

Back home, others were having a good time too. Apart from his grotty job, Gill was quite pleased with life at the moment. He was beginning to enjoy living in his new digs although it was far from a palace and his relationship with Julie was going from strength to strength. He knew he'd changed quite a lot over the last few months but Julie had almost become a different person.

Smiling to himself, Gill thought about the prissy young girl who'd first walked up the path to Byker Grove. If she hadn't been so pretty, he knew he wouldn't have bothered talking to her. Now she was standing her ground more, he was proud of her. Except that she sometimes bossed him around too!

He was on his way to meet her now, although he'd set off early to do some errands on the way. As he walked along he noticed a brand new Porsche parked by the roadside. Its owner was standing beside it looking anxious. 'Hey, son. Any idea where the nearest garage is?' he asked. Gill wondered what the problem was and the man told him he had no idea, the car had just 'died' on him. Wanting to get his hands on the engine of such a stunning car, Gill asked if he could have a look at it. Its owner was happy to oblige, anything to get his pride and joy on the road again.

First he turned the key in the engine and listened to the engine noise. Then he looked under the bonnet and finally took the petrol cap off. Bumping the car, he put his ear to the open petrol tank and listened carefully.

'What is it?' the man asked hopefully. Gill responded without hesitation. 'No petrol,' he said. The man found this hard to believe as his petrol gauge showed he still had half a tank, but Gill was insistent. At this point the man's car phone rang. Picking it up he began talking, then fished in his wallet and handed a £20 note to Gill. 'Be a good lad,' he told him, and fetch me a gallon. At least get me mobile.' And he carried on with his conversation.

Gill hurried off towards the garage, his mind racing. He could do a lot with twenty quid – take Julie somewhere nice, for a start. The bloke was a mug for trusting a stranger, serve him right. He pocketed the note and walked quickly past the garage.

But then he thought about what would have happened if Julie had been with him. He *knew* she'd insist on getting the petrol. Maybe she was right. Turning round, he headed back to the garage.

'So what do you do then, son?' the man asked, as Gill poured in the petrol. Gill filled him in about his YTS scheme, including the fact that he hated it. 'This is what I'd give my right arm to do,' he said, stroking the Porsche's brilliant red paintwork. 'Work on cars like this.'

The bloke reached into his pocket and took out a business card which he handed to Gill who read it out loud. 'Neville Fletcher, Fletcher's Automobiles, authorised dealers.' He explained that his company sold and serviced cars. Then he asked Gill to come and see him the following Monday and they'd have a chat about a job. 'I'm not making any promises, mind,' he said quickly, 'but at least you seem to be an honest lad.'

Neville Fletcher got in his car and drove off, leaving Gill open-mouthed at his good luck and the thought that he'd very nearly blown it.

As it turned out, that wasn't the only surprise he was getting, this particular Saturday. As he waited for Julie to arrive, he casually eyed up a bird dressed from head to toe in black leather who was strolling towards him. He got the shock of his life when she came closer and he saw that it was Julie.

'What the heck have you done to yourself?' he asked, not bothering to hide his dismay. Julie was less than pleased, telling him he sounded just like her dad.

She was hurt too, as she'd thought that Gill at least would approve of her new get-up. Realising that he'd said the wrong thing, Gill attempted to smooth things over, muttering, 'It's . . . different.'

Julie was getting quite irritated by now and told him it

was *meant* to be 'different.' 'I was sick of the old me,' she added. But Gill found himself saying he'd quite liked the way she was – which didn't help matters at all.

By this time Julie had had enough. 'Oh brilliant!' she shouted at Gill angrily. 'I do all this for you and you hate it.' Realising that calming tactics were in order, he told her, 'No, I don't, it's just a bit of a shock that's all.' Then he added with a grin, 'Can't call you Duchess any more in that get-up, can I?' But Julie didn't smile back.

Suddenly he remembered the business card and the offer that Neville Fletcher had made. Hoping to change the subject, he told her about his good deed that morning and then showed her the card. He was chuffed at how excited she was for him but thought it wiser to stay quiet about it himself. Unfortunately this landed him in hot water yet again.

'Why do you always have to be Mr Cool?' Julie demanded. Again, Gill tried to calm her down. He explained that he didn't like to get too worked up about things because he'd been knocked back in the past.

But Julie wasn't letting him off that easily. 'This could be something fantastic. Don't you care? She wanted to shake Gill to make him realise what a great opportunity he'd just been given.

Seeing that he was going to get no peace and quiet until he showed some enthusiasm, Gill replied that of course he cared. And, yes, he wanted this job more than anything he'd ever wanted in his life. 'If I don't get it I'll probably top meself, jump off the blimmin' Tyne Bridge . . . now are you satisfied?' He looked at Julie. She smiled. She knew that, joking apart, he meant what he said.

In the Byker Arms living room, Lisa, Donna and her dad were finishing lunch. Jim had just asked if Polly was all right and Donna was milking the situation for all it was worth.

'She's dead miserable, Dad. If you could have seen her this morning . . . poor Mam.' Her father looked concerned and asked if her ex-boyfriend had hurt her badly. When Donna replied that he'd 'beaten her up something rotten,' Lisa, who could see where this scheming was leading to a mile off, interrupted. 'I thought you said he just slapped her face?' But Donna wasn't being thrown that easily. She made some excuse that that was just her mother being brave before Donna had gone round and actually *seen* the injuries.

Lisa couldn't stand to listen any more so she cleared the plates and went into the kitchen. Grabbing the opportunity while her father's sympathies were with Polly, Donna said, 'I think you should go round and see her, Dad.' Jim Bell wasn't so sure. He reminded his daughter that whenever they did get together, sparks flew. But Donna put on her little girl voice and pleaded with him, while Lisa listened, feeling sick in the stomach, from the kitchen door.

The doorbell rang. Donna leapt up, saying it would be Jan. Her dad hesitated, then said to her, 'I wouldn't get too keen on him, love.' Donna asked what was wrong with him and her father carefully pointed out that Jan would be going back to Denmark one day and he didn't want his daughter to get hurt.

Cockily, Donna replied, 'I won't be. Jan and me are special.' For Lisa's benefit she added loudly, 'Just like you and Mum used to be.' Then she opened the door to her boyfriend.

Outside the Grove, Gwen's battered old car pulled up and the three girls piled out.

'Thanks Gwen. That was brilliant,' Spuggie and Kelly

told her, before running into the Grove. But Nicola stood on her own on the pavement, deep in thought.

'How about you Nicola?' Gwen asked curiously. 'Did you enjoy the trip?' Nicola, who'd been miles away, hardly seemed to hear the question. 'I can't help thinking about all those creatures dying. It's not right, 'she said, looking troubled. Gwen couldn't have agreed with her more.

Together they went into the Grove where Speedy and Robert were already questioning Spuggie and Kelly about their day out. Both girls were full of tales about the puffins, cormorants, gulls and seals.

What Robert most wanted to see was the terns because they dive-bombed anyone they thought was attacking their nest. Speedy volunteered to take him one day but Robert said it wouldn't be possible while he was in a wheelchair. For once he sounded fed up. Kelly wanted to know when he would be able to walk again. He told them that he'd be getting about a bit in a couple of months but it would take him a while before he could walk properly again.

Speedy explained that Robert had been playing for the Newcastle under-sixteens when he'd taken a low header, collided with the goalpost and severely bruised his spine. Both girls cringed at the thought of it. Then Spuggie remembered to get the shells she'd collected for Robert.

Looking genuinely pleased, he told Spuggie that he was going to put them with some pebbles in a big glass jar, then make a lamp out of it for his foster mum. Speedy listened with admiration. 'Robert's dead good at making things,' he said.

In a quiet corner of the general room, Donna and Nicola were having a heart to heart. Only each of them was discussing different things. Donna was trying to tell Nicola about her mum being bashed around. But Nicola only wanted to talk about Farne Island and pollution. In the end Donna got fed up with talking to a brick wall and, exasperated, asked her friend, 'Nicola Dobson, are you listening to me or what? This is serious.'

'So's this,' Nicola replied indignantly. But she did concede that what Donna was telling her *was* serious for once. When she asked if Polly was all right, Donna said she was but she'd be a lot better if her dad would go round and visit her. 'You know, when it was my birthday,' she confided, 'that's what I wished for, that they'd get together again.' Then, embarrassed at having told Nicola, she changed the subject. 'How'd you get on with Miss Miseryguts anyway?' she asked.

Not wanting Donna to make any more of her cutting remarks about Gwen, Nicola simply answered, 'All right.' Donna didn't believe it. To her, the woman wasn't 'all right', she was 'a pain in the whatsit'. Leaping to Gwen's defence, Nicola told her that she was actually very good company. And what's more, she knew an awful lot of stuff.

Donna was scornful. 'Oh yeah? What about?' she asked.

But Nicola wasn't prepared to let the conversation go any further. 'Nothing you'd be interested in,' she replied truthfully.

Outside the door to the general room, Julie looked anxiously at Gill. She'd decided not to admit to him that she was nervous. He'd only tell her she should go back to the way she'd looked before. As luck would have it, the first person to see her was Donna Bell.

'Blimmin' heck, get a load of that! What's *she* come as?' Was the predictably cutting remark. Donna remembered the outfit from the time she'd been shopping with Julie and Hayley. She was envious then and she was envious now.

She's only jealous because I'm looking trendier than her, Julie thought and decided not to take any notice. But Donna, wanting to make Julie feel really uncomfortable, asked Jan what he thought.

'I think it's very different,' he told her. Not sure how to take this, Donna nevertheless commented bitchily. 'That's what people always say when they think something's dead revolting.' But Jan was quick to put her straight on that. He explained that he thought it took courage to make a big change and he admired that.

While the boys seemed to be on her side, Julie thought she'd add Gill's approval to the list. 'Anyway, Gill likes it, don't you Gill?' she asked, although it was more of a statement than a question.

Gill looked uncomfortable and shuffled his feet for a moment before confessing that it was all right but actually he liked her the way she was before. A furious Julie exploded at Gill, telling him she'd only done it for his benefit. 'I don't know why I bothered, fat lot you know. All *you* know is working on stupid building sites!' she shouted before running out of the room, leaving Donna with a smirk that stretched from ear to ear.

It was early evening and Jim Bell had been thinking about the conversation with his daughter all afternoon. He knew that getting in touch with Polly usually ended in disaster. But he *did* feel sorry for her and he did want to know if she was all right. She wasn't a bad old bird when all was said and done and the past was the past.

In the end he picked up the phone and dialled. Polly seemed delighted to hear from him – she hadn't sounded so friendly in years.

As they talked, Donna came in from the Grove and realised who her dad was talking to. Not wanting to interrupt the conversation, she stood in the doorway eavesdropping, excitedly.

'I was wondering if it would help to talk about it, Polly,' her dad was saying. Donna crossed her fingers and closed her eyes tight, wishing as hard as she could. 'Maybe we could get together over a drink,' he added.

Donna's birthday wish was going to come true, she could feel it in her bones.

CHAPTER FIVE

Jim Bell had arranged to take his ex-wife out the following Saturday. That morning Donna was escorting Polly round the shops, trying to persuade her to buy something sexy for her rendezvous. As they looked in the window of a trendy fashion shop, Donna pointed to a rather flashy dress. 'That'd look fantastic on you, Mum,' she said. 'Knock me dad's eyes out tonight,' she added craftily.

Laughing, Polly reminded her daughter that he was only popping round for a drink. But Donna had news for her. She'd persuaded Jim to take Polly out for dinner, telling him it was the least he could do after the way that animal had treated her. Amused, her mother commented that Donna always could wind her dad round her little finger. But she didn't like Donna calling her ex-boyfriend names. 'He only gave me a shiner,' she reminded her daughter. Glancing at her reflection in a shop window, Polly saw that the bruising was still showing. Oh well, she'd look better when she'd had her hair done, she told herself.

Nicola came to join them, holding a bottle of spray cologne. 'I hope she likes it,' she said anxiously. Mary, her grandmother, had suddenly been taken ill again, and this time she'd been rushed off to hospital. It had been a shock to Nicola and her sisters to see their normally super-active granny looking so weak and pale.

Taking a last look at the dress in the window, Polly finally gave in and said to her daughter, 'All right, bossy. I'll try it on.' But Donna wasn't listening. She appeared to be glued to the spot, staring at someone in the distance. The three of them looked over to see who it was.

Lisa was too close by now to dodge them but Donna was determined to pretend she wasn't there. Nicola, however, automatically said 'Hiya, Lisa.' Taking a deep breath, Lisa came over and asked about Nicola's gran. 'She's not too good,' Nicola told her. 'They're keeping her in for tests.' She showed Lisa the cologne she'd just bought. Then there was a horribly embarrassing silence while Donna stubbornly refused to introduce her to Polly. Finally Lisa asked Nicola to send her best wishes to Mrs O'Malley and walked away.

'So that was Lisa,' Polly said, staring after the tall, slim and *very* attractive girl rapidly disappearing into the crowd. Donna glared at Nicola and clumsily tried to pretend that she was Brad's girlfriend. But her mother wasn't that stupid. 'You told me she was ugly,' she said.

'She is,' was all Donna could think of to say. Polly smiled sadly as she told her daughter, 'Lovie, I know you mean well but you can be a silly girl at times.' Furious, Donna glared accusingly at her friend. This was all *her* fault.

A furtive-looking Spuggie approached the leek allotment. Looking round to make sure the coast was clear, she took out a tape measure. Then she got on her hands and knees and began measuring the height and girth of the leeks. Taking a scrap of paper and a pencil from her pocket, she hastily scribbled a note of the measurements she'd taken. Once again Spuggie was risking life and limb on a daring mission to discover the size of Denton Burn's leeks.

Five minutes later secret agent Spuggie was being unceremoniously chucked out on her ear by a whole gang of Denton Burners. One of them, Greg, had discovered what she was up to. 'Just hop it, blimmin' little snoop!' he shouted after her, his jeers echoed by the others.

Only one person, a girl called Charlie, stuck up for Spuggie. 'Leave her alone, Greg,' she shouted. 'Maybe she isn't a spy at all.' But Greg wasn't taking any notice. The fact that she was measuring their leeks was proof that she was a spy, as far as he was concerned. Spuggie tried in vain to defend herself. But Greg wasn't letting up. He told her to tell her mates at Byker Grove that they might as well dig up their leeks and make them into pasties 'because they've as much chance of winning the competition as our cat.'

Everyone began to jeer again and Spuggie was close to tears. Why did she always end up in trouble when she was only trying to please people? Charlie angrily shouted at everyone to stop the jeering. 'You should be ashamed of yourselves,' she told them. 'All this fuss over a few stupid vegetables. Meanwhile Spuggie was walking down the road, trying very hard not to cry. Charlie called after her to come back but it was too late. She had already disappeared round the corner.

Donna breezed into the Byker Arms living room, announcing for Jim's benefit that she'd been shopping with her mum. Then she turned to Lisa. 'Thought it'd be a bit embarrassing if I introduced you,' she said innocently. 'You didn't mind, did you?'

Through gritted teeth, Lisa said of course she didn't. Wanting to make the most out of the situation, Donna told her dad that Polly had brought a smashing frock for that evening. 'I hope you're taking her somewhere nice,' she said, with a meaningful look.

This dinner date was news to Lisa who turned to Jim and asked him what it was all about. Awkwardly he explained that they were just going for a bite at a local restaurant. 'Least I could do after that bloke duffed her up last week,' he mumbled, hoping this would satisfy as an explanation.

But Lisa wasn't so much upset about them going out together, it was more the fact that he hadn't told her. Jim frantically tried to play it down, telling her that Polly had had a rough time lately. And, after all, they *had* been married for thirteen years.

'Fine,' Lisa told him. It obviously wasn't fine with her. Far from it. But she didn't want that little cow Donna to see how upset she was.

Donna smiled sweetly at her father as soon as Lisa had left the room. 'She's very selfish, isn't she? I bet me mum wouldn't behave like that if it was the other road round.'

Through the open living room door, Lisa caught the comment that Donna intended her to hear and felt even more upset, while in the living room, Jim Bell looked at his wide-eyed daughter and thought about Lisa and his wife. At that moment he didn't know what on earth to do about the whole mess.

Gwen and Nicola were busy tending the leeks. Gwen was feeding them with fertiliser while Nicola came along behind her and watered them. Kneeling down beside a leek, Gwen examined it closely. 'I think they're looking very good,' she pronounced after a detailed inspection.

Nicola grinned at her, 'So long as we can stop Winston and his pals digging 'em up to hunt for buried treasure . . .' She broke off mid-sentence as she realised that Gwen wasn't listening. Instead she was gazing wistfully across the grounds to where Brad had just leapt out of his car.

It didn't take long for Nicola to put two and two together. 'You like him, don't you?' she asked Gwen, although she already knew the answer. Embarrassed, Gwen told her not to be silly.

This didn't put Nicola off. 'Why's it silly? He's very tasty,' she replied bluntly. Gwen didn't know what to say. She didn't want to lie to Nicola who was the first of the kids she'd made friends with at the Grove. But on the other hand she didn't want to tell the truth and risk being made fun of by everyone. And most of all, she didn't want Brad finding out.

'I suppose he's all right, if you like that type,' she said in an offhand sort of way. Then she added a little more honestly, 'Anyway, he's keen on Alison.'

Nicola smiled. So it *was* true. Her heart went out to Gwen and, just to give her some hope, she told her that Alison already had a boyfriend called Mike.

Matter-of-factly, with only a trace of jealousy, Gwen said, 'I suppose she's always had heaps of men after her. She's very pretty.'

'So are you,' Nicola replied loyally. However Gwen was under no illusions on that score. She knew she'd never win any beauty contests but she appreciated Nicola's kindness all the same.

Suddenly curious, Nicola asked Gwen if she had a boyfriend. Busying herself with the leeks, Gwen muttered something about having too many interests to waste her time flirting. 'I leave that sort of thing to your friend Donna,' she added. Nicola wasn't fooled for a minute. She could see that Gwen was dying for a boyfriend but she would never admit it.

Inside the Grove, Debbie and Robert were busying themselves sorting stuff out for the jumble sale that Byker Grove were organising to raise money for a video recorder. It had been Speedy's idea but he'd roped Robert and Debbie in to knock on doors, asking for old clothes. Now Debbie held up a particularly untrendy woolly cardigan and pulled a face. 'Yuck,' she said. 'Who the heck'd wear this? It's out of the ark.'

Alison pointed out that not everyone had to be trendy. 'At least it's warm,' she said. 'Some old person will be glad of that.' Debbie pulled another face and said that she'd hate to be old. She told Alison and Robert that her gran had been carted off to hospital because she was old.

Hearing this, Robert told her that you didn't have to be old to go to hospital. He'd been in one for three months. And he still had to go to physio every three weeks. Debbie asked him if he minded being in his wheelchair.

At first he put on a brave face. But then he remembered how he'd felt earlier today. The local radio station had told Geoff they wanted someone to go on air and give details of the jumble sale. Robert would have loved to have made the announcement, and he knew he could have done it really well, but the radio station was on the first floor and there was no ramp for the wheelchair. Eventually a *very* reluctant Speedy had been persuaded to go on air instead. Robert went quiet for a moment and then admitted reluctantly, 'Yeah. Sometimes you get well cheesed off.' But he wasn't the type to stay down for long. Grabbing a balaclava from the 'woolly' pile, he stuck it over his head and told Debbie, 'Let's be Bonnie and Clyde. You hold 'em up, I'll drive the getaway chair!'

While they were careering around, Spuggie slunk in, trying not to be noticed. She'd obviously been crying.

Alison, who spotted most things, saw her first.

'Spuggie, pet, whatever's the matter?' she asked, concerned.

'Nothing,' came the sniffly reply.

Debbie Dobson looked at her closely. 'You've been

crying,' she announced. Of course Spuggie immediately denied this. Seeing that a more sensitive approach was needed, Alison told Debbie to leave her alone, then suggested they go and talk in the club room which was empty.

However, Spuggie couldn't wait that long to spill out her feelings. She suddenly errupted, telling them, 'I'm never going back to Denton Burn, never ever. I don't care if we *don't* win the blimmin' leeks! Astonished by this outburst, Debbie demanded to know what had happened.

But Alison said what Spuggie needed right now was a nice hot cup of tea and a choccie biscuit. Taking Spuggie off to the snack bar, she left Debbie speculating wildly to Robert about the Denton Burners descending on Spuggie like some howling pack of wolves and beating her up.

Robert wasn't listening, he was making sure the radio was tuned properly for Speedy's radio debut.

Speedy had brought along his Byker Grove support group. But as Fraser, Duncan and Geoff sat waiting in the radio station reception with him he wished he'd been on his own. At least then none of them would have seen how scared he was. Or asked him . . . 'You scared?' The question came from Duncan.

Geoff interjected hurriedly, 'Course he's not,' he said confidently. 'Are you lad?'

'Yes,' Speedy replied, clearly petrified.

The next moment Geoff was called into the studio to have a quick chat with Dave, the DJ. Speedy peered at the piece of paper he was screwing up in his hand and read from it, for the umpteenth time, 'Don't miss the chance to come to Byker Grove's jumble sale tomorrow afternoon at . . .'

A laid-back, confident-looking boy of about fifteen wandered past. He overheard Speedy's hesitant news bulletin and came over. 'Here, mush, let's have a look at that,' he said, grabbing the piece of paper. He quickly scanned its contents, his mind working rapidly. Finally he delivered a sales pitch for the jumble sale that would have had even Fraser rushing down to the Grove.

The boys were impressed, although Speedy was slightly doubtful. 'It's only a little local jumble sale,' he told the boy, who introduced himself as Peter Jenkins, known to all as P.J.

This fact didn't seem to worry P.J. 'You've got to make a pitch, man. Hype, that's the name of the game, right?'

Geoff rejoined them, telling Speedy he was 'on'. 'Dave says you've nothing to worry about. It's a piece of cake,' he added encouragingly.

Nevertheless, as Speedy followed Geoff into the studio, he looked like he was about to be led off to the guillotine.

P.J. started to give Fraser and Duncan his opinion of Dave, the presenter, saying he was OK but he was no Bruno Brookes. Fascinated by this outgoing character who seemed to know so much about the radio station, Fraser asked him if he worked there. P.J. explained that they let him hang around, doing messages and other bits and pieces.

'Why?' Fraser wanted to know.

"Cos it's what I'm going to do when I leave school,' came the answer. Duncan was puzzled. Why would anyone train to be a messenger? P.J. laughed out loud at his question. 'No, divi. Run my own radio station . . . And not just local, I'm going to go global. Be the boss, man.'

Fraser and Duncan stared at him in amazement. They were hugely impressed, both by P.J.'s dream and by his cool confidence that he'd achieve it.

Paperwork was beginning to get the better of Alison as she sat in the office wondering which form to tackle next. Brad walked in and perched on the desk. 'Any decisions yet?' he asked in a casual sort of way.

Alison closed her eyes for a second. She still didn't know how to deal with this situation. She tried to tell Brad that now wasn't a good time – she had a million things to do before the jumble sale.

'Stop putting it off, Ali,' he said gently. 'You're not being fair on any of us, me, Mike or yourself . . .' He broke off as Spuggie came in. Not a minute too soon as far as Alison was concerned. She knew that Brad was right but she simply couldn't make a decision at the moment. Goodness knows she'd lain awake at night often enough these past few weeks.

Spuggie had come to tell them to get a move on as Speedy was going to be doing his interview in a minute or two. As she ran out to join the others round the radio, Brad commented that she certainly seemed to have cheered up. Then he had to smile as he saw the look on Alison's troubled face. He reached over and kissed the tip of her nose lightly before she could stop him. 'I'm glad somebody has,' he said lightly.

Walking along the corridor to join the rest of the gang, Gwen saw the kiss and hurried on her way.

Everyone else was already clustered round the radio when Alison and Brad came to join them. Dave had just finished announcing the last record leading up to the news. 'But before that, this . . .' he said. There was a general chorus of cheers and shushes and then Speedy was on the air.

His voice was high at first and cracking with nerves but he'd written down the new spiel P.J. had given him and it sounded great. 'Bargains, bestsellers and bric a

106

brac at Byker Grove. I don't believe it, yes, they're giving 'em away – well, almost . . .'

As Speedy finished his sales pitch, another round of cheers and murmurs of surprised approval went up from the gang.

Only Robert remained unsurprised by Speedy's sudden transformation into a radio whizz kid celebrity. 'Good on yer, Speedy! Said you could do it man!'

P.J. had been giving Fraser and Duncan a tour round the radio station. As they got back to reception, Fraser thanked him. But P.J. seemed to think he should thank Fraser more for the info he'd been giving him on the technicalities of radio. During the tour he'd arranged to meet Fraser again to find out more.

'See you tomorrow and we'll suss it out together, right?' He thrust out his hand in a businesslike fashion. Fraser hesitated briefly, then returned the handshake, though he wasn't quite sure what he was getting himself into with this likeable dynamo.

Speedy came out of the studio, relieved that the ordeal was over. 'Hey, did you hear me, how was I, was I OK?' he asked excitedly.

'Philip Schofield eat your heart out,' P.J. grinned in reply.

Geoff was patting Speedy on the back and telling him what a great job he'd done when the receptionist interrupted, looking worried.

'P.J., did you see anyone come through here in the last few minutes?' she asked anxiously. P.J. replied that he hadn't as he was showing the boys around and he'd only just got back himself. The receptionist told him that she'd been to get a cup of coffee and when she got back, her purse had vanished.

P.J. was sympathetic but could only repeat that they

hadn't seen anybody. 'Have we, lads?' he asked the boys. Fraser and Duncan shook their heads.

Lisa was sitting at the Byker Arms bar looking fed up. Jim had gone out with Polly and she didn't know what to do with herself. She was trying not to feel jealous or to be angry with Donna for fixing the whole situation. But she wasn't being very successful.

Brad came in, also looking a bit glum. He saw Lisa and, remembering her from the football match, went over to say hello. 'It's Lisa isn't it?' he asked, not quite sure.

'Only to my friends,' came the uncharacteristically cool reply. Brad was a bit taken aback but then realised that she might not remember him. He explained that he helped out at the Grove and reminded Lisa where they'd met before.

Thawing instantly, she apologised, explaining that she thought Brad might be one of the flash Harrys they sometimes got at the Byker Arms.

Brad smiled at this. 'Do I look like a flash Harry?' he asked.

Lisa had to smile back. 'No, not really.'

Brad asked where Jim was and Lisa told him drily, 'He's taken his ex-wife out for a cosy little dinner.'

'In that case,' Brad said, 'can I buy you a drink?'

Back at the Grove, everyone was busy setting up stalls for the next day's jumble sale. Nicola and Donna were working on one together when Gwen came over. 'That's looking very enticing,' she told them encouragingly, looking at their wares.

Donna laughed at her, saying it was a load of old junk. Gwen tried to tell her that not everyone was as fortunate as she was. But Donna only mimicked her as she walked away, which irritated Nicola.

'She's right,' she told Donna. 'I don't know why you have to keep having a go at her.' Nicola was fed up with her friend's attitude towards Gwen. 'What's she ever done to you?'

But Donna simply dismissed Gwen as boring, looked at her watch and said it was time she was off. Robert called over to ask her to pick up some more stuff for tomorrow. But Donna told him that Nicola could pick it up as she wouldn't be coming.

Nicola looked at her in amazement. 'What do you mean, you won't be here? It's the jumble sale.'

'I *know* it's the jumble sale, petal,' Donna replied patronisingly. 'But I won't be here because Jan's taking me to Cragside for the day. Any more questions?' With that she got up and walked out, leaving Nicola feeling thoroughly exasperated and more than a little jealous.

A short while later Donna was walking up the drive to the Byker Arms when she suddenly spotted Brad and Lisa laughing together as they left the pub. She could hear Lisa saying to Brad, 'Curry, Chinese, fish and chips, kebabs, anything. You choose.'

When Brad asked if she was sure, Lisa told him that the glass of wine she'd just drunk had gone straight to her head as she hadn't had a bite to eat all day.

'Big mistake,' Brad told her.

Lisa suddenly stopped laughing. 'Yes, well, sometimes when you're mithered you get too choked up to eat.' Then Brad became serious too – he knew the feeling only too well. With a decisive air, he grabbed her arm and led her to his car.

Donna stood watching them, a smug smile on her face. This was an unexpected bonus to her scheming.

Early the next morning, Nicola was helping Donna pile some of her unwanted clothes and jewellery into a binliner for the jumble sale. She couldn't believe some of the stuff her friend was giving away. Most of it was almost new. When she asked what was wrong with a pair of earrings Donna had bought two weeks ago, she was told, 'Nothing, I'm just tired of them. You can have 'em if you want.'

Nicola was tempted but decided she didn't want Donna's charity. Putting the earrings in the binliner, she returned to the subject they'd been discussing – Donna's sighting of the night before.

'Why shouldn't she go out for a curry anyway?' Nicola asked.

''Cos she's *meant* to be me *dad's* girlfriend, that's why,' Donna replied virtuously. Nicola still didn't see what she was so indignant about, pointing out that her dad *had* taken her mum out. But Donna told her that was different.

'I still don't see why you have to tell him,' Nicola persisted. She felt sorry for Lisa, knowing that Donna was doing everything she could to break her and Jim up.

Donna was still being self-righteous, saying that her dad was entitled to know if Lisa was going out with other men behind his back. This was really over-the-top as far as Nicola was concerned. She pointed out that Lisa had *only* been spotted with Brad. But the way Donna saw it, she could have been cheating on her father ever since they started going out together. Nicola refused to believe that. And what was more, she didn't think it was up to Donna to snitch on Lisa.

With a look of disgust, Donna turned to Nicola. 'You know something, Dobson,' she told her. 'You're getting more like your boring pal Gwen everyday.' Then she picked up the binliner stuffed full of clothes and led the way out of the room.

Downstairs Lisa had just opened the door to Jan as

Nicola and Donna walked in. Jim Bell joined them from the living room, wished them a good time and told Jan what a great place Cragside was.

Donna said she didn't know what time they'd be back as they'd probably have a bite to eat out. Then she turned to Lisa, all innocence, and asked, 'Was the place you went to last night with Brad any good, Lisa?'

There was a long awkward moment before Lisa replied through gritted teeth, 'Yes thank you, Donna. It was very nice.'

Still the soul of sweetness, Donna added, 'Brad's gorgeous, isn't he? I bet you had a smashing time.'

Embarrassed by the silence that followed, Nicola said that she'd better get off to the Grove with Donna's contribution. And, satisfied that she'd really put the cat amongst the pigeons, Donna asked Jan to help her get the picnic stuff out of the fridge.

Left alone in the hallway, Lisa looked at Jim and finally told him, 'We were both at a loose end, that's all. We just went for a curry.' She bitterly resented feeling that she had to justify what she'd done. Even when Jim told her she didn't have to explain, she replied angrily, 'Oh don't I? After the way Donna just put the boot in.'

Jim tried to tell Lisa that Donna hadn't done it deliberately but *she* knew the truth. Her boyfriend might be blind to his daughter's schemings but *she* knew Donna was doing everything she could to split them up. Feeling hurt and angry and not knowing what else to say, Lisa grabbed her coat off the banister and stormed out.

In the kitchen, Donna, who'd been stuffing sandwiches and cold drinks into a rucksack, had overheard the row. She clapped her hands together silently to applaud it, looking thrilled to bits. Everything was going according to plan.

111

Later that day Donna and Jan were wandering happily among the rhododendron-lined paths at Cragside. Jan carried a camera and the rucksack on his back. Donna stopped, picked up some pinky-mauve rhododendron flowers which had fallen, and stuck them behind her ears. This was a really brilliant day, Donna thought, as she looked over at her handsome boyfriend. Sometimes she couldn't believe her luck. She posed against the blaze of colour behind her while Jan took her photo.

'Wasn't I right about this place?' she asked. 'It's like fairyland.' Jan very matter-of-factly told her he'd enjoy it far more when they'd eaten their lunch. Giggling, Donna pelted him with rhododendron flowers and teased him for being unromantic, calling him a 'lump of Danish bacon.'

Perhaps he wasn't being very romantic, he admitted, but *she* wasn't the one carrying the rucksack.

'It's not heavy,' Donna told him without thinking. Predictably the response from Jan was, 'Good. Then you have a turn.' He began to hand the rucksack over to her. But Donna protested. 'Not blimmin' likely – that's your job.'

Jan said in Denmark they believed in equality.

'In that case when we get married we're living here,' she told him, then stopped abruptly as she saw the smile disappear from his face. Hastily she told him she was only joking and suggested they go to see the Cragside house. Skipping ahead happily, she didn't see the apprehensive look on Jan's face.

Having looked around the house, they carried on walking until they reached a terrace overlooking a tranquil lake surrounded by a blaze of rhododendrons and azaleas. Jan was impressed. 'It is very beautiful,' he said.

'Do you think *I'm* beautiful?' Donna asked him. Modesty had never been her strong point. He smiled at the question and told her that he thought she was attractive. Donna pouted jokily and pursued her question. 'But not beautiful?'

Realising that he was going to get no peace unless he said something that pleased her, Jan told Donna that he thought her hair was beautiful. He loved the colour, 'like a flame', which he'd never seen until he came to England.

Donna wanted to know what colour hair Danish girls had. Jan replied that it was mostly blonde and straight, then suddenly went quiet. Too busy trying to look sexy, Donna offered to bleach hers if he liked blondes better. She was serious too. 'I'd do anything for you, Jan,' she told him as she moved closer. Jan hesitated for a moment, then leant towards Donna and began to kiss her.

After a lengthy embrace they had their lunch, then spread a small ground sheet on the grass and were soon engrossed in another steamy clinch, the remains of their picnic scattered around them. As they parted for breath, Donna was genuinely carried away by her feelings. For once she wasn't flirting as she looked into Jan's eyes.

'Jan . . . I meant it when I said I'd do anything for you,' she told him softly. Attempting to keep the situation light, Jan joked that he liked Donna's hair the way it was, although he knew that wasn't what she was talking about.

But Donna persisted, what she was saying was important to her, 'I'd not be scared, not with you.'

Jan lay back, not knowing how to handle the situation, and pretended he hadn't heard.

Frustrated, Donna asked Jan if he was listening to her.

113

'I *love* you,' she told him. 'I've never really loved anyone before.' She confided how with Cas they were just a pair of children playing games but with him she felt different, not a stupid kid any more. As she lay back dreamily on the grass, Donna was so carried away by her own emotions, she didn't notice that Jan had gone very quiet.

Back at the Grove, Brad came into the general room carrying two long planks. He stopped for a moment, watching the activity which was growing more frenzied by the minute. Shyly, Gwen walked up to him and asked, 'Are you all right, Brad?'.

Still feeling frustrated over his last conversation with Alison, he said rather abruptly that yes, he was fine, and why was she asking anyway?

Gwen hesitated, then told him she couldn't help noticing that he'd left early the previous evening. Brad wasn't quite sure what that was supposed to indicate but he once again assured Gwen that he was OK.

Now she stood in front of him feeling awkward and embarrassed. Searching for something to say, she asked, 'What are those for?', nodding at the planks. He explained that they were going to make some ramps for rooms which had steps up to them so that people in wheelchairs could get about more easily.

Gazing up at him with admiration, Gwen said, 'That's a marvellous idea, Brad. You're so thoughtful.'

Brad dismissed her praise, saying it was Geoff's idea. 'But yeah,' he added. 'It's a good'un. We should have thought of it before.' He was about to say something else when Alison walked past. 'Morning,' he said casually. Alison's very cool 'Good morning' wasn't lost on Gwen.

Brad and Geoff had soon finished making a ramp up the front steps. Speedy was 'test driving' it by pushing Robert up, while Spuggie and Fraser stopped to watch.

They cheered as Speedy easily made it to the top. Spuggie wanted to have a go at pushing Robert but Speedy protested, telling her, 'He's not a blimmin' *doll*.'

Spuggie, nothing if not persistent, asked Robert who agreed 'as long as you don't let me roll all the way down into the road.'

As the two men walked off to fix more ramps, P.J. arrived. He looked approvingly up at the Grove and commented to Fraser, 'Not bad, man. Not bad at all.'

Spuggie, of course, wanted to know who he was. Fraser explained as briefly as he could, then wandered off to show P.J. round.

As they passed, Debbie Dobson who was carrying some hoopla stands for the hoopla stall, watched them go inside, then rushed over to Spuggie. Both girls had immediately been impressed by this cool-looking boy. Debbie wanted to know who he was *and* what he was doing there.

'Dunno,' Spuggie told her.

Debbie looked at her scathingly, 'Didn't you ask?'

Spuggie replied equally scathingly, 'I'm not nosy like some people.'

Duncan came up the path at this point and Spuggie shouted over to him, 'Where the heck have *you* been?'

Looking very uncomfortable, Duncan muttered that he'd had stuff to do.

'What stuff?' Spuggie wanted to know. But all Duncan would say was, '*Stuff*, that's all.'

Up on the Grove roof, Fraser was also looking uncomfortable as P.J. gazed out over the rooftops. 'Perfect,' P.J. told him. He'd decided that this would be an excellent place to transmit a pirate radio station.

Fraser was doubtful. 'Isn't it against the law?' he asked. P.J. simply shrugged off the question, saying that no one would find out. He examined the roof with a professional eye, pointing out where they could run the aerial. Fraser wondered about the equipment but P.J. told him that was no problem either as he already had all the gear.

Beginning to feel excited, Fraser asked, 'What'll we call it?' They began playing around with names. P.J. wanted to use something 'spacey' but he wasn't sure what.

'Satellite. Jupiter. Venus. Mars. Challenger. Voyager . . .' Then P.J. suddenly got it, they'd call the radio station 'Radio Rocket'. 'Welcome to Radio Rocket, going where no station has gone before, and now let's blast into orbit with . . .' He continued with the spontaneous spiel that had first impressed Fraser so much.

Curious about this newcomer to the Grove, Spuggie had decided to follow him and her brother. Now, crouched below the small doorway leading onto the roof, she was listening to every word of their conversation.

Down below, the jumble sale was soon in full swing. Speedy's radio announcement seemed to have worked wonders – the place was crowded both inside and out.

Everyone had really gone to town on the stalls. There were stalls selling everything from clothes to cakes, fancy goods to bric a brac. Robert was wheeling himself around selling raffle tickets. Speedy was in charge of 'Guessing the number of beans in the jar'. Brad was manning the photo booth. And Geoff and Alison were wandering amongst the stalls supervising it all.

Nicola was amazed to see Polly and Jim Bell approaching her stall, apparently the best of friends. They came over to say hello to Nicola and remarked on how well it was all going. Polly added that it was a shame Donna wasn't there.

'Her look-out,' Nicola replied, then asked casually,

'You and Mr Bell just bumped into each other here, did you?'

Polly smiled as she told Nicola, no, they'd come together to support the Byker Grove cause. 'We *are* speaking, you know,' she added, looking over at Jim Bell fondly.

Then she grabbed him by the arm and took him over to the hoopla stall where he gave Speedy some money for five rubber hoops. Polly threw a hoop which landed on a prize. She laughed as happily as a child and kissed her ex-husband lightly on the cheek – for old time's sake!

Brad had finished taking photos and was wandering around looking at what the other stall holders had on offer. Gwen, who'd been manning the snack bar, had asked Duncan to help out while she had a ten-minute break. When they bumped into each other at the hoopla, Gwen suddenly became all girlish and tongue-tied. Not knowing quite what to say, Brad offered to buy her an ice-cream.

'I'd *love* one,' Gwen gushed as though he'd just offered to buy her a diamond ring. 'That's if you're not too busy,' she added.

'Never too busy for a ninety-nine, that's my motto,' he replied, as they walked towards the ice-cream cart. Gwen laughed and began to relax but Brad's smile faded as he saw Alison walk past. 'Er, excuse me a moment,' he said lamely as he dashed off after her. Gwen just stood there looking crushed.

Meanwhile Brad pulled Alison away to a quiet corner of the grounds and pinned her gently against a tree.

'Crunch time, Bright Eyes,' he said. He couldn't handle not knowing any more and had decided he had to have a decision – whatever it was.

Alison looked at him with pain in her eyes. 'I've

117

thought about it and . . .' She couldn't finish the sentence. Brad prompted her. He *had* to know.

'I'm staying with Mike,' Alison told him finally. 'I love him and I can't hurt him.'

Brad couldn't believe what he'd just heard. Realising that he'd been sure she'd choose him, he suddenly felt very stupid. He turned on his heel and walked away. Alison watched him go with tears in her eyes.

Walking through the chattering crowd of people, Brad passed Gwen, who was still waiting hopefully.

'Could we go for the ice-creams now, Brad, only I have to be getting back to . . .' But he didn't even hear her as he walked away down the path and out of the Grove.

The jumble sale finally ended late that afternoon with the last visitor deciding to call it a day and wandering off, pleased with her purchases. Robert wheeled himself over to Speedy and congratulated him. 'So you do have *some* bright ideas occasionally then.' Speedy grinned at him, he was feeling very chuffed with himself.

Adding her praise, Nicola said that it had been a fantastic day. 'Geoff's counting the money now,' she told Speedy.

He agreed that it had all gone very well. 'Bet Donna'll be dead cheesed she missed it.' Then he added charitably, 'But at least she'll be chuffed about her mum and dad getting back together again.'

Nicola looked at him in surprise, this was news to her. '*Are* they?' she asked.

'Oh, yes,' Speedy replied confidently. 'I saw 'em kissing.'

A little later Geoff asked Alison to come to their office – immediately. She rushed in to find a grim-looking Geoff with piles of notes and coins in front of him on the desk. Gwen was standing next to him, and she seemed upset.

'Some money's been nicked from the snack bar,' he told her.

Gwen, who somehow felt that she was to blame, added that she'd only been away five minutes.

Not wanting to believe that such a successful day could end on this sour note, Alison asked him, 'Are you sure?' But Geoff was certain.

'Don't say anything to the kids yet,' he told them both. 'I want to make a few enquiries.'

That evening, a euphoric Donna burst into the general room with her news. Pulling a chain out of her T-shirt, she showed Nicola the costume jewellery ring threaded onto it. 'Look what he bought me,' she said.

Nicola, who still hadn't forgiven her for skiving off would only say 'very nice'. But Donna was too carried away with it all to be put off.

'It's me engagement ring!' she told her friend, adding that of course it wasn't real but that once Jan was qualified and had a proper job he'd get her a real one.

For once, Nicola was shocked by Donna. Surely she couldn't be so stupid. 'You're not serious?' she asked her, not bothering to disguise her amazement.

Donna had a ready answer, telling Nicola that if girls can get married at sixteen then why couldn't they get engaged at fifteen? She dragged Alison, who was passing by, into the discussion.

'Girls can get engaged at fifteen, can't they?' Donna asked. But Alison, who was distracted both by Geoff's news and her own problems, wasn't really listening. 'I suppose so. Why?' she asked vaguely.

''Cos she is,' Nicola told her. Donna pretended that she was annoyed her secret was out of the bag. But she was too happy to be really cross.

Suddenly jolted out of her own problems, Alison asked, 'Is it true, Donna?' Donna proudly replied that it

119

was and showed her the ring, adding, 'Only don't tell me dad, he'd go spare.'

Alison suddenly found herself feeling very irritated by Donna. 'I wouldn't blame him, at your age,' she said in an uncharacteristically patronising tone.

But Donna wasn't letting *anyone* spoil her moment of glory. 'What difference does age make?' she wanted to know. She pointed out to Alison that people didn't behave any better as they got older, in fact they behaved worse. 'Look at Lisa,' she said. 'Meant to be me dad's girlfriend and she's two-timing him with Brad.'

Not wanting to believe it, Alison asked Donna to repeat what she'd just said. Shamelessly embroidering on the truth, Donna told her, 'Oh, they've had lots of cosy little dates together. Didn't you know?'

CHAPTER SIX

Donna couldn't wait for school to be over so she could go round to her mum's. As soon as the final bell rang, she shot out of the classroom and headed straight for Polly's flat. When she arrived, she banged on the door loudly. Eventually a window was flung open upstairs and Polly peered out to see who it was. She was dressed up to go out and, from the look on her face, she was clearly expecting someone else. But Donna was too excited to notice.

'Where the heck *were* you yesterday?' she asked her mother. 'I came round about ten times!' Polly explained that she'd gone to the Lake District with an old friend. By this time Donna was bursting with her news and asked her mum to let her in quickly as she had something fantastic to tell her.

As it turned out, Polly wasn't quite as thrilled about the engagement as Donna would have liked. Donna showed her mother the ring and Polly said, 'I hope you're not thinking of getting married for a few years?'

Donna replied teasingly that she was just worried about becoming a grandmother. And Polly confessed that she wasn't exactly over the moon about the idea. She preferred it when everyone took them for sisters.

Donna chattered on about how she and Jan were going to write loads of letters to each other when he went back and then they'd visit each other in the holidays. She was dying to see Copenhagen. Then she stopped and looked at her mother. 'Oh, Mum, I love him so much. Say you're happy for me.'

Not knowing what else to tell her, Polly said of course she was. 'You've always been mature for your age,' she told Donna. And she realised that she hadn't been much older when she'd fallen for Jim. Thinking about him, she smiled. 'I bet he went spare,' she said.

Donna had to admit that he didn't know and she made her mother promise not to tell him either. Polly pointed out that he'd have to know eventually.

'But not yet,' Donna urged. She knew he'd only try and stop it and no one was going to come between her and Jan being together, not even her dad.

Polly had to smile. 'You're your mother's daughter, all right, pet,' she said fondly. 'You do everything with a passion.' Then she looked at her watch and opened the door for Donna to leave, telling her they'd talk about it some more tomorrow.

Not wanting to go yet, Donna asked, 'Can't I stay for tea?' But her mum explained that she'd already made arrangements.

Walking back to the Byker Arms, Donna couldn't help feeling disappointed that, once again, her mother wasn't really there when she wanted her.

In the office, Geoff, Alison and Gwen were discussing the theft. Gwen was miserably blaming herself for leaving the snack bar unattended. But Alison told her, rather irritably, that it wasn't her fault and these things happened from time to time.

'In the meantime,' said Geoff, 'keep it to yourselves for a while. I know what you women are.'

Indignantly, Alison asked him just what he meant by that last comment. Geoff grinned in reply, telling them to keep their eyes and ears open and their mouths shut. He was about to add something else when Spuggie walked into the room.

'Are you on about the money that's gone missing?' she asked. She, Speedy, Robert and Nicola had been discussing the rumour on their way to the Grove, and Robert had said he thought it might be the same person who'd tried to pinch Spuggie's purse. Geoff pulled a face at Gwen and Alison. He might have known that this kind of thing couldn't stay secret for long.

'All right, who's been talking?' he asked in a resigned voice.

'You have,' Spuggie replied innocently, much to the amusement of both Gwen and Alison who tried unsuccessfully to hide their smiles. Spuggie went on to remind Geoff that he'd told Debbie Dobson's dad in the pub who'd told his wife and . . .

Geoff interrupted her at this point, well aware that 'Debbie Big Ears' would have done the rest of the gossiping. He held his hands up to Alison and Gwen, saying, 'OK, I plead guilty.'

Gill checked his reflection once more in the mirror, before leaving the flat. He was looking unusually smart, having swapped his jeans and leather bomber jacket for a shirt and a good pair of trousers bought specially. This was the big day – he was going for his interview with Neville Fletcher at Fletcher's Automobiles and he was as nervous as anything.

Walking up the road, he bumped into Fraser and P.J. who were on their way to the Grove, each carrying a large cardboard carton. Feeling in an unusually good mood, Gill said hello to Fraser who he wouldn't normally have bothered with. 'Been robbing a bank?' he asked, nodding in the direction of the cardboard boxes.

Fraser muttered that it was just some stuff they needed. Then, changing the subject, he said he thought Gill was doing a YTS scheme. Gill explained that he'd been given time off for an interview. Then, bursting to tell someone, even Fraser, he said, 'I tell you it's a biggie, man. I get this and it's strictly life in

123

the fast lane for Gillespie's kid.' With that he sauntered off up the street.

P.J. watched him go, looking amused. 'What a poser,' he said. But Fraser was more concerned with how they were going to get their boxes up the stairs at Byker Grove without anyone noticing. That didn't seem to bother P.J. As usual, he had a plan.

They were walking up the front path of the Grove when Fraser groaned loudly. He'd spotted his sister, Spuggie, who'd been weeding the leek trenches. Even worse, she'd seen *them*. 'She's *everywhere*,' he moaned to P.J. 'I sometimes think there's clones of her all over the place,' though he had to admit he was grimly amused at the thought of an army of Spuggie clones.

But Spuggie surprised him by for once *not* asking questions. She was too full of her own news. 'Hey, Frase, guess what?' she started. 'Gwen's got me a Saturday job helping her brother, he's a vet . . .' And she went on to reel off a list of all the animals Gwen's brother had ever treated.

Fraser was genuinely pleased for her but he was also anxious to get the boxes upstairs and out of sight. They were almost up the front steps when Spuggie called out, 'Hey, Fraser? What's in them boxes?'

Acting as the reconnaisance party, P.J. went into the building first to check where Geoff was. Peering into his office, he was relieved to see that it was empty. As he headed along the hallway he bumped into Robert wheeling himself along. 'Just the guy,' P.J. told him. 'Any idea where Geoff is?'

Robert said Geoff was changing a light bulb in the kitchen, and P.J. asked if he could do him a favour and keep Geoff there for a few minutes.

'How?' Robert wanted to know.

'Jam the gears on your Batmobile,' P.J. replied.

Robert grinned at him, enjoying being part of a conspiracy and wheeled himself off towards the kitchen.

P.J. rushed out through the front door and returned with a box, closely followed by Fraser with his box. They scooted quickly up the stairs.

Just then Spuggie rushed in from outside. 'It's all right, you don't need to tell me what's in 'em,' she shouted after them with satisfaction. 'I already know.' They didn't bother to reply but, standing at the bottom of the stairs, Spuggie grinned smugly to herself.

Taking P.J. at his word, Robert had gone and got his wheelchair well and truly jammed in the kitchen doorway. Geoff was trying to move it from inside the kitchen. He seemed rather harassed, more than necessary under the circumstances.

'Come *on*, Robert,' he said irritably. 'I can't see anything wrong with the brake.' Robert stayed calm and simply continued to stall him, stretching out the manoeuvre of getting out of the doorway for as long as he dared.

When Geoff was finally released from inside the kitchen he dashed along the corridor to his office. Once inside, the first thing he did was look at his desk where he'd left two fifty pences. But the trap had already been sprung and the money had gone. Blow it, he'd arrived just a bit too late.

Debbie Dobson was browsing in the Metro Centre with a couple of schoolfriends when she spotted Jan using one of the public phones. Deciding to impress her friends, she told them she knew the tall blond boy with the film star looks and shouted 'hello'. But Jan was far too engrossed in his phone call to hear her. Annoyed at being shown up in front of her giggling friends, she was about to walk on when she noticed the affectionate tone of Jan's voice. Her friends carried on without her.

He was speaking in what Debbie presumed was Danish to someone called Kirsten. Then he changed to English, telling this Kirsten, 'Yes, of course I miss you.' Debbie was all agog. 'I think of you every day,' he continued, 'But soon we will be together again . . .'

Running to catch up with her friends before Jan spotted her, for once in her life Debbie Dobson was at a loss for words.

Still looking radiant, Donna swept up to Nicola, Speedy and Spuggie in the general room at the Grove. She told Nicola she'd just been to tell her mum the news about 'you know what' and Polly was tickled pink. Speedy turned to Spuggie, saying that *he* knew why Donna was in such a good mood.

'Oh, do you, Cleverbonce,' Donna replied, only mildly annoyed. 'I s'pose *she* told you?' she said nodding at Nicola.

But Speedy denied this. 'Nobody told me. I saw them.'

Donna was baffled now and asked just who Speedy had seen. Equally confused that Donna didn't know what he was talking about, Speedy explained that he'd seen her mum and dad at the jumble sale kissing. 'I expect you're dead glad they're back together,' he added.

A delirious Donna whirled Nicola round by the waist. She wouldn't have believed she could have felt so happy. Everything was coming up roses. That was why her mum was dressed up, she realised. She was probably going out with her dad. 'They're in love all over again just like me and . . .' She stopped, remembering that her engagement was still meant to be a secret. But Spuggie filled in the missing word. 'Jan,' she said smugly. Then she told Donna that Debbie had seen her ring.

'Can't keep no blimmin' secrets round here!' Donna giggled. But she was much too happy to mind.

Donna was soon rabbiting on, while Nicola sat with her, looking very bored. 'If they get married again I'll be bridesmaid, I'll wear a turquoise frock like Melanie Griffiths did in *Working Girl* . . .'

But Nicola wasn't listening. She was looking at Alison who had just walked in. She didn't seem very happy. 'You shouldn't have said that to her the other day,' she told Donna who asked what she was going on about.

'About Lisa going out with Brad,' Nicola explained.

Donna didn't see what the problem was. As far as she was concerned, Lisa *had* gone out with Brad. The fact that it was only once made little difference. Even when Nicola said that Alison looked miserable, Donna's only comment was, 'I don't know why, she's meant to be Mike's girlfriend.'

But Nicola wasn't letting her off that lightly. She pointed out that Donna *knew* she liked Brad and had even encouraged them at camp. 'You can't just go round telling people things that'll upset them,' Nicola told her friend crossly. 'How would you like it if somebody did it to you?'

'It wouldn't bother me,' came the reply. 'Anyway,' she added, 'What could upset me? I've got everything I want.'

Sometimes Nicola wanted to smack her round the face for her selfish arrogance, she really did.

Up in the Grove attic room, Fraser and P.J. were unpacking P.J.'s equipment from the cardboard boxes. Bit by bit they brought out a transmitter, mikes, turntables, a cassette deck, tapes and the rest of the gear they needed to set up their radio station.

'What we need now is a call sign,' P.J. was saying. 'Something with a beat.' And he began experimenting with a rap, clicking his fingers at Fraser. When the rap line started to take shape, Frazer joined in, 'First you rip it, then you rap it, then you rock it on Radio . . .'

They broke off suddenly as they heard the sound of Geoff's voice in the club room below them accompanied by several other excited voices. P.J. rushed out of the room to see what was going on, with Fraser following behind. In the club room they found a gang gathering round to admire the new video recorder which had just arrived. Geoff put a plug on it and asked Fraser to tune it when he'd finished.

'What was the racket I heard as we came up the stairs?' Geoff asked. Fraser looked helplessly at P.J. He was as bad at inventing stories as P.J. was good at it.

True to form, P.J. had an answer, explaining that they were going in for a competition where they had to write a jingle. Geoff thought that was a great idea, especially as Fraser had a good record of winning competitions. He'd won a watch in a computer magazine competition only a few months ago.

Spuggie piped up. 'That's not the only good idea he's got, is it, Frase?' For which she was rewarded with a sharp kick in the shins from her brother. Offended, she asked, 'What was that for? I wasn't going to say anything.' But Fraser wasn't taking any chances. The kick, he told her, was just to make sure she didn't.

A very quiet Alison was serving Nicola and Donna at the snack bar when Brad came in. He gave them the good news that the video recorder was up and running, then asked Alison if she wanted to come and see it.

'No thank you, I'm busy,' came the cold reply. Equally cool, Brad said she could suit herself and walked out, leaving Alison looking even more unhappy.

'See what you've done?' an angry Nicola hissed to her

128

friend. But Donna was unrepentant and simply shrugged.

Spotting Gwen across the room, Alison asked if she would take over for a while and rushed outside. She had to get some air, get out of the building. Although it was huge, it seemed at the moment that wherever she was, Brad was too. And she couldn't handle it.

Yet again, Spuggie was back weeding the leek trenches. And she'd roped Duncan in to help. Alison had to smile. Spuggie was getting so attached to the leeks which were in the same place as the sunflowers she had once been so upset about. Walking over, Alison asked, 'Are our leeks doing well?'

Spuggie told her proudly that Mr Dobson had said they'd got some real prize-winners. As she rabbited on, filling Alison in on every single detail of what Mr Dobson had told them, Alison noticed that Brad had followed her out of the Grove.

'That's wonderful,' she told Spuggie and said she'd keep her fingers crossed but she wasn't really paying much attention. Brad came up to her and asked if he could have a word about 'the stationery requisition'. Gritting her teeth, she had to agree in front of Spuggie and Duncan. She allowed Brad to lead her a little way away then hissed, '*What* stationery requisition?'

With a hint of a smile Brad said that he thought it had sounded businesslike, then asked, 'Why the cold shoulder, Ali?'

Alison wondered what to do. Should she make up some excuse or should she tell him the *real* reason? She decided to go for the truth. 'Obviously I made the right decision choosing Mike,' she told Brad angrily. But why had he gone through the charade of not wanting to share her when all the time *he* was seeing another girl, Alison wanted to know.

129

Looking stunned, Brad asked, 'When I was *what*?' But as far as Alison was concerned, the conversation was over. As she started to move away he grabbed her by the arm and asked her what other girl.

'Jim Bell's girlfriend, Lisa,' she told him coldly. 'I know all about it.' And with that she walked back towards the Grove, leaving Brad too gobsmacked to do anything.

Gill was coming up the drive, bursting to tell someone his great news. He could hardly believe it himself but he'd actually got the job. Dying to tell someone, he'd tried to phone Julie but her dad had said she was visiting her mother and slammed the phone down before Gill could ask when she'd be back. Now, seeing Alison, he shouted over to her that he'd just got a brilliant new job. But she was too wrapped up in her emotions and she didn't even hear him as she went inside. Undaunted, Gill saw Brad walking towards him.

'Brad, you know when I told you I was keen on working with cars and you said . . .' But Brad, looking like thunder, also disappeared inside the Grove.

'Oh brilliant, Gill, I'm dead chuffed for you, Gill, well done, man,' Gill muttered to himself as he stood alone, feeling hurt and let down. Little did he know he wasn't the only one.

Donna and Nicola were both putting on make-up in the girls' loo when Debbie came in and told Donna she'd just seen her boyfriend in the Metro Centre. Donna immediately presumed he was buying her a pressie because 'he's dead sweet like that.' But Debbie Dobson soon put her straight. 'No, he was talking to some girl on the phone.'

Trying to sound casual, Donna asked her how she knew it was a girl.

'Because he called her Kirsten,' Debbie said impatiently. 'That's not a blimmin' boy's name, is it?'

Donna was still attempting to stay calm while she asked Debbie what else Jan had said. This prompted Debbie to do a soppy impersonation of everything she'd overheard, ending with Jan saying, '. . . But soon we'll be together again . . .'

Donna's anger was showing now as she shouted at Debbie that she was a lying little pig for making the story up. But Debbie simply shouted back at her that it was the truth. 'Ask him if you don't believe me,' she said finally. Donna glared at her and then stalked out.

Nicola was furious with her sister, asking her why she always had to go stirring it. Full of injured pride, Debbie replied that she'd only told the truth. 'If Her Highness doesn't like it, hard blimmin' cheese,' she added, before stalking off herself.

Later that day the club room was in darkness. A small gang of boys sat huddled round the video occasionally giving low gasps and making horrible noises at a revoltingly gory horror film.

The door opened quietly and Debbie Dobson crept in.

Knowing who it was without even looking round, Gill shouted, 'Out, pest! How many more times? No birds allowed.'

But Debbie wasn't to be got rid of that easily. She pointed out that they had all helped to get the money for the video. And then she played her trump card. 'Anyway, if you don't let me watch I'll tell Geoff.'

This was enough to shut the boys up. Debbie elbowed her way to the front of the huddle, showing great bravado, but after about two seconds she put her hand over her eyes and peered out at the horror film from between her fingers.

*　　*　　*

Donna stood outside the terraced house and took a deep breath. Then she knocked on the door and waited. Jan's landlady, a large, middle-aged woman, answered. Discovering that Jan was out, Donna rapidly made up a highly convincing story about urgent news for him. Eventually the landlady let her in and showed her to Jan's room.

As soon as she was inside the bedroom, the first thing Donna spotted was a framed photo of a pretty blonde girl on the bedside table. It was inscribed 'Med kaerlig hilsen, Kirsten'. Although Donna couldn't speak Danish, its meaning was made very clear by the long row of kisses next to the girl's name. Donna picked up the photo and stared at it before putting it back on the table. The she sat on the bed and waited.

When Jan walked into his room later that afternoon he was surprised to see Donna. He'd thought they were meeting at the Grove.

Icily, Donna asked him, 'Who the heck's she?' Jan's eyes followed her to the photo.

'She is my girlfriend in Copenhagen,' Jan replied. Donna couldn't believe what she was hearing. And she certainly didn't want to hear what Jan started telling her about how long they'd been going out and where they'd met.

'What about *me*? You said you loved *me*!' she wailed. By now Jan was getting tired of the world of fantasy that Donna had been living in ever since they'd met. Deciding it was time for a few facts, he pointed out that *Donna* was the one who had talked about love, *she'd* been the one to persuade Jan to buy the ring and *she* was the one who'd called it her engagement ring. 'I thought it was just one of your games,' he added, meaning it.

Donna couldn't believe what she was hearing. She refused to see it Jan's way and instead accused him of leading her on. When Jan told her that perhaps she was leading herself on, Donna pointed out that he hadn't exactly run away.

'Because I *liked* you. You are a funny, lively girl . . .' he replied.

'But you love Kirsten,' Donna said bitterly.

'Yes,' Jan agreed. Donna flew into a rage, shouting at Jan that she hated him, tearing her ring off its chain and throwing it at him. She started to run towards the door, then stopped and picked up the photo.

'And I hate *her*. Dopy, grinning thing . . .' she said, before hurling the photo at Jan. He ducked, it hit the wall and the glass shattered. Donna ran out of the room.

It was much later that evening when Polly got out of the Escort laughing. She called goodnight to her companion and began to fumble for her key in her handbag. As she walked up to the front door she was amazed to find a miserable, tear-stained Donna hunched up on the front door step.

'Donna, lovie! What on earth . . .???' she began, before Donna flung herself sobbing into her mother's arms.

When she came out of the bedroom with a box of Kleenex an hour later, Polly had heard the whole sad story. Donna, her tears finally beginning to dry, was telling her mother what a lousy, rotten, two-timing stinking bum Jan was.

'I'd forget him, lovie, best way,' Polly said. 'Remember, you're a survivor like your mum. Feeling any better now?'

'A bit,' Donna sniffed. Her mother said she was going to make them a cup of tea, then it was time she was off, as her dad would be worried. Should she give him a ring, she wondered? Donna said it was OK, she'd go

133

soon, then told Polly, 'That's the only good thing, you and him getting back again.'

Startled, Polly asked her daughter where she'd heard that from and Donna explained how they'd been spotted at the jumble sale kissing.

'Oh that!' Polly exclaimed. 'That was just a peck for old time's sake.' The she added dreamily, 'I'm seeing Tony now.'

Donna couldn't believe it. She felt in danger of bursting into tears again when she asked who the heck Tony was.

'An old flame from way back,' her mother told her. Then she went on to explain that his marriage was over too, they'd bumped into each other again and had picked up where they'd left off years before. Donna put two and two together and realised that he was the person who'd dropped her mum off earlier.

Polly was quiet for a moment, before telling her daughter that Tony lived in Manchester . . . and he wanted her to go down there with him for a while to see how they got on. 'I thought I might,' she finished. Seeing the look on Donna's face, she added, 'It's not Mars, lovie. And you can come and stay with us in the holidays . . .'

'No thanks!' was all Donna could say. This was the final straw. Her mother began to tell her how she'd got her own life to lead and she wasn't getting any younger . . . But there was no point, Donna was already on her way out.

Later that night, a very tearstained and bedraggled-looking Donna walked into the Byker Arms. She could hear voices coming from the living room.

'Dad? Dad, I need to talk to you . . .' she shouted as she opened the living room door.

Her father and Lisa were kissing and cuddling on the

134

couch. When they saw Donna they pulled apart slightly but Jim kept his arm fondly round Lisa's shoulder. Not noticing that Donna had been crying, he commented on the fact that she was late but presumed that she'd been with Jan. Then he told her happily, 'Me and Lisa are back together again, and this time I want us all to be friends . . .'

This was the last straw. She bolted out of the room and rushed upstairs to her bedroom where she locked the door and flung herself on her bed. After a couple of moments, her father came knocking on the door. 'Donna, sweetheart, don't be silly . . . what's the matter . . .?' he shouted but Donna made no move to answer him. She just lay on the bed sobbing her heart out.

The Dobson household was always noisy and chaotic in the morning. There was usually someone who'd lost something and someone else who was late. This particular morning Mrs Dobson was reminding her kids that she wanted the house tidy as their gran was coming home from hospital today. 'Is she going to be all right now?' they asked.

Kath Dobson told them that she would be fine as long as she didn't overdo it. At which her husband grinned, 'Knowing your mother she'll have a duster in her hand before she's got her coat off.'

Debbie was the Dobson child who was late today. Her mother yelled up the stairs, telling her that she wasn't calling her again and if she was late for school, it was her own look-out. Eventually a bleary-eyed Debbie wandered in, yawning loudly.

Without much sympathy, Nicola commented, 'I'm not surprised she's tired after the way she had us all up in the middle of the blimmin' night.' Hearing this, Jemma,

135

the youngest Dobson, piped up hopefully, 'What was she screaming for? Was it a burglar?'

But her mother explained that Debbie had had a nasty nightmare, that was all. 'What about?' Jemma asked, all agog.

'Never you mind,' she was told briskly. 'And get on with your breakfast otherwise you'll be late for school.'

Over at the Byker Arms, Donna was still lying in bed at twenty to nine that morning. She hadn't slept all night and her eyes were red and swollen. Her father knocked at the door, telling her she'd feel better once she was at school with her friends. But Donna didn't bother to respond. She just carried on staring at the ceiling.

A couple of minutes later there was another gentle tapping at the door. This time it was Lisa, who'd made her a cup of tea. She asked if she should leave it outside the door but got no response. In desperation, Jim Bell suggested that he phone her mum. 'If you won't talk to us will you talk to *her*?' he asked.

This finally stung Donna into a response. 'No!' she shouted through the door. 'She's the last person I want to see. She doesn't love me, you don't, Jan doesn't . . . nobody does . . . I wish I was dead . . .' And with that she broke down once more.

Jim and Lisa looked at each other helplessly. Then, softly, and with genuine compassion, Lisa murmured, 'Poor Donna. Poor kid.'

Donna had so recently had everything she wanted in the world. Now that whole world seemed to have come crashing in on her. She didn't want to see *anyone* ever again.

Jan was taking his usual short cut on his way to school that morning when he bumped into Nicola. He anxious-

136

ly asked her if she'd seen Donna. Not since the previous afternoon she said, then asked him why.

'She was very angry with me last night,' Jan confessed. Nicola put two and two together and realised that her little sister had been right after all.

'It's true, then? About you and this other girl?' she asked. Jan, looking embarrassed, asked if everyone knew about it. Nicola told him that you couldn't keep anything a secret at Byker Grove.

'I wasn't trying to keep Kirsten secret,' Jan protested. He told Nicola that they'd agreed they were each free to go out with other people while he was away. She knew all about Donna, he added.

'But Donna didn't know about her,' Nicola commented drily – Jan tried to explain that he'd thought it was just a holiday romance. He thought that Donna would move onto the next boy when he left, just as she'd moved from Cas to him. 'I didn't know she was going to talk about love and engagements.'

Nicola couldn't help teasing him a little. 'You should've stuck with me,' she grinned. 'You'd have been a lot safer.'

Feeling genuinely sorry for the upset he'd caused, Jan apologised to Nicola for making 'a right cow's ear of things'. She laughed as she corrected him, 'Pig's ear, you wally.' But then, looking more serious, she told Jan not to feel bad about it because Donna had set herself up for being hurt from the start. He took her point but said that he still couldn't help feeling sorry for her. After a moment's silence Nicola said, 'I know. Me too.'

After school that afternoon, Mary O'Malley was welcomed back to the Dobson household as though she was the Queen. Although the kids were loath to admit it, they'd missed their gran and her bustling presence in the house. Nicola gave her a hug and asked if she was feeling OK. Mary said that she would be once she'd had a good night's sleep in her own bed. At this, Nicola glared at Debbie and pointedly hoped that they'd *all* get a good night's sleep tonight. The she lowered her voice and told Debbie accusingly, 'Donna was off school sick today . . .'

'What's wrong with her?' Debbie asked innocently.

'I think she's suffering from an attack of Big-gob-itis,' Nicola replied pointedly. 'Somebody *else's* big gob.'

Debbie Dobson told her sister there was no need to give her filthy looks, *she* wasn't the one who'd done the dirty on Donna.

'No, but you were the one to tell her,' Nicola pointed out. At this, her gran's ears pricked up and she wanted to know what was going on.

Instantly, Nicola and Debbie united against the common enemy of gran's nosiness as they replied in chorus, 'Nothing, Gran.'

Very quietly Donna tiptoed out of her room. It was late afternoon and she'd thrown on an old sweater and a pair of jeans. Her hair was a mess and she wore no make-up. She crept downstairs, relieved that no one was apparently in sight. As she walked out of the front door, the living room door opened a crack. Lisa had heard her.

Lisa followed Donna for a little while until she came to a nearby piece of parkland. The she saw her sit on the grass, knees hunched up to her chin, staring unseeingly at the view.

'Go away,' Donna said when she realised that Lisa was standing next to her. Ignoring her, Lisa crouched on the grass too. 'You've been on you own too long as it is,' Lisa said.

'So? Who cares?' Donna challenged. Lisa told her that everyone did, her dad, her mum, her friends, and she did too. But Donna didn't believe a word of it.

Gently, Lisa let her know she was sorry about Jan, she'd heard all about him from Polly.

Donna replied rudely, 'What do *you* know about it?'

'I know how much it hurts when you love someone, and you think they're rejecting you for someone else,' Lisa told her quietly.

Suddenly Donna realised that Lisa was talking about her dad. And she found herself listening with new understanding as Lisa told her honestly how it had all got to her when she'd thought he wanted Polly back.

Then Donna said tonelessly, 'She's going off with some new bloke to Manchester.'

Lisa already knew about that. Polly had called in to say goodbye – she couldn't wait, as she had a train to catch.

'Me mam's always got a train to catch,' Donna commented in the same hollow voice. Suddenly all her anger was gone as she turned to Lisa. 'Do you think I'll end up like her? Different feller every week?' She paused for a moment, then looked scared. 'I don't want that.'

Hesitantly, Lisa reached out to stroke Donna's hand and Donna didn't move it away. Lisa began to tell her that one day she'd fall in love and, with any luck, it would be for keeps. 'But until then,' she told her, 'you've got so much fun to have, so many places to see, so many exciting things to do . . .'

The first glimmer of a smile appeared on Donna's face as she added, 'So many fantastic lads to meet . . .'

Lisa smiled back at her and asked, 'You didn't really want to get married at sixteen, did you?'

Not quite ready at first to admit how stupid she'd been, Donna demanded to know why not. But, now that her whole daydream had collapsed around her, she had to agree, 'No, 'course I didn't.' After a pause in which she began to imagine all the good things to come, she added, 'Not on your blimmin' life!'

Then she got up, stretching. And suddenly she became aware of the expanse of greenery around her – she just wanted to run and run. Halfway down a hill, Donna flung her arms in the air. 'Not on your blimmin' life!' she shouted to the world.

Other **Byker Grove** titles to look out for . . .

BYKER GROVE

Adele Rose

Julie Warner seems to have it all. She's pretty and clever and lives in a comfortable house in Wimbledon. But when her dad's work takes the family up to Newcastle her safe little world falls apart. Julie hates Newcastle. Everything's so different – it makes her feel like an alien from outer space.

Then she goes to Byker Grove a wonderful old house where kids can do what they want. Before she knows it, she's met charming Cas, slow-on-the-uptake Speedy, spoilt Donna Bell, understanding Hayley, wideboy Winston, gutsy little Spuggie, and lots of others.

But the person who really draws Julie back is good-looking, moody Martin Gillespie. He spells big trouble but somehow she can't keep away . . .

BBC BOOKS

TURNING ON, TUNING IN

Don Webb

When you're fifteen and you enter a competition with a friend to sing on the backing track of a youth club's record, the last thing you'd expect to happen is to be offered a recording contract.

But that's just what happens to Marilyn Charlton, the newest member of BYKER GROVE. Soon Charley and Hayley find joy and heartbreak combined when they meet Steve Rottega, local medallion man.

Charley also finds that she is falling in love with Robert, even though their interests are worlds apart as Robert struggles to walk again after a serious footballing accident.

There's also the mystery of Spuggie's strange friend and Duncan's obsession, and Gill and Julie in love again, and the brooding presence of Carl, who casts a dark shadow over the kids of BYKER GROVE.

BBC BOOKS

ODD ONES OUT

Hugh Miller

Everything goes horribly wrong for Bill after Julie leaves him. Worst of all, a joyride in a stolen car ends in disaster when Gill and Winston get involved in a hit-and-run accident. Gill swears his friend to secrecy, but as the police net tightens, the strain on Winston mounts to breaking point.

When Nicola meets Paul, she finds someone even more committed to 'green' issues than she is. However, it's not only Paul's convictions that attract her.

These are also unsettling times for Spuggie and Fraser as they have to adjust to life in Speedy's foster home. Fortunately, Spuggie makes friends with Joanne, a Vietnamese orphan, whose greatest wish is to meet her brother, who is still in a refugee camp.

And Donna can't believe it when she hears that Jan is showing his Danish girlfriend around Newcastle. Being Donna, her reaction is immediate – and explosive . . .

BBC BOOKS